A PLACE OF SAFETY

Also by Natasha Cooper

Creeping Ivy
Fault Lines
Prey to All
Out of the Dark

A PLACE OF SAFETY

Natasha Cooper

St. Martin's Minotaur New York

www.minotaurbooks.com

ISBN 0-312-31936-3

First published in Great Britain by Simon Schuster UK Ltd
A Viacom company

First St. Martin's Minotaur Edition: September 2003

10 9 8 7 6 5 4 3 2 1

ACKNOWLEDGEMENTS

Suzanne Baboneau, Mary Carter, Broo Doherty, Jessica Gulliver, Jane Gregory, David Scrase, Felix Turner, Sheila Turner and Melissa Weatherill all provided essential information, advice, and support while I was writing this novel. Occasionally their information had to be adapted to fit the needs of fiction. I would like to thank them all.

Natasha Cooper

For

THE OTHER UNUSUAL SUSPECTS

Leslie Forbes, Manda Scott, Michelle Spring, Andrew Taylor and Laura Wilson, without whom life just wouldn't be the same.

Prologue

France 1916

The guns crashed. Helen woke and was half out of bed before she remembered. Then she turned her head to look at Jean-Pierre, still lying against their shared pillow. His eyes were open and as bright as ever. He propped himself up on one elbow and held out his other hand towards her.

'Calm, *ma mie*, stay calm. It is only eight-thirty. You are not on duty this morning. Come back to bed.'

Wanting whatever he wanted, she let herself lie down again. The linen sheet felt rough, as though every single thread had a new force of its own against skin peeled back to its thinnest layer.

Last night she had felt so powerful that she could have embraced the whole world. Now it was different. Now the threats were back in place and she had no strength left. But for another few minutes, she would try to remember that one moment of safety and rest with the length of his thigh pressing against hers.

He stroked her face, pushing the heavy hair away from her eyes, then kissed her again.

You were supposed to be afraid the first time, she knew. All the whispers she had ever heard had told her it would hurt. But Jean-Pierre had not hurt her once. Last night there had been no fear at all, only comfort, then pounding excitement, and finally almost unbearable pleasure. Perhaps for her, fear was now so tightly tied to the barrage and the gas, the puffy gangrenous flesh she had to dress, the bone splinters and the spilling brains and guts, that she couldn't be afraid of something as simple as a man touching her.

She knew all about men's bodies now. She had been washing, splinting and suturing them for two years. She had seen everything bullets could do, smelled the pus, understood the pain, and hated knowing how much the men had to suffer before merciful unconsciousness set them free for a while. When you knew all that and watched them sometimes holding themselves for comfort, you couldn't be afraid of letting one of them near you. Especially not when you loved him and he wanted you so.

She thought of explaining that to her sister and knew she would never even try. On her last leave, she had hoped to tell her family the truth about the war, only to find that none of them would listen. Outside the house, dank, sulphurous fog had hidden everything she had once loved about London. Inside, the loathing and disapproval had been as bad. Both her parents had been shocked when she'd described her work with the smashed bodies of the heroes they talked about with such odious sentimentality. That, and their preoccupation with respect and marriageability, had seemed unutterably childish in comparison with what the men had to endure hour after hour, day after day, so Helen had snapped and made her mother and sister cry. Remembering the tears now, she sighed.

'This *will* end,' Jean-Pierre said, as though in answer to the sound of unhappiness. 'There *is* a future for us. You must have faith in that, Hélène, *ma mie*.'

As she looked into his dark eyes, she saw an intensity of love that she had never known. It was infinitely more important than her family's rejection.

'I will,' she said, making it a promise.

Jean-Pierre relaxed his supporting arm, and let his body sink against hers. The way he laid his face against her breasts told her how much he needed her to hold on to him, so she wrapped her arms around his back and let her lips brush against his hair. She felt as though she had somehow leapfrogged the twenty years that divided them, to become the older of the two.

His lips moved against her skin, but she couldn't hear what he was saying. She released her hold on him and pushed his head up a little way, squinting to bring his face into focus.

'What did you say, Jean-Pierre? What? I didn't hear you.'

'Only that I love you,' he said, almost despairing. 'And I wish we could have found each other in a better time, and in a better place.'

'So do I,' she whispered, pulling him back against her. 'But you're right: there *will* be peace, and time to live sanely again. We have to hold on to that.'

'We will, please God. It is mad and impossible, I know, but I want to take you away from here and look after you, protect you from every shadow, every breeze.'

The guns seemed nearer now, which meant the wind had changed. Helen winced. He changed position so that he could put his hands over her ears, but she couldn't forget what she had heard. That sudden extra-loud crack in the relentless thudding always made her feel as though she had been hit herself. She hoped the army wasn't using gas as well as bullets today. If so, the shifting wind would blow it right back into their own lines, to burn out the men's lungs, blister their skins and blind their eyes as well as everything the enemy was doing to them.

The casualty station was too far from the front for gas to be a risk for her and Jean-Pierre this time. She wouldn't have to pull on a mask this morning, to smell the sick-making rubber or hear her own voice booming round inside the canvas. She gently pulled his hands away from her head so that she could hear clearly again.

'I know,' he said, kissing her forehead. 'I am sorry. You do not need my protection – or anyone's. When I watch you work I see such courage, Hélène, and such compassion, too. I think I would have loved you for your courage alone, even if I had never spoken to you.'

Chapter 1

London, 2002

'Trish? That you?' Antony Shelley's voice was quick with satisfaction over the phone. 'They're going to settle. We're off the hook.'

'Oh, sod it!' she said, her whole body tingling with wasted adrenaline. She'd been expecting to leave for court any minute now, even more keyed up than usual because it was such a big case.

'Sod it? You should be pleased. The clients are.'

'I am. Of course. But Antony— Oh, hell! It's not fair. I wanted them to have their triumph in public. Now nobody except us will ever know exactly what those bastards did to them.'

He laughed. 'Such passion, Trish. When am I going to teach you to be less emotional? Didn't you abandon family law precisely so that you wouldn't have to anguish over your clients' fate? Be like me: I never care which side wins or who knows it.'

'You are such a cynic, Antony,' she said, knowing she could never feel as little about anything.

She had to care about her clients to do her best, and, caring, minded what happened to them. This lot had been abominably treated. In her view, no financial settlement could ever make up for that.

'I feel all let down,' she said, trying to be professionally casual. Then she shivered. 'I've always hated anticlimaxes.'

'I know. But don't worry. You won't have to endure this one for long. Henry Buxford was on the phone only last week, asking whether I thought you'd do a little private research for him. I told him to keep his sticky fingers off you until we'd got the case under control.' Antony laughed. 'He sounded so disappointed you ought to be flattered.'

'I am. But research? What sort of research? And why does he want a commercial barrister for it?'

'No idea. Why not give him a ring and find out? I know he'd pay well for your time.'

That should help, Trish thought, remembering all the big bills she'd have to pay after Christmas.

Although she would eventually get the whole of her generous brief fee for the case that had just settled, there would now be none of the daily refreshers for time spent in court. Until last year that wouldn't have mattered because she had earned more than enough for the kind of life she wanted to live. Then she'd taken her 9-year-old half-brother, David, to live with her and her expenses had rocketed, along with her anxieties.

'It all sounds very mysterious,' she said.

'Only because I wasn't listening properly. Hang on a minute. I've got his direct line at Grunschwig's here somewhere.'

Trish waited, pen in hand, until he came back with the number.

'Thanks,' she said when he had had dictated it. 'But, you know, I really ought to spend the time with David. I've been neglecting him even more than usual over the last few weeks.'

'Small boys need freedom far more than sororal attention,' Antony said. 'Take it from one who knows. And don't forget that Henry's a powerful man. They're always worth helping – even when they're not friends of mine.'

Trish bit down hard on the words that hovered around her tongue. She hated the trading of favours that was second nature to her head of chambers. And she hated recognizing her own reluctance to piss him off. Her career had boomed after Antony had started to take an interest in her, and she wasn't high-minded enough to risk losing that.

Even so, she didn't want to look like a complete pushover. 'OK, I suppose I could talk to him; see if I might be able to fit him in.'

Antony laughed and put down the phone.

Direct line or not, Trish found herself talking to Henry Buxford's secretary at the merchant bank of which he was chairman, then hanging on for five minutes before he'd freed himself to speak to her. When he did come on the line, he said he was very pleased she'd called. Trish reminded herself to feel flattered.

'I'd like to explain what I need face to face,' he went on. 'Because it's a complicated story. I've got a rare window between 5.30 and 7.00 this evening. Is there any chance we could meet for a drink?'

All year Trish had fought to keep that particular slot free for David, even when she'd had to go out or back to work on her case papers afterwards. Still, now that the case had settled she could fetch him from school and have tea with him. That might do instead.

'I could rejig a few things. Where should we meet? El Vino?' It wouldn't take long to get back to Fleet Street from her Southwark flat.

'Too many hacks and barristers to eavesdrop there,' said Buxford. 'Do you know a friendly basement wine bar off Leicester Square called the Cork & Bottle? Could you get there by 5.30?'

An image of Procrustes' bed started to flicker on the margins of Trish's mind, like an irritating icon on a computer screen. During the last year she had become obsessed with the ancient Greek myth of the robber who waylaid travellers, measured them against his bed, and then either cut bits off them or stretched them out until they fitted exactly. For Trish, the 21st century equivalent was time itself. One day, she thought, the stretching will go too far and I'll snap.

'Is that a problem?' Henry asked into the silence.

'Not if I can get a babysitter. I'll let you know.'

When he'd gone, Trish picked up the phone again to call Nicky, who would have been David's nanny if he'd been young enough to need one. They had none of them been able to think of a way of describing her job and so she was just Nicky, who did all the things at home that Trish would have done if she'd been there. Nicky had a busy social life of her own, but she was saving up for a laptop and so she was usually happy to work overtime when she could.

'Sure,' she said when Trish asked if she could stay on until eight tonight. 'Or all evening, if you like. I'm not going anywhere and your TV's bigger than mine. Your sofas are more comfortable, too. Why don't you take George out, to make up for cancelling that dinner last week?'

'Are you sure, Nicky? That would be great.'

There were no words fit to describe George's role in Trish's life either. He was the most important person in it, even though they didn't actually live under the same roof and would have eaten raw nettles rather than share a bank account.

Trish phoned his office to tell him about the case's settlement and find out whether he'd like her to book a table at their favourite restaurant to celebrate.

'You mean you're abandoning David today as well as Wednesday?' he said, making his voice sizzle with amazement. 'How will he survive?'

'Oh, shut up,' she said, having in fact forgotten that she'd agreed to dine with one of his clients later this week. As the senior partner in a big firm of solicitors, George had to do a fair amount of client entertaining. Trish always tried to help when she could, but it often bored her. 'You know why it's important for him to be able to trust me to be there whenever he needs me.'

'Come on, Trish. I was teasing. OK, given that you've decided to allow us a night off, is eating really what you want to do? What about the theatre? Is there anything good on at the National?'

The idea that George might prefer a play to food was surprising. But if the theatre was what he wanted, that was what she would try to give him. She was well aware that she'd been short-changing him as well as David in the last few weeks.

'I don't know. But I could find out.'

'Great. And if you like the look of something, book it. I have absolute trust in your judgement.'

She laughed and told him she'd had plenty of evidence to the contrary in the five years they had been together.

'Most of the time,' he amended. 'Trish, I've got to go. I'm due to chair the partners' meeting in five minutes. 'Bye.'

The phone rang again as soon as she had replaced the receiver. Hearing her clerk's lugubrious voice, she waited for him to tell her about a stunning new brief that would catapult her into the ranks of the really big hitters, like Antony himself. Then she wouldn't have to do favours for anyone.

'One of your old clients is asking for you,' Steve said, deflating the fantasy in an instant. 'And you've got time to sort her out now the case has settled. It's Legal Aid, of course. Will you do it?'

'Who is it?'

'Tamara O'Connor.'

'Oh, no!' Trish remembered the drawn, anguished face of the most dispiriting woman she had ever represented. 'I thought she was safely in prison after that last soliciting charge.'

'She got out four months ago, but she's in police custody again and probably on her way to Cookham Wood. It's worse than usual this time. She's been caught at Heathrow with twenty-two condoms of cocaine in her gut. She says she needs you to see her through the bail application.'

Trish detested everything about the drug world and all the people involved in it. But most of all she hated the men who persuaded poor, usually naïve, women to become their mules, smuggling the stuff through customs. Only a few of the mules had any idea of the kind of prison sentences they were risking, or the sometimes permanent separation from their children. Even so Trish did not want to get involved with this one.

'You know perfectly well I don't do crime now, and Tamara doesn't need counsel for a bail application anyway. Her solicitor can do it.'

'She's convinced you'll be able to get her bail.' Steve didn't sound as though he shared the client's opinion. 'And once you've done that, she wants you to go on to get her kids back for her.'

'With her record? She hasn't a hope. They were taken into care for about a million very good reasons. And I don't do family law any more either.'

'The theory is,' Steve said, as though he hadn't heard her interruption, 'that she's going to give the police names of some big drug dealers this time, and she thinks that'll make the authorities look kindly on her. The police have told her they can't do any deals, but she doesn't believe them. Are you on? I need to know. Susie Brown, her solicitor, is on the other line now.'

'Oh, all right then. I'll do the bail application, but someone else will have to deal with the rest of it. I really can't take Tamara on again long-term. When do they want me?'

'She's scheduled for early afternoon tomorrow. Now don't forget: in success, humility; in failure, grit; and . . .'

'. . . in everything, hard work,' Trish said, interrupting his favourite Churchillian quotation because she'd heard it far too often. She put down the phone before he could retaliate.

Chapter 2

The Cork & Bottle was more crowded than a rush-hour tube station. As Trish peered down from the spiral staircase and across the jumble of heads, she saw an elegant arm waving. Looking more closely over the thin iron banister, she followed the arm down and saw Henry Buxford's face.

As usual, she was amazed at how young he looked. She knew he was at least sixty, but no stranger would ever guess.

There weren't many lines on his broad-cheeked face; just enough to show the places where his smile creased up the skin around his dark brown eyes and strong, still-sexy mouth. Only his silver hair betrayed the fact that he was more than middle aged. He moved his arm so that he was pointing to an empty chair opposite his own.

Trish waved back and negotiated her way through the press of bodies. It was typical of Buxford to have kept a whole table to himself in a place as popular and informal as this. She sank into one of the free chairs in relief. There was an opened bottle of Gicondas in front of him and a plate of different cheeses to eat with it.

'You've changed your hair,' Buxford said, pouring wine into the empty glasses. 'It suits you.'

Trish still felt self-conscious about the loss of her short gelled spikes. The story she'd told her colleagues was that once pop stars and actors had started to adopt a style very like hers she'd had to have a new look. In fact, she'd had it done in case David should be teased about her eccentricities at school.

The resulting geometric cut took much more time to keep tidy than the old spikes, but it didn't make her beaky nose look as idiotic as she'd feared. And the style was still sharp enough to stop anyone thinking she'd been domesticated. She would have hated that. But she didn't want to waste any time discussing it now.

'Sir Henry, Antony said you have some kind of private research you want me to do for you.'

'I wish you wouldn't indulge in all that "Sir" stuff,' Buxford said, with a glinting smile. 'It doesn't suit an Angry Young Woman like you. Call me Henry.'

'Thank you.' She tasted the wine, liked its spiciness, and waited to hear what he wanted.

'Have you ever heard of the Gregory Bequest?'

'Of course,' she said, surprised. 'It's that private gallery near Southwark Bridge that has somebody-or-other's lost art collection in it. Wasn't there something in the papers about it the other day?'

'Yes, there was,' he said with a grimness that surprised her even more.

'George and I keep meaning to go and have a look because it's only just across the river from my flat, but we've never found the time.'

'You and most of London,' Buxford said. 'Still, that's the least of my problems at the moment.'

'I had no idea you were involved.' She drank again. 'I thought music was your thing, not art.'

'It is. I got roped in because of old Ivan Gregory, whose collection it was. We were friends in the City.' Buxford paused, looked at his perfect fingernails, then added: 'I owe him a lot.'

More favours, Trish thought crossly. I should have known.

And I should have said no at once and stayed at home. She took a huge swig of wine and almost choked herself. Buxford waited until she had got the mouthful under control, then said:

'As I told you on the phone, it's a long and complicated story, but I'd like you to hear it in full because it'll make you understand why I need you.'

'OK,' she said, avoiding a surreptitious glance down at her watch.

'My involvement started about five years ago, after Ivan Gregory had had a stroke. As soon as I heard he was back from hospital, I went round to his house to see how he was getting on.'

Buxford looked over the top of Trish's head, as though staring back into the past. She waited, not sure where the story was going.

'I found him huddled at the bottom of his attic stairs in tears. His nurse-cum-housekeeper couldn't understand a thing he said and he wouldn't let her touch him, so she'd had to leave him sitting there in a heap on the floor. She practically fell on my neck, poor woman.'

He wiped a drip of wine from the stem of his glass with one finger, as gently as though he was mopping up a child's tears. Trish, who had always thought his charm hid total ruthlessness, was intrigued to see how much the memory still moved him. Some of her irritation leached away, and she settled more firmly in her chair to listen.

'I hadn't expected anything so bad,' Buxford went on, 'even though I'd known Ivan would be fragile. At first I couldn't make out what was worrying him so much. He kept muttering about betraying his father, and debts he wouldn't be able to pay, and wasting his life's work, over and over again. It took hours to tease out what he meant.'

This time Trish supplied a prompt, saying: 'And what was it? What had he done?'

'Nothing, in fact.' Buxford looked at her, as though making sure she was still prepared to listen. She nodded and watched his face relax into a more natural smile. He wiped his finger on a paper napkin, making sure every trace of wine was rubbed away and paying particular attention to the cuticle.

'The collection belonged originally to his father, Jean-Pierre Gregoire, who was French, obviously, and had met Ivan's mother when she was a nurse during the First World War. He was killed at some time before the Armistice, but we don't know exactly when or where because no body was ever found. That wasn't an uncommon story at the time.'

'I understand what you're saying,' Trish assured him, in the phrase she'd used so often with clients who needed encouragement that it had become a reflex action whenever anyone waited for her to say something.

'Good. At some point he must have decided that the Germans were going to overrun France because he had his paintings shipped over to London for safety and put in the care of his wife.'

'We're still talking about Ivan's mother, I suppose.'

'Yes; she anglicized their surname to Gregory after the war. According to the account I eventually heard from him, she never touched the paintings herself in all the fifty-odd years she had them under her control. She refused to accept that her husband must be dead. In fact, she seems to have convinced herself that he would come back one day and that it was her duty to keep his collection exactly as he'd sent it – right down to the original packing – until then.'

'She must have been mad.'

'Deluded, anyway. And unhappy.' Buxford's eyes had softened again. 'When she died in the late 1960s, no one knew anything very much about the paintings, and Ivan simply left them where they were.'

'But *he* must have known his father was dead.' Mental

arithmetic had never been one of Trish's skills. 'He'd have been about a hundred and ten by then.'

'Not quite. More like ninety-something. The First World War isn't exactly ancient history, Trish.'

'It is to me. I was born in 1965.'

'Good lord!' Buxford laughed. 'One forgets. Anyway, Ivan told me that he barely gave the pictures a moment's thought. The probate valuers who'd had a look at them after his mother's death hadn't been impressed, so that didn't give him any incentive to do anything. And he was always so busy. It was only after his stroke that he remembered them and panicked.'

'Why panic?'

'He was depressed. It often happens after a stroke, I gather. I eventually found out that he was spending half the time terrified that he would die and the other half that he wouldn't. He thought his executors might chuck the paintings out as so much rubbish after his death, destroying his father's life's work. But he also thought someone might discover they were worth millions after all, and accuse him of conspiring to defraud the Inland Revenue when he inherited them from his mother. For a man of his integrity, that was the real killer.'

Trish had had her own brush with depression in the past and could see exactly how such contradictory fears might feed on themselves until they had overtaken every scrap of normal rationality.

'He could barely walk at that stage,' Buxford went on, 'but he'd tried to get up into the attic to unpack the pictures and see what they were. Of course he fell. Then he couldn't get up again. He was in a terrible state. The only way to calm him down was to promise I'd take over. I said I'd deal with the Revenue if the collection did turn out to have any real value, and that I'd make sure it was properly exhibited and due credit given to his father.'

The casual announcement took Trish's breath away. She had

a pretty good idea of how much work must have been involved. This was no trading in favours.

'I'd like to help,' she said at once, 'if I can. But what is it you want me to do?'

'I haven't quite got to you yet.' Buxford refilled her glass. 'I'm sorry it's taking so long.'

'That's OK,' she said, liking him much more than she'd expected.

'Good. Once I'd got an expert to look at a few of the paintings and discovered that Ivan's instincts had been right and some of them were worth really quite a lot, I cleared the position with the Revenue. Eventually Ivan set up a trust, with three of his other friends joining me as trustees, to preserve the paintings and ensure their permanent public exhibition.' He picked up his glass.

Trish watched the corners of his mouth turn down after he'd swallowed, as though the mouthful of wine hadn't pleased him as much as usual.

'Because none of us knew anything much about art,' he went on, 'we advertised for a director to run the gallery and oversee the whole rolling process of conservation. Eventually, after three rounds of interviews, we took on Toby Fullwell, the art historian. He's been doing a good job, and we're about three-quarters of the way through the unpacking and cleaning of the paintings now.'

'Why is it taking so long?' Trish made an effort to stop frowning. She'd heard far too much from George about how ferocious she looked when her forehead tightened and her eyebrows clenched across the top of her nose. Ferocity could be useful in court, but not when dealing with something like this.

'It's not that long. Ivan had his stroke five years ago and we'd got enough paintings restored and ready to open the gallery with two years later. I think that's positively speedy myself.'

Seeing that she'd insulted him, Trish put an apology into her smile to save time.

'There's a hell of a lot involved, you know,' Buxford went on, as though he hadn't noticed. 'First, the paintings have to be unpacked, which is such delicate work it has to be done slowly and in controlled conditions. Then the good stuff has to be sorted out from the dross, which is disposed of through provincial salerooms straightaway. The more valuable canvases are sent for cleaning and restoration as necessary.'

'How is it all funded?' Trish said because her usual gap-filling phrase seemed overworked.

'Ivan donated a sum to get it started, then, as soon as we realized what we were dealing with, the trustees sold a couple of seriously important paintings. They raised enough to convert his house into a gallery – he had moved to a nursing home by then – make a flat for Toby and his family in the attics, and—'

'So where are you keeping the packages that still haven't been unwrapped? I thought they were in the attic.'

The skin around Buxford's eyes crinkled as he smiled. 'Antony always says you listen well. We tanked the basement and moved them down there. They don't need daylight; Toby and his family do.'

'That makes sense,' she said, itching to tell him to get a move on.

'I'm almost there, Trish. Be patient a little longer. When we set up the trust, we made sure that there was a provision to allow the director, whoever he or she might be, to sell not only the dross but also better stuff, if and when funds were needed.'

'Ah, of course,' she said. '*That's* what I read in the papers. He sold a painting a couple of weeks ago, didn't he? And raised a fortune.'

'Five million pounds.'

'Wow!'

'It was a Pieter de Hooch. You know, the not-quite Vermeer

bloke who did street scenes with fat women sweeping and a lot of sunshine.'

Trish smiled. Buxford was laying it on a bit thick, even for a man who professed to know nothing about art.

'And that's where you come in, Trish. I want you to find out why he did it.'

'But there must be all kinds of reasons.'

'None that makes sense. There's enough cash in the kitty to last for years at the normal rate of expenditure.' Buxford pushed both hands back over the sides of his immaculately cut silver hair. 'And so—'

A woman in very high heels lurched past their table just then. Trish grabbed her glass to keep it out of the way of the woman's swinging shoulder bag. The movement distracted the woman and she tripped, flinging the contents of her own glass of red wine all over Henry Buxford's impeccable suit.

'Oh, Christ!' she said, lurching the other way and bouncing off one of the people leaning against the bar. 'I'm so sorry. God! I don't know how that happened.'

She grabbed a paper napkin from under the cheese and was attempting to dab at his suit, depositing smears of Reblochon on the wine stain.

'Will you please leave me alone?' he said in a voice so harsh it made Trish stare at him. He produced a rueful grimace and pushed back his chair. 'Shall we go?'

'Sure. Whatever,' Trish said.

He thrust three twenty-pound notes under the wine bottle and waved to the man behind the bar, who nodded. As Buxford urged Trish through the crowd towards the exit, she heard the woman who'd emptied her wine over his suit telling her friends what had happened.

'And he looked at me like a complete psychopath,' she said. 'I feel sorry for his girlfriend.'

'I'd feel sorry for her anyway,' said a new voice. 'She must be half his age. Still he looks rich. That must be some compensation.'

'Ignore them,' Henry said from behind Trish. 'They're plastered.'

Outside, the pavements around Leicester Square were almost as crowded as the wine bar.

'Shall we go to the Garrick?' he said, shivering and driving his hands down into the pockets of his dark-blue overcoat. He pulled a cashmere scarf out of one and thick leather gloves out of the other. 'It may be a bit stuffy but at least no one flings wine over you there.'

This time Trish did look at her watch. 'I wish I could, but I've got to be at the National Theatre in half an hour.'

'Oh. Pity. Well, why don't we walk in that direction? We can talk on the way.'

'OK.' Trish pulled the sides of her long black coat together and did up the buttons. It didn't help much. The cold seeped up under the sleeves and through every seam. Stuffing her hands in her pockets, she wished she'd brought a scarf and gloves like his.

'You must have asked your director why the trust needed the five million pounds,' she said through clattering teeth.

'Of course we did,' Buxford said. 'And at the relevant meeting, all the trustees accepted his answer – probably too easily – that there were a lot of unexpected costs coming up. It was only afterwards, when I looked at the bank statements, that I realized how much money there already was in the trust's accounts. So then I asked him, privately, for a few more details.' He paused again.

'So,' Trish said, 'what did he tell you this time?'

'That I was right and there was no immediate need for extra funds, but that the painting was a second-rate work the gallery didn't need because we have a much better one, which is insured for ten million. He'd heard of a rich foreign buyer, who was in London for only a short period and was thought to be prepared to pay over the odds for a de Hooch. His interest would undoubtedly push up the price of ours if it were to be put into the next old master auction at Goode & Floore's, and it would have been madness to miss such an unusual opportunity. I'm not exactly quoting, Trish, but that was the gist of it.'

'It sounds quite feasible to me. Why didn't you believe him?'

'Because it wasn't the story he'd given us at the meeting. And because I've never seen a man look so frightened.'

'Ah. I see.'

'Yes. All the blood drained out of his face when I put my question, and his voice shook like an old man's as he answered. He's up to something, Trish, and I have to know what it is.'

'Where's the five million now?'

'Still sitting safely in the trust's account. I know, I know,' Buxford said, although she hadn't made any kind of protest. 'If it's still there, he can't have stolen it, or used it to pay debts he's been hiding from the trustees, or anything else of a nefarious nature. But he wouldn't have been so scared if he wasn't doing something he was ashamed of.'

'Like what?'

'I've no idea. And I need to know. I should have been more challenging at the meeting when Toby first told us about the proposed sale. It's too late to do anything about that now, but if there's trouble coming, I need to know so that I can deal with it before it blows up in our faces. I can't have Ivan's last years ruined by any kind of scandal. *Will* you help, Trish?'

'I'd like to, but I'm not sure that I'm qualified. I know nothing about old masters or the art market. Not at that level anyway.'

'Perhaps not, but you can spot a gap in documentary evidence quicker than anyone except Antony Shelley, and I'll send you all the paperwork.' Buxford smiled. 'You can also make almost anyone talk to you, and without scaring them. Unlike me.'

'Thank you. But I can hardly waltz in and ask your director questions about his Pieter de Hooch sale without letting him know that I've come from you and scaring him in spite of myself, can I?'

'Of course you can, if you drop into the gallery early one weekday morning, when no one else is around. He's bound to show you the paintings himself, because he loves doing that. You could get chatting that way.'

'And while we're chatting, I just casually drop in a question about what he's planning to do with his five million pounds?' Trish said. 'Come on, Henry. He'd smell a rat at once.'

His eyes crinkled up again as he laughed. 'I know you can be a lot more subtle than that, Trish. Don't forget, I watched you in court with Nick Gurles last year. But if there's a problem, you could always use your personal connection.'

'What? I've never even met the man.'

'His younger son is in your brother's class at Blackfriars Prep. Didn't you know?'

This time Trish didn't even try to stop the frown.

'They call him Mer, short for Meredith,' Buxford went on cheerfully. 'If you were to organize a joint family expedition, I'm sure you could get all sorts of stuff out of Toby without letting him have any idea I'm involved.'

'No,' Trish said, stopping in the middle of the pavement. 'I can't take that sort of risk.'

Buxford had walked three paces beyond her before he realized she wasn't following. He wheeled back to stand in front of her. The light from a street lamp shone on his face, making it look glowingly innocent.

'There's no risk here, Trish. It's only money. What are you afraid of?'

'Anything that might make David's life more difficult than it has to be.'

He looked so puzzled that she realized she was going to have to explain and tried to keep it short.

'I only have him living with me because his mother was murdered last year and there isn't anyone else to look after him.'

'Trish, I'm so sorry. I had no idea. The poor child. Did he see it happen?'

'No, thank God. She had a kind of warning and got him away in time. But that doesn't stop the world looking like a very frightening place. He's only nine.'

'I understand. You don't have to plead. All right, forget the idea of using him to get to Toby, and see what you can do just by going to the gallery. You will, won't you? There's no one I'd rather trust with this than you, Trish. And it's important.'

They had reached the Aldwych now, and both stopped on the edge of the pavement.

'Oh, OK,' she said at last, looking up at him. 'I'll have a go.'

'Thank you.' A taxi lumbered up the Strand towards them, and Buxford summoned it with a brief, imperious gesture. 'Let me know as soon as you've got anywhere,' he said just before he slammed the door.

Trish's face was tingling as she watched his taxi drive away. It wasn't the cold, she thought, that sent the blood prickling under her skin, but the sense of having been dismissed as soon as she'd given him what he wanted. The lights changed and she stalked across the road, making her way towards the river.

London looked even more glorious than usual in the frosty darkness. If George hadn't been waiting, she might have dealt with her crossness by idling along the edge of the Thames. But not tonight. He hated people being late. He'd once said in a burst of fury that it was the worst kind of selfishness. If she made him miss the first act of tonight's play, he would go berserk.

* * *

Helen watched until Jean-Pierre was out of sight. The sun was a huge, bright orange disc in a sky that looked almost white. He had waited here at the inn until she came off duty again and then held her in his arms, barely moving, while she fell into sleep. Only when she'd woken of her own accord had he told her that he had to leave today. She had clung to him for a moment, then forced herself to let go. Now she had only her own body to wrap her arms around.

Jean-Pierre had told her that there was very little chance he would be able to get any messages to her while he was away. When she'd asked him where he was going, he'd laid his fingers across her mouth. His black eyes had been as gentle as his voice when he'd said:

'You know I cannot tell you that, *ma mie*. But what I can tell you is that I have never loved a woman as I love you, and that nothing and no one will keep me from coming back as soon as I am able.'

Staring down the road after him, listening to the guns, she shuddered.

'You're a nurse,' she told herself the next instant. 'Control yourself.'

It did not take too long. Her eyes were dry again and her head was up as she walked into the ward to smile at her frightened patients.

Chapter 3

'And if it hadn't been for the longbows, Trish,' David told her on the way to school next morning, shouting against the wind that was roaring up the Thames from the sea, 'the English would have been beaten hollow at Agincourt. But they were just so much more flexible than the French crossbows. And as for those knights with all their armour! Well, they just got stuck in the trees.'

'Oh, I see,' Trish said, wishing he wouldn't offer her these streams of adult-sounding information whenever they were alone together. Was it to make sure she didn't ask intrusive questions?

She had plenty of those, rattling around in her brain, but she had seen how much they distressed him when he had first come to live with her, and she'd stopped voicing them months ago.

The wind forced its way through the fabric of her clothes and slapped her face. She shuddered. David didn't complain, but then he never complained about anything. He was the most cooperative child she had ever encountered, and it scared the wits out of her.

'It sounds as though you're liking this project better than last term's Greek myth one,' she said hopefully.

'Yes, I do like it much more.' He looked up with a shy, earnest smile that made her long to tell him he didn't have to try so hard. There were tears in his eyes, but she knew they were only the result of the wind. He had never cried in front of her since she had taken him to live with her, even when George shouted at him. 'War's much more fun than all those stories about families.'

That's one way of looking at the Greek myths, she thought. Procrustes had no counterpart in her family, but David had seen things and felt things that were right outside her own experience.

He stopped to lean over the edge of the bridge, calling back against the wind: 'Look, Trish. Look!'

She peered over his shoulder, to see three River Police launches bouncing around on the wind-stiffened waves. One uniformed officer was leaning over the side of his launch, apparently shouting, while two others conferred on the leeward side.

'Something big must have dropped off one of the barges,' Trish said. 'They'll have to get it out before it sinks one of the other boats.'

'What if there's already been a shipwreck?' He hoisted himself up against the balustrade, showing enviable gymnastic skill, then turned to look at her. His eyes were huge. 'D'you think they all drowned?'

'No, of course not. Don't lean over too far, David. There'd be bits of wood floating about, wouldn't there? If a boat had already been damaged.'

A head bobbed up through the water, sleek and dark as a seal's. Then a naked hand pushed up the diver's mask and its owner said something to the nearest policeman. Trish and David were too far away to hear anything. After a moment the diver tipped himself down again. David laughed to see his flippers wave above the surface. Trish was glad to see his ideas about drowned bodies hadn't spooked him.

'He must be freezing. Did you see? He didn't have any gloves.'

'Come on,' Trish said, tugging at David's sleeve. 'We mustn't be late for school.'

'No. I'm sorry.' He dropped down from the parapet at once, bouncing a little as his feet hit the pavement, and he sped off towards the far end of the bridge.

She hoped it wasn't just obedience that made him keen to get to the school she'd picked with such care. George kept telling her that the boy would be safer, and probably happier, at boarding school, but she didn't believe it. She'd seen – and felt – enough of the emotional suppression George had had to impose on himself to deal with the shock of being sent away from home at the age of eight to want that for David. He suppressed far too much as it was.

'Here we are,' he said cheerfully. 'Thanks for bringing me, Trish.'

'I enjoyed it. And I like the sound of your new project. Maybe we should go to the Imperial War Museum one weekend. It might be useful.'

'That would be great,' he said. For once the black eyes that were so like her own showed real excitement. 'I'd like that a lot. They've got a dugout, you know, from the Blitz. You can go in it and hear the sirens and the bombs. One of my friends was telling me. And a trench, too, from the First World War.'

'We'll definitely go, then.'

When she had seen him safely inside the school's stout gates, Trish turned her back on her usual route to chambers, and set off for the Gregory Bequest Gallery. The sooner she got Henry Buxford's odd little enquiry out of the way, the better.

She found the place without difficulty, a tall double-fronted eighteenth-century house, sandwiched between two hideous 1960s brown-glass-and-concrete office blocks. Originally it must have been part of a street or square of matching buildings, but there had been a lot of bombing round here in the Second World War and now it was the only one of its kind.

An engraved brass plate told her that the gallery was open on weekdays from half past nine until half past five, which meant there was still more than half an hour to wait. It was much too cold to hang about out of doors. Retracing her route to the nearest coffee shop, she ordered a large latte and took it, with one of the newspapers the place provided, to a deep leather chair.

Warmth soon transferred itself from the thick mug to her hands. Steam from the coffee also made her cold nose drip, which was less satisfactory. She sniffed, wishing she had a handkerchief, and opened the paper.

Half past nine came and went. It seemed mad to go out into the icy bluster again when she could stay here all morning. She remembered the police diver's bare hands and told herself that if he could plunge into the water on a day like this, she could certainly walk a few hundred yards.

The glossy black door was still shut when she got back to the gallery, but that could have been to conserve heat. She banged the knocker and heard footsteps almost at once.

The woman who opened the door must have been in her early twenties. Her thick blonde hair was caught back in a velvet hairband and her black trousers and pink twin set looked expensive. She had ordinary little gold studs in her ears and a single baroque grey pearl hanging from a slender chain around her neck.

Sleek was the word for her, Trish decided. Sleek and rich. But then you had to be rich to work in places like this. The pay was always awful.

'Come on in and let me shut the door,' the woman said, shivering. 'I don't want to lose all the heat.'

Trish bought a ticket and an expensive catalogue to the exhibition.

'I'll just tell Mr Fullwell you're here,' the young woman said. 'He likes to take people round himself, especially on their first visit. This is yours, isn't it?'

'Do I look that lost?' Trish asked with a smile.

'No. But I recognize most of the regulars.' She giggled. 'There aren't all that many. If you go through that door on the right, you'll find the Dutch pictures. I'll get him down, and he can join you in there.'

'Thank you.'

The large light room must originally have been the house's main drawing room, Trish thought. Its walls, shutters and austerely carved cornice were off-white, and the floor was a warm honey-coloured parquet. Everything had been subdued to display the magnificence of the paintings. She was impressed.

She was even more impressed a moment later to see what looked like one of Rembrandt's self-portraits. In spite of her careful disclaimer to Henry Buxford, she knew enough about the art world to be aware of the recent downgrading of a lot of supposed Rembrandts. There had been plenty of deliberate copyists, as well as artists choosing to work in his style, for centuries. Maybe this was a copy, too.

Peering at the label, she saw that the Gregory Bequest's director was claiming the work as genuine. He had given the painter his full name and dates, and there was no suggestion of 'school of' or 'after' to water down the attribution.

Trish stood back again, to get a better view, and wished she knew more. This was an effective portrait of an elderly man, looking out at the world with a mixture of pity and dread. He had the familiar bulbous nose, brown stuff gown and soft white cap of other self-portraits she already knew from illustrations and exhibitions.

'Wonderful, isn't it?' said a light male voice from behind her.

Trish swung round and saw the director smiling at her from the doorway. He was quite tall, maybe a couple of inches more than she was, which would have made him about six foot, and good-looking in a slightly droopy way. His well-cut pleat-front flannel trousers were topped with a mid-blue sweater over a crisp white shirt. Large horn-rimmed spectacles balanced on the end of his nose completed the picture of elegantly casual European scholarship. As he moved, his dark-brown hair flopped against his broad pale forehead.

'Marvellous,' she agreed, wondering whether an image-consultant had advised him on his clothes. 'I can't think why I've never come here before. You've been open quite a few years now, haven't you?'

'Three. How did you hear about us?' he said, giving her the perfect opening.

'I read all the stuff in the papers at the beginning, when the collection was rediscovered,' she said, 'but somehow never got round to coming to have a look. It was the reports of the sale of your Pieter de Hooch that reminded me you were here. It must have been an awful wrench to sell something like that, even though all those millions must come in handy.'

'Oh, absolutely,' he said, showing no sign of anxiety, let alone the kind of fear Henry Buxford had described. 'Now what would you most like to see? The collection is far too big to hang in its entirety, so there's only a selection here. Even so, it's probably too much for one visit. One can only take in a few pictures at once. This is obviously the Dutch room. The Italians are upstairs and the French across the hall. Where shall we start?'

He had a good smile, Trish decided, genuinely humorous and friendly.

'Why not here? I had no idea there was so much. How could anyone have forgotten they owned it all?' she asked to edge him back to what she needed to know.

He shrugged as he came further into the room. 'It does seem extraordinary, doesn't it? But it's a wonderful story, you know. Jean-Pierre Gregoire, the man who built it up, was French.'

'So I'd heard.'

'His life's work was to create a collection that would represent all the major developments in European art, and he scoured the Continent for the best examples before the First World War. How he beat Berenson and Duveen to some of them, I'll never know. It's tragic that they remained hidden for so long – and that he was killed before he could see them exhibited. There's no justice, you know; there really isn't.'

'Except that the paintings did survive,' Trish said. She was enjoying herself, which she hadn't expected. 'And, when you think about it, that's amazing, given how much bombing there was round here. The whole lot could have gone up in flames in the Blitz, with no one any the wiser.'

'Oh, don't,' Fullwell said, putting a hand over his heart as though to calm its racing beat. 'I can't bear the thought. Now would you— ?'

A mobile phone began to ring with an irritating little jingle. His pleasant smile twisted into a grimace. Trish sympathized: she hated the endless interruptions of mobiles herself. Then she realized it was her own phone that was ringing and apologized at once. She grabbed it out of her bag and was about to switch it off when she recognized the chambers' number on her screen.

'This is one I have to answer. I'm so sorry. I'll go outside.'

'There's no need,' he said coldly and turned his back.

She wasn't sure whether he was giving her privacy or signalling his detestation of the mobile menace.

'Yes, Steve?' she said into the phone.

'We've had a call from your brother's school,' her clerk told her in a voice loaded with disapproval. 'He's been involved in a fight and they want you to call them straightaway. D'you want me to give you the number?'

'I've got it, thanks. I'll ring them now,' Trish said. If David were hurt, Henry Buxford's job would have to wait. 'Mr Fullwell, I'm really sorry, but I'm going to have to go now.

May I come back another time, if I promise to keep my mobile switched off?'

'I very much hope you will,' he said, smiling again, as though to show that he'd forgiven her solecism. 'There's a lot here you would enjoy, and you haven't had full value for your ticket. If you bring it with you when you next come, Jo will let you in again.'

'How kind! I'll see you again, then.'

Trish hurried out of the building, already pressing in the code for the school. The secretary answered before she'd reached the street and she was through to Hester More, the head teacher, a moment later.

'Is he hurt?' she said, without any kind of greeting.

'David is no more than bruised,' Mrs More said with her usual careful formality, which always sounded as though she was reproaching the rest of the world for its sloppy speech.

'How did it happen?' Trish couldn't believe the gentle, cooperative child she knew could have got into a fight with anyone.

'Neither of the adversaries is prepared to tell me, and it seems that no one else saw the fight start. I have, therefore, no alternative but to keep David in for a detention this afternoon.'

'Only David? That doesn't sound quite fair.' Trish knew how hard he worked to stay out of trouble, and how much he would hate this. 'What about the other boy?'

'Unfortunately he has had to go to casualty.'

Shock made Trish stop moving. 'David hurt him *that* badly? I don't believe it.'

'I am afraid you must. He's had to have two stitches just above his left eye. It could have been very nasty indeed if David had caught the eye itself.'

'But he didn't.' Trish had enough real worries without letting anyone implant this kind of retrospective anxiety in her mind. She walked on with the phone clamped against her ear. 'And two stitches doesn't sound too bad.'

'That is a matter of opinion, Ms Maguire. It is extremely important that we all make David see how lucky he is that he did nothing worse, and so I hope you will cooperate. The detention will keep him here until four-thirty today. I think it would be a good thing if you were to collect him then yourself, so that you can talk to him while the incident is still fresh in his mind.'

'All right,' Trish said, pulling her diary out of her bag and fighting the wind that tried to turn the pages to the end of the year. Oh, shit! she thought. I'd forgotten Tamara O'Connor.

'I have to be in court in the early part of the afternoon, but I'll do my best to get back in time. If I can't make it, Nicky will fetch him and I'll talk to him later. Unless— Look, why don't I come in to see him now, just in case I am held up this afternoon?'

'I'm afraid that would be most undesirable. I do not wish to have his day interrupted any further.'

Trish was paying the woman a fortune to oversee her brother's education. It would be mad to undermine her now, but she couldn't leave it here. 'Who was the other boy? Has there been any trouble between them before?'

'No. His name is Stephen Johnson and he is two years senior to David. I'll expect you this afternoon. If you cannot come yourself, please telephone my secretary to make an appointment to talk later in the week. Goodbye.'

Trish clicked the phone shut. It sounded to her as though this Stephen must have started the fight. He was older, after all. And even the anxious social worker assigned to David's case after his mother's death had told Trish he was unlikely to be violent.

'Obviously he will have some behavioural problems,' she'd said when she was trying to make sure Trish knew what she was taking on. 'You may be lucky and face nothing worse than underachievement at school, with a bit of lying or truancy thrown in. But stealing is a distinct possibility, and arson could be a problem later. Fourteen is the prime age for that. But with luck you'll have got him straightened out by then. D'you think you'll be able to cope?'

Trish had thought she would. She still thought so, but it would have been a lot easier if David had been prepared to talk about himself. Sometimes she thought that even tantrums would have been less daunting than his quiet determination to hide all his feelings and act as though the past had never happened.

Chapter 4

Toby shut the door and checked that the lock had caught. Another phone was ringing upstairs, on and on. The sound made him feel as though someone was tightening a clamp around his head. 'Jo!' he shouted. 'Answer the phone.'

He ran upstairs to the office and pushed open the panelled door. She was gazing at her computer screen, oblivious to everything else. He nearly hit her.

'When will you learn to answer the fucking phone?'

Jo looked round, her usually sweet face ugly with contempt. 'What phone? There isn't one ringing.'

Toby looked round the room. His lungs were pumping so fast they seemed to tear at his chest and still left him without enough oxygen to breathe. She was right.

'They've rung off,' he said, fighting the thought that he might have imagined the sound because it frightened him so much now. 'I've told you before, you *must* answer within four rings; otherwise they give up. It could have been important. I can't cope with this much longer, Jo. You're going to have to take your job more seriously or leave.'

'I do take it seriously,' she shouted. 'And *I'm* not mad. Or deaf. This phone has not rung all morning.' She turned away and muttered something he couldn't hear. Then she looked back, her expression marginally more gentle. 'What's happened to you, Toby? You never used to be like this. At the beginning I even thought you were the perfect boss. Now all you do is shout at me. Why?'

'You're imagining things.' As Toby wiped his sweating forehead, he dropped his glasses. Stooping to pick them up, he knew that his face would redden as the blood rushed down into it. He hoped the colour would stop her noticing that he was in tears again, too.

'Make sure you answer the phone as soon as it does ring,' he said sharply, to counteract his weakness. 'And for God's sake remember to take proper messages in future. I can't believe you let Peter go last night without at least taking a phone number from him.'

'I told you, I tried.'

He didn't believe her. He could always tell when someone was lying. But why should she lie now? What on earth could she be hiding?

'But he refused to leave any details,' she went on, not meeting Toby's eyes. 'He said you'd know who he was, and you did, didn't you?'

Toby nodded. Then he took off his glasses again to rub the corners of his aching eyes. She was right about that. Her description had made it entirely clear that the mystery caller was Peter Chanting, whom he hadn't seen for eighteen years and whose letters had stopped coming nearly a decade ago.

'So why do you keep blaming *me*?' She tossed back her hair. 'If you'd been here at five o'clock, like you promised, you'd have seen him yourself. Anyway it's no big deal. He said he'd come back again. It's not my fault you haven't seen him.'

Or mine, Toby thought, remembering the traffic that had clogged the Embankment yesterday afternoon.

'But why didn't you phone me when he came back the second time?' he said. 'You know I always have my mobile switched on when I'm away from the gallery.'

'Because you make so much fuss whenever a phone rings and

bang on and on about how you hate them,' Jo said with a snap. 'I didn't want to get another earful about not disturbing you. Why's he so important anyway?'

Since he couldn't tell her that, Toby went to sit in his own office and stared at the pile of post she'd put there when she arrived for work. Peter Chanting was important because he'd put the whole of Toby's life at risk by blabbing the secret they'd both sworn to keep till they died.

Had it been a mistake or a deliberate betrayal? Toby had asked himself the question a hundred times in the two months since his persecution had begun.

At first it hadn't crossed his mind that the well-spoken, well-dressed man who had appeared at the gallery on that dreadful, never-to-be-forgotten Monday morning could be dangerous. Toby had even been pleased to see him. There weren't usually many visitors so early in the week, and the man had bought a catalogue without even raising an eyebrow at its price, which was rare. He had also seemed flatteringly excited by the idea of being shown around the collection by its director.

Toby had hated his own gullibility ever since, and now burned at the memory of his eagerness to tell the good-looking visitor the sad romantic story of Jean-Pierre Gregoire and his English widow. He had led the man on from canvas to canvas, revelling in his unusually intelligent questions and apparently genuine admiration of what he saw.

Then it had started to go wrong. Looking back, Toby tried to pinpoint the moment when the first tiny shiver of fear had made him pause. He thought they'd been standing in front of the Rembrandt when the visitor had put his simple, unemotional question: 'Have you got any Clouet drawings in the collection?'

Toby had said no easily enough, before moving to the next canvas he wanted to show off. But the man hadn't paid much attention. Within five minutes he'd gone back to asking questions about Clouet drawings, questions which had soon shown him to be terrifyingly well informed. Toby had had to keep looking over his shoulder to make sure that neither Jo nor any other visitor had sneaked in to eavesdrop.

The one thing he could still feel good about was the length of time he had resisted the man's attempt to make him incriminate himself. Toby had stuck to his story for what felt like hours until the visitor, who later said his name was Ben Smithlock, had said:

'So if the story I've been told about those so-called Clouet drawings you found at Cambridge is all untrue, you won't be afraid if I go to the papers with it.'

He had taken a mobile out of his pocket and stroked it, adding: 'The papers and your trustees, of course. I have Sir Henry Buxford's private number programmed into my phone, so it'll be the work of a moment to tell him what kind of sleazy criminal he's got running his favourite charity. You'll be out on your ear in no time. And probably in prison soon afterwards.'

Gaping at him, Toby hadn't had a clue what to do or say.

'Your wife'll leave you, too.' Ben had said. 'There's no way a glamorous, intelligent woman like Margaret would stay if she knew the truth about you.'

'Don't be ridiculous.' Even now, Toby could hear the hoarseness that had made his voice rasp as he'd forced out his pathetic protest. Still more humiliatingly, he'd felt spit dripping from his lower lip and had had to fumble for a handkerchief to wipe it off his chin and his cashmere sweater. Ben Smithlock had just laughed.

'Of course, if you were to do me one small favour, I'd be more than grateful enough to suppress everything I know about you. D'you want to hear about it?'

Even then Toby hadn't quite understood that what was happening to him was no more or less than straightforward blackmail. Nor had he realized Ben was not working alone. It had been at least a week before he mentioned his boss and even longer before he'd hinted that they had enforcers working for them, too.

Sitting at his desk now, Toby retched and put his hand over his mouth to control the impulse to vomit. He'd been certain all along that Peter had betrayed him. Only now did he let himself contemplate the even worse possibility that Peter might be the blackmailer-in-chief.

Had he come to the house yesterday to bring the latest demand in person?

Too restless to sit still, and too sick to do any work, Toby went to the window to gaze down at the small paved garden with its few bare trees and empty urns. Wouldn't it be better just to open the window and fling himself down on to the elegant paving stones? Even Henry Buxford couldn't be cruel enough to punish Margaret and the boys for what he'd done if he were already dead. And her father was already paying their school fees and would make sure they had everything they needed.

The thought of the pain that would rip through him as his body hit the ground was enough to send Toby two paces back from the window. It was humiliating to find that he was too much of a coward even to take the most obvious way out.

Upstairs in the private flat that came with his job, his wife was talking to someone. The sound of her soft American voice buzzed through the floorboards, even though he couldn't distinguish the words. There'd be no help from her either. If he went up now, she'd only ask why he was so jumpy, and he couldn't tell her, any more than he could tell Jo or Henry. He was alone, just as he'd always been, except for the three years at Cambridge, when he and Peter had been inseparable.

Toby had once hated the sloppiness of people who talked about getting their heads round things, but now he understood what they'd meant. Somehow he had to get his head round what Peter had done to him.

They'd met in their second term. The first had been hell, as he'd struggled with the unfamiliar work and his inability to find anyone who wanted to have anything to do with him. He'd tried clubs and pubs and university societies, and he'd always got it wrong, making jokes when everyone else was serious or taking literally what turned out to be hysterically funny anarchic humour. Then Peter – rich, good-looking and wildly popular – had whisked him up and, almost overnight, turned him into a different being.

Toby had learned how to talk to girls then and to ask them out. Pretty soon he'd even taken one successfully to bed. He'd learned to drink in vast quantities and make other men laugh. And later, when he and Peter had started to talk about things that mattered, Toby had also learned that being unhappy was neither unique nor any kind of failure.

That was how it had started, with their shared confession of growing up in a welter of misery. Then they had begun to trust each other. And later, when they had worked out their great money-making plan together, it had never occurred to Toby that trusting Peter might be stupid.

It had all started as a kind of a game. Toby couldn't now remember whose idea it had been in the first place, but it didn't matter. At that point it had all been 'what if?' What if we faked an old master drawing and took it to one of the big salerooms in all innocence to ask them what it was? What if they decided it was genuine – or near enough to get past their usual punters' scrutiny? What if it was put into auction and raised a lot of money? Wouldn't that be a gas?

Then they'd started to work out how they could do it. Neither belonged to the sort of family with grand attics full of ancestral rubbish that might yield valuable art, so they'd had to think up another way. Bit by bit the plan had become more and more elaborate until one day they'd had to try. They'd picked François Clouet because Toby could already draw in his style, and his figures were so lacking in personality and emotion that they seemed easier to copy than anything more interesting.

The scam had worked so easily that neither of them could believe it. At every stage they'd been ready to give up and admit it was just a rag, but there had been no need.

Peter had laid out the money to buy four big sixteenth-century books with blank flyleaves they could cut out, and Toby had prepared and prepared until he was confident that he could draw exactly like François Clouet. He'd done all the necessary research to ensure the hats and doublets he was going to include were accurate. Even he had been impressed with the finished product.

He had dirtied the drawings up a bit and framed them in crappy cheap gilt frames under low-grade cracked glass, before flogging them as prints to a bottom-feeding dealer, who wouldn't have known a Clouet from a Corot. Peter had breezed into the shop later that day and bought them at a rapacious mark-up, which still came nowhere near their cost of production, let alone the price the real thing might raise.

Then the fun had really started. Toby had talked to a few friends about the amazing find he thought Peter had made. Together they had taken the drawings, now out of their frames again, to Goode & Floore's in London and asked humbly at the front counter whether they might show them to an expert.

It had been the expert who had first pronounced the name François Clouet. Toby hadn't made any suggestion at all; he'd merely said that he thought the drawings might be interesting, but that he didn't know enough to make even a wild guess. The expert had got very overexcited and almost insisted that the drawings went into the next old master sale. He'd been even more pleased than Toby and Peter when they'd made a record price for the artist.

That night the two of them had celebrated with wines finer than any Toby had dreamed of tasting, and they had solemnly renewed their oath never – ever – to tell. Even when Peter's father had guessed there was something wrong with the drawings and thundered and shouted about criminal records and a lifetime of shame, Peter had stood firm and made Toby stand with him.

When the old brute had left them alone again, Peter had insisted that so long as neither of them admitted anything, ever, or paid out too much of the money at once, or tried a similar scam, no one could touch them. The story was that they'd bought the drawings in good faith and it was Goode & Floore's expert who had claimed they were by François Clouet. So long as they stuck to it and never tried to fake anything else again, they'd be safe. After a while, even Toby the terrified had come to believe it. And they'd gone swanning off on their holiday of a lifetime that summer without a care in the world.

Remembering it now, Toby shuddered. He should have known as soon as the trip turned into a disaster that it was an omen, warning them that they wouldn't get away with the scam for ever. But he'd had too much else to think of, as he'd been sucked down into the hell of amoebic dysentery and the certainty that he would die.

A lorry thundered by outside, breaking off his memories. His head wasn't anywhere near round them all, and he still had no idea how deeply Peter was involved. So far the only one of the blackmailers he'd met face to face was the appalling Ben, but Peter had to be in it somewhere. No one else had known all the details of how the Clouet drawings had come into being, however much some, like Peter's father, might have suspected.

Without those details, Toby still believed he might have followed the original line of never admitting anything. He'd still be safe. He wouldn't have been forced to pretend the blackmailers' faked de Hooch was part of the Gregory Bequest collection, and he wouldn't be sitting on five million pounds of their money now, ready to buy the next forgery they wanted to establish as genuine.

At least the de Hooch had been reasonably convincing. It was one of his many nightmares that they would force him to bid – in public – for something that wouldn't deceive a child. When he'd first understood what Ben was going to make him do, he'd tried to recommend a restorer who could be relied on to produce a really top-class job. Ben had laughed and told him they were much further on than that and had already got their fakes ready and waiting to be fed on to the market.

Who was he working for? The whole of the London art world had been worried for years about the supply of old masters dwindling to nothing, but Toby couldn't think of anyone with the brazen dishonesty – or the balls – to dream up something like this.

Everything about the operation was clever. Even he had to admit that. And picking a middle-ranking expert like him to add legitimacy to the fakes had been the masterstroke. He had just enough influence to carry the right weight, but none of the security that would have allowed him to tell them to bugger off when they'd first tried to blackmail him into working for them.

Jo was moving about in the outer office now, probably getting ready to go out to lunch. As far as he could tell, she did less and less work every day, as though she'd sensed his ever-growing vulnerability.

'Have you finished those letters yet?' he called through the closed door, to re-establish his authority.

There was no answer, so he went out to see what she was up to, and asked the question again.

'Nearly,' she said, but she didn't look round from her computer screen. He saw there was a half-typed letter on it, which was something. But she'd probably spent all morning chatting to her mates on the phone, stopping all the important calls coming through, and leaving her work untouched.

'Well, hurry them up. They're urgent. And don't forget to run the spell-check this time. You know you always make mistakes, and you'll only have to print all the letters out again if you don't correct them on the screen first.'

As she turned to look at him, he flinched at the fury in her eyes.

'I am the best secretary you have ever had, or are likely to have,' she said. 'So stop making excuses to blame me for whatever it is that's eating you. *I* am not the problem.'

Toby hadn't the energy to deal with her now.

'I'm going down to the basement,' he said, turning away. 'Buzz me on the internal phone when you've finished the letters or if my call comes through.'

There were only a few barristers in the clerks' room when Trish got back to chambers, but even one would have been enough to stop her going in. She couldn't have her rivals knowing that her only brief at the moment was Tamara O'Connor's tiresome bail application this afternoon. As she passed the open door, she overheard Steve talking to young Sam Makins about one of his other cases.

'And if you get stuck, talk to Trish Maguire. She dealt with the family for years and knows the background.'

'OK,' Sam said in the husky voice that sounded as though he must get through at least forty full-strength cigarettes a day. In fact Trish had never seen him smoke anything while he was her pupil, and his skin had always had the taut clear look that came from perfect health and fitness.

'As you know, she's good,' Steve went on. 'Anything she says is worth listening to.'

That's something, Trish thought, moving quietly on down the corridor. Maybe Steve will get me more real work soon. And with luck he'll get a move on with calling in all the unpaid fees. Otherwise I won't be able to pay my January tax bill. Or David's next set of school fees.

In her own room, she sat down, trying not to resent the fact that her father had left her with all the responsibility for his son. A DNA test had proved Paddy's paternity, and yet he had never agreed even to meet David.

Trish knew perfectly well that she had played a part in his stubbornness, but, at the time, she hadn't understood what she was doing. She'd been trying to put it right ever since, but so far Paddy had held out against her, as well as leaving her to pay all the bills.

'All the more reason to find out what Henry Buxford wants to know quickly,' she muttered, opening up her laptop and plugging in the modem.

Even so, there didn't seem any point going back to the gallery this morning, now that she knew the director wasn't going to faint at her questions about the de Hooch – or answer them. With luck she would learn something useful from the papers Buxford had promised to send her. Once she'd read them, she could try interrogating Toby Fullwell again. You always got more out of people if you had a few facts to use as a lever.

The first email she read was from George, saying simply: 'You haven't forgotten dinner at the Carfields tonight, have you? Do you want me to collect you or shall we meet there? They live on the river, just by Tate Modern.'

Sighing, Trish clicked on 'Reply' and told him she'd meet him there, if he'd send her the address. That way, neither of them need hold the other up if work got in the way.

She had never met their hosts and didn't like going to formal dinners in the middle of the week, but Jeremy Carfield was the founder of a huge software company and one of George's biggest clients, so he had to be kept sweet. And it wasn't as if she had to get up early to work on any case papers now.

Knowing that George would forget to buy them anything, she made a mental note to get something herself. Wine would be insulting and silly for a man as rich as Carfield, she thought, and chocolates were a bit ordinary. Flowers might be all right, except that they always got in the way when hosts were busy greeting their guests and pouring drinks. The whole business of giving presents to people who didn't need them and would probably recycle them or take them to a charity shop irritated her, but everyone else did it, so she had to join in.

Her phone rang. It was Steve, wanting to know whether she could accept a brief for a dispute between a catering company and some manufacturers of kitchen equipment. It sounded small and deadly dull, and it was going to be heard in Guildford of all places, but at least it was something.

'All right.'

'Good,' he said, adding as a reward for obedience: 'There's more in the pipeline. I'll put the papers in your pigeonhole. You've already got a bunch of personal stuff in it. You ought to come and empty it. It's messy when it overflows and you know I don't like mess in the clerks' room.'

There was the faintest hint of a smile on Trish's lips as she put down the phone. Now that no one would think she was hanging around in the hope of picking up some crumbs from the silks' table, she didn't mind going in to collect her post.

Her pigeonhole wasn't quite overflowing, but it was full. There was the traditional pink-tied brief for the catering dispute, as well as a bunch of ordinary-looking post and an expensive, stiff cream-coloured document envelope with her name and address in equally expensive handwriting. This must be Buxford's information about the Gregory Bequest.

A quick look at the catering company dispute told her she need not start on that yet. She almost wrenched her forefinger from its socket as she ripped open the envelope, so thick was the paper. As she slid out the neat pile inside, she saw a handwritten note on the top.

> Dear Trish,
> Thank you for agreeing to take this on. As you will see from the board meeting minutes and the other documents, the whole business of the trust is very simple. But if there is anything you need to ask, please don't hesitate.
>
> Yours ever,
> Henry

Nice and clear, she thought, but then it would be. Anyone with his responsibilities would have learned long ago to waste neither time nor words. She turned quickly through the top sheets, adding each one to the neat pile when she'd finished with it.

In the past she had had to discipline herself to keep her papers tidy; now it was second nature. She could work much more quickly with neat, clearly identified bundles than with the mess she'd allowed herself in her early days.

The first interesting item was the probate valuation of Helen Gregory's estate after her death in 1969. Trish saw that she had had very little money, and her only assets had been her house and its contents. As Henry had said, the valuers hadn't thought much of the paintings, but the phrasing they had used struck Trish as unnecessarily contemptuous:

'Sundry cardboard tubes containing oil paintings of doubtful provenance and value. Those examined proved to contain nineteenth-century copies in the style of various well-known artists. Notional value one thousand pounds.'

A yellow Post-It stuck to this had another handwritten note from Henry: 'Even the experts can sometimes get it wrong!'

There was also a copy of Helen Gregory's will, leaving everything she possessed to her only son, Ivan, without specifying what that was. Below the will came the documents drafted to set up the trust, which were a great deal more professional than the first probate valuation. That, too, was typical of Henry Buxford.

Trish turned on to see the advertisement that had been sent to all four broadsheet newspapers, inviting applications from men or women suitably qualified to be director of the collection, Toby Fullwell's letter and c.v., a copy of the trustees' letter appointing him, and his contract. Below those were his preliminary report of the state of the collection and second opinions from other experts on some of the most important paintings, including the Rembrandt.

All the other experts agreed that it was indeed genuinely by Rembrandt Harmensz van Rijn, even though it was painted on canvas and not on panel. Trish learned to her surprise that canvas, being so much cheaper than wood, had rarely been used at that date except for copies, but that in this case the X-rays had confirmed that the painting was indeed the master's own work.

Apart from the probate valuation and the brilliance of the deal Buxford had negotiated with the Inland Revenue once he and the other trustees had discovered some of the gems in the collection, there weren't many surprises in the papers he had sent. Trish read on for the rest of the morning, making notes at intervals and listing the very few questions that occurred to her.

She was taken aback by the price of expert restoration of old masters, but compared with the sums Antony Shelley, for example, cost his clients it wasn't so much. And she was surprised by the amount of freedom the board had given Toby Fullwell.

In the minutes of the latest board meeting, she read his report of the sale of the de Hooch. She couldn't see anything in it, or anywhere else in the papers, to make her doubt what Toby had said or give any reason for the fear Buxford thought he had seen.

'And yet he must know what's he talking about. He's spent his whole adult life assessing other people,' Trish muttered, moving on to the next sheet in the bundle. 'And he must have terrified enough young bankers in his time to know fear when he sees it.'

'What's that? Talking to yourself again?'

She didn't need to look up to know that the gibe had come from Robert Anstey, her biggest rival in chambers. He was doing his best to achieve the kind of reputation Antony Shelley had as one of the most brilliant generalists at the Bar, accepting cases of all sorts. Trish occasionally wondered whether her determination to keep her practice entirely commercial was quite sensible, but she wasn't going to let Robert see any of her doubts. Or let him know how little work she had at the moment.

'Did I disturb the great brain with my chatter?' she said, making her expression wide-eyed and innocent. 'So sorry. Now I come to think of it, I'm glad you dropped in. There's something I wanted to ask you.'

'You're not telling me that you've finally come to accept the fact that I really do know more than you, are you, Trish? Wonders will never cease.'

'Yes, Robert, amazing though it may seem, there are some things you have that I do not.' She watched him preen. 'You were at Cambridge, weren't you?'

'I was. I've always felt sorry for people who had to go to one of those ghastly red-brick horrors. Oh, God! Trish, I'm so sorry. I keep forgetting that you're one of them. How awful of me!'

She gave him a look that should have reduced him to ash but only made him giggle.

'You must be much the same age as a bloke called Toby Fullwell. I don't suppose you remember him, do you?'

'Vaguely. He was friends with a flamboyant chap called Peter Chanting, and everyone knew *him*. But they mixed with an arty crowd. Not really my sort. How have you come across Fulwell? He's not a client, is he?'

'No. But I've been reading about this rather glamorous little gallery he runs,' Trish said, knowing how Robert hated hearing about other people's successes and hoping that would make him talk. 'He seems on the young side for quite so much responsibility, so I was wondering how he'd done it. You must remember something about him.'

'Not a lot. He was a nonentity who ran about doing favours for rich blokes in the hope they'd pay some of his bills. I don't think it worked, except with Peter Chanting, who was grateful enough to stump up for Toby to join him on an exotic trek one summer. Tibet or Kathmandu or something.'

'That sounds pretty generous.'

Robert laughed. 'Doesn't it? One or two people wondered if Toby could've been his bumboy, but in spite of the artiness he was always into girls.'

Only a dinosaur like Robert could make a remark like that, Trish thought, as he said:

'Why are you so interested?'

'Oh, any red-brick graduate like me just loves hearing gossip about *proper* universities, Robert,' she said, batting her eyelashes at him. Then she caught sight of the time. 'Shit. I've got to go. Can we finish this later?'

She picked up the tidy pile of papers and slid it into the thick envelope, without looking back at Robert. He was still there. She could hear his breathing and smell the faint whiff of medicated shampoo that hung about his hair these days. At least it had stopped the flaking dandruff that had once made his shoulders look like a freshly dusted chocolate tart, but someone should have told him to rinse his hair more carefully if he didn't want to smell like a chemist's. Slapping the envelope into her briefcase, she added her laptop and moved to fetch her overcoat from the hanger behind the door.

'Could you move, do you think? I really do have to go.'

'Why? What's so important? Some little domestic errand, I suppose, for that boy you've adopted. You want to be careful, Trish. Pseudo-maternity is blunting your edge and only the sharpest of the sharp get to do commercial cases with Antony Shelley.'

Trish turned to smile over her shoulder. She wasn't going to admit she was off to represent a pathetic client in the magistrates' court. 'Actually this isn't anything to do with my brother. Antony asked me to sort out something privately for Henry Buxford.'

Helen closed her aching eyes. She was exhausted, having been on her feet for nearly twelve hours. They'd just moved her back on to day shifts, and so she hadn't got much rest last night. She always found it hard to adjust to sleeping in the dark again.

The kidney bowl in her hands felt very cold, and gripping it helped to keep her mind working properly. Any moment now the doctor would call for her and she'd have to get back to work, but for a minute or two she could stare out of the window at the road down which Jean-Pierre had walked away from her.

Even though the sun had sunk behind the horizon at least an hour ago, there was enough moonlight to see everything for a hundred yards or more. Thick black shadows were thrown by the bushes at either side of the white road. Sometimes they seemed to move. Once or twice, she thought she could see a man-shaped shadow leaving the bigger blobs of the hedges and coming towards her, but it always turned out to have been a mirage when she looked a second time.

Would he ever come back?

'Nurse! Nurse!'

She went to do her job.

Chapter 5

Half an hour after she'd left chambers, Trish was sitting with Susie Brown, Tamara O'Connor's solicitor, in one of the cells below the magistrates' court, watching their client struggle to stop crying. Tamara was shaking and there were needle tracks up and down both arms, as well as long scratch-marks from her ragged fingernails. She was sharply thin, and her grey, doughy skin was blotched with picked spots.

Who could have thought she'd be a suitable mule? Trish asked herself. Everything about her screamed 'heroin addict'. Any woman who looked like this, flying in from anywhere that produced drugs of any sort, was bound to be stopped and searched.

'Have a fag,' Trish said, pushing an open packet across the table. She herself had never smoked, but her painful years in crime and family law had taught her always to have a packet ready for her clients and today she'd bought one specially.

'Thanks.' Tamara wiped her hand under her nose. She sucked on the cigarette, then had to put it down again to cry properly, dropping her face on to her arms. Trish brushed Tamara's hair away from the lighted cigarette end.

'OK, Tamara. Now, have you really got names to give the police?'

''Course,' she said from inside the circle of her arms.

'You do understand the risks you'll be taking if you become an informer, don't you?'

The woman lifted her face. Trish understood the meaning of the word ravaged in a way she never had before.

Oh for the day the state decides it's lost the war on drugs and legalizes the lot! she thought. At least then the fools who choose to destroy their own lives with smack and coke and everything else can get on with it and leave the rest of us in peace.

There would be no mules then, no dealers, and none of the other crimes that always attached themselves limpet-like to the first one. Prices would be controlled, so burglary and street crime would be less common. And maybe, just maybe, some of the drug-takers would lose interest when their habit was no longer glamorously wicked.

'Of course,' Tamara said, dragging Trish back into her job. 'But it's the only way I'm ever going to see my kids again.'

'Who told you that?' As Tamara started crying again, Trish cursed herself for sounding so sharp. It wasn't the client who was making her angry. She tried again, much more gently: 'Have the police been telling you they'll get your kids back for you if you help them?'

Tamara shook her head. 'No. They haven't said anything. But my boyfriend said I would. That's why I told them I'd talk after this, when they've let me out on bail.' Her voice tailed off, and she sniffed. 'Can I have my fag back?'

Susie, who had rescued it, handed it over. Trish started to explain that there was no way the police could make Social Services give Tamara back her children while she was in this state, however many names of drug dealers, importers or manufacturers she might give them. Before she had got very far, watching Tamara's blankly stubborn expression, she had to give up. Susie shook her head and pointed at her watch.

'We'll be called any minute now,' Trish said. 'Your solicitor and I have to go up now. But whatever happens we'll see you afterwards. OK?'

On her way upstairs, Trish phoned Steve to ask who would

be dealing with Tamara after today. He laughed and told her that Robert had agreed to take on the case.

'That's not even funny, Steve. Be serious: who will be doing it?'

'Young Sam Makins. He's taking on most of your old clients. Tamara will be all right with him, if you really won't do it.'

Susie tugged at her arm.

'Got to go, Steve. I won't see you this evening; I'm due to fetch David from school, but I'll let you know how it goes when I see you tomorrow.'

Trish settled her shoulders and went into court to do her job. Not remotely to her surprise, the magistrates were unimpressed by her practised advocacy and remanded her client to custody.

Tamara's wails were still ringing in Trish's ears as she rushed from her cab to Blackfriars Prep at twenty to five. She tried to distract herself as she rang the bell at the top of the ostentatious flight of stone steps by thinking how lucky the pupils were that their school wasn't part of the state system. If it had been, such a potentially profitable piece of real estate with a river view would have been turned into loft apartments by now, with the children sent to classes in a leaky prefabricated building on the edge of a car park somewhere infinitely cheaper.

'Ms Maguire,' said Mrs More a few minutes later, holding out a well manicured hand, 'thank you for coming. Do sit down. David will be released in a few minutes.'

'How is the boy who was hurt?' Trish asked.

'Shocked, of course, and in some pain. His mother has taken him home. But you will be glad to hear that the doctor in casualty said there would be no scarring on the eyebrow. All the tests have confirmed that his sight has not been damaged.'

'And David?'

'Stoical, of course. He's a brave child and, usually, a pleasure to teach.'

Trish felt her face relax a little. Breathing became easier, too.

'But rules are rules and discipline is important, so I had to keep him in today. Now, do please sit down.'

'Thank you. You know, I just don't understand this. Fighting is so unlike him.'

Mrs More rubbed her hands against each other. There was a rustling sound, as though the skin of her palms was as dry as tissue paper.

'That is why I am so concerned. Given his history, he must have a great deal of repressed aggression, which might be why he was so violent when he let go.'

'I suppose that's possible. But couldn't it just have been an accident?'

'I can understand why you would like to believe that. We haven't been able to persuade David to say anything, and so I should like you to try. Will you tell me if you get anywhere? It is important for us to know exactly what happened.'

'I'll do my best,' Trish said, 'but he's always reluctant to tell me anything.'

'Which brings me to the other reason why I wanted to see you. Have you considered getting some counselling for him? I think you should.'

'I did consider it, yes,' Trish said. 'But his social worker thought he was too young to benefit and that it could simply add to his difficulties. I'm holding it in reserve. And I do not believe this episode is significant enough to justify it.'

'Ah, I see. I was going to recommend a very good woman we use in serious cases like this. Let me know if you change your mind.' A bell rang. 'That's the end of detention. You'll find him in the courtyard in about two minutes. Good luck.'

'Thank you.' Trish was relieved to have got away so lightly, but she didn't look forward to the cross-examination she was supposed to carry out now.

Seeing how forlorn David looked, and limp, with his bright blue and yellow rucksack dangling from his hand and bumping into a muddy puddle, she knew she wouldn't force him to talk if he didn't want to. She couldn't imagine him in a fight with anyone.

'I've always thought that child was spooky,' said a voice behind her. 'Now I know why. The attack on Stephen was vicious. I'm not surprised she looks so scared.'

Trish knew she'd been supposed to hear the comment. But it didn't make the accusation true, any more than the suggestion in the wine bar that Henry Buxford was a psychopath had been true.

She smiled at David and saw his lips quiver as he smiled back at her. All she wanted to do was hug him, but she fought to keep her hands to herself. Very early in their dealings, she had consulted George about what a 9-year-old boy could and could not accept in the way of public shows of affection, and she tried conscientiously to remember everything he'd said.

'How are you feeling?' she asked calmly, as she took the boy's rucksack and walked out of the courtyard beside him. 'Those bruises must have hurt. How did it happen?'

David shrugged, his face turned towards the bridge and the blue plastic hoardings that hid this particular bit of Trish's favourite view of St Paul's and the river. They seemed to have been up there for ever.

'David?'

'I'm OK.' They walked in silence for nearly twenty yards before he added, in a voice scratchy with effort: 'Have you heard what the divers were looking for this morning?'

'No,' Trish said, as determined to keep him talking about the fight as he was to get her off the subject.

After a while, getting nowhere, she had to give up and tried to think of something easier for him to answer. 'You had a rehearsal for the Christmas play today, didn't you? How did it go?'

'It was OK. Mer was stupid, of course. But he always is.'

'Mer?' This had to be Toby Fullwell's son. There couldn't be two people with such a peculiar name.

'He's got the part of the tramp.' His voice was as polite and gentle as ever, but Trish was aware of an unusual antagonism.

'Don't you like him?'

'No.'

'Why not?'

'Why d'you want to know?'

'Only because someone at work knows his dad, so I was thinking of asking him to tea. But if you don't like him, I won't.'

David kicked the raised edge of an uneven paving stone, scuffing the carefully polished leather of his black uniform lace-ups. 'Good. Because he's stupid.'

'So you said, but he can't be that stupid if he's in your class.' Trish was glad she'd already told Buxford she wouldn't try to get to Toby this way. 'It's the top set.'

'He can't keep up. I heard Mr Phillips say he'll have to be put down if he doesn't shape up. And everyone hates him. He's always trying to make the cast go to tea with him after rehearsals. He says his dad's got a secret basement full of treasure, but no one wants to go. He eats rust, too.'

'What?'

David looked up at her, his black eyes earnest, as though he had to prove that he wasn't about to be stupid himself. 'You know the netting round the playground?'

'Yes.'

'Well, some of it's rusty. Mer picks off the rust with his handkerchief, then he gets the bits out and eats them. I've seen him do it.'

'Hasn't he got any friends?'

'I told you.' He sounded as nearly cross as she'd ever heard him. 'No one wants to go to his house.'

'What's the matter?'

He didn't answer. His mouth was turned down at the corners and his eyes were sullen. He kicked the pavement again. Trish remembered the light in his smile this morning, and his bouncy conversation about war.

'Will Nicky be in when we get home?' he asked.

'She should be. She said she was going to make flapjacks for tea.' They'd reached the iron staircase that led up to Trish's front door now.

'I've got my key.' David ran up the stairs to unlock the door, then waited for Trish to precede him. 'Thank you for fetching me today.'

'I was glad to have the chance. It's always fun to walk back with you. Aha, I can smell the flapjacks. Hello, Nicky.'

Trish walked on into the narrow galley kitchen, which was really too small these days. Maybe she and George would soon have to take the plunge and buy something bigger together. No one was sure when the next property crash would come in London, but if interest rates went up, there might soon be a buying opportunity.

But would George want to live with her after all these years of refusing to give up her own space? Would he be able to put up with David all the time? And what would she do if he found he couldn't? There was no way she could pass the child on to anyone else. He had had more than enough to bear without a rejection like that. But what about her? What would it be like to try to live without George now? Looking back to the days before she'd known him, she could see that she'd inhabited a kind of tundra, semi-frozen and bleak as hell.

'Those look just as good as they smell,' she said, telling herself not to worry about things that hadn't happened and probably never would.

'D'you want one?' Nicky said, looking pleased.

'Better not.' Trish smiled. 'I've got a client dinner with George tonight and I'll never be able to eat enough to be polite if I've filled up on tea first. I've got some work I ought to do now. Will you two be OK?'

'Of course,' David said, much happier now that he was in Nicky's consoling company.

Trish left them to it. Sitting at her desk, she phoned chambers to tell Steve about Tamara O'Connor's bail application.

'Fine. I'll let Sam Makins know,' he said. 'While you're on the phone another two likely briefs have come in. We can discuss them in the morning. I can't see that you'd need a leader for either of them, but you'll want to check that for yourself.'

Trish lay back in her chair and smiled at the ceiling. She told herself she hadn't really been worried that she'd never get any more commercial work. But it was good to know new briefs were coming in so fast, even though there was nothing nearly as big as the case that had just settled.

Toby couldn't think why it was so hard to draft a simple letter to a teacher who thought he should admit her pupils for nothing just because her school had no budget for expeditions to art galleries. How did she think his would survive if everyone tried that on?

He heard the phone in the outer office ring, once, twice. Jo picked it up. This morning's talking-to had obviously worked. He waited, listening.

'Yes, he is here,' she said. 'I'll put you through.'

The extension on his desk rang. As soon as he picked up the receiver, Toby heard Jo's voice, sharp with sarcasm, telling him that he had a call. She knew he would have heard everything she'd already said. The partition wall was very thin.

He thanked her and waited until he'd heard the click of her phone, before saying quietly: 'Toby Fullwell.'

'Hi, Toby; this is Ben.'

Toby's guts tightened into a sharp tangled mass, like a steel pan-scourer. He couldn't speak.

'We need to talk,' Ben went on. 'Your secretary will be leaving any minute now, unless she's changed the habit of a lifetime. As soon as she's gone, I want you to come and meet me at the corner of Bread Street and Cheapside. OK? I'll be waiting there in fifteen minutes' time.'

There was no chance to say anything before Ben cut the connection. Toby tried to breathe, stretching upwards to rid his stomach of the scourer. Every movement set up a new pain somewhere else in his body. He listened to Jo packing up and going downstairs.

Once, she would have called out a perky 'good night', but these days she was too sulky for that. He heard the front door bang, then rang Margaret on the internal phone to say he had to go out for half an hour or so but would be back well before half past six. She didn't sound surprised, or even very interested.

Outside the front door, he looked both ways, like a child fresh from his first lessons in road-crossing. No one was paying any attention, still less spying on him. Huddling himself into his coat, which had been far too expensive even in the sales but at least made him look like the director of an important art gallery, he walked to the rendezvous.

The streets were so full of people struggling to get home from work that he understood why Ben had waited until now to summon him. No one would notice them or bother to eavesdrop in all these crowds.

'You're late,' Ben said when Toby reached the corner. 'Let's walk.'

They set off in the direction of Moorgate, heads down against the cold like everyone else.

'OK, Tobe. There's a Hieronymus Bosch in next week's old master sale at Goode & Floore's. We want you to buy it. It's lot number 50, the only Bosch in the catalogue, so there can't be any confusion.'

Toby had already been sent the catalogue and had noticed the Bosch. They didn't come up very often. But he hadn't paid much attention because it was only a dull religious panel, not one of the complex allegories.

'Did you hear what I said?' Ben demanded.

'I heard. But I can't do it.' Toby couldn't believe what he'd just said. He'd had no intention of rebelling when he'd left the house. Muscles in his legs twitched and he put down a hand to hold over the worst one in his thigh. Where on earth had his subconscious found this terrifying courage?

'Either I'm not hearing you properly,' Ben said quite calmly. 'Or you've forgotten who you're talking to.'

'No, I haven't. I should have told you to publish and be damned in the first place. But I'm doing it now. You can tell my board of trustees and every bloody newspaper in the country the truth about the Clouet drawings, if you want. I don't care. But I am *not* going to buy or sell any more of your fakes. OK?'

Ben laughed. Toby had his freezing hands behind his back now. They were already painful, but he dug the nails of the right hand into the palm of the left to keep his courage up. He felt Ben's hand tucking itself cosily into the crook of his elbow. His resolution slipped, along with his grip on his own hands, and he asked himself what he thought he was doing.

'My boss keeps wanting me to give you one of his demonstrations,' Ben said in the easy voice an old friend might use about his plans for a children's party, 'but up till now I've managed to persuade him that you'll do what he wants without anything like that. You will, won't you, Tobe?'

'No. I know I'll lose my reputation, my job, my home, and most of my friends, but so be it. Anything would be better than helping you flood the market with fakes.'

'I doubt that,' Ben said. 'Not that it matters now. You see, the stakes have risen a bit. I didn't want to have to tell you, but I see I've got to. It's not just your reputation you're risking. Not any more. My boss hasn't decided yet which one of your boys he'll go for, but it's usually the youngest. He's found that's the quickest way to make any parent do what he wants. Could you bear to watch your young Meredith screaming as first his arms are broken, and then his legs, and then God knows what else is done to him?'

Ben spoke so casually that it was a moment before Toby understood what he'd heard.

'You *bastard*.'

Toby wanted to grab Ben's neck and throttle him, but there were too many people around, and Ben was bigger and stronger than he was, and he was a hopeless coward anyway.

'Now, now. There's no need to be offensive,' Ben said. 'Do as you're told and you'll be safe. So will your sons. Rebel again, and they will be hurt.'

Where exactly was Peter in all this? Toby asked himself. Did he know what Ben was threatening now? Had he sent him to do it? Could anyone have changed that much, even in eighteen years?

Ben reached across the narrow space between them to flick his fingers against Toby's cheek. The patch of skin stung.

'Concentrate,' he said. 'And remember that it usually takes only one child killed to make anyone toe the line.'

'Christ! You're unreal.'

'You wish. Don't forget, Toby, I'm all that stands between you and my boss. If you screw up, or if you so much as breathe a word of this to the police or anyone else, he'll pick up one of your boys straight away and take him to pieces in front of you.'

Toby shut his eyes. He could feel the helpless, humiliating tears seeping out through his lashes. This couldn't be happening to him. He'd made mistakes, been a fool – worse than a fool when he'd faked the Clouet drawings with Peter – but he hadn't done anything nearly bad enough to warrant this.

'Oh, don't be so pathetic.'

When Toby opened his eyes again Ben had gone. But he'd left behind a kind of miasma. Toby had never felt anything like it. He wanted to rush home and scrub his whole body under the shower to get rid of every trace of it before it could contaminate him.

Chapter 6

When Trish reached the Carfields' huge penthouse flat at ten past eight, she found that she was the first of the guests to arrive. She handed over her present – a beautiful glazed jar of red Camargue rice, and left her coat on what was obviously the spare bed, an uncomfortable-looking brushed-steel platform covered in pristine pale-grey suede. That didn't do anything for her, but the amazing living room made her writhe with envy.

It was nearly twice the size of hers and furnished with the kind of perfect simplicity that must have cost nearly as much as the flat itself. She was glad she was wearing her one plain black designer dress this evening, instead of her usual trousers, and had even put on some mascara.

Standing at one of the enormous, uncurtained windows beside her host a few minutes later, she looked out at the inky river, and the jewel-like lights strung on garlands along the edge.

'God, London's gorgeous.'

'Isn't it?' Jeremy Carfield sounded warmly approving. 'Angelique yearns for Paris. She's always on at me to move there, but I couldn't bear to leave all this.'

'It may look pretty,' his wife said in charmingly accented English, 'but it is violent beyond belief. The sooner we leave, the better.'

'Oh, nonsense, Angelique. London's as safe as any European city. Now, Trish, champagne or a margarita?'

'Champagne, please,' Trish said. She loved margaritas and might have found it difficult to pace herself safely if she'd started on them. Champagne didn't do nearly as much for her and she could usually make a single glass last all evening.

She hoped George would arrive soon. It wasn't that she needed his support or would let herself talk to him for more than about two seconds at someone else's dinner, but these were his clients and she knew nothing about them. It would be all too easy to pick a tactless subject if she had no guide.

'Of course, London is more violent than Paris,' Angelique said, with a stubbornness that belied her delicate prettiness and breathy voice. 'Only this morning they have found a body in the river, just by the bank there. With a bullet in its head.'

'You're not serious,' Trish said.

'But yes,' Angelique said. 'They picked it out at seven-thirty this morning. I heard the police boats coming, so I watched them to see what was happening.' She waved to a beautiful antique brass telescope, which provided the only ornament on a deep window seat that ran under the windows. 'I couldn't see anything, but later I heard it on the news.'

'I saw the boats myself,' Trish admitted, thinking so much had happened since this morning's walk with David that it could have taken place a week ago. 'But that was later. About half-past eight. If they'd already found the body, what were they looking for then?'

Angelique shrugged. 'Evidence to identify it – it was naked, you see – and for the gun.'

'I wish I'd had time to listen to the radio this evening.' Trish thought of everything she knew about the shortage of police officers and about all the incident rooms that were dealing with three or four murders at once. How could they have spared all those officers and boats and divers to look for something to identify a single body? They must believe this death was part of something much bigger than that.

She saw both Carfields looking at her in surprise, so she quickly said. 'How awful!'

'Except that if they were searching for a gun it sounds much more like suicide than murder,' Carfield said, returning with a glass of champagne for Trish. 'No killer would throw away a useful weapon.'

'How could it possibly have been suicide?' Trish said without thinking about the effect of her sharp question on George's client. 'No one's going to be able to walk naked through London to shoot himself on the edge of a bridge without being stopped – or at least seen on a security camera. No, no. This is murder. It has to be.'

Her imagination sent pictures of what might have happened flashing through her brain. Even the least brutal of them was so shocking it made Toby Fullwell's reported fear over his five-million-pound sale seem ludicrously trivial. As Buxford had said, that was only money. At the very least, this story of the naked body must have involved real terror. The thought of it turned the residual taste of champagne nauseatingly metallic on Trish's tongue.

'It *must* have been suicide,' Carfield said with an edge that told her to keep quiet. 'So none of us needs worry. The mad and miserable have always used rivers for release, in Paris just as much as London. There's the bell, Angelique darling. Why don't you let the others in?' When his wife had gone, he turned back to Trish. 'You must be local if you were crossing the bridge this morning.'

She told him obediently where she lived, gazing out at the ravishing black-and-gold spectacle in front of them and trying to deal with the fact that someone had committed murder within ten minutes of her front door. A barge pushed its way up river, thrusting the water away from the bows in two fans that looked brilliantly white against the blackness of the river.

'Was the body male or female?' she asked.

'Male,' Carfield said, watching her over the rim of his champagne glass. 'Why?'

'I was thinking of the suicide figures,' she said at random. 'Statistics show that far more men than women kill themselves these days.'

Carfield said coldly that he supposed she must come across that kind of information in her work. Remembering her duty to him as George's client, Trish forced the thought of the body to the back of her mind and tried to ask intelligent questions about the future of software until Angelique introduced her to the new guests.

They were a couple who owned a company that made pop videos. Their whippy bodies told Trish that they must spend a long time in the gym, and their superconfident aura that their company was successful. It wasn't their fault that they didn't share her horror of the story about the body, but she found their imperviousness unpleasant.

Failing to find any points of contact with them, Trish soon abandoned the idea of a real conversation and asked about their skiing plans. She had already forgotten their names and thought of them as the He-producer and the She-producer. Luckily they were flying off just after Christmas and had an elaborate programme of off-piste skiing already arranged. Telling her about it lasted right through George's appearance and the much later arrival of the last two guests. At last, Angelique announced that dinner was ready.

The food was good, and conversation soon became less laboured. No one said anything more about the body in the river, although Trish thought, looking from one face to the next, that she wasn't the only one who found it hard to forget.

Carfield talked well, and eventually Trish made everyone

laugh with an account of one of her more eccentric cases. The main-course plates had just been collected when the front-door bell rang.

'Who's that?' Carfield asked sharply, as though his wife had X-ray vision.

She shrugged elegantly and turned away to consult one of the two young Asian women who were distributing pudding plates among her guests. Trish noticed that the video producers were exchanging complicit glances.

'It should be our contribution to the evening,' the She-producer said. 'I knew we mustn't bring flowers because of Angelique's hay fever, and chocolates are so suburban. One of us had better answer the door or they won't make the delivery.'

'How very generous of you,' Carfield said. 'Go ahead. Hold the pudding Angelique.' He went to a concealed cupboard below the window seat and took out a small stack of mirrored-glass squares.

Trish understood the video producers' sly smiles and felt more uncomfortable than ever. How was she going to get out of this without offending George's client? Inspiration struck her as she remembered the last dinner she had given, when three of the guests had refused to eat one or other course because of their allergies and food intolerances.

'Not for me, Jeremy,' she said, fixing him with the same kind of sadly accusing stare she'd seen on their faces. 'The awful thing is I'm allergic. I just can't take cocaine.'

'You can't be,' said the He-producer, laughing at her. 'You're probably just inexperienced and afraid. Have a go. I'll talk you through the process. You'll enjoy it, believe me.'

Trish smiled at him and saw even more complacency in his pale eyes, and enough arrogance and contempt to make her hate him.

'No, thank you,' she said sweetly. 'I've met too many of the mules who have to swallow the stuff before they smuggle it in. If you thought about how they excrete it and then pick it out of their own shit, you might be allergic, too.'

The She-producer looked at Trish with as much disgust as though she had just expelled a fart. Trish turned in apology to her host.

'I don't want to be a party-pooper,' she said, 'but I've got to get into chambers early tomorrow, so I should probably leave you to it.'

George was getting to his feet, too. Trish frowned at him, slightly shaking her head. He ignored the gesture, thanked Angelique for a superb evening and made his own excuses.

'You didn't have to do that,' Trish said as they reached the marble and glass atrium at the foot of the building. 'I'd hate to cause trouble with one of your best clients.'

'Don't worry. I've said worse things to Jeremy in my time, and I was glad of the excuse to get out.' He put his arm around her shoulders. 'I've had a hell of a day. What about you?'

This was clearly not the moment to tell him about David's fight. She didn't think she'd bother him with Buxford's peculiar little enquiry either. Not yet anyway.

'Not too bad. I must say I was amused by the delivery,' she said, leaning against him. 'I thought that was a kind of urban myth.'

'Or a wish-fulfilment fantasy.' He sounded more like himself. 'I'm sorry it had to happen when you were there. I know how strongly you feel about coke.'

'Only because of the number of people whose whole lives have been wrecked in order to produce a momentary pleasure for self-indulgent tossers like that.' Trish shook herself like a wet dog. 'You know, I hate the snobbishness of cool almost more than the sort that comes from owning the same five thousand acres for four hundred years.'

'I know you do. It's one of the reasons I love you. May I stay tonight?'

They'd reached the glass doors out into the street. A uniformed doorman let them out. The cold was like a fist punching into their faces. Trish revelled in it, breathing so deeply that she had a moment of dizziness and had to lean against him.

'Of course. It would be mad to go back to Fulham now.'

'Yes, and David will be asleep.'

Next morning, she had a difficult time with David at breakfast, dealing with more questions about what the divers had really been doing in the river. It turned out that he'd known all about the naked body when they were walking home yesterday, and about the bullet, because he'd heard about them at school. Now all he wanted to know was when the murderer would be caught.

His voice wobbled on the word 'murderer'. Aching for him, trying to make him feel even a little safer, Trish talked gently about the way the police ran their investigations, and the kind of evidence they would be trying to find now. She wished she had some facts she could use to reassure him and did her best with generalities.

It didn't work, and he soon stopped talking altogether. The walk to school felt twice as long as usual. Today he kept to the very edge of the pavement, even when lorries thundered past, as though he was afraid to get anywhere near the parapet or look over at the river.

When they reached the school gates, he ran straight in, and didn't even produce his usual wave when he reached the door into the juniors' part of the building. Trish decided to phone his godmother, Caro Lyalt, who was an inspector in the Met, as soon as soon as she got to chambers. If anyone could help now, it would be Caro.

But she found Robert Anstey blocking her way. He smiled at

her with an expression of such self-satisfaction that he looked like a camel. She knew he wanted her to ask what he was looking so pleased about, so she smiled at him and kept her mouth shut. Clearly disappointed, he sauntered into Antony's room and shut the door behind him.

Trish went straight to the clerks' room to find out what was going on.

'Nothing to worry you,' Steve said, pursing his mouth to show that he was going to tell no secrets.

'Come on. It's obviously a big case. Tell me about it.'

'It's crime.' He bared his teeth in what might have passed for a smile. 'And you keep telling me you don't do crime any more, so it can't be of any interest to you.'

'What sort of crime?'

'A solicitor's been charged with laundering money for a client,' Steve said, casually shuffling some papers on his desk. 'We're for the defence.'

'That doesn't sound like Antony,' Trish said, remembering the disdain with which he had once talked about the lower end of the legal and accountancy professions, where he'd claimed money-laundering was rife. 'Who's the solicitor?'

'Monica Carrell, the youngest partner at Flyte Wilson. They only made her an equity partner last year. Must be regretting it now, mustn't they?'

That explained it. Flyte Wilson was a huge international firm with a great reputation and a vast list of commercial clients. But it didn't explain why Antony had picked Robert to be his junior.

Trish thought furiously of the hours she'd put in on Antony's cases over the past year, sacrificing huge amounts of time she could have spent with her family to do it. They hadn't lost a single one of those cases and yet Antony had still dumped her for Robert. Presumably he'd had this planned when he'd thrown her Henry Buxford's trivial little job as a kind of sop. Bastard!

Hating him and Robert, and Buxford too, Trish stomped off to her own room to get hold of Caro. The phone rang for nearly a minute before she answered, sounding breathless and harassed.

'Trish,' she said. 'What's up? I haven't got long to talk.'

'I'm sorry to bother you, but I'm worried about David. He's heard all about the body your colleagues fished out of the Thames. Not surprisingly, he's in a great state about it, and I want to reassure him, but I've nothing to do it with.'

'Nor have I.' Caro's voice was brisker than usual. 'All I know is what I've read in the papers, just like you, and so far there's been nothing to suggest they have any idea who did it. What exactly is David afraid of? A killer coming for him in the night?'

'Probably. I think if I were his age and my mother had been bludgeoned to death, I'd find any hint of another killer near where I lived pretty terrifying. Wouldn't you?'

'Almost certainly. And not just at David's age. How is the fear taking him?'

'It's making him aggressive.'

'David? You're joking.'

'No.' Trish told her about yesterday's fight, adding: 'There has to be a connection, but I can't get him to talk about it. You would probably do better. He's so much easier with you. I suppose you wouldn't like to come for an early supper with us, would you? You and Jess, obviously, if she isn't working.'

'She is, but it's television, so she's often free in the evenings. We'd love to come. When?'

'Tonight or tomorrow? It's only pasta today, cooked by me, but tomorrow George is doing his famous fish pie. If you're both free then, I'll tell him to get enough for all of us.'

'I'd go a long way for George's cooking.' Caro's voice relaxed a little. 'And I am free tomorrow. I'll get Jess to phone you if she's got a problem.'

'Good. I'll tell him. See you then. As early as you can make it.'

Trish felt a little more optimistic. David adored Caro, and she had spent enough time in the child protection unit to know how to deal with children far more damaged than he was.

Accepting the fact that there was nothing more she could do for him now, Trish pulled Buxford's papers out of her desk, hoping she would find something she could use to satisfy him. When Robert's unmistakable footsteps slowed down outside her open door, she arranged her face with care and looked up with a brilliant smile, as though he'd just given her a stunning present.

'Congratulations, Robert. I gather you're about to star in a huge case with Antony.'

'Cow,' Robert said, before sticking out his tongue at her. 'You might at least *sound* jealous.'

Trish laughed. 'I am, of course. Money-laundering is a huge gap on my c.v. I know virtually nothing about it, and—' She stopped suddenly, distracted by the thought of Toby Fullwell's unneeded five million pounds.

'And you're planning to augment your pathetic fee income with a little cleaning-up of criminals' money yourself, are you?' Robert suggested with an evil grin.

'It's true, isn't it,' Trish went on, not bothering to answer, 'that you can get seven years in prison for just not reporting your suspicions that money you've been paid might have come from drug dealing? Even if you yourself weren't involved in any crime whatsoever?'

'Absolutely. You have to file what they call an STR with the police, a Suspicious Transaction Report. Of course, you can get twice that for actually doing the laundering. Which is why all bankers and solicitors are so paranoid about checking where their clients' money comes from these days. But it's one of the few things you won't have to worry about as you struggle on at the Bar, Trish. None of us ever has to handle clients' money.'

'What?' she said vaguely, pretending she hadn't been listening to him.

He looked so disappointed that she nearly laughed again. Despairing of a good fight to get his cerebral juices flowing, he gave up and ambled off to his own room.

Trish went back to the papers Buxford had sent her. There was nothing to suggest that any of the trustees had even raised a question about the source of the money Toby had received for the de Hooch. Maybe there was no reason for them to worry about it. But Henry must have questioned it once he'd become so suspicious of the sale itself.

She had always thought better with a pen in her hand, so she started to doodle. Pictures of sacks of money appeared in a circle on the paper in front of her, with arrows joining one to the next. She wished she'd thought of all this before she'd talked to Robert so that she could have sucked out everything he knew about money-laundering while he'd been in her room.

All she knew was the obvious stuff: that the profits of drug dealing had to be disguised. After all, if you had no obvious source of income and yet were seen to be spending – or investing – a fortune, people would start wondering where you'd got it. Pretty soon the police would be round asking inconvenient questions; as, in due course, would the Inland Revenue and Customs & Excise.

The easiest answer would be that you'd been gambling, but you might have to show some proof. If so, you might persuade the owner of a dodgy casino to take in a suitcase of your ill-gotten cash and give you back a cheque, which you could wave at the police as evidence of legitimate winnings at the table. Casino owners paid cash into their banks all the time, so no one would bother to ask one of them where he'd got a particular bundle. You'd have to pay him a commission, of course, but no business was ever without its costs, so you'd wear that. Then you'd start putting your relatively clean money through a whole variety of other transactions to make it even harder to trace back to the original crime.

Could the art market provide an alternative to the casino? Trish asked herself, drawing a stack of framed paintings beside her money bags.

As far as she could see, the answer had to be 'yes'. You could spend the profits of your latest crime on a painting, bidding through an intermediary and insisting on the kind of anonymity common in the art world. When you later chose to sell the picture, you would get back a cheque from the auctioneers, which would make your money look perfectly respectable to anyone who wasn't actively tracking it from transaction to transaction.

A clumsy picture of a club-like implement appeared on the paper in front of Trish as she tried to draw an auctioneer's gavel. Then she added a huge question mark as her mind produced an objection: what would happen if you'd bought a dud? No one else would want it and so, instead of nice clean money, you'd be left with a worthless piece of painted canvas on your hands.

It would be much safer if you had several pictures and continually bought and sold them through various nominees, making your money look more and more legitimate each time.

And it would be better still if one of those nominees could be the director of a well-established institution run by a trust of the greatest and the best the Establishment could provide.

'I wonder,' Trish said aloud.

She thought back to Buxford's original description of the Gregory Bequest collection. As far as she could remember, he had made it pretty clear then that no one had any idea what was in the packages that still hadn't been unwrapped. Which would make it remarkably easy for someone with money to launder to pretend that his own paintings were part of the collection.

Buxford was one of the most intelligent people Trish had ever met. He was also at the top of one of the professions that had to take the greatest care to avoid unwitting involvement in money-laundering. He must have thought of this for himself. So why hadn't he said anything about it in all that long briefing in the wine bar?

Helen's hands felt raw by the end of her shift and her eyes were smarting. She told herself it was tiredness not tears that made them burn and water like this. But it happened every time she watched another eviscerated boy die in front of her. Some of the nurses managed to distance themselves, but she hadn't yet learned the trick of it.

If only Jean-Pierre had come back, she thought, she might have been able to bear it more easily. Sometimes when she woke in the night she wondered whether she had been mad to believe she would ever see him again.

Perhaps she had bored him last time he had been with her. That wouldn't be so surprising. After all, what had she got to offer a man like him? She knew nothing about art or architecture. She barely spoke his language and had never even been to Paris. She was young and ignorant and unsophisticated. It had probably been nothing but stupid vanity that had made her believe he could love her.

She pulled the handkerchief out of her sleeve and scrubbed her eyes with it. It only made the tears fall faster. The huge white moon was a shifting blur as she stared up at the sky, fighting for control.

Chapter 7

The fish pie was ready before Jess arrived at the Southwark flat on Thursday evening. Trish had provided the small amount of help George allowed and she'd laid the table and opened the first bottle of wine, while Caro let David show her the latest treasures in his room.

'Let's not wait for Jess,' Trish said, taking the empty tray back to the kitchen. George had the tight look about his mouth that meant irritation wasn't far away. 'She knows David needs to eat and get to bed. She won't mind if we start.'

'It's just that fish pie goes so gluey if one leaves it too long,' he said.

Trish stuffed the tray in its rack and straightened up to remove the drying-up cloth he had draped over his shoulder so that she could hang it over the rail in front of the double oven.

'No, it isn't,' she said cheerfully, kissing him. 'It's that you can't bear people being late.'

'Nag, nag, nag,' he said, taking her head between his hands and kissing her properly. She let her lips open and wished they were alone. George's hands brushed her nipples.

'You're quite right, of course,' he said, when they'd forced themselves to pull apart. 'D'you really think Jess won't mind if we start?'

'Not half as much as I'll mind if you get grumpy.' Trish

brushed his hair back from his face. 'And Caro can sort her out if she does. Caro can sort out anything.'

'Let's hope so, in view of the boy's current agitation. OK. You'd better tell them that we're about to eat.'

Caro was sitting cross-legged on the floor of David's room, while he stood behind her, showing her his drawings of the different sorts of bowmen at the Battle of Agincourt, and leaning against her strong back. Trish thought she'd never seen him so relaxed.

They both looked up. Caro was obviously tired, but in the child's company she seemed more peaceful than usual. Her brown eyes never faltered, but there were times when the lids looked like hoods, protecting them from too much horror. Tonight they were just ordinary eyelids, with unfairly long lashes, brushing up against the brow bone as she smiled at Trish.

'Hi!' she said. 'Are we making too much noise?'

'No. It's just that supper's ready and we thought we might start without Jess, so that we don't crash bedtime. Have you washed your hands yet, David?'

'No. I'll go and do it now, Trish. I won't be long.'

There was a bathroom attached to his bedroom, which had once been Trish's only spare room. She and Caro left him to it and strolled through the big living room towards the chimney and the open hearth beneath, with its illicit wood fire crackling out comfort. On the far side was the long refectory table, which would have seated fourteen without too much trouble. The five laid places looked a little sad, Trish thought, all up at one end.

'Has he said anything?' she asked Caro, having made sure he wasn't just behind them.

'Not yet. And I didn't want to rush it. We'll see what transpires over supper. If necessary, I'll put him to bed for you and raise it then. OK?'

'Sure. How have you been, Caro? You look tired.'

She wagged her head from side to side in a familiar gesture, which meant that either work or her relationship with Jess had been giving her problems, but that she wasn't going to moan about them. Her face was much broader than Trish's, but that was only because the bones were bigger. Caro had as little spare flesh as anyone who trained for forty minutes in the gym three times a week and ran for light relief at weekends. She kept her hair short, too, layered around her beautifully shaped head and just curling forwards from behind her ears.

Tonight her earrings were the gold anchors Jess had once given her. The first time Trish had seen them, she'd liked them so much she asked where they came from. Caro had surprised her by blushing; then she'd said:

'Oh, Jess had them made for me. She always says that I'm her anchor.'

'That's good, isn't it?' Trish had said, noticing the hesitation in her friend's voice.

'Maybe, but I'm not sure I like the subtext. An anchor is right down there under the water, stuck in the mud, while the ship's dancing away on the surface, usually in the middle of a flotilla of admirers.'

That had been the closest Caro had ever got to complaining about her partner. Trish had watched them afterwards, and decided that Jess, like a lot of other actors, was so insecure that she had to flirt with everyone to get the reassurance she needed to believe herself worth anything at all. Trish had tried to tell Caro that she didn't think there was any need to worry. As far as Trish could see, Jess was safely besotted with her.

'So,' George said three minutes later, as he was ladling out vast helpings of fish pie. 'What have your people discovered about this body in the Thames, Caro? Presumably it was murder.'

Trish closed her eyes. She and George had always differed over the best way to help David. She wanted him protected from everything that might remind him of his mother's death, but George thought that merely stopped him growing the kind of shell everyone needed to survive. He thought the situation called for what he always described as 'a little ordinary insensitivity'. And boarding prep school.

'I don't know, George,' Caro said, without even blinking. 'But then the case isn't being handled by my bit of the Met and I don't know any of the officers involved. Frankly, you probably know as much as I do from the papers.'

'At school,' David said, surprising Trish with the firmness of his voice, 'they're saying the man was probably an illegal immigrant, killed because he was going to tell the police about the traffickers who'd brought him in.'

'I suppose that's possible, but it's not a theory I've heard before. What else are the Blackfriars Prep Irregulars saying?'

'I haven't talked to them, Caro,' David said, looking worried again. 'And I don't know who they are.'

'It was just a joke,' Caro said. 'In some of the Sherlock Holmes stories, Holmes uses a group of boys to find things out for him and he calls them the Baker Street Irregulars. Are there any other theories at school?'

'Yes. They think he could be a drug dealer killed in a turf war with another gang.' David kept his gaze fixed on Caro's face, while his fork mashed the fish into a disgusting-looking paste. 'But I didn't know there were any gangs round here.'

'Don't play with your food,' George said sharply. 'If I've given you too much, just put your fork down tidily and leave it alone.'

David bit his lip.

'If you're stuck, may I have it?' Caro said. 'I missed my lunch and I'm starving.'

He looked up at her with something close to worship. He lifted his cutlery in one hand and shoved the almost-full plate towards her, accepting her clean one in return.

'That's great. Thank you. And you mustn't think that because the body was found at Blackfriars, that's where it went into the river,' Caro said, forking up the pulverized fish and potato. 'There are ferocious tides in the Thames, which could have brought it here from miles away.'

Trish watched blood returning to David's bitten lip and pale cheeks.

'I never thought of that,' he said, picking up his water glass. When he had swallowed, he added: 'It was really good, George. I'm sorry I couldn't finish it. Thank you very much.'

Jess arrived just then and distracted everyone. When Trish had poured her a glass of wine, and invited her to sit down on David's other side, she followed George into the kitchen.

'I know, I know,' he said, standing with his back to the oven, before she could even open her mouth. 'I shouldn't have snapped at him. But there are times when his pickiness drives me mad.'

Trish didn't answer. She wasn't going to tell him it didn't matter, and there was no point repeating what she'd already said so often in the past about how threatening food could seem to people like her and David.

'Will you take the dish in while I get another bottle?' George said calmly. 'We're running a bit low.'

When he had followed Trish to the table, he bent to kiss Jess's cheek.

'I'm sorry I'm so late, darling,' she said, pushing back her streaky blonde hair, and gazing up at him, much as David had gazed at Caro. 'There was another producer hanging around today with news of a new classic serial they're about to cast. I couldn't pass up such a good schmoozing opportunity.'

Trish glanced back at Caro, to see her stolidly eating her way through the second plateful.

'Caro, have you ever had anything to do with money-laundering?' Trish said, mainly to draw her attention away from Jess's antics. 'Or the art market?'

'No. They're both far too specialized for me,' she said, looking up in surprise. 'Why?'

'Oh, just some El Vino's gossip I overheard. Someone was talking about the connections between the art world and organized crime. Money-laundering was the only one I could think of. I wondered if there were more.'

'Definitely,' Caro said, looking happier. 'Artnapping's the thing these days. Far more common, too.'

'What?'

'Oh, you know, Trish; like kidnapping. They steal well-known paintings and offer them back to the owners or the insurance company for a ransom. It's easy enough to do, and most insurers will pay up. There aren't many experts who would happily see a Van Gogh destroyed just to save money. But we don't usually have anything to do with it. You're not allowed to pay ransoms in this country, even for pictures.'

'No,' George agreed, reaching for the bottle again. 'Although it's easy enough for private individuals to do offshore. David, you ought to be in bed. You've got school tomorrow.'

David looked at his plate, then glanced sideways up at Trish, who nodded quickly and said she'd forgotten to watch the clock. His lower lip edged forward.

'I'll take you,' Caro said brightly. 'If you like.'

He put his hand in hers and dragged her towards his room.

'Why are you really interested in money-laundering?' George asked when they'd gone. He refilled all the wine glasses.

'There's a case that's come in to chambers,' Trish said. 'Even though it's not mine, I was curious, but I don't want to bore Jess.'

'You couldn't,' she said with a blinding smile, before turning back to George. 'Does it come your way much?'

'I hope not,' he said with a short, barking laugh. 'It's one of my many nightmares. In the old days, before all solicitors had compliance officers tracking every bit of money that comes in, criminals would just send in a whacking great cheque, before phoning up a couple of weeks later to say that it had been mailed in error. The accounts department would go through their books, see that the individual concerned didn't owe the firm any money, and write out a cheque of their own straightaway. Bingo! Clean money.'

'How amazing!' Jess said with all the fervour of a child watching a firework extravaganza. Trish thought of Caro's careful avoidance of all exaggeration and unnecessary emotionalism and felt even sorrier for her.

'It's not so easy now.' George smiled at Jess. 'But, as Trish said, it's a dull subject. How were the rehearsals today, Jess?'

Trish hardly listened to the answer as she mentally drafted the questions she was planning to put to Henry Buxford.

Caro and Jess got up to leave two hours later, and Trish escorted them to the door while George fetched their coats.

'Thank you for sorting bedtime, Caro,' Trish said while he was out of the way. 'It could have been a sticky moment. Did David say anything more about the body?'

'Not much. But I really don't think you need worry. He's a bright boy and he'll be fine. He'll forget it as soon as something else exciting happens at school.'

Trish hugged her, then turned to say good night to Jess. She seemed to be treating George like a climbing frame as she reached up to kiss his cheek. He looked over her shiny blonde head at Trish and smiled with such a familiar look of mock terror in his eyes that she only just stopped herself laughing out loud.

We will be all right, she told herself, once he and David have shaken down and I've stopped trying so hard to keep them both happy at the same time.

Chapter 8

The Hieronymus Bosch didn't look too bad, Toby decided as he passed it for the fourth time. He could probably bid for it without raising too many suspicions. If he hadn't known it was a fake and had been thinking of buying it for real, he would have had it X-rayed to examine the under-drawing. Given Bosch's habit of constantly changing his mind as he painted, it should have been easy to see whether this was genuine or a copy. Then to be absolutely sure, he would have taken the panel to the Prado to compare it in detail with the real thing. As it was, he hoped there was no one else interested enough to take any such precautions.

On the other hand, he thought as his breakfast muesli churned in his stomach, if no one else were interested at all, he would never be able to get the price high enough to satisfy Ben's boss. You couldn't go bidding in millions when no one else was prepared to offer more than a few hundred quid, which was probably all this wretched fake was actually worth.

He wondered who had painted it, and where they'd got the panel itself and the paints. There must be a mini-factory somewhere, breaking up rotten old coffers for wood of the right date, and making their own paints to ensure they used only ingredients known at the time the pictures were supposed to have been painted.

Ben had promised from the start that they'd be fed on to the market slowly enough to look convincing. Even he had been able to see that one 'lost' painting might come up every so often but that if you put two or three into every old master sale you'd lose all chance of persuading buyers they were real.

All in all, it wasn't such a bad plan, Toby told himself, trying to make it seem ordinary and bearable so that he could forget the threats to Mer. At least Ben's team had had the wit to pick a dullish subject that might well have escaped notice in some church or other over the past five hundred years.

Toby walked on and stood for much longer in front of a very dubious Dürer drawing, peering and shaking his head, before ostentatiously checking the glossy catalogue.

'You're not really interested in that bit of old tat, are you, Toby?' said a voice from behind him.

He turned to see the arts correspondent of the *Daily Mercury*, a waspish man called Mark Sapton, who was always on the hunt for gossip and scandal. Toby felt faint with relief that he hadn't been standing in front of the Bosch when Sapton arrived.

'God no!' he said, sharing a cheerful sneer. 'I just couldn't believe the catalogue description.'

'I know. Standards are slipping horribly, aren't they? I can never decide whether it's wishful thinking or straight dishonesty. You busy? What about lunch?'

'I wish I could,' Toby said, lying easily, 'but I've got to get back. Too much to do. Next time, maybe.'

'Sure. See you.' Sapton walked on in search of an easier target.

This was definitely not the time to have another look at the Hieronymus Bosch, Toby thought. He hoped he'd spent long enough in front of it to satisfy whomever Ben had sent here today to spy. Now all he had to do was bid for the wretched thing, and pray that he could push the price up high enough to please Ben and so keep Mer and Tim safe.

As he walked down towards the Embankment so that he

could pass Blackfriars Prep on his way back to the gallery, Toby tried to persuade himself that Den's threats hadn't been serious. It was ludicrous to think that anyone, however criminal, would really torture or kill a child just to get a better price for a faked old master.

There was no sign of anyone in the school courtyard, so Toby rested against the broad granite balustrade and stared out across the river at the Oxo Tower, trying to hold on to hope. He'd always thought of good as the opposite of evil before; now he knew goodness wasn't enough. Only hope could keep you fighting.

The stone felt like ice under his clasped hands. He pulled them back to stuff them in the pockets of his expensive coat and felt his teeth chattering as he shivered. That reminded him of Nepal, even though it had been fever then, not cold or fear, that had made his whole body shake.

How could Peter have treated him with such gentleness then, fought so hard to keep him alive and wanting to live, and now do this to him? Had Peter nursed a grievance for eighteen years and been thinking of the cruellest possible revenge? Had he blamed Toby for his exile? Or had he thought Toby insufficiently grateful for everything that had been done for him?

Voices, high and excited, broke into his misery. There were clattering feet too, and the heavy rhythmic slap of a kicked football. Dragging himself back into the present, he turned to look. Boys in the familiar uniform were pouring down the grandiose steps in a yellow-and-grey river. He stared, squinting, until he caught sight of Mer hopping down the steps beside another, even smaller, boy. Moments later he saw his brother Timothy, too. Thank God. Both of them were still safe.

Toby turned east without trying to attract their attention and set off towards the gallery. His phone rang before he'd got as far as the pedestrian crossing all the boys used. The sound made him feel as though icy spikes were being driven into his spine. Even though the number on the screen was unfamiliar, he knew who was at the other end of the phone, just as he knew he had to answer.

'Toby Fullwell,' he said, trying to believe it could be an ordinary call from someone who didn't matter, but knowing it wasn't.

'Nice to see Mer's in such a good state, isn't it?' Ben's sarcasm sharpened the spikes and dug them further into his spine. Toby's hand clenched so hard on the phone he heard the plastic casing crack. He looked behind him, but there was no one there.

'Don't bother,' Ben said. 'You won't see me. But I can see you. I've been watching you as you mooned over the river. What did you think of the Bosch? I know you've just been to Goode & Floore's.'

'You bastard!'

'There's no need for that. Treat this as a business transaction and you'll find it easier to keep your head. So, what *did* you think? We went to a lot of trouble to make it look right.'

'It's just about convincing enough for me to buy,' Toby muttered.

'Good. And you should sound a lot happier about that. Don't forget it means you'll have less to worry about. Not nothing, mind, but less. And your boys will be safe.' Ben cut the connection.

Toby looked all round, but he couldn't see anyone obviously watching him. Of course, Ben's heavies could be anywhere, hidden in one of the buildings or tracking their quarry from one of the hundreds of cars that were inching along the Embankment. A man on a motorbike, dressed all in black leather with vicious-looking studs, sneered at Toby from across the road. Was he one of them? Or the man who looked like a low-grade sales rep, picking his nose at the wheel of a red Vauxhall?

It could be either, or any of a hundred others. There was no way of knowing. Toby felt as though he was living inside a net, ready to be hauled out of his real life at Ben's whim. How was he ever going to get free? And how was he ever going to keep Mer and Tim safe if Ben was keeping this close a watch on them all?

They'd have to leave London. There was no other way. Margaret would have to take them somewhere and hide them until this was over.

Ten minutes later Toby was standing in front of her in the middle of the main gallery. His hand was stinging and Margaret was holding the side of her face. He knew he must have hit her, but he couldn't remember doing it. He couldn't remember anything since the moment he'd come in and found her here in front of the Fragonard, waiting to tell him that Henry Buxford had invited himself to lunch on Sunday.

Her lips were moving now, pulled from one side to the other, although she wasn't making any noise. She was obviously exploring the inside of her mouth with her tongue. Could she be tasting blood?

'Have you gone mad, Toby?'

'Don't be ridiculous.' Shock had wired his jaws together so that his voice was thin and hissy and his cheeks blew out like balloons with every syllable. He forced his teeth apart so that his mouth opened properly. 'I'm only trying to make you understand that this is important.'

'So is my life. And the boys' education. Take them out of school and drive them up to your bloody mother's? It's only three weeks since half term. And they hate her as much as you do. You *must* have gone mad.'

'Margaret.' He stopped and breathed hard through his nose. Somehow he had to make her sense the urgency without giving her any clue to what was going on all round them. He knew he looked ridiculous, while she stood swaggeringly beautiful in front of him. Her flowery scent made her seem even more superior now that he smelled of fear all the time. He tried to straighten up and his vertebrae crunched. His face hurt. His back hurt. His sore hand twitched. Somewhere another phone was ringing, as though to remind him how close Ben must be. Not that he needed any reminding.

'If you hit me again,' Margaret said in a voice like a knife, 'I will call the police.'

He turned away, to face the Fragonard. He'd once loved the idea of the frothy woman kicking her legs on a swing. Now he hated her for her insouciance, just as he hated Margaret for her stubbornness.

'Why can't you ever listen?' Toby said, trying to put some authority into his voice. 'You *have* to take the boys to Scotland, Margaret. Today.'

'Who the hell do you think you are to give me orders?'

Hot tears were bubbling up round his eyeballs. He knew if he tried to speak they would leak out.

'What's the matter?' Her voice had softened, as though she might still care a little, but that made it harder to hold on.

His lips felt stiff, as though they'd been sprayed with local anaesthetic. He licked them and forced some sound out of his throat: 'Nothing. I told you, I want you and the boys out of London for the next two weeks. Scotland's the obvious place. I'll phone when you can come back.'

Margaret looked as beady as she always did when she was deciding how to win her current argument. Toby had never been a target before. In the past her most effective insults had always been flung in his defence.

'Is this about Jo?' she said nastily. 'Do you want everyone out of the house so you can screw her in peace?'

'Don't be stupid.'

'I'm not. When she first came to work for you, she wafted around the house, looking at you as if you were some kind of love god. And you enjoyed it.' Margaret laughed with the kind of cruelty he hadn't heard from anyone since the last time he'd been up to Scotland himself. 'I wouldn't have thought you had it in you. Not that I'm bothered. I know she won't get much of a bang for her buck.'

The ache between his shoulders sharpened. If he'd been able to tell her the truth about Ben, she might have softened. But he couldn't. It would be far too dangerous. She might insist on standing up to Ben or going to the police or doing something equally fatal. He knew now that Ben could get to them at any time, so there was no way the police could keep them safe, even if they wanted to.

Only getting her and the boys away from London would give him the slightest hope of protecting them. Even that might not work. But it was their only chance.

'It's just work, Margaret,' he said, knowing he sounded feeble. 'Far too much work. And I can't get it done while you and the boys are here.'

That might persuade her. She knew he had to satisfy the trustees if he were to keep his job and the flat. Oh, God! Henry. How could he sit through a whole meal with Henry cross-examining him all over again about the de Hooch and why he'd wanted five million pounds? Margaret would have to phone him back and say he couldn't come.

'Why not?' she demanded, making his eyes hot and wet all over again. He swallowed hard.

'Because I don't want him here.'

'Him? Who? You really are cracking up, Toby. We're talking about your ludicrous conviction that the boys and I might stop you working. When has anyone ever stopped you doing anything you want? We never come down here or to your sacred basement without an invitation as it is.'

'You know that's not true,' Toby said, feeling better now he had some justification for what he had to say. 'Mer followed me down there again only yesterday, in spite of everything

I've always said, getting in the way and putting his fingers in—'

'Is that what all this is about? Poor Mer's attempt to get a little fatherly attention after weeks of alternating blankness and snapping?' The pupils in her toffee-like eyes grew smaller as she peered into his face. 'Just exactly what have you got in the basement, Toby? Body parts? Or are you adding exciting signatures to second-rate canvases down there?'

He grabbed her shoulders and started to shake her. He couldn't see her any more, only the paintings turning into a bright kaleidoscope around them as his head rocked in time with hers. Her shoulders were dense under his hands, and her weight threw them both off balance.

'Stop it. Stop it. Stop it.' Mer's voice battered at his ears.

Toby's hands tightened, then let go. His eyes cleared. He saw his younger son crying in the doorway. Margaret was wiping her face. She coughed and straightened her hair, moving round him as she tucked most of the thick dark-red curls behind her ears.

'It's all right, Mer. Daddy and I were just arguing. You go on up to Tim. I'll be up in a moment. It's not a problem. Run along.'

Mer scuttled off.

'I'll take the boys away all right,' Margaret said, slicing the edges off each syllable with a viciousness that made her seem almost as cruel as Ben. 'But not to your bloody mother's. Or to anywhere else you might think to look, so don't even try to find us.'

Nicky put a full mug of coffee down on Trish's desk in the flat, asking: 'D'you want a biscuit or anything to eat with that?'

'No, thanks.'

'OK.' Nicky dragged over the spare chair and sat down, facing the desk. 'I asked David about the fight on the way to school this morning. And I think you're worrying unnecessarily. Stephen's back in school and very proud of his stitches. The only thing scaring David now is that you might be so cross with him for getting a detention that you'll let George persuade you to send him to boarding school.'

'Oh, shit! I didn't think he knew anything about that.'

'David knows everything,' Nicky said, sounding as though she pitied Trish for her delusions. 'Haven't you got on to that yet? He's incredibly bright anyway, but he also watches everyone all the time, and listens to everything that's said. He knows all about you and George and what George thinks about him living here.'

Trish frowned, trying to remember the worst things George had said about him. There wasn't anything she could do about that.

'But I will find a way to make him see that I'll never send him away,' she said aloud.

'That would help. It's his biggest nightmare. Far worse than the body in the river.'

'OK. By the way, Nicky, have you ever heard him mention a boy called Mer Fullwell?'

'Often. David thinks he's awful.'

'Why?'

'He hasn't said. D'you want me to ask?'

'Only if it crops up easily. I don't want him worried by questions.'

'I'll be careful.'

Trish blew Nicky a kiss. 'I couldn't do it without you, you know.'

'Good. I love it here,' she said with even more warmth than usual. 'And I love David. He's the nicest boy I've ever looked after. Now shouldn't you be in chambers?'

'Slave-driver,' Trish said. The insult made her think of Buxford and the questions she had rehearsed with such care. 'I've got one phone call to make before I leave.'

When Nicky had gone down the spiral stairs to sort out the mess in David's room, Trish rang Buxford's office, only to hear his secretary saying that he would be out of the office until Thursday. He'd given Trish his home number, too, although not a mobile, so she tried him there.

'I'm afraid he's away today,' said a smooth female voice that sounded old enough to be his wife's. 'But he'll be back at the weekend. Can I give him a message?'

'Could you say that Trish Maguire called? I need to talk to him. He's got all my numbers.'

'I'll make sure he gets the message. Goodbye.'

Chapter 9

Saturday was rugby day. The alarm brought Trish out of a tangle of duvet, gasping for breath. Choking, she grabbed a Kleenex from the box by her bed and blew her nose. She hated colds for the way they slowed down her brain. This one must have been incubating inside her all week.

'You OK?' George pushed himself up the bed.

'Sorry to make such a noise,' Trish said, blowing again and blinking to clear her sore eyes. 'What a way to wake you up! I seem to have a cold. I hope you don't get it.'

'I don't usually. But you'd better stay in bed today.'

'No, I must get up. It's rugby. David needs breakfast first.'

George flopped back against the pillows. 'Why did we decide to give Nicky Saturdays off? Remind me.'

Trish laughed through the ache in her head and the blockage in her nose. 'Because it gives us the chance to have Sundays in Fulham on our own. Maybe not this weekend, though. The least I can do is leave your house free of germs.' She put one long bare leg out of bed. 'Thank heavens for central heating.'

'No, I meant it, Trish. Don't get up. I'll take him to rugby today.' George was already on his feet and wrapping his scarlet towelling dressing gown round himself. 'I'll bring you breakfast in bed. LemSip or coffee? Or both?'

'Oh, both, please. You are a saint.'

'I know. I won't kiss you because you're disgusting when you have a cold.'

'Such charm, George! You will be gentle with him on the way to rugby, won't you? You know he's having a rough time at school.'

'What d'you think I'm going to do? Torture him?' he said from the door. 'I only told the boy not to play with his food.'

That was a mistake, Trish told herself as she listened to him thump down the spiral staircase to call David.

Nearly an hour later, when they'd gone, she had a bath instead of taking her usual quick morning shower. She usually avoided the waste of time involved in lolling in hot water, but this morning it was comforting. She leaned back, enjoying the coolness of the enamel against her neck and the steam sorting out her nose.

The whole process had such a good effect that there seemed no point going back to bed. She filtered some more coffee and took it to her desk, wondering whether Buxford would ring today. She couldn't keep the lines free just on the off chance, so she picked up the phone to make her usual Saturday morning call to her mother.

'How's Bernard?' Trish asked, after they'd swapped the week's news.

'Fine, apart from the sciatica, which makes him rather bad tempered.'

'Poor you,' Trish said with real sympathy as she thought of George's recent bouts of irritability.

'Bernard's the sufferer, Trish,' Meg said firmly. 'Not me. Now, how's your brother?'

'Oh, OK. Does the sciatica mean— ?'

'Trish.' Meg's voice was even more firm. 'I know you don't think I should be burdened with your anxieties about him, but your father and I had been divorced for decades by the time he had his affair with David's mother. And even if we hadn't been, it's not the child's fault. He's the most important thing in your life at the moment. Don't shut me out of that.'

Throughout Trish's childhood, Meg had always done everything she could to counteract the way Paddy had deserted them soon after Trish's eighth birthday. It seemed amazingly generous of her to go on trying to make everything right, even now that her daughter was an adult and definitely ought to have been able to cope on her own.

'Come on,' Meg said. 'What's up? Tell me.'

So Trish gave her a full account of the body in the river and David's playground fight, got the usual dose of warm common sense in return and felt a lot better for it.

'And don't push him to talk,' Meg added at the end. 'If he's anything like you were, that'll make him even more stubbornly silent. You were always the original clam whenever there was something I particularly wanted to know.'

Trish laughed, remembering her efforts to keep her worst misdemeanours to herself. 'Now, when am I going to see you?'

When they had eventually said goodbye, she dialled her father's number. He wasn't there, but his answering machine invited her to leave a message. Fighting the fury that would make him even less likely to pick up any of his responsibilities, she tried to make her voice sound reasonably friendly.

'Paddy?' she said. 'Trish here. It seems ages since we met, and I miss you. What about coming round here for a drink sometime? Or dinner, maybe? David and I need to see you soon. Let me know. 'Bye.'

It was ironic that she now had to be the suitor in their relationship. Was Paddy taking revenge for the years when she'd refused all his overtures? Or was it just that he still couldn't handle the fact that he had a son he had never seen, by a woman he'd left even before he knew she was pregnant and who was now dead?

Whatever it is, Trish thought, he'll have to get over it.

She poured herself more coffee to sharpen her mind in case Buxford called, but she couldn't think what to do while she waited. *The Times* was spread all over one of the black sofas, showing plenty of signs of George's touch. For someone who was so neat in the kitchen, he was extraordinarily heavy-handed with newspapers. Every page was crumpled and out of line with the rest. But he'd finished both the cryptic and the baby crosswords, in spite of everything he'd done for her and David. She couldn't have done that in the time.

An impending sneeze made her dive for the box of tissues at the far end of the sofa. When she emerged from the bundle of paper, she caught sight of her face reflected in the mirror over the fireplace. She looked terrible, like a sodden, red-eyed witch. If she didn't get out of the flat soon, she would drown in a trough of self-pity.

She looked at the clock. There was plenty of time to go back to the Gregory Bequest and have another go at Toby Fullwell before the end of the morning's rugby.

On her way out, she saw a bundle of post on the doormat and riffled through it. There was a postcard from Emma Gnatche, an old friend now working in the States. Beneath that were a couple of expected bills, and three charity appeals. Nothing that couldn't wait. She dumped the pile on her desk and went out.

Toby opened the door to the gallery himself this time. He did not look welcoming and obviously had no idea who she was.

'I came here last Tuesday morning,' Trish said, holding out the torn ticket she had bought then. 'Do you remember? I had a work emergency and had to leave. You told me I could come back to see the rest of the pictures without buying another ticket.'

'Of course.' He produced a smile that made the skin of his face twitch and flicker like a horse getting rid of flies. 'Come on in. What would you like to see?'

'You said something about a French room, I think,' Trish said, wondering how soon she could get on to the subject of the five million pounds and whether it was really such a good idea to broach it on a day when her mind was sluggish. 'I'd love to see that. The original collector was French, wasn't he? So French pictures must have been particularly special to him.'

Helen looked down at the little package in its flowered paper, then up again at Jean-Pierre.

'I don't need a present,' she said. 'All I've ever wanted was to know you're safe.'

'But I need to give you one, *ma mie*,' he answered, tracing the line of her lips with one soft-tipped finger. 'I cannot give you a ring yet, so it had to be something else, and something small enough for you to keep safe while you are here. This seemed best. Are you not going to open it?'

She untied the knotted ribbon that held the paper together and parted the flaps to reveal a flat gold oval about two inches by one and a half.

'What is it?'

'Turn it over, Hélène.' His voice, gentler and more seductive than ever, made her eyes blur again.

She had never expected love to make her so weepy. In the old days she had despised girls who cried all the time, girls like her stupid sister, whose latest letter had been even more self-pitying than usual. She sniffed.

'Don't cry, *ma mie*,' Jean-Pierre said, taking out his own handkerchief to wipe her eyes. 'There is no need. All will be well. Look at it properly.'

She turned the gold oval over and saw a frame set with clear stones that could have been diamonds, which worried her dreadfully. They surrounded a tiny portrait of a dark-haired man, who looked so like Jean-Pierre that after a moment she could think of nothing else. Both had the same dark eyes and beautiful tender mouths, but the painted man wore his hair long and had a large pearl hanging from his ear.

'Is it you?' she asked, delight at last pushing aside all her fears. 'In fancy dress?'

He laughed. 'No. It was painted about three hundred years before I was born, by your English Nicholas Hilliard. But I have always thought it looked like me, which is why I chose it for you.'

'Then it's much too valuable,' she said, holding it out, balanced on her outstretched palm like a sugar lump for a carriage horse. 'I can't take it, Jean-Pierre.'

'But you must. I want you to have something that is *very* valuable to me.' He put one hand under her outstretched wrist and laid his lips over the fluttering blue veins. Then he kissed her properly.

'It was one of the first paintings I acquired,' he said, folding her fingers over the miniature, 'and so I wanted it to be the first one I gave to you. I thought you could wear it on this chain, under your bodice. No one else will know, but you will feel it all the time against your skin, and think of me, and know that I will always return.'

More tears swelled in her eyes and she felt them dripping down on to her cheeks, but she smiled too, even though she couldn't speak.

'Ah, *ma mie*,' he said, gathering her into his arms. 'Don't be so sad. We will be together properly one day. I promise you.'

'You can't,' she said, her words muffled against his chest. 'No one can promise anything any more.'

The guns crashed in the distance. And nearby a man shrieked in agony.

Trish learned nothing useful from Toby Fullwell, except that he was not prepared to talk about buying or selling paintings or exactly what he had found in Jean-Pierre's packages.

Each time she asked a direct question, he either pretended he hadn't heard it, or chattered on about painters' techniques regardless. It happened too often to be coincidence. She heard a lot more than she wanted to know about brush strokes and composition, and the way painters built up different sorts of glazes to achieve the light effects they needed. But she saw no sign of fear.

All she took away with her in the end was confirmation that Buxford hadn't imagined everything, even if he had exaggerated Toby's terror. The man definitely had something to hide, but Trish still had no idea what it could be.

Leaving the building, she wondered whether it might have had something to do with Jean-Pierre himself. At first she had accepted the story that his huge collection had been forgotten. Now that seemed incredible. Why hadn't anyone asked what had happened to his paintings? She decided to go to her favourite library in St James's Square in search of information about him.

There she discovered that none of the three types of catalogue – the old bound ledgers, card index or the computer – turned up a single reference to Jean-Pierre or his paintings. Nor did any of the directories or reference books in the reading room.

Not prepared to go away without anything, she scooped up a random selection of general accounts of the art market, and some memoirs of the First World War. Even if they didn't help her learn more about the origins of the Gregory Bequest collection, she thought, they might come in handy for David's project, so they wouldn't be wasted.

All the cabs seemed to have disappeared when she re-emerged from the library, which meant she had to walk up St James's to Green Park tube. The books didn't seem very heavy at first, but they began to weigh her down as she waited on the platform. When the Jubilee Line train eventually arrived, it was stuffed with people and luggage, and she had to stand all the way to her stop, in a crowd of tourists on an outing to Tate Modern. By the time she was riding the escalator up through the magnificently soaring concrete halls of Southwark Station, her arms were aching so much that she had to keep shifting the pile of books, like a baby, from arm to arm. The walk back to her flat seemed much harder than usual.

'Come on, Trish,' said George's voice from behind her, as she reached her own street. She felt his arm around her shoulders and leaned back for the comfort. 'Why on earth didn't you stay in bed?'

'I was too restless,' she said, turning to smile at him. Then her voice sharpened: 'Where's David?'

'Having a pizza with a friend and his parents. They'll bring him back by seven.' He was hustling her up the iron stairs. 'Which will give us both peace and quiet and you time to rest properly.'

Trish opened the door and silenced the alarm. 'It's only a cold, George. I'm not ill.'

'I know. But it's a sign that you're run down. You've spent the last year dashing about looking after everyone else and working far too hard. Go and lie on the sofa and let someone else look after you for once.'

That was pretty rich, she thought as she kicked off her shoes. George was always telling her what she ought to do for her own good. But he was right, irritatingly enough. As soon as she lay back on one of the two big black sofas in front of the fireplace, blood drummed in her ears and she felt as though bullets were ricocheting around the inside of her head.

Toby had made himself a cheese sandwich, but he couldn't eat it. He longed for Margaret to phone so that he could be sure she and the boys had got away safely. Now that it was far, far too late, he realized how easily Ben could have picked them up as they left the house.

He could be keeping them somewhere so that he could bring

them out one by one, if Toby tried to rebel, and force him to watch them being tortured. He kept imagining he could hear their screams. He knew he'd never be able to hold out if he heard them for real, but that didn't matter a toss when he thought about what they might have to suffer before he had convinced Ben he would do anything he was told.

Through the open door of the kitchen, Toby could see two of the five skylights in the flat. He'd once revelled in the lightness and airiness of the place. Now it just felt exposed and dangerous. He wanted to hide for ever.

But he couldn't. In only four hours, he'd have to go out to do the *Live Arts* programme on Radio 4. In the old days, before Ben had ruined everything good Toby had ever done, he had enjoyed *Live Arts*, and it had produced a handy little bit of money to bulk up his pathetic income. Now he hated the idea of even that much exposure. And leaving the flat would mean deactivating the alarms and opening the front door to face whomever Ben had waiting for him.

Toby knew they were already outside the gallery. He could feel their presence.

If only the BBC had thought him important enough to send a car! Then he would have had some kind of protection. But they didn't. Maybe tomorrow, if the *Sunday News* did run the interview he'd given their arts correspondent, he might be seen as slightly more important.

Or maybe, he told himself looking at the cheese sandwich in disgust, I'll be exposed as a fraud and a forger.

Maybe that wouldn't be so bad. He'd be sacked, of course, and he'd never get another job in the arts, but that would mean Ben would have no use for him any longer. And if the exposure had come from a third party, Ben couldn't blame him for it, so there'd be no reason to take revenge on the boys.

* * *

At night now whenever she could not sleep, Helen would reach under her thin pillow to touch Jean-Pierre's miniature and try to forget that he had told her he could not give her an engagement ring. He had not said why, and her mind kept inventing more and more horrible reasons to explain it.

During the day, just as he had promised, the sensation of the fine smooth gold against her skin was a constant reminder that he loved her, even if he did not want to marry her. At night now, it just made her sure she would never see him again.

Chapter 10

By mid-morning on Sunday, Trish knew she was on the mend. She looked even more witch-like than she had yesterday, but she felt a lot better.

Lying flat in bed last night had been too uncomfortable, so she'd propped herself against her banked pillows and skimmed through several of the library books while George slept beside her. The art histories had been turgid and even a cheerful journalistic account of fakes and forgeries hadn't held her attention. Only when she had started to read about the war had she become interested enough to forget her own discomfort.

Life in the trenches sounded surreal. According to the memoirs of one officer, regular deliveries of post from London direct to the front line had brought him and his friends their favourite literary magazines, fine wines, Fortnum & Mason hampers and cigars, while all around them rats were fattening on half-buried decomposing corpses. They must have added an unbearable stench to the fumes of mustard gas and the stink of urine, excrement and sweaty bodies.

There had been no drainage in the trenches, which had at times been so badly waterlogged that the men had had to be issued with waders. Lice infestations had been constant and brought dangerous infections with them. Appalling wounds had had to be treated in makeshift tented hospitals with inadequate equipment and drugs. Worse than all the rest must have been the unrelenting, mind-destroying terror of living under continuous bombardment, punctuated by even more terrifying sorties across no man's land into a storm of bullets.

'The effects of machine-gun fire on the human body have been grossly exaggerated,' one of the home-based warmongers had written, which had made Trish shake with rage as she read it.

More and more surprised that Helen Gregory could have met a French art collector in the middle of such a war, Trish had read on in search of clues. There had been very little about nurses in any of the officers' memoirs, even when they wrote about their various stretches in hospital. Presumably they were so accustomed to being cared for by women that it didn't occur to them to mention these ones. But Vera Brittain's *Testament of Youth* had given a vivid picture of the kind of life Helen must have lived.

It made Trish ashamed of even noticing her poxy little cold. But it also gave her some clues to Helen's indifference to the collection she had inherited. Maybe she hadn't been mad to leave it untouched. Having watched the suffering of men who'd died in such conditions, even the greatest of paintings must have seemed trivial.

Trish blew her nose and in the sudden freedom caught a hint of the scent of roasting meat, sharpened by the unmistakable smell of grated horseradish root. George must be performing his usual alchemy with the unpromising ingredients of the traditional English Sunday lunch.

In their early days together, it had surprised her to find him such an efficient cook. She had only gradually come to understand that he used dealing with food as a way of getting rid of all the aggression that built up in him as he worked with clients he loathed but had to placate, clients as unreasonable and demanding as Jeremy Carfield.

'Anything I need to read in the *Sunday News*?' George asked, emerging for a moment.

There was flour all over his blue-and-white apron. Trish admitted that she'd been falling behind and hadn't done more than browse through a few of the sections. Promising to have something to report over lunch, she tidied and closed the financial pages she hadn't been reading carefully enough, and dropped them on the floor beside her sofa.

'Great,' George said, turning back to his pots and pans. 'I wouldn't want to think you were slacking off while I'm hard at it.'

Laughing, because he loathed interference in the kitchen when he was in charge, Trish picked the next part of the paper, which turned out to be the news, and skimmed over the front page. The biggest headline led into an account of a shooting in North London.

A woman had been killed in a tube station newsagent's by a 15-year-old who'd demanded change for a ticket machine. Witnesses who'd been in the station at the time had all told the police that the boy had been angry and jittery from the start. When the woman behind the counter had refused to give him change, he'd pulled a revolver out of his pocket and shot her in the head. The other people in the station had all been too shocked to prevent him running away, but the police were confident of being able to pick him up soon. For once they had a good picture from the CCTV cameras.

Sodding drugs, Trish thought. He must have been high on crack, or coming down from a high and desperate for more.

George had often told her she was neurotic on the subject and saw drug addicts everywhere. But, as she'd told him, that was only because they were everywhere, even at the Carfields' dinner party.

Oh shit! she thought. I should have written to thank them. Tough. I bought the present and he's not *my* client. George can write this time.

She turned on through the paper, in search of something less depressing than yet more accounts of drug-related crime, and was pulled up short by the sight of Toby Fullwell's name in the list of contents of the Review section.

There was an instantly recognizable caricature of him wearing a bow tie, beside a headline quote that read: 'Running the Gregory Bequest is the job of a lifetime. I can't imagine ever wanting to do anything else.'

Remembering the tiny salary he was paid, Trish thought that was unlikely. Unless, of course, he really was using the collection to generate illicit cash for himself.

She had already established to her own satisfaction, if not yet to anyone else's, that he could have found a way to launder money through the trust. But there must be plenty of other income-generating scams he could have been running.

It would be easy, for example, for anyone in his position to siphon off a drawing or painting each time he opened one of the packages in which they had been stored for so long. Only he knew what they contained, after all. But then that wouldn't have explained why he had sold the Pieter de Hooch on the trust's behalf.

Trish's mind began to work a little faster, as though the cold was releasing its last grip on her brain, and she saw another reason why he might have done that.

Some time ago she had met an art expert at one of Antony Shelley's glamorous dinners, and he had told her that London art dealers were going to the wall at an unprecedented rate because the supply of important paintings had dried up. With the Gregory Bequest offering a whole new source of forgotten old masters, Goode & Floore's, the auctioneers Toby had used, might well have thought it worth offering him an inducement to sell some of the treasures through them.

A seller's premium of, say, 15 per cent of the five million pounds raised by the de Hooch would have come to seven hundred and fifty thousand pounds. A kickback of even a fraction of that could have been a serious temptation to a man on Toby's salary.

Wishing she had more to go on, Trish picked up the interview again in the hope of learning more.

The journalist had not been able to persuade him to say much about his family or upbringing, beyond the fact that one of the great advantages of being an only child was that you could create a private world in which you could always lose yourself. Trish was surprised. She was an only child too, but all her energies had gone into trying to *find* her self.

Toby had told his interviewer that he had discovered his sanctuary in the history of art. His parents had had quite a good collection of books of their own and lived near an excellent library, so he had spent much of his solitary childhood becoming acquainted with the great painters of the past, their models and their patrons. According to the journalist, this experience had stood him in very good stead when he was deciding which career to follow after his straightforward history degree, and in even better stead when he was still at university and identified some original crayon drawings by François Clouet.

'Clearly surprised that I knew the story, and reluctant to boast,' the journalist had written, 'Fullwell said very little about his great coup.'

The article went on to explain that the drawings had been sold as prints by a local antique dealer, who had not been able to see past the grimy glass and poor framing to what lay beneath. That dealer must have been spitting tacks when the undergraduate's attribution was confirmed by the auctioneers Goode & Floore's, who sold the drawings on for a record price a few weeks later.

'I asked Toby Fullwell whether he had made many similar discoveries,' the journalist had written, 'and he laughed modestly saying: "You don't get that kind of opportunity more than once in any career. Of course, I'm always on the lookout, but I'm not optimistic. I only wish it had been I who bought the so-called prints. Unfortunately, all I did was identify them." '

The sound of footsteps on the iron staircase made Trish look up from the paper, and a brisk knocking at the door had her pushing herself up off the sofa. She shuffled across the polished wooden floor in her thick socks.

George reached the front door before she had even passed the fireplace. He was still wearing his huge blue-and-white butcher's apron and now had a gravy-stained tea towel draped over his shoulder.

'Ah, good morning,' said a rich familiar voice. 'My name's Henry Buxford. I—'

'Of course. Come on in. I'm George Henton. We met at dinner at the Shelleys', didn't we?'

'So we did. That apron distracted me.'

George laughed, much too secure in his position as one of the leading solicitors in London to worry about being caught in such a domestic guise.

'I'm sorry to disturb you, but I was in the neighbourhood, and I know Trish was trying to speak to me yesterday. Might I have a quick word with her?'

'Sure,' George said. 'But it doesn't have to be quick, does it? Stay for lunch. There's a huge amount, and the Yorkshire puddings will start to spoil in about—' He looked at his watch. 'Ten minutes. Come in, Henry, and have your word with Trish while they cook.'

'I suppose it is lunchtime,' Buxford said. 'But I'm afraid I can't stay. I'll be as quick as I can.'

Trish walked forwards to shake hands and apologize for her red nose and stockinged feet.

'I hadn't realized you were ill. I'm sorry to be disturbing you.'

'It's only a cold. I'm fine.'

'You don't look it. Hadn't you better sit down or something?'

She took him round the great fireplace and offered him a drink, which he declined.

'What have you got for me?' he asked as she stretched herself out on one of the big black sofas. He sat down opposite her. 'I know you've been trying to phone. I should have given you my mobile number.'

'It's only speculation so far, but there was something I wanted to ask you.'

'Fire away.'

'Are you afraid that Toby could be involved in money-laundering?' she said straight out.

He didn't flinch, or even look particularly worried. 'No, I'm not,' he said. 'I'm not surprised you've come up with the idea, Trish. In fact, I would have been worried about your judgement if you hadn't, but I really don't think it's a runner. For one thing Toby has shown no signs of paying the five million out again, and obviously he'd have to if he were laundering it.'

'He hasn't had much opportunity yet. The de Hooch sale only happened about three weeks ago. Couldn't he just be waiting for the right moment? Or maybe he's got cold feet.'

'I doubt that.' Buxford smiled at her, looking kind as well as honest. 'I've been round all this myself, Trish, believe me. If Toby had got involved with people who wanted money laundered, he'd be working for men involved in organized crime, and that sort are remorseless. He wouldn't be allowed to have cold feet. What else have you come up with?'

She ran through all her other ideas, watching him make notes when she reached the possibility that Toby could have been taking bribes. At the end of her account, Buxford said:

'That's a good start, Trish. You've done well.'

'It's kind of you to say so, but I haven't come up with any evidence of anything. And I don't think I'll be able to without a proper inventory of the collection.'

'Well, you're not going to get that, I'm afraid. There isn't one. It would have made all our lives a lot easier if there had been.'

'But there must have been one at some stage. I've been wondering whether Ivan Gregory could have burned it when he was in that post-stroke panic you described so vividly.'

'Not possible.' Buxford sounded certain. 'Even half-mad with fear and misery, Ivan would never have destroyed an important document. He was a banker for heaven's sake! Everything about his life and training would have forbidden it.'

Trish tried not to laugh as she thought of all the financial scandals of the last few years, and all the reports she'd ever read of shredded documents and misplaced evidence.

Before she could say anything, David and Nicky reappeared from their walk and had to be introduced to Henry. By the time they had gone to get rid of their outdoor clothes, Trish had moved on to one of her other doubts:

'You told me that you'd had three rounds of interviews for the directorship of the gallery, Henry.'

'Yes?'

'I've been wondering what it was about Toby that made him seem so peculiarly suitable, and so trustworthy, that you felt you could give him all this power over the collection.'

'He was easily the best of the applicants, judged by any criteria,' Buxford said in the voice of one who would accept no contradiction. Then he pushed back the sides of his immaculate grey hair in the gesture she was coming to believe he used whenever he was feeling particularly uncomfortable, and added: 'But he is also my godson.'

More sodding favours, Trish thought, which made her voice irritable as she said: 'Ah, I see. Now I know why you wanted a private investigation of what he's up to. I couldn't understand why you didn't call in the police straightaway.'

'That's not fair.' He was brushing back his hair again. 'If I'd had any evidence of crime, I would have gone to them. But, as you've pointed out, there isn't any evidence. I hoped you'd find some.'

'Then I'm sorry I haven't done a better job.'

There was a clattering sound from the kitchen. Buxford stood up.

'Your lunch is clearly ready, and I must go anyway. Your idea about kickbacks is clever. Convincing, too. I wish I'd thought of it myself. I'll look into it. And you will call me if you come up with anything else, won't you?'

'Of course. But you know, I've been thinking: the idea of bribery only brings us right back full circle to where you started, albeit on a more personal scale. Why would Toby want the money?'

'We don't pay him much,' Buxford said, without any of the embarrassment Trish thought he ought to feel.

'Exactly. So you'd notice if he were spending above his income, wouldn't you?' She paused.

'True.'

'So why would he be tempted by a bribe he couldn't spend? Unless, of course, he wanted it for something illegal and untraceable.'

'Like drugs, you mean.'

She could hear George's voice in her mind: Oh, come on, Trish. You're obsessed. You see drugs everywhere.

'Yes.'

'It's possible but unlikely. I've seen no signs of addiction in Toby. There are no needle tracks, and I've never seen him display any of the aggression or idiocy cocaine produces.' Buxford checked the time on his watch. 'I really must go now. Phone me again whenever you need me. My wife will always take a message at home if you can't get me on the mobile or at the bank.'

Trish showed him out, then took her place at the lunch table, where David soon showed signs of having as healthy an appetite as George himself. That was one worry out of the way. They must have got on well over yesterday's rugby expedition.

'Pretty good to have a man like Henry Buxford on dropping-in terms, Trish,' George said, refilling her wineglass. 'I'm impressed.'

'Amazing, isn't it?' she said, laughing at his obvious envy.

'How did it happen?'

'Antony asked me to look into something for him. But I haven't done very well. I just hope that's not going to piss them both off.'

George refilled her wineglass. He was too accustomed to guarding his own professional secrets to ask her for details. 'So what if it does? Antony Shelley is not your boss. You're a self-employed member of the Bar, for heaven's sake. I know you think he's only one rung short of God, but you ought to have grown out of that kind of hero worship by now.'

Several answers suggested themselves to Trish, some of them almost as sharp as his voice had just been. She saw that David had put his knife and fork together, even though there was still at least a third of the food on his plate, so she took the easy way out and grinned at George, ignoring his tone.

'I worship all my heroes, as you very well know, O Most Heroic of the Lot.'

He laughed, looking a little ashamed of himself, and blew her a kiss. David started to eat again.

Chapter 11

Helen's back felt as though it was about to snap in two. She put her hands behind her, massaging the muscles either side of her spine. All the orderlies seemed to have disappeared, so she was having to cart buckets full of stinking dressings to the incinerator. She could hardly bear to bend down again. The smell made her gag, and the weight dragging at the pain in her back was almost unbearable.

'Nothing's as bad as the men suffer,' she muttered aloud. She couldn't work out why everything was so much more difficult than usual. Maybe now that Jean-Pierre was back and she knew what being happy was, the usual semi-miserable life she'd always had in the past was that much harder to bear.

'Hélène?'

His voice made her smile, even though she'd just caught the full whiff of the dressings. Gangrene, she thought. There was no mistaking that smell. She let the buckets clank down on the muddy ground again and straightened up.

'Let me help you with those buckets.'

'They're foul.'

'All the more reason. Walk with me. Show me the way.'

He did it all for her, using his beautiful hands to manipulate the heavy tongs much more effectively than she'd ever been able to do. The revolting dressings spluttered and began to burn. The smell was even worse. She gagged and turned away.

When he had finished he came to find her again.

'You are exhausted,' he said. 'You should be lying down. And you should be off duty now, unless they've changed the shifts suddenly.'

She rubbed the back of her hand against her sweaty forehead. 'No. But we're even more short-staffed than usual. I can't go off duty yet. We're still on the morning dressings, and it's already six o'clock. We can't leave the night shift to do them all.'

'All the more reason for you to rest. I will tell the sister you must lie down.'

'No,' she said in sudden panic. If anyone guessed what there was between them, she would be shipped straight back to England, and she really would never see him again. 'I'm almost finished. You go on ahead. I'll follow.'

'As soon as you can, *ma mie*.'

She smiled. If they had been alone, she would have kissed him, and she could tell from his eyes that he knew that.

It was nearly two hours before she reached the small inn where they always met now. The landlord had known him for years, Jean-Pierre had explained, and he was well paid to keep his mouth shut. It was the safest place to meet for miles around.

'Ah, Hélène,' he said, laying his lips against her skin, just above the miniature. 'You are still wearing it.'

'It is all I have to remind me that you're not part of a dream when you are away. Oh, Jean-Pierre, I love you so much.'

'And I, you, *ma mie*,' he said, peeling away her dress before starting to take down her hair. He loved pulling out the pins and watching the blonde mass cascade down over her naked shoulders. Her whole body ached for him and as his lips travelled over her skin they lit a fuse of tingling delight.

Much later, he lay back, breathing heavily. She curled herself against his side, laying her hot face on his shoulder. He patted her head with his other hand, then fell into the kind of sleep that made her feel lonelier than ever. She still had to school herself to wait until he woke.

There was no reason to feel alone, she told herself as she had so often before. From this absence at least, she knew he would return.

It was only ten minutes this time, much less than usual, and so her muscles had not even begun to stiffen. He took her head between both his hands and kissed her.

'I am sorry that I could not get back here any sooner this time,' he said when they were lying side by side, her hand tucked into his. 'I hope you have not been working too hard without me to remind you to rest. I could not believe they have been making you burn the dressings now.'

'We have been very busy, but I have had a little time off. Last Saturday Myrtle and I walked to the next village.' She wasn't going to tell him that she had been trying to learn as much as she could about art and architecture. That might only underline the ignorance of which she was so ashamed. 'One of the men had told me there was a beautiful church there, but when we found it we saw that it has been wrecked.'

'Blown up?' Jean-Pierre said.

'No. Much worse than that. It was deliberate. The crucifix has been bent forwards so that it lies dangling just above the altar, some of the glass has been smashed, and all the paintings are riddled with bullet holes. It made me understand why you are so worried about yours.'

Jean-Pierre shivered in spite of the heat, and his hand tightened on hers.

'I'm sorry,' she said at once. 'I didn't mean to remind you, or make you worry even more.'

'It's not the paintings that make me afraid now,' he said. 'It is you, *ma mie*. Walking so close to the Line with only Myrtle to protect you? It is mad. Far, far too dangerous. You could be—' He pulled himself up, coughed, then started again more calmly: 'Anything could happen to you, Hélène. Promise you won't take risks like that again. You matter far more to me than any painting. You must promise.'

Helen rolled over on to her side, so that she could see his face properly. He looked terrified. She brushed his face with her hand, as though she could remove the fear. But his expression did not change.

'I'm afraid for you all the time now, *ma mie*. You must promise.'

'All right, Jean-Pierre. But you must promise, too. It is harder for me to bear the fear when you go away and I don't know where you are or when I will see you again. You at least know exactly where I am and what I am doing.'

'Hélène,' he said as he leaned forwards to kiss her, pushing his knee so gently between her legs that she barely noticed what was happening. A moment later, he was hanging over her, his lips brushing her eyebrows, her lids, the end of her nose, her lips. He had never wanted her again so soon. Nothing mattered now but him.

Toby stood in the middle of the basement, staring at Jean-Pierre's treasure store. His privileged access to it had once seemed like a certificate of his worth. Now it was the opposite, a continual reminder of every way in which he had fallen short of what he should have been.

Once, long ago in Cambridge, he had thought of art forgery as mischief rather than crime and forgers as gentle, scholarly types. Now he knew those were only the amateurs. Professionals were like Ben, in it for big business, prepared to stop at nothing and as brutal as any other criminal.

Someone was knocking on the door again. Couldn't they read? The sign clearly stated that the Gregory Bequest collection was closed on Sundays.

There was a spyhole in the front door, but he wasn't going

to risk leaving the basement while there was someone outside. The hall floorboards creaked and would betray him to anyone with working ears.

His mobile rang. He looked at it lying on the workbench, a small harmless black-plastic rectangle with a crack in it, and he hated the thought of what he might hear through it. Was it Ben? He didn't think so. He couldn't feel the same iciness digging into his spine today. So maybe it was Margaret, offering news of the boys' safety. He grabbed the phone.

'Ah, Toby, good! It's Henry Buxford here. Everything all right?'

Shaking with a mixture of relief and dread, he licked his cracking lips and winced at the small pain. 'Fine, fine. Why? Where are you?'

'Outside your house, dear boy, hoping to come in and have a chat. Where are you?'

'Halfway to Cambridge, I'm afraid,' he said, turning his back to the outside wall of the basement. Thank God for mobiles! He was pretty sure that sound couldn't leak out up to street level from here, but if it did, maybe Henry would take it as an echo from his own phone.

'Oh. Margaret and the boys with you?'

'No. They're away, I'm afraid.'

'She never told me she was going anywhere when she phoned to cancel lunch today. Is she all right?'

Oh, God! Toby thought. What has he heard? Aloud he said: 'She's fine. She just had an invitation to take the boys to stay with friends and couldn't resist it.'

'In the middle of term? That doesn't sound like Margaret. She's always been so keen on their education.'

'Not this time,' Toby snapped. He couldn't help it. Didn't he have enough to cope with? Even if the management of the gallery was Henry's business, the boys' education was not.

'What's going on, Toby? I know something's the matter.

You sound all over the place. I wish you'd tell me and let me help.'

'I'm fine. I don't need any help. It must be the reception that's making me sound odd. Can I phone you when I'm back in London?'

'Yes, do. We need to talk. I've got to fly to New York tomorrow and I won't be back until Wednesday night, so it'll have to be Thursday. Could you come in to the bank at, say, eleven o'clock on Thursday? I'll make time to talk to you then.'

Anything to get you off the phone, Toby thought. 'Yes, sure, whatever you like, Henry. What do you want to talk about?'

'We'll discuss it on Thursday.'

Suddenly he remembered why he couldn't go anywhere on Thursday morning. The cheese sandwich he'd had for lunch seemed to have got stuck halfway to his churning stomach and felt as though it was burning a hole in his gut.

'Damn!' he said, trying to sound lightly irritated instead of on the point of being sick again. 'No, I can't come on Thursday morning. There's a sale at Goode & Floore's I have to go to.'

'You're not selling something else, are you?' Henry's voice quickened with suspicion. What did he know? 'You didn't tell me.'

'No, I'm not selling anything. But there's a fantastic buying opportunity,' Toby said, grabbing the scalpel he'd been using to cut some mounting board. He tried to make himself feel normal so that nothing in his voice would alert Henry. 'There's a Hieronymus Bosch in the sale, which I think we could get for a pretty reasonable price. And we haven't got anything by him. It would really help raise the profile of the collection if we could buy it.'

There was silence on the phone. Toby wondered whether they'd been cut off. 'Henry? Are you there?'

'Yes, I am. What time is the sale?'

'Eleven o'clock. The Bosch is lot 50, so they're not likely to get to it for three-quarters of an hour or more. I suppose I could come to your office afterwards, if it's really that important.'

'No, don't worry about it. It would be much more sensible for us to meet at the sale. It's time I learned more about the art market in any case. I'll join you at Goode & Floore's.'

Oh, God forbid! Toby thought as he said: 'But, Henry—'

'No, don't say a word. It's not fair to drag you over to the City, and I know I haven't been giving you enough support at the gallery. This can be the beginning of a new regime. I'll come to the sale and we can talk afterwards. Goodbye, Toby.'

Toby dropped the phone on his cutting board. There was a piece of cloudy glass at the back of the workbench. It showed him the loathsome meekness in his eyes and the miserable droop of his lips. He could hear his mother's voice now: 'Why *must* you always be so wet, Toby?'

She had never touched him, or locked him in his room, or even punished him, but then she'd never had to. Her voice had been her weapon. She could make it crack like a whip, and it hurt like a whip. Every time. Even now. And if he flinched, she would lose her temper. In the old days, it had nearly always ended in the same way. 'Oh, for heaven's sake, stop crying, you loathsome child.'

He jammed the scalpel so deep into the cutting board that the blade snapped.

Chapter 12

Caro's colleagues can't have got very far with their investigation of the naked body in the river, Trish thought as she stood behind David, shielding him from the wind and the traffic. They've had a whole week. They should have come up with something by now.

David was reading the text of one of the large yellow metal notices the police set up to ask for information or witnesses to violent crime. So far the sandbags that weighted this one down had been strong enough to keep it upright, in spite of the gale.

As the wind insinuated itself up Trish's skirt and between her thighs, she wondered why she hadn't grabbed trousers in her rush to get dressed this morning. She tugged the skirt nearer her knees and hunched her shoulders.

'At school yesterday they were saying there are probably lots more bodies under the bridge,' David said, still staring at the sign. 'And that there's a serial killer like Hannibal Lecter living near here.'

Trish felt as though she could see light through the first tiny chink in his armour. This was the first anxiety he had willingly shared with her. She put her hands on his shoulders, trying to give him as much security as the sandbags gave the notice.

'Then they're being very silly,' she said clearly. 'Serial killers are incredibly rare, and there definitely aren't any here. There is only one body, and it probably didn't even go into the river from this bridge. Don't you remember Caro saying that it had probably been washed down here by the tide? You don't have anything to worry about. George and I will keep you safe.'

'Then why did the police put this up?' He moved restlessly, as though the weight of her hands disturbed him, but she didn't let go. 'They wouldn't have if they didn't think someone on the bridge saw something. So there must have been something to see.'

I've always wanted him to be intelligent, Trish thought, but this would be so much easier if he were not so bright. She thought it would probably frighten him more if she started to lie than if she took his fears seriously.

'That may be true,' she said, 'but you must try not to think about it. One of the most useful skills to have in life is the ability to turn off your worries. Now we'd better get on or you'll be late.'

He said nothing else until they had reached the school gates, then he stopped dead.

'Why's the Head beckoning? What does she want?'

'I don't know, but it's OK. She and I often chat. Here's your rucksack. Have a good day. And try not to worry too much about anything. You're a great chap, and you're doing so well here that I know it's the right place for you. You'll be able to stay here till you're thirteen, then move on to the senior school, if that's what you'd like.'

'Great! Thank you, Trish.' His eyes stilled for a moment and his fingers brushed her hand as he took the straps from her. 'Don't you mind talking to the Head?'

'No. I like her. I'll be fine.' She ruffled his hair, then wished she hadn't, as he hastily flattened it again. 'It'll be Nicky picking you up this afternoon, but I'll see you later in the evening. And don't forget, Jamie Bagnall is coming back for tea.'

'OK. See you tonight,' he said and darted off to the far side of the building, pausing to wave shyly before he went in through the door.

Relieved to see the old friendly gesture, Trish went over to Hester More to find out what she wanted.

'Ah, Ms Maguire, I've been hoping to consult you about something. Have you a moment?'

'Of course.'

'It's nothing to do with David.'

'Fine.' Trish smiled encouragingly.

'I wanted to ask your advice about the mother of one of the boys in his year,' said Mrs More. 'She has a black eye. She claims it was caused by a swing door, but I don't believe her. I think her husband must be hitting her.'

'Poor woman.'

'I have been worried about the family for some time because both children have been displaying signs of disturbance, of the kind you described so vividly in your book about domestic violence.'

Trish felt absurdly flattered that the Head knew she'd even written it, but she did not want to get involved in any more unhappy marriages. She had seen more than enough to last a lifetime.

'Their mother's inside now, talking to the school nurse about them. I wondered if you might talk to her when she comes out, persuade her to admit what's happening and get some proper help.'

'I can't do that. I have no right to ask her questions, and no standing. Besides, if you can't persuade her to accept help, I'm hardly likely to do any better.'

'I think you might. Any woman like Margaret Fullwell is going to respond much better to a lawyer than to her children's teacher.'

'Fullwell? Mer's mother?'

'Yes.' Mrs More's grey eyes had sharpened. 'Does that make a difference?'

Trish produced a small, unamused laugh. Everything seemed to be conspiring to keep her involved with Buxford's anxieties. She had an uncomfortable sensation that her life was no longer her own, as though accepting his commission had somehow let in forces she could not control.

'Only in that I know some people she knows,' she said, trying to sound casual. 'I suppose I could have a go. Is that her now?'

A tall woman with a thick mass of curly reddish-brown hair had emerged from the pupils' entrance. She was wearing a rakish black suede jacket over straight black jeans tucked into ankle boots with little cuffs. Anyone with shorter or fatter legs would have looked stumpy. Noticing the athletic way she ran up the three steps to the courtyard, and the freedom with which she moved, Trish thought she had never seen a woman who looked less like a victim.

Hester More half-turned so casually that no one watching would have thought she was doing any more than checking the clock on the wall behind her.

'Yes.'

'I'll do what I can.'

Trish walked slowly back towards the ornate gates that led out on to the Embankment. Reaching them, she stopped, balanced her briefcase on her knee, opened it and started scuffling among the papers. As the other woman walked towards her, she allowed some of them to fly out.

'Let me help,' Margaret Fullwell said, as a gust of wind blew some out on to the pavement. Her voice had an attractively clear Bostonian accent.

Trish hadn't realized the woman was American. Maybe that explained Mer's surprising name. Meredith could have been Margaret's surname before she married.

'Sod it,' Trish muttered aloud, hoping she hadn't let out anything important with the rubbish that was now floating out to be mashed beneath the wheels of the usual rush-hour traffic into the City. She shut the case, dumped it on the ground and rushed to collect every piece of paper she could.

Toby felt his hands curl into fists as he stood with his back to the Embankment, watching the school gates. He knew exactly what the thin dark-haired woman must be up to and he could have killed her. He kept seeing her now, wherever he went, and he knew she had to be one of Ben's watchers, monitoring everything he did. She didn't give him the same sensation of creeping evil as Ben did, but that was probably because she was only an assistant.

Maybe that was why he hadn't picked her out of the crowds originally. Or maybe it was just because he'd been looking for men, and of the kind whose knuckles grazed the ground. Wondering how many other innocuous-looking women Ben had following him, he wanted to shout out a warning to Margaret, but, of course, he couldn't. It was a miracle she hadn't already seen him.

How could she have been so obstinate as to stay in London? If it hadn't been for Henry's call yesterday, Toby would never have believed that she might care so much for the boys' education that she'd merely pretend to take them away. But here she was, bringing them to school at the same time every day and giving Ben the perfect opportunity to get at them, whenever he wanted.

For about a second, Toby thought it would be a good thing if Ben's heavies did try to do something to Mer. Maybe that would make Margaret understand and do as she was told.

'Here.' Margaret Fullwell handed over a bunch of dusty sheets. 'I think that's the lot.'

'That's great. Thank you,' Trish said, straightening up and smiling. 'I'm sorry to have been so clumsy. I just suddenly remembered something I needed for a meeting and thought I'd left at home. But I should have waited till I got to my desk. I'm Trish Maguire, by the way.' She held out her free hand.

'David's mother?' Margaret asked, automatically shaking Trish's hand.

'No. His half-sister.' Trish thought about the discussions she'd had with David before they'd agreed that he would use her surname. 'How d'you know him?'

'I don't myself, but one of my boys talks about him as a great hero. My name's Margaret Fullwell.'

Trish shook hands, distracted from everything else by this news. 'A hero? You do surprise me.'

'Haven't you heard how he refused to tell the Head what happened when he was beaten up in the playground?'

'No.' Trish felt the old frown pulling down her eyebrows. 'The only playground beating-up I've heard about was the fight in which David injured another boy so badly he had to go to hospital.'

'That's the one. David was thumped when he refused to play the drowned victim in a game some bigger boys were playing on the awful day when that body was found in the river.'

Trish momentarily closed her eyes. Why hadn't he told her what had happened?

'But he didn't cry, as Mer always does when he's picked on,' Margaret went on, 'and he refused to hit back, too. That infuriated Stephen Johnson, who's a terrible bully, so he took another swing at David, who very sensibly dodged. Stephen overbalanced when he met no resistance, and he cut his eye on a sharp stone on the playground.'

Trish felt like rushing straight back to school to bang several heads together and said so.

'You can't blame the staff. There's a ferocious anti-sneaking culture this term,' Margaret said. 'Haven't you come across it yet? Mer was very impressed that David stuck to it even though it got him a detention.'

But Mer had no friends and ate rust in the playground, Trish thought, so he would probably have been impressed by almost anything. She wondered why he was so despised and solitary.

'I'm really glad to know,' she said. 'Thank you. Are you on your way somewhere? Or would you like to have some coffee?'

Margaret looked surprised, but after a moment she smiled. 'Why not? Mer will be impressed to hear that I've had coffee with his hero's sister. Where shall we go?'

'There's always Pret in Fleet Street. We can walk up through the Temple, and I could drop off my briefcase in chambers on the way.'

'So you're a lawyer, are you? What kind of work d'you do?'

What a lead, Trish thought, and settled down to an account of how dealing with the miseries of dysfunctional marriages and abused children had eventually driven her out of family law.

'I think the thing I hated most,' she ended truthfully, 'was going through all those agonizing cases, in which women finally got the self-esteem together to give evidence against their violent husbands, only to go back to them a month or so later. Sometimes I see them processing through my memory like the dead kings in Macbeth, with their wounds still dripping. Every single one of them thought her husband would reform, but of course he never did. It used to make me want to shake them till their teeth rattled.'

'Never?' Margaret said, just as they were passing Plough Court.

Trish decided she didn't want to risk losing the fine thread that connected them by dropping off her papers and so she walked on, the leather briefcase heavy in her hand.

'I never dealt with a case in which a violent husband – or wife – reformed,' she said, still honestly. 'And some of the aggressors *are* women. I hate admitting that, but it is true.'

'Why do they do it?'

'The aggressors or their victims?'

'The violent ones.'

'It sounds like a cliché, but I can't think of a single case I dealt with when it hadn't had something to do with the way they'd been treated in childhood, although it was usually made worse by drink or drugs. Occasionally the trigger was some particular stress in their current lives. Why? You're beginning to sound as though—'

'Did Hester More set this up?' Margaret stopped and turned, effectively barring the path that would lead out into Fleet Street. She looked like some mythical winged warrior, ready to flatten all her enemies. 'I thought she was looking a bit too interested in my black eye. Was that paper spillage by the gate pre-arranged?'

Was this the moment to lie? No, Trish thought, looking into Margaret's hot, hurt eyes.

'I'm sorry to be so obvious. You're right: she did ask me if I might be able to help you.'

'Well, she should have come straight out and given me your name, not snuck behind my back like this.'

'I'm sorry if it seems like sneaking,' Trish said, far too experienced to feel any kind of embarrassment. 'I gather she did try to talk to you, and she was worried enough about your response to try another way. Couldn't I help, even if only with advice?'

'I doubt it. My husband is not a wife-beater.' Margaret scowled. 'And don't look at me as though you think I'm in denial. It is true that he hit me, once, and that is why the boys and I have moved out. Toby has to know he can't push me around. But the physical assault was a one-off. I'm certain of that. You can't be married to a man for fifteen years and not know whether he's violent by nature.'

'No,' Trish said, smiling through the other woman's anger. 'I don't suppose you can. Will you still have coffee with me?'

Margaret laughed, but the tautness of the muscles in her strong face made it clear she wasn't giving in. 'All right, so long as you promise to tell Hester More to keep her bulbous nose out of my life. It's none of her business.'

'Except in so far as it affects your boys, who are in her charge.' Trish wasn't prepared to soften her message, even in the interests of finding out more about Toby Fullwell. She was too worried by the little she'd heard about poor, frightened Mer.

When she and Margaret were perched on a couple of high chairs in the window of Pret à Manger, with cups of cappuccino in front of them, Margaret apologized for snapping.

'The stupid thing is,' she added, 'that I have wanted to talk to someone about what Toby did to me, so I should have jumped at the chance. But it's humiliating to think of your children's teacher talking to a complete stranger about the black eye your husband gave you.'

'I'm sure. How did it happen?'

Trish listened to a halting account of an argument that didn't sound too bad, followed by a blow, unfortunately witnessed by Mer (who had always acted as a kind of lightning conductor whenever anyone shouted in anger), followed by Margaret's exasperated walkout.

'Could he have been drunk?' Trish asked, understanding more about poor Mer. 'A lot of otherwise calm men do become violent with alcohol.'

'Not Toby. We share a bottle of wine every so often, but that's as far as it goes.'

'Then what about drugs? Some are notorious for making people aggressive. Cocaine derivatives, in particular.'

'Toby?' Margaret burst into peals of laughter, which reassured Trish. 'I really can't see him in a crack den, you know. I shouldn't laugh because you have no idea what he's like, but he's far too frightened of authority to do anything illegal. And he's far too clean.'

'Are you sure? A lot of men – and women, come to that – have secret habits, which—'

'Not Toby. Take it from me. I would know if he were on anything.'

'OK,' Trish said. 'In that case, do you have any idea what did make him hit you?'

'I think maybe he was trying to tell me something. He'd been morose for weeks. I'd done the usual "what's the matter darling?" stuff at the beginning. All he did in return was snap at me. So I ignored his bad temper and hoped he'd recover eventually. Now I'm wondering whether he wanted me to go on asking questions. That could have done it, don't you think? Because I wasn't showing enough interest in whatever was tormenting him?'

'Possibly. Have you any idea what it could have been?'

'There's never been a shortage of things that worry Toby.' Margaret's lips hardened. 'You know what I really resent is all those years I spent telling him he was OK, that his mother had been wrong all his life, that he *was* good enough, that he *could* hack it, that he ought to go for the kind of job he really wanted. And then after all that support, when he'd got the right kind of job at last and I'd put my life on hold to help him do it properly, all he could do was turn on me and give me a black eye.'

'I'm sorry.' The obvious question almost forced itself out of Trish's mouth: 'Are you sure he didn't misinterpret what you intended as support? Maybe some of your reassurance came across as contempt. Or nagging.'

She worked hard to keep her face blank, but Margaret was already on to another track and paid no attention to anything Trish said.

'No. I think he felt guilty and wanted me to guess why and tell him it was OK and didn't matter.'

'Guilty about what?'

'The obvious.' Margaret shrugged. 'An affair. If it hadn't been so out of character, I'd probably have seen it earlier.'

'D'you know who— ?'

'At first I thought it must be his secretary; now I've realized it has to be an outsider. There had been some weird phone calls. If I answered, the phone would go dead, which is a giveaway in itself. And it came to the point when I had only to walk into a room for Toby to break off his call, blushing and mumbling excuses about wrong numbers. It's so obvious now I look back that I can't think how I missed it for so long.'

'Maybe,' Trish said, thinking that it was a pity Margaret and Henry were both so sure Toby couldn't be on drugs.

Calls like that could easily have come from a dealer, phoning to demand payment or to arrange the next pick-up. Or, of course, to use the addict's need for the next fix to force him to do anything the dealer wanted.

'I must go,' Margaret said, putting down her cup. 'We'll meet again at the Christmas play, won't we? I know David has a big part.'

'Yes. I'll definitely be there. I'm sorry I haven't been more help.'

'Oh, I don't know. I've been able to talk about Toby and you've given me some good advice. Thank you for that.'

Trish wondered if that comment had been sarcastic. As far as she could remember she hadn't given any advice at all. The half-drunk cappuccino was cool now, and the foam clung unattractively to the inside of the cup in beige festoons. She abandoned it, unobtrusively walking behind Margaret back through the Temple and out on to the Embankment. There she ignored the rough sleepers in their sad, urine-smelling heaps and turned straight into Temple tube station.

Trish decided to stay with her a little longer. She felt a bit of a fool, and hoped Margaret would not look back and catch her out.

There was only one dangerous moment, as they emerged from the tube at Sloane Square and Margaret paused by the flower stand to buy a bunch of well-berried holly. Trish turned her back and pretended to study the tube map just inside the station. Later, walking at a more discreet distance along the King's Road, she followed Margaret to a house in Radnor Walk and watched her unlock the door.

So, Trish thought, she must be staying there. It shouldn't be too hard to find out who owns the house.

What would be hard, though, would be forgiving herself for the waste of so much time. She'd learned nothing useful and now she had to get back to chambers fast. There would be Steve's irritation to face, as well as all the work she hoped would be piling up for her.

Forty minutes later, she found not only the work but also Sam Makins, sitting in the sagging visitor's chair opposite her desk and frowning over some papers.

'Hello,' she said. 'What can I do for you?'

He smiled, with his chin tucked into his neck like a shy girl. 'Sorry to hang about like this, Trish, but I wanted your advice.'

'Sure. What's the problem?'

'It's this Tamara O'Connor case. You remember she's in Cookham Wood on remand?'

'Yes. Probably a good thing if she's given the police names of the Jamaican dealers she told me about. She'll be much safer there than out on the street.'

'I know. But I wanted to ask if you think I'm going nuts to assume there must be more to the story than she's told us. I mean why would anyone pick such an obvious addict to be a mule?'

Trish smiled at him. Steve had told her Sam had the right mixture of brains and kindness to deal with Tamara, but this was the first direct evidence she'd had.

'I don't know. But I have been thinking about it ever since the bail application,' she admitted. 'All I've come up with is that this Jason character she was talking about could have set her up to be arrested, having primed her with the names of his rivals over here. It would be a neat and original way of winning a London turf war, wouldn't it?'

'But why would he bother? It's easy enough to shoot someone on the street these days and get away with it.'

Trish thought of the body in the river and shrugged. 'Maybe

he's decided that turf wars turn into blood feuds and he doesn't want to risk his family. Or maybe there's just been a change in the way the drug world is operating now. If so, it's long overdue.'

The phone rang. It was her catering company's solicitor, wanting to check that everything was in place for next week's hearing. Sam waited until she'd finished the call, then said:

'D'you think it's worth mentioning in my plea for mitigation, Trish? That's really what I came to ask.'

'Tricky. You could always try, I suppose. "M'lord, my client deeply regrets that she was stupid and starry-eyed enough to let herself be sucked into a double-dealing plot—" I'm not sure it would work, Sam, even if you didn't put it quite like that.'

'Then I don't know what I am going to be able to do for her.'

'Very little, I'm afraid,' she said. 'Tamara is a walking disaster show. The one consolation is that she really is unlikely to be worse off in prison than on the streets. She's not going to get her kids back in any case.'

'That's a counsel of despair.'

'I'm afraid so.'

'You know how Antony and Robert are acting for this solicitor who's being done for money-laundering?'

'Is that as much a *non sequitur* as it sounds, Sam?' Trish asked, as she forced herself to keep smiling. She couldn't believe he would say something like that to needle her. Needling took Robert's kind of self-satisfaction. And Sam was far too young to see himself as her rival.

'No, it isn't. Her crime – alleged crime – is barely different from Tamara's. They were both working for men involved in major drug-smuggling operations. But the rich solicitor gets the head of chambers, the most senior junior, and a good chance of getting off, while Tamara gets only me, on Legal Aid, and a foregone conclusion. It's class all over again, Trish, and it *stinks*.'

'A lot of what we do stinks,' she said, realizing that she must have taken on a little of Antony's self-protective cynicism after all. She felt sorry for Sam and all the years of angst he faced before he gave in to it too. 'You have to put up with that if you're not to go mad.'

The door was flung open, making Sam jump and revealing Antony, still talking to someone else over his shoulder. Sam pulled himself out of the only spare chair, grimacing. Trish nodded to him and watched him wait uneasily until their head of chambers turned at last, saw him, and gave him room to get out.

'So, Trish, how are you getting on with Henry Buxford's problem?' Antony said as he took Sam's place in the sagging leather armchair.

'Not well. It's trickier than I'd expected, and has very little to do with any kind of research. If I'd known what I was in for at the beginning I don't think I'd ever have agreed to see him, let alone taken it on.'

'Don't make excuses. And don't forget that Henry's not a patient man. He has a very low tolerance of both failure and shoddy work.'

'I don't do shoddy work,' Trish said, biting back her fury at the allegation. 'And I don't do failure. I talked to him yesterday. He seemed perfectly happy with what I'd given him then.'

'Good. I told him you'd be able to sort it out, so I'll be in deep shit if you let me down.'

Oh, don't, she thought, even as she kept the confident expression on her face, I've got more than enough pressure as it is. The phone on her desk rang. Antony waved at it, giving her permission to answer.

'Trish? That you? It's Henry Buxford here. I'm calling from New York.'

'Hello. Antony's here. He and I were just talking about you.'

This was Antony's cue to leave her to have the conversation in private, but he didn't take it.

The way he leaned back and crossed his legs showed he was determined to listen to every word. Was he monitoring her performance or checking that she showed his grand friend due deference?

'Are you in court on Thursday morning?' Henry asked.

'No, although I've got a hell of a lot of paperwork to do.'

'Good. There's to be a big sale at Goode & Floore's, and I'd like you to be there.' The line crackled. 'Sorry. I'm not getting a very good signal.'

'Why d'you want me there?' Trish asked, raising her voice above the crackle. She thought of her practice and the importance of satisfying all her instructing solicitors, as well as keeping Steve happy. She couldn't go frolicking off like this without a very good reason. Antony was looking boot-faced, presumably at her even daring to question Henry Buxford.

'To observe. Toby has told me he's proposing to buy a painting.'

And get rid of the five million pounds perhaps, Trish thought. In which case my first idea of what he's up to *is* right, whatever you want to believe. But this didn't seem a good moment to say so.

'Don't make me beg, Trish.'

'What time d'you want me there?'

'I told Toby I'd be there round about eleven o'clock. It would probably be better if you and I didn't acknowledge each other in front of him.'

'Fine.'

'Were you being deliberately difficult?' Antony asked when she put down the phone.

'No. I have a lot of real work to do and I can't go rushing out of here on frivolous errands every time anyone asks me to, even Henry Buxford. I had to be sure it was important.'

'I hope you're taking this seriously enough, Trish. It may not be part of your practice, but it matters.'

To you maybe, she thought, reminding herself of George's point that she was an independent self-employed professional and not some kind of skivvy, slaving away in Antony's basement. She clicked on to the diary in her laptop to enter the appointment at Goode & Floore's.

'Of course I'm taking it seriously,' she said when she was satisfied. 'Now, what did you want me for, Antony?'

'Only this.' He paused by the door. 'Oh, and if you see Robert, would you ask him to drop into my room? I want to check a few things in his excellent notes before our conference this afternoon.'

Trish looked resentfully at his departing back. That last crack had to be deliberate. It was not her job to run errands for either Robert or Antony.

Helen woke out of a nightmare, pouring sweat and gasping. Jean-Pierre had been carrying his priceless paintings to safety across no man's land and was now lying on the ground, with his intestines bulging out of an appalling stomach wound. She had been crawling towards him, dragging a medical bag after her, and the harder she'd dragged and the further she'd crawled, the greater the distance between them. She had never even reached him.

She got out of bed to pour herself some water from the chipped carafe on the table between her bed and Myrtle's.

'It's only a dream,' she whispered. 'He isn't wounded. He will be back.'

Under her thick nightgown, she could feel the miniature hard against her skin. One hand crept up to hold it through the flannel. Somehow she must hold on to her faith that he was still alive, too. Otherwise, what point would there be in doing any of it?

Chapter 13

'Morning, Felicity,' Toby said on Thursday morning, as he passed the front desk at Goode & Floore's, with its familiar bunch of beautiful trainees of both sexes.

For the first time he wondered if it could have been his lack of good looks that had made the directors refuse him a gap-year job here all those years ago. At the time he'd taken it as yet more evidence of the world's hostility and hated them for it.

'Good morning, Mr Fullwell.' Felicity offered him her customary radiant smile, so he must have achieved a reasonable version of his old jauntiness.

It didn't help him force himself up the stairs to the principal saleroom. Every step was such an effort that he thought he might have to haul himself up by the banisters. He'd often seen elderly collectors do that, with their sticks bunched in their free hand and their faces contorted to hold in the pain. Just now he felt weaker even than they had seemed.

'Hi, Toby!' He didn't recognize the speaker for a moment, but raised a hand and a smile for him. 'You buying or selling today?'

'There are one or two things I like the look of. You?'

'Of course not,' said the man, looking at him as though he was mad.

Oh, yes, of course, Toby thought, wondering how he could have forgotten. Was he losing his memory now, along with everything else? This was Mark Sapton, in search of dirt for his column in the unspeakable *Daily Mercury*.

'There's plenty of money around today by all accounts,' Sapton went on. 'So you may have stiff competition if you do decide to bid. Good luck.'

'Thanks.' Toby passed the desk where customers without his reputation and backing had to register, provide details of how they would pay for anything they might buy, and be given a number with which to bid.

He walked on through the anteroom, where the less important lots were still hanging. The Hieronymus Bosch he had to buy would already have been taken down, ready to be carried in by the porters and put on the great easel in front of the auctioneer when he reached its lot number.

Toby wished it could have been the first lot, so that he could get it over with quickly, but important paintings were never put on so early. The auctioneer would want to warm up his audience first. They'd have to feel money flowing before they would spend with the kind of freedom he'd want for a serious piece like the Bosch.

Here was the saleroom door. Toby hesitated on the threshold, feeling like a boy on his first day at boarding school. He wanted to turn and run, but he knew he had to stick it out. Several faces turned towards him. Most were smiling. A lot were familiar. He couldn't see Ben and wondered if he'd sent someone else to spy for him.

There was no sign of Henry Buxford either. Maybe he'd been held up in the States. That would be a relief. It was bad enough having to pretend in front of everyone else.

Familiar icy needles began to prickle and he knew Ben must be somewhere in the building. Then he saw the tall, thin, dark woman again. She was pretending not to look in his direction.

How many more of Ben's people were there in the room, ready to cut him off if he tried to escape?

'Are you all right, old boy?' said another acquaintance, whose name Toby couldn't remember. 'You ought to sit down.'

'Thanks. A bad oyster last night,' he said, grabbing the first excuse that occurred to him.

'You ought to be in hospital then. I was once poisoned by a dodgy oyster and was on a drip for days. It could have gone either way, you know.'

'Mine's not nearly as bad as that. And I couldn't miss a sale like this,' Toby said, sure that his smile must look like the rictus of a corpse. 'But I'll be fine. I'm all drugged up.'

'Sensible fellow. But you ought to find yourself a seat soon or you'll pass out, drugs or no drugs.'

A stranger was sitting in Toby's usual seat at the aisle end of the fourth row, perfectly placed to catch the auctioneer's eye, so he had to make do with one on the wrong side of the room, and six rows further back.

Looking around, he could see six of the younger members of Goode & Floore's staff behind the telephones that were ranged to the right of the auctioneer's rostrum. That meant a lot of interest from absent buyers. Dealing with phone bidding was expensive. The auctioneers never allowed it for trivial sums. Several people were looking at their watches. Any minute now.

The chatter round him quietened. A slim man in his forties walked unobtrusively into the room and took his place on the rostrum. He was wearing a perfect but inconspicuous suit. Some of the auctioneers behaved like conductors of major orchestras, expecting flurry and fuss to greet them wherever they went, but not Marcus Orgrave.

Toby believed he was the best in London: he knew a lot; he never went in for theatrics; and he never faked a bid. There were plenty of his rivals who would pick non-existent bids out of the air to encourage the real punters. But not Orgrave.

Trish relaxed as she watched Toby sit down. She'd been afraid he might pass out after he caught her eye and all the blood drained away from his face. Now she understood why Buxford had been so worried. She had never seen anyone pale so quickly and sway like that. Who did he think she was? And what on earth was he up to that scared him so much?

She saw Henry Buxford stroll into the big room and watched him walk unhurriedly behind the auctioneer and choose a seat in the second row. Toby flinched and shrank back in his seat, almost as though someone had hit him.

Trish didn't think Buxford's choice of seat was very sensible. He wouldn't be able to watch anything Toby did from there, unless he twisted round like an ill-disciplined guest at a church wedding. But then from her position, she could see only the back of Toby's head and about a quarter of his face, as well as the movements of his hands on the catalogue.

Watching carefully, Trish saw nothing useful until the auctioneer knocked down lot 48. Then Toby's shoulders tightened and his head lifted, which made him look like an animal that has felt its hunter's breath on the back of its neck.

He'd never make a poker player, she thought, wishing she could see his eyes as well.

Toby felt almost paralysed by terror. He knew he wasn't going to be able to bring this off. And when he failed, Ben would turn on Mer. The thought of what they might do to him sent Toby's guts into spasm, as though he really had been poisoned. The icy needles were sharper, too, as though Ben was coming closer.

Lot 49 was knocked down for five hundred and forty thousand pounds. Toby forced himself to check his catalogue to see what painting had just been bought. That's not a bad price, he told himself, fighting for calm. Mark Sapton had been right: there was money in the room today. Thank God for that. At least it should mean he wasn't going to have to fling a bid of several million pounds into an empty auction.

He braced himself. Any minute now he would have to do his stuff, convincing Ben and the auctioneer and Henry and the other trustees that he was acting in everyone's best interests, while still not betraying his bids to anyone else in the room.

Trying to keep the familiar bored expression on his face, he looked up towards Orgrave to make sure he understood that there would be gestures of interest later. Orgrave gave his usual, almost imperceptible signal of acknowledgement and Toby looked down again, leafing through the catalogue, as though he was looking for some later lot.

What a stupid pantomime it all was! He'd never seen that in the past, only enjoyed the brilliance of his own performances in salerooms like this, buying or selling for other people. He'd never had the money to buy anything for himself.

'And now we have a very exciting painting. Lot number 50, ladies and gentlemen. A very fine Hieronymus Bosch of the Holy Family.'

The blue-aproned porters brought in the panel and hoisted it up on to the easel.

'Paintings of this quality do not come up very often. So who will start the bidding at one million pounds?'

Toby didn't move. Everyone else seemed to be holding back, too. He couldn't be the first. The auctioneer said something else, but Toby didn't listen. He was waiting for the numbers to start rising. You had to come in once the money had begun to get big, but not until then. One of the women taking phone bids raised her hand and they were off.

The bidding moved quickly through two million eight hundred thousand pounds and Toby raised his head. He knew Orgrave would have been looking towards him as each new sum was reached. There was a rare air of excitement about him today, which suggested that a lot of people were bidding. Thank God for that.

They were already past four million now and Toby knew he

had at least two rivals in the room. He wished he knew who they were and what their resources might be, but he couldn't look round. In any case, there would be no point; they'd all be hiding their interest in exactly the same way he was hiding his. But he could see that three of the phone bidders had dropped out.

'Four million five,' Orgrave said, beginning to look happy. They must be way past the reserve now. 'And six. Thank you. And seven,' Orgrave said, looking back at Toby. 'Four million seven?'

Toby gave his signal, but when Orgrave came back to him with the bidding way over five million he had no idea what to do. He could see Henry's face, twisted round to look at him. And in his mind he could see Mer and Tim bleeding and broken in front of him. He could even hear their screams. But how could he bid more? There was no more money to spend. Even at four million seven hundred thousand pounds the collection would be badly out of pocket, paying buyer's and seller's premiums on the two paintings, with VAT added, on top. He had no credit anywhere to cover the shortfall. He couldn't do it. And then there was the tax to pay on the de Hooch sale, too.

Ben must understand. Toby tried to believe he wouldn't mind much in any case. After all, today's auction had already served his purpose. The fake was now established in everyone's mind as genuine and extremely valuable. Even more important, the name of its supposed owner had also been established in public as that of a serious collector.

But would Ben see it like that? The chills and pain in Toby's spine didn't give him any confidence.

Orgrave was still looking at him. He couldn't have moved, even if he'd known what movement to make.

'Any more?' Orgrave said, pushing him to bid again. 'We have five million six for this superb example of the work of Hieronymus Bosch. Ah, thank you.' He was no longer looking in Toby's direction. 'Yes, five million eight, and nine, and six million. And one and two and three. Any more? All done? We're all done at six million three hundred thousand pounds.' The gavel came down.

Toby knew his legs wouldn't hold him up if he tried to stand now. Had he just signed his son's death warrant?

Trish watched Toby battle for control and felt all the admiration that any display of real courage aroused in her. Whatever he was doing, it terrified him, yet he was fighting the fear with everything he had.

He hadn't looked like any kind of money-launderer today, and certainly not a voluntary one. No one tough enough to have chosen to be involved in organized crime would let himself appear so vulnerable in public – or draw so much attention to himself.

Trish still didn't see what she could do to help him or Henry Buxford. He should have gone to the police in the first place, or even Customs & Excise, who dealt with all forms of smuggling and their financial implications. Only they had the power to bug a suspect's phones or have him watched. She didn't think anything less would turn up the evidence of whatever Toby was doing now. Or being forced to do.

Toby could see Henry shifting in his chair. Would he have the wit to wait? Or would he storm out, letting everyone in the world know that he had some connection with either the seller or one of the bidders for the Bosch? No, he obviously knew better than that.

The bidding on the next few lots was desultory, as though no one had any interest left, but it picked up again at lot 56, which was the iffy Dürer drawing. At last Toby could go. He ostentatiously flicked through his catalogue and made a mark against a very much later lot, idly looked at his watch, shrugged and got up to shuffle out of the row. At the doorway, he looked back and saw Henry hold up a hand. Toby nodded. He waited at the top of the wide staircase. Henry caught up with him two minutes later.

'You had me frightened in there,' Henry said. 'Would you really have paid several million for that rather ordinary-looking religious picture?'

Toby wasn't sure he was going to be able to speak, but the words came out without conscious thought. 'For a Hieronymus Bosch? Of course. They're bloody rare, you know, and we ought to have one if we're to be taken seriously.'

'But how do you know we haven't already got one? There are still tubes you haven't yet been able to open, which means you can't yet have identified all the paintings inside them. Mightn't there be a Bosch among them?'

Toby recognized the answer emerging whole and convincing in his brain. Perhaps this ease with Henry was the payoff for fighting the terror Ben had inflicted on him. Perhaps today had been a kind of rite of passage, through which he had at last achieved the toughness he'd always wanted.

'Bosch painted on panel – wood, you know – not canvas, which is presumably why our Jean-Pierre didn't include any in his rolled tubes.'

Henry laughed. 'That would certainly explain it. But perhaps that's a reason for us to avoid anything on panels, too. We can't possibly expect to cover every aspect of European art, whatever Jean-Pierre Gregoire wanted when he started collecting. Shouldn't we confine ourselves to works on canvas, too?'

'That's definitely something I'd like to discuss,' Toby said, wondering whether Ben would see the point, too. He was somewhere close by. Toby could feel it. He had to get rid of Henry fast. 'But I'm afraid I can't stay to talk about it now. I've got to get back straightaway.'

'But we agreed we'd talk this morning,' Henry said, just as

the familiar tall, thin, dark-haired woman brushed past him, murmuring 'excuse me'.

'I know. But I really can't do it now,' Toby said, fighting his urge to kick the woman down the stairs and scream obscenities after her. 'My secretary's holding the fort this morning, and I don't like leaving her on her own for too long. She's not exactly reliable. I'm sorry, but there's no option, Henry.'

'Well, as I said, I need to talk to you. What about dinner tonight? The Garrick perhaps. You'd probably enjoy that more than Brooks's.'

Henry was looking so suspicious that Toby knew he wouldn't get away with refusing a second summons.

'Thank you. Yes, I like the Garrick very much.'

'Good. I'll book a table for eight o'clock. Margaret and the boys all right?'

Shut up, shut up, shut up, Toby said in his head, even as his mouth produced the usual polite sounds. 'Yes, yes, they're fine. Staying with friends. I must dash. See you tonight, Henry.'

'Hi, Toby!' Ben's sickeningly familiar voice made him freeze. A second later Ben appeared in front of him, dressed and sounding like every other denizen of Bond Street and St James's.

'Pity you missed out on that lot in there. Are you leaving? I'll give you a lift.'

Toby said nothing, but he looked from Henry to Ben and back again. He longed to beg Henry to save him, but he knew he couldn't. With his spine almost crumbling under the assault of the icy needles, Toby followed Ben down the stairs. Halfway down, he turned back to see Henry watching them with a dangerous expression in his eyes.

'Oh, don't,' he whispered under his breath. 'I need you on my side.'

'Careful, Toby. Careful,' Ben said, putting his hand under Toby's elbow. Toby shuddered.

Ben didn't comment, even though he must have felt the

tremor, or say anything else at all until they were sitting side by side in a taxi, heading down towards the Embankment.

'What the fuck is going on, Toby?' Ben's voice was completely different now. There was no jaunty charm, only a harshness that made Toby cringe against the back of the seat. 'You were told to buy that Hieronymus Bosch. Why did you drop out of the auction?'

'I had to. You told me to bid up to what I got for the—' He thought of the driver, listening in, and mumbled, 'You know, for the other one.'

Ben slapped Toby's face, hard enough to knock his head against the side of the cab, missing the window only by millimetres. Dreading the next blow, Toby gazed at the driver, trying to will him to turn and see what was going on. There was a movement. Any minute now, he would be safe. He put everything he could into his expression and stared at the driving mirror, silently begging for help.

In its reflection, the cabbie caught his eye and laughed. Oh, God! He must be one of Ben's heavies.

Miraculously, just then, Toby saw a couple of police officers strolling towards the cab along the pavement. He reached up to bang on the window.

'Oh, no, you don't.' Ben seized his arm and bent it agonizingly behind his back. 'Keep still, arsehole, or it'll hurt even more. You've seriously pissed off my boss. You know what that means, Toby.'

'Don't hurt the boys,' he said. His eyes closed, as though if he couldn't see Ben, that might make him less real, less dangerous. 'Please don't hurt the boys.'

'You've left me no choice. Here we are,' Ben said. 'Get out. And next time I tell you to do something, fucking well do it.'

Toby couldn't move. He thought of Kathmandu. Even vomiting up his very guts and shitting nothing but bloody water hadn't been as bad as this. Oh, why hadn't he died then?

'Get out.' The viciousness in Ben's voice made him move and he stumbled out of the cab.

A moment later, he was inside the gallery and racing upstairs to the private flat, ignoring Jo, who came out of the office as he passed the open door, looking as though she was about to say something. He fled on upstairs.

The flat was still locked and the alarm activated. But that didn't mean much. At last he got himself inside his own front door.

There was no sound and no smell he didn't recognize. Even so, he went through every room, searching for any sign that Mer or Tim had been brought here. There was nothing. He took the mobile from his pocket and rang Margaret's.

As always, the voice mail clicked on. As soon as it started to record, he said:

'Margaret, for pity's sake, phone me. I have to know you and the boys are all right. I can't bear this silence. It's driving me mad. Please, please phone.'

'Toby? Toby?' Jo was shouting up the stairs.

The garage, he thought suddenly. What if they've got Mer in there?

He flung himself down the stairs, wanting to swear at Jo for shouting at him. Couldn't she see this was important and just sodding well wait a moment? His right hand was shaking so much as he reached for the key to the garden door that he had to grip it with the left for a moment. At last it seemed functional again and he slid the key into the lock.

It jammed. Was he going to have to get some oil now? No, there it was, turning at last. He pocketed the key and ran across the mossy York stone towards the garage, slipping twice. The second time he actually sprawled on the ground, cracking both knees against the stone. Scrambling up, dusting down his trousers, he saw they had green stains on them now.

Here was the pedestrian door, the only way into the garage

from the gallery itself. You walked in here, then drove out under the up-and-over door opposite, straight into the backstreet. His fingers slipped on this key, too. At last it turned. He wrenched open the door, tearing a strip of skin off his hand as it caught on the harsh spines of *Rosa filipes* 'Kiftsgate', which Margaret had insisted on planting when they first arrived to cover the ugliness of the brick garage. He stuffed the side of his hand into his mouth to suck the wound and gagged. He'd forgotten the thin but sickly taste of blood.

Wrenching open the garage door he grabbed for the lightswitch. There was nothing to see except a broken chair and a few bits of waste paper. It was just a bare concrete box, with old oil stains on the floor and no screens or cupboards to hide anything.

'Have you gone completely mad?' Jo's voice was heavy with contempt. He turned to see her standing on the garden path behind him. 'First you tell me to give you your messages the instant you come through the front door, then you charge all over the house, ignoring me when I try to tell you about them.'

'What?' He knew he was on the point of crying. 'What are you talking about, Jo?'

'Today's phone calls,' she said, hating him just as everyone else had always hated him.

'Has Peter rung?'

'No. But Margaret phoned just now to say she and the boys are fine and she's getting fed up with all your messages. She'll phone you soon. But she wants you to wait until she's ready.'

'Oh, Christ!'

Jo backed away from him as though he had really gone mad.

Chapter 14

Toby's taxi drove away as Trish waited for Henry. After a while he emerged, pulling on his gloves. Another taxi appeared at the end of the street and he raised his hand in the familiar imperious gesture. She called his name and he turned. Waving off the cab, he came towards her.

'There you are,' he said. 'Good. I assumed you'd gone.'

'No. But I couldn't talk to you while you had Toby with you. I think—'

'It's too cold to stand out here. And I need lunch. My body clock is all over the place after being in the States for three days: too long to avoid jet lag and too short to get properly acclimatized. Will you come and eat with me? We can talk much more easily in the warm.'

Trish followed him reluctantly into a restaurant without noticing which it was or anything about it. She asked for an omelette because it was the lightest thing on the menu. As Buxford gave the order to their waiter, Trish rehearsed what she had to say to him.

'You look very serious,' he said. 'What are you thinking?'

'That you're right: Toby is involved in something that terrifies him. I've never seen it before because each time I've been to the gallery he's been in control. Now that I have seen it, I'm seriously worried about him.'

'I wish to God he'd had the guts to come to me for help in

the first place,' Buxford said. 'I could have had it all sorted by now. Still, he's coming to dinner with me in the Garrick tonight. That may do the trick.'

Trish remembered the last time she'd been a guest in the club and felt the weight of centuries of wealth and status bearing down on her. It wouldn't have made her want to tell anyone anything, least of all a man as rich and powerful as Henry Buxford. But then she was a natural rebel.

Unlike Toby, she thought, as Robert's mocking voice echoed in her memory.

'I have been told that while he was at Cambridge,' she said aloud, 'he used to run around doing favours for richer undergraduates to make them like him. You might try to tap into that part of his character.'

'He'll have grown out of all that by now.' Buxford sounded impatient. 'People change, you know, Trish.'

'I don't think they do, not in fundamental ways.' She thought of an old photograph of herself as a fat 3-year-old standing under a garden sprinkler and gazing up at her father. At some level she would always be that child, who would have done anything to make Paddy love her because that was the only thing that would make the world safe for ever. 'It could have been that habit which got Toby into this mess in the first place.'

'What on earth do you mean? Here's your omelette,' Buxford said. 'Tuck in.'

'All art collectors are rich,' she started, thinking it through as she spoke, 'and Toby will know most of them. After all, they've been coming to him for years whenever they've wanted expert advice on paintings to buy or sell, haven't they?'

Buxford nodded, but he didn't look impressed.

'What if one of them, maybe a stranger in London, once asked him to get hold of some drugs?'

'He wouldn't have had a clue what to do,' Buxford said

snappily, picking up his knife and fork. 'Your omelette's getting cold.'

'It's not hard to find out who the best dealers are,' Trish went on. She thought of the video producers she had met in Jeremy Carfield's flat. 'I hate and detest that whole world, but I'd know exactly who to go to if I needed to buy some drugs. And if I do, anyone would. Even Toby.'

'I wish you'd eat.'

She realized that he was waiting to start on his steak until she had had some of her omelette and obediently forked up a crisp corner.

'Any dealer would make enquiries before supplying a new customer,' she went on as soon as she'd swallowed her small mouthful. 'And if Toby's supplier discovered that he has this astonishing amount of power over the Gregory Bequest, he'd probably have done anything he could to get his hands on it.'

'You're back to money-laundering again,' Buxford said, even more irritably. 'I wish you weren't so obsessed. There's no evidence that Toby has ever had anything whatsoever to do with anyone who sells drugs.'

'But it's the only thing that fits the few facts we have. Think, Henry. There's no other reason for Toby to have taken in five million pounds a couple of months ago and then tried to pay it out again this morning.'

'He wasn't ever going to pay it out,' Buxford said, cutting deeply into the centre of his steak and watching it ooze thin red blood. Then he looked up with something like the old, charming smile. 'Didn't you notice how he dropped out of the bidding long before he could have been landed with the painting?'

'No,' she admitted. 'But then I couldn't see much from where I was sitting.'

'Then take it from me. I watched him the whole way through. He clearly wasn't there to spend any money, let alone five million pounds. All he was doing was ramping up the price for the auctioneers, presumably in return for one of those kickbacks you warned me about.'

'Taking kickbacks isn't nearly serious enough to make anyone look as frightened as Toby did,' Trish said. 'At one moment I thought he was going to pass out. Or have a heart attack.'

'Aren't you exaggerating?'

'I don't think so.'

'I do. Now I come to think of it, he looked exactly like a secretary my wife once employed. She hadn't even taken bribes, just been a victim of the great carbon-paper scam. But she was terrified of being found out.'

Trish cut off another corner of the omelette and ate it. If Henry were not prepared to accept what looked increasingly obvious to her, there didn't seem any point saying any more.

'You're probably too young to have seen anything of it,' he went on, as though she'd asked a question. 'I suppose it started about thirty years ago. It was ultimately fairly trivial, and the effect on the victims quite disproportionate to what they were actually made to do. A bunch of wide boys used to bully secretaries in small businesses into believing they'd ordered millions of sheets of carbon paper without meaning to. When they protested, they'd be led to believe they would be sued if they didn't go ahead with the deal. Most of them were so frightened they let it go on.'

'That's absurd.'

'Possibly. But it was effective. Went on for years. I should have thought of Sad Sue and her mountains of carbon paper when I first realized how scared Toby was. I wonder what Goode & Floore's have been holding over him to make him look so like her.'

'If he really had taken bribes from them,' Trish said reluctantly, still certain that Buxford was underestimating the problem, 'mightn't that be enough in itself?'

'Could be. Yes. I don't suppose it occurred to him that there was anything wrong with taking a commission for giving them the de Hooch to sell. I wonder when he realized what a dim view the trustees would take of that.'

Trish could see how much more comfortable Henry would feel with this than if he had to face the fact that his godson had been forced into laundering drug money through the trust of which he himself was chairman. But she wasn't going to encourage it.

'So,' he said, untroubled by her silence, 'all we've got to do now is show that Toby's got much less to fear from telling me than letting it go on. You could help there, Trish.'

'I? How?'

'By going back to the gallery this afternoon and softening him up for my encounter with him this evening. I'd like you to ask him about art-market manipulation and mention the penalties involved in rigging auctions. Make him think you know exactly what he's up to and could be on the point of reporting him to the authorities. I can then be kind and comforting, like a poultice, and bring out all the poison.'

Trish had always known Buxford was ruthless, but this shocked her. She put down her fork.

'I think that's a high-risk strategy,' she said at last, 'considering the state he was in this morning. It could tip him right over the edge.'

'There's no need to look at me as though I was Attila the Hun. It's for his own good. What on earth do you imagine he might do?'

'Almost anything, if he were frightened enough. You do know he can be violent, don't you?'

'Toby? Rubbish.'

'He's already been hitting his wife.'

'I don't believe it.'

'You have to. He gave her a black eye.' Trish almost felt sorry for him. 'She told me about it herself, and she has no reason to lie. That's why she's taken the boys away to stay with friends in Chelsea. Putting extra pressure on him now would be madness.'

'I can't get him out of this mess until he talks to me. I'd hoped you'd be able to persuade him to confide in you by friendlier methods, but you haven't. This is the only way, Trish.'

That was probably true, but it didn't make her any happier. She thought of Antony and his determination to make her jump whenever Buxford so much as breathed on her. What on earth would life be like in chambers if she lost the last vestiges of his favour? Steve's crucial approval wouldn't survive without Antony's backing.

She saw that she hadn't changed much from the fat child she'd been under the sprinkler, longing for approval from the most powerful man around.

'Oh, come on, Trish. I thought you were more sensible than this,' Buxford said. 'And why should you care so much? It's not as though you owe Toby anything, after all.'

'Oh, all right,' she said, despising herself. 'I'll try. But if the first attempt doesn't work, I won't do it again.'

'Fair enough. Now, pudding?'

'I couldn't.'

By the time Trish reached the gallery, Toby had changed out of the dark suit he had worn to the auction, and he was calmly showing five people around the collection. The miasma of acrid sweat that had emanated from him at Goode & Floore's had been replaced by something infinitely sweeter, which suggested he might have raided his wife's dressing table.

Trish tagged on to the back of the group he was escorting around the gallery and listened to him talking easily about the paintings and about Jean-Pierre's romantic story. Toby seemed almost normal, once again the charming well-informed man she had encountered the first time she'd been here. She was beginning to let herself believe that she had exaggerated his fear when they came face to face as he swung round to lead the group into the next room.

Once again the blood drained from his head and he put his hand against the wall as though he was afraid he might fall. Trish produced her best client-calming smile and saw that it had no effect whatsoever.

'I didn't realize you were here,' he said in a voice hoarse with tension. 'Who let you in?'

'Your assistant.' Trish went on smiling, even though she saw affronted astonishment on the faces of his visitors. She took her ticket out of her pocket. 'I've paid again, I promise. I just couldn't resist coming back to have another look at some of the pictures you showed me last time I was here. Don't you remember our talk then?'

His eyes looked dead, and his roughened voice dragged as he said: 'I'm afraid I don't remember. But I can't waste time discussing it now. Ladies and gentlemen, here we have most of the French work. This is a Watteau. Please notice the gleam of the silk, here and again here in the dress, and the freshness of the colours.'

Trish waited for him to take a breath, then broke in: 'I'm so fascinated by this collection and how Jean-Pierre Gregoire managed to buy all these wonderful paintings in the teeth of all the other dealers who must have been competing with him before the First World War. I've been reading about the ways in which some of them manipulated the market, and I was really shocked. Does that kind of thing still go on?'

'I don't know what you're talking about,' Toby said. His voice vibrated somewhere in his throat, making it high and much more uncertain than usual.

'Oh, things like bribing experts to belittle paintings belonging to other people so they could pick them up for next to nothing. Smuggling them through jurisdiction after jurisdiction. Even altering pictures of ugly women to turn them into the kind of beauties rich collectors want on their walls. Most people would call that forgery, but they all seemed to be at it. Does it still go on?'

Toby's face looked grey. 'If it does, I know nothing about it.'

'You were at this morning's sale, though, weren't you?' she went on, pretending she hadn't noticed either his reaction or the impatience of the other sightseers. 'Do you suppose any of the lots in that had been tampered with?'

'I have no idea. But I think it's most unlikely.' He looked round, as though searching for something more to say, and added with a kind of desperation: 'Goode & Floore's has an excellent reputation. They've always been my favourite saleroom.'

'I can imagine,' Trish went on, obediently trying to spook him with a pretence of knowing far more than she did. 'After that fantastic price they achieved for those Clouet drawings you sold when you were still an undergraduate. I was reading about them in the paper last weekend. It was Goode & Floore's who sold them for you, wasn't it?'

Toby's head snapped up. Now it was hostility, not fear, that was pumping out of him. At last she could see him as someone capable of blacking Margaret's eye.

All around them were irritated rustlings from the other visitors. Trish shot a general smile around the group before concentrating on Toby again.

'It must be such a help for someone in your position to be on good terms with successful auctioneers like them. I imagine they must often need to pay experts like you for all sorts of little tasks.'

She watched his jaw soften and his shoulders loosen. He looked as though he'd just been let off something he dreaded.

'We can't discuss it now. There's a lot to see this afternoon,' he said, turning away. 'I don't want anyone to miss anything.'

'Of course. I'm sorry I interrupted.' Trish smiled apologetically around the group. 'I'll keep out of your way now and look round on my own.'

Sitting in his office when everyone but the thin woman had left, Toby thought blood might burst out of his head. All the arteries around his skull were pulsating and his skin and hair felt very thin. He touched one throbbing blood vessel in his right temple and winced.

The woman had refused to leave with the others. He hadn't dared order her out. She was ostensibly looking again at all the paintings that had most interested her, but Toby knew better.

What was she going to do next? Toby switched on the closed-circuit television screens until he found her, apparently still staring reverently at the Watteau. Then he saw her gaze flick towards the camera lens and she smiled a secret, nasty little smile to show him she knew he was watching her.

Toby felt his right hand aching and looked down. He was gripping the stapler together as though it was a pinless grenade that would explode as soon as he let the two parts spring apart. He put it down and wiped his hands on his trousers again. Oh, God! He'd have to take the mossy pair to the cleaners. Margaret usually did that kind of thing, so his mind just wasn't geared up for it. But he didn't have enough pairs of trousers to leave them dirty.

He heard the main door bang and made himself move to the front window to look out. The thin woman had gone at last. His mobile rang. He knew it would be Ben, watching from somewhere close by until his employee had done her stuff.

'OK, Toby.' The sound of Ben's voice made him thrust one knuckle between his teeth, so that he could stop himself crying out. 'You've been lucky. Your punishment is to be no more than a taster this time. But if you screw up again, you'll get the full works. There'll be another of our paintings in the sale the week after next. We'll give you the details later, but you are to bid for that one and get it, whatever it costs. If it goes over the five mill., we'll get you the funds before you have to settle with Goode & Floore's, so there'll be no excuse for a repetition of today's fuck-up. OK?'

Toby knew he mustn't mention the tax that the trust would have to pay on the proceeds of the de Hooch sale, even though that was now waking him in the night, too.

'And when I've done that, will you leave me alone?' He might have saved himself the trouble of speaking. Ben had gone.

The phone beeped with the short burst of sound that meant a text message was coming through. Toby looked at the small screen. As the letters formed, all his joints seized up with a single agonizing jolt.

Mer's arm brkn 2 plcs. Wnt sy hw. Mre nws l8er. Mgrt

Toby laid his face against the leather top of his desk and howled. All the tears he'd been fighting for weeks poured out in a hot disgusting flood as he thought of Mer being hurt to give him Ben's 'taster' of punishment.

Chapter 15

Trish collected the mail from her pigeonhole, trying to ignore the thought of what Toby might be doing now that she had obediently put the frighteners on him. It was dawning on her that he'd reacted far more strongly to her comment about the Clouet drawings than all her insinuations that Goode & Floore's might be paying him to rig the market for them.

Had there been something wrong with the Clouets? Could they, rather than drugs or the fear of losing his job, be the source of the pressure that was making him so afraid? Had he had evidence that they weren't genuine when he'd originally taken them to Goode & Floore's? Evidence that someone else had now uncovered and was being used to blackmail him?

Steve was muttering behind Trish about how no one could guarantee success at the Bar, but only deserve it. Usually his Churchillian exhortations made her laugh, but today she had too much to worry about to be amused by anything. On her way out of the clerks' room, she paused to say:

'Did you know that your hero once told Siegfried Sassoon that man's natural activity is war?'

'No,' he said, looking more favourably on her. 'Where did you find that?'

'In *Siegfried's Journey*. You know, by Sassoon himself. But do you know what Churchill added after that first bit? "War and gardening".'

Steve rattled his cheeks at her. She left him to his outrage and went to the door of Robert Anstey's room. It had been a point of honour throughout their battles of the past few years that she never, ever, went to ask him for anything. That had made each of his invasions of her room in search of help or evidence of her weaknesses a victory in itself. Now she was going to have to yield to Robert. She hoped it would be worth it.

He looked up. A smirk slid across his face like a stain on a tablecloth.

'Well, well, well. This is a real mountain and Mohammed moment, Trish. What can I do for you?'

'Give me more on your old university friend.'

'What? Who?'

'Toby Fullwell.'

'I told you. He was no friend of mine. What has he got that you could possibly want?' The smirk turned into something considerably nastier. 'It's not sex rearing its ugly head again, is it? I say, Trish, are you being unfaithful to that rich solicitor of yours? Not a good move, I'd have thought.'

It's a routine bit of baiting, she told herself as she tried not to rise. Usually she could laugh at anything Robert produced. But for some reason this particular idiocy grated. She took a moment to gather her wits, then said:

'I was intrigued by the story in last Sunday's papers about how Fullwell found fantastically valuable pictures in a junk shop while he was at Cambridge. I wondered if it was a bit of handy spin. Someone said the hack who interviewed him occasionally embellishes her profiles with the odd fantasy like that.' Trish hoped that the journalist wasn't a friend of Robert's. It would be a nuisance if she got to hear of the slander.

'Not this time. I'd forgotten the story myself until I read that piece. It brought it all back though, and I remembered exactly how angry Toby was when he didn't get a fair share of the profit from the resale.'

'Oh? Who did get it?'

'His best friend.' Robert's lips thinned and his eyes looked mean. 'It was about the only time I ever felt sorry for Toby. Peter Chanting was rich already, which was why he was buying pictures in the first place, and without Toby's sharp eye, he'd never have made such a killing.'

Trish had not heard Robert sound so sympathetic about anyone else in years. 'Isn't that the man you said took Toby on an expensive holiday one year? Maybe that was the kickback.'

'I think it probably was. But handing out lavish presents isn't the same as paying a legitimately earned finder's fee. And poor old Toby was always strapped for cash.' Robert added, not looking at Trish, 'Like most of us.'

'Not you, though,' she said, thinking of her own early years of scraping by with part-time jobs and a diet of black pudding and rotten bananas, which was all she'd been able to afford at one time. 'You had it easy with your parents funding you until you were earning enough for a mortgage.'

Robert had always given the impression of having plenty of money, and he'd certainly never had to take on freelance work to pay his way through pupillage as she had. Each December she had marked exams into the small hours, as well as offering year-round coaching and anything else that would earn enough to cover her basic bills.

'Still got that chip on your shoulder, Trish?' He laughed, with a typically Robert-like hooting of derisive merriment. 'Isn't it time you grew out of it?'

'Sod off,' she said, wondering whether she had imagined the hint of sensitivity, and went back to the clerks' room. She needed to find out more about the Clouet drawings before she talked to Henry Buxford again, and Peter Chanting would be the obvious source of information. Toby clearly wasn't going to tell her anything.

'Yes?' Steve said coldly, looking at her over the top of his glasses. He had never minded her teasing in the past. This could only be yet another sign that Antony was withdrawing his protection. 'What can we do for you now?'

'I only wanted to borrow Debrett's *People of Today*.'

Steve reached behind him and handed it to her. 'I hope this means you're preparing tomorrow's case. I know it's small and dull, but you can't expect to change your whole practice without taking several backward steps.'

'I know. Thanks, Steve. I'll bring this back.'

Trish turned to the Cs as she walked along the dark corridor. There was no Peter Chanting listed, only a Martin Chanting, whose date of birth would have made him seventy-four. He could have been the father of one of Toby's university contemporaries, but there was no mention of any children. His late wife was named in the paragraph and the date of her death given as last year. He was a retired actuary, presumably included in the directory because he'd written a series of textbooks. He had given his address in Godalming. There was a phone number, too.

Back in her own room, she keyed in the number. As she listened to the phone ring, she practised her opening remarks.

'This is Martin Chanting speaking,' said a voice with enough of a tremor to sound right for his age.

'I'm so sorry to disturb you,' Trish said, before giving her name and adding that she was a barrister, which she had usually found helped to persuade people she was a safe confidante. 'I'm trying to track down an old university friend, Peter Chanting, and it's such a rare surname that I thought he must be a relation of yours. I wondered whether you could give me a phone number for him.'

'I thought everyone knew that I have not seen my son for seventeen years. Goodbye.' He cut the connection without another word.

So there is something odd about Peter Chanting, Trish

thought, quickly dialling Directory Enquiries. They, too, had no record of anyone of that name. She walked reluctantly back into Robert's room to ask whether he knew what had happened to his old university acquaintance.

'No idea,' he said. 'What *is* all this about, Trish?'

'I told you,' she said, through gritted teeth. 'I'm fascinated by the goings on of the gilded youth at ancient universities. Come on, Robert, don't you remember *anything* about what this Peter bloke did after you all left university?'

'Not a thing. Sorry.'

She didn't know whether to believe him.

'And I really haven't time to chat,' he added, smirking again. 'I've got a report to finish for Antony. I'm dining with him and his wife tonight and I don't want to show up without having finished it.'

Trish hadn't had an invitation to the Shelleys' Holland Park palace for months, and she clearly would not get another one until she found out what Henry Buxford wanted to know. Robert's voice stopped her by his door.

'He doesn't give anyone a second chance, you know.'

Trish turned back to look at him. 'What exactly does that mean, Robert?'

'It's a friendly warning.'

'No, it isn't. I'm not that stupid. What did you mean?'

'It is, in fact, a friendly warning.' Something unusual in his smile made her wonder if he could be telling the truth. If so, it was the first good thing that had happened today. 'I overheard him talking about you the other day, and it didn't sound good.'

'Oh yes?' Trish hadn't felt this grim for a long time. 'And who was he talking to?'

'They were on the phone, so I don't know.' Now Robert's smile made her feel as though someone was pouring thrice-used cooking oil all over her. 'All I know is what Antony said:

"Trish? No, I don't believe I've oversold her. But I admit it is unlike her to be so slow. I hope she's not being distracted by this child she's taken on."'

Robert's attempt at Antony's light academic drawl was a failure, but that didn't help much.

'There was a bit of a pause, presumably while he listened to whoever was at the other end, then he laughed in that nasty way he has and said: "I know. They spend half their time clamouring for equal treatment, then they go and land themselves with responsibilities no bloke would dream of taking on, and still wonder why we prefer dealing with other men."'

'I do not believe you, Robert. Antony is far too wised-up to lay himself open to a sex-discrimination claim by saying anything so stupid.'

'That was the sense of it, even if I haven't got the words in the right order. 'Bye, Trish. Have a good evening. I'll think of you sharing fish fingers and alphabet spaghetti with your infant as I shovel in the foie gras.'

'Give me fish fingers any time,' she said blowing him a hate-filled kiss. 'I loathe foie gras.'

The other party in that phone conversation had to be Henry Buxford, she thought, which made it hard to ring him now. But she had to talk to him again before he had his dinner with Toby. And she had to show him that she was not the slacker he and Antony seemed to think her.

'This is what you get for doing favours for people,' she muttered, reaching for the phone. Next time she would resist any blandishment Antony might use. If there ever were a next time.

For once Henry was in his office and answered his direct line himself. It seemed ironic that this was the one time when she would have preferred to leave a message with his secretary.

'What's happened?' he asked. 'Did you tip him over this edge you're so afraid of?'

'Not quite,' she said, drawling a little in the effort to contain her dislike of what his so-called little research job might be doing to her career. 'But he did say something that surprised me. Has he ever talked to you about those Clouet drawings he identified for his friend Peter Chanting when they were at Cambridge?'

'No. But then it's not surprising. I barely knew him before he came to London to work. I was the usual hopeless British godparent and did nothing but produce a silver spoon at the christening and cheques for birthdays and Christmases after that.'

'Pity,' Trish said. 'I think you ought to ask him about them tonight. There's definitely something fishy about them, and about this Chanting bloke. Even his father won't talk about him. I think it's possible the Clouet drawings were fakes, which could open whole new lines of enquiry.'

'I thought you were convinced Toby was involved with a gang of millionaire drug dealers, Trish,' Buxford said, sounding more mocking than she had ever heard him. 'It's a bit rich to start trying to interest me in fakes and forgeries at this late stage, isn't it?'

No it sodding-well isn't, she thought, determined to make him grovel for that sneer one day.

The tender pheasant turned to unswallowable pap as Henry waited for an answer. Saliva poured into Toby's mouth, hot and frightening. He grabbed his big wineglass and gulped some claret. That helped him force the food down his throat.

Margaret hadn't texted him again yet, and she was still refusing to pick up her phone. He'd had no more news of Mer since that first cruelly brief message. He didn't even know which hospital his son was in. He'd tried phoning all the obvious ones, but he hadn't been able to find any trace of Mer. He'd even contemplated phoning Ben for help until he realized how much extra power that would have given him. And now Henry was asking questions about all the most dangerous subjects. If it hadn't been for Mer, Toby might have given in, if only to stop the questions. But how could he, with his son in such danger?

All around them in the dark, glossily polished room, were rich-sounding, happy-looking members of the most glamorous of the old London clubs, which somehow made it worse. Henry had put Toby up for the Garrick years ago and he'd once dreaded the moment when he reached the top of the waiting list. In the old days he would have given almost anything to be a member, and he'd burned with humiliation at the thought of admitting he couldn't afford the subscription. Now, it didn't matter at all, not in a world in which a grown man could break a 9-year-old's arm to force his father to commit a crime.

'Peter Chanting was my best friend at Cambridge,' he said, hoping he would be able to keep the food down and stop Henry harassing him. He gritted his teeth and tried to remember the old days, when he'd still been able to trust Peter. 'He saved my life.'

'Good lord! How?'

'We went to Nepal together in our second summer at Cambridge, and I got dysentery. There was no help or shelter anywhere. You know, not even a tree to shit behind. If it hadn't been for Peter, I'd have lain down and died. He kept me walking, gave me virtually all the water we had, and got me to sanctuary in a run-down kind of ashram, where he eventually nursed me back to health.'

'That must have been a frightening experience, and a very dramatic one. Why did you never tell me about it?'

Toby gulped down more wine. He wasn't even going to try to eat the rest of the food on his plate.

'I suppose because it had such a depressing sequel,' he said, glad to be able to rely on the truth for once. At least some of the truth. 'Peter found something in the ashram he'd never had before. He talked about peace and gentleness and a kind of mystical fulfilment. I could understand the first because he'd had the sort of life with his father that I'd had with my mother, but not the last. I felt—'

Peace and gentleness, Toby thought, looking down at the mess of pheasant and gravy and red cabbage in front of him. What an irony!

He felt sicker than ever. His plate looked as though it was covered in blood and guts.

'Left out?' Henry had stopped sounding like a judge. 'Betrayed even?'

Toby looked up and thought he could see sympathy in the usually critical face. He almost let go. Then a nightmare landscape of terror and recrimination and disgrace opened up in front of him, like the mountains of doom in the Fitzwilliam Museum's Cézanne. He could just see Henry as the huge, stalwart hero figure and himself the drooping pallid villain being dragged to hell.

'So, what happened to your friend?'

'He tried life in England again, and stuck it out until we graduated. But when his father started forcing him towards some kind of City job, he couldn't bear it. So he went back to the ashram. At the beginning he used to write, but a few years ago the letters stopped.'

Toby saw the ghosts of sympathy in Henry's eyes turn into mocking demons just like the ones at the edge of the Cézanne. Hoping to banish them again, he added: 'I've missed him ever since.'

The demons did retreat, and a smile of extraordinary gentleness curled Henry's lips. 'That's tough. In my experience one doesn't get that kind of friendship more than once in a lifetime.'

Toby had to blink for real now, to clear his own eyes of a sudden embarrassing wetness. It was one thing to cry in front of Jo, even if it did make her sneer and tell him he needed to see a shrink. It would be quite another to pour out tears here in this bastion of hideously confident old-style masculinity. He tried to distract himself by wondering who Henry's friend had been and whether he still had him. Probably. Henry was lucky in everything else, so why not this too?

'And it was this Peter, was it, who bought those drawings you identified as being by François Clouet?' Henry went on, apparently quite unmoved by his own memories or emotions.

Coming without a warning like that, the accusation made Toby's hand shake so much that he had to put down his claret glass. How was he going to get through the rest of this evening if he could neither eat nor drink without betraying himself?

'Yes. But why do you want to know?' He could hear his voice shaking, too.

Any minute now Henry was going to smash right into the truth and then everything would be over.

'Someone was asking me about the Clouet drawings the other day,' Henry went on cheerfully, 'and I was ashamed to have to admit that I knew nothing more about your great coup than I'd read in the Sunday papers. I wish you'd tell me all about it now. It sounds brilliant.'

This couldn't be coincidence. Was it Ben who'd been asking Henry about the Clouets? Or the dark woman? She'd brushed past the pair of them while they were talking after the sale. Had she snaked back after Ben had taken him away, to drip her poison into Henry's ears?

He was saying something else now. Toby tried to forget the woman and listen properly. Henry was asking him whether there was anything he wanted to say, in the tones of a man asking his wife if she wanted to confess adultery. How much had he guessed? Or did he already know the whole story? Was this going to be another long-drawn-out torture?

Unable to speak safely, Toby shook his head, staring at the mess on his plate.

'You do know,' Henry went on, drilling like a dentist, 'that you can always come to me if you're worried about anything, don't you? If you're in some kind of trouble, Toby, I can almost certainly help. I do have a lot of resources.'

Toby risked looking up, hoping for another gentle smile, but all he could see was hard speculation and contempt. Whatever Henry said, he knew he was on his own, just as he always had been. Everyone he'd ever thought might love him had turned away. First Peter had betrayed him, and now Margaret had gone, too. If she ever found out it was his fault Mer had been hurt, she'd never come back. He had no one.

Helen lay in Jean-Pierre's arms. For once he had not gone straight to sleep after they'd made love. He was nuzzling her hair and murmuring the most wonderful words to her. Her own French had got so much better now that she could understand nearly all of them and was mentally translating as he spoke.

'I'll always love you. You are the most perfect woman. I'll never leave you. You have restored my faith in love. The world is worth saving because you are in it. I would do anything for you. I love you. I love you. I love you.'

She laid her face against his chest and told him she had thought she would never be loved like this, that she would do anything for him, too. Anything. Whatever it cost her.

Chapter 16

Trish thought that if anyone touched her she might snap like an icicle. She couldn't believe she would ever be warm again. The thirty little boys in front of her were rushing about in the mud of Clapham Common like worker ants, while the two hearty solicitors who coached them were running alongside, bellowing instructions and encouragement. Whistles bounced against their ample chests as they ran.

Trying to warm herself with the remains of her fury over Henry Buxford's last sneering comment, Trish considered various ways of finding out enough to make him admit she'd been right all along.

One miserable, blue-kneed child tripped and fell face down in the icy sludge, reminding her that here, at least, she ought to forget Buxford and Toby Fullwell. Two other children flung themselves on top of the first. A woman in the small parental crowd moved forwards but was restrained by her husband. Trish overheard him mutter something about not making a wimp of the boy.

She was glad it hadn't been David. He didn't look happy, and his knees and shorts were as muddy as everyone else's, but he hadn't fallen and he was neither shivering nor snivelling. When he scored a try, she found herself cheering as loudly as any mother.

At the end of the match, she told him she was proud of him and was glad to see some pleasure in his face. But by then the cold was getting to him, in spite of all the exercise he'd just taken, and making his teeth chatter against each other. His lips were grey. She handed him his fleece and walked him back to her car as briskly as possible, fighting the urge to do anything embarrassing like warm him up in her arms or put her own coat round him.

In the car, she turned up the heating as high as it would go and felt in the glove compartment for the bar of chocolate she kept for emergencies. She knew his mother had never allowed him to eat sweets and usually she tried to follow all the old rules, but the cold today had been savage. David must need something inside him, and she couldn't bring herself to carry around a bag of peeled carrots, as though he was a horse.

'That was a really good try,' she said, hoping she wasn't being too effusive. 'I'm so glad I saw it. And that I haven't infected you with that beastly cold I had last weekend.'

'I never get colds,' he assured her. The chocolate was making his voice sound squelchy. 'I'm glad you're better. You seemed really ill.'

'Not ill; just stuffed up and uncomfortable. How was yesterday's rehearsal?'

'Not bad at all,' he said, shooting a half-smile at her. He must have overheard her the other day suggesting that George might occasionally allow himself a rather more colourful compliment than that when she'd dressed up specially to please some of his clients.

'I'm glad to hear it,' she said, enjoying the hint of cheekiness. 'And how's Mer doing in his part?'

Oh, stop it, Trish, she thought. You're obsessed with the Fullwells. This is David's time.

'He's got a broken arm.' All the gleam and pleasure had gone from his voice. He turned his head away, too, to look out at the seedy-looking shops that lined this bit of the main road. Did he know she was trying to pump him? Or was this just the old reluctance to talk about Mer? 'He says a man did it, but everyone knows it isn't true. He's stupid.'

'A man? What man?'

'He says it was a giant with red hair and yellow teeth, who put his arm across his knees and broke it. But it's a lie. Mer's a stupid, snivelling, little liar. Everyone knows that. And there aren't any giants. I hate him.'

'But why? Why aren't you sorry for him? You're usually much kinder than this, David.'

He still didn't look round. Trish tried again:

'You know I wouldn't ever try to make you tell me anything you didn't want to talk about, don't you?'

'I s'pose.' He shrugged, still looking out of the window.

'Good. Then I will just ask once what it is about Mer that makes you so uncomfortable.'

'I told you.' The dismal view might have been of paradise for the way he kept staring at it. 'He's stupid, and a liar.' Trish took a hand off the steering wheel to lay it gently on his cold, dirty knee. He pulled away from her.

They finished the rest of the drive home in silence. Trish asked herself savagely what she thought she'd been doing. She was usually far better at cross-examination.

'George should be here by now,' she said as she pulled up outside her building. That made the boy turn back at last. She saw that he'd been crying. 'Oh, David.' She was about to apologize, but he got the words out first, hiccuping a little.

'Trish, I'm sorry. I didn't mean to make you angry.'

Now she did risk putting an arm round him. His body was rigid. She kissed the top of his head. 'You haven't made me angry. You don't have to tell me anything. And I won't ask any more questions about Mer. I promise.'

He didn't relax, so she knew she'd have to let him go uncomforted. She hoped being back in the flat would help him feel safe again. Later, while he was having his post-match bath, she went to find George and confess her latest idiocy.

'Don't worry so much,' he said at once. 'He's more robust than you think. All he needs is a bit of ordinary insensitivity to make him see that he needn't be on his best behaviour all the time, not all this pussy-footing and apologizing.' He kissed her head, in much the same way she'd kissed David's and, she thought, for much the same reason. 'Open the wine, will you?'

After lunch, George drove David to a friend's house, while Trish did the washing up. She was still at the sink when he came back to hug her properly. His body was warm and very comforting. She dried her hands and turned in the circle of his arms.

Ten minutes later they were still there. The edge of the sink was pressing into her back and her hands were sliding up inside his shirt while he pushed down the straps of her bra.

'Let's go upstairs,' she said, barely able to speak.

'Wait, Trish, wait,' he murmured as he bent to kiss her breast. But she couldn't wait. She wanted him with an urgency she hadn't felt for years and arched up towards him.

Later, when they had made it up the spiral staircase to bed and she felt him building the once-familiar dizzying excitement in her, she forgot Toby and Henry Buxford and her career and even her brother. Later still, with George lying spent in her arms, she knew that nothing and no one mattered as much as he did.

For once she slept, and it was he who woke her. She smiled up at him, back where she belonged.

'You look glorious,' he said, straightening her tousled hair. 'Absolutely glorious. And I *love* you.'

'Me too.'

On Sunday George decided he had to work, so Trish stayed in Southwark instead of spending the day at his house in Fulham. David and Nicky had had an expedition planned for weeks and left early. Trish took her time finishing breakfast, then phoned her mother and left another message for her father. With no other obligations to fulfil, she booted up her laptop and clicked on to Outlook Express to read her accumulated emails.

Her fingers slipped off the keys as she saw the name Ivan Gregory at the top of the list.

My dear Miss Maguire,

Henry Buxford sent me a note last week, asking me to write to you about my father's collection of paintings. I am afraid that I am not going to be able to give you what Henry believes you need. You see, there has never been any kind of inventory of the paintings. At least, I have never seen one.

To understand my ignorance, you would have to understand my mother. She was a remarkable woman. I, of course, knew her only as she was once the great adventure – and tragedy – of her life was over. But its effects never left her, and she devoted the rest of her life to the shell-shocked survivors of her war. She had seen their life in the trenches in close up, you see, and could never forget what it had done to them.

She and I lived together in the house my father had bought her, on the very edge of the City, where the gallery now is. When I was young we had lodgers too. I do not know when my father bought it, although I imagine the deeds must include a date. I can't remember ever having looked at them myself.

She used to tell me about his paintings when I was a small boy, and how she was keeping them safe for him, for when he returned to her. Even when it became clear that he would not return, she could not bring herself to touch them, let alone unpack them to make any kind of list.

As you must know, he never did return. We think he was probably killed some time before 1918, but obviously after her pregnancy forced her to confess her secret marriage and leave the army nursing service.

She never met any of his family while she was serving in France, and it may be that he had no opportunity to tell them about her before he was killed, which may also be why no one ever informed her of his death. But I do not know.

She tried to find them, just as she tried to find him, writing to everyone she could think of who might have been able to tell her. After the Second World War was over, she even went over to France to search for clues, but found nothing.

All she ever had were her memories and the paintings themselves. Perhaps in the end it was her sadness that made her leave them untouched, as though they were but a poor substitute for the man she had so greatly loved.

It has been on my conscience that I took my attitude from hers and did not even think to look at the paintings. After I had my stroke, I began to see that we had betrayed his legacy by leaving it in the dark. During my recovery I became obsessed by the need to put that right, although in my almost speechless and semi-paralysed state there was very little I could do.

Young Henry Buxford saved me and took on the burden of my father's legacy. He even found this place for me to live, where the women who care for us are kind.

He has allowed me to make some kind of peace with my father's ghost, if that is not too sentimental a way of putting it. Of course, it will only be when the last painting has been unpacked and restored that I will feel completely at ease, but this is the kind of thing that is slow work when it is done properly, as our director Toby Fullwell is doing it.

I am afraid there is nothing more that I can tell you about the paintings or about my father's intentions for them. All I have ever known is what my mother told me about her magnificent Frenchman, who appeared one day at the dressing station behind the front line, where she was working.

As always, it was appallingly short of every kind of staff, from doctors right down to orderlies. He rolled up his sleeves and joined in with whatever needed doing. He had no medical training, but he carried stretchers and soil buckets, stoked incinerators, held wounded limbs while the doctors worked on them, which, my mother said, was something most orderlies couldn't stomach and left to barely trained VADs. Everyone loved him, she used to say, and he did much to restore the reputation of his countrymen in the eyes of the men he served.

There was a great prejudice amongst our forces against the local peasants, you see. There they were, my mother used to tell me, only a mile or two from the hell on earth that was the front line, living their comfortable prosperous little lives and rapaciously overcharging the suffering soldiery for the small comforts they could provide.

But Jean-Pierre Gregoire was not of their kidney. He was heroic in the quiet, unflamboyant way that my mother loved. And, although he was well over fighting age, he was waging the dirty secret war no one could speak of. She said he must have been in his early forties when she first knew him in 1916, and so when she went in search of him in 1949, he would have been seventy-four or five, only ten years younger than I am now. But as I say, she found no trace. Not of him, nor of his family.

I am becoming repetitive. Please forgive me, my dear Miss Maguire, and do let me know if there is any further help that I can give you.

Yours sincerely,
Ivan Gregory

No wonder Henry likes him so much, Trish thought, and is so determined to protect him.

The old man's mention of the deeds of the house interested her. There must have been a marriage certificate, too, if his mother had inherited his father's house and paintings, and another certificate to show that he had been officially presumed dead. Henry ought to know where they were. In fact, Trish thought, it was odd that he hadn't included any such documents in his original, wholly inadequate, bundle. Just as so many other things about Jean-Pierre's life and collection were beginning to look extremely odd.

She had no difficulty believing that the body of a man killed in the First World War might never have been found, but she was less convinced that his widow would have been unable to find any trace of his family if she had really tried. Or that his family would not have made any efforts to trace his collection. Or that his widow would never have looked at it, however sacred a charge it might have seemed.

'You're getting side-tracked,' Trish muttered to herself.

Jean-Pierre Gregoire was not her problem, and his son was clearly safe in the place Henry had found for him. Only Toby was in any kind of danger now. And Trish was still sure the danger was a great deal worse than Henry was letting himself believe.

The threat had obviously been very close at the Goode & Floore's sale, so it seemed only sensible to start there. As Trish had told Henry in the beginning, she knew very little about the world of old master dealing, and she needed a guide.

She thought of the man she'd sat beside at a dinner of Antony Shelley's. If only she could track him down, he might be able to help. As far as she could remember, he had been intelligent and reasonably open about the eccentricities of some of his colleagues.

He had certainly had a lot to say about the behaviour of some of the more aggressive dealers he knew. He'd talked of one in particular who would give absurdly exaggerated attributions in order to secure the sale of a big painting for his gallery. 'Like a greedy estate agent,' Trish had said and watched the expert's eyes warm up with laughter.

It took a moment longer to retrieve his name. Gerard Radsden, she thought. That should be enough to find him.

She had a disk with details of everyone who had been on the electoral roll at the end of the 1990s and she was sure he'd be there. Even if she had to contact dozens of people with the same name, she'd get him in the end.

Her computer whirred as it loaded the information, much more slowly than it should have done. Maybe she'd nearly filled up the hard disk. If so, she ought to bin some of the data. Otherwise they might clog it up terminally.

At last the screen invited her to type in the name she wanted traced. Only one Gerard Radsden came up. The address in Chelsea looked appropriate for the kind of man he'd seemed, and there was a phone number. She dialled it. The phone was picked up and a male voice recited the number.

'Oh, hello, my name's Trish Maguire,' she said. 'I'm hoping to talk to Gerard Radsden.'

'This is he. Trish Maguire, did you say?'

'Yes. We met at dinner at Antony Shelley's once, and I was hoping to ask your advice about something.'

'So we did. You're a barrister, too,' he said after a moment. 'In Antony's chambers. Tall and thin and dark. That's right, isn't it? And we talked about the Hunting Prize.'

'We did. I'd just bought one of the short-listed paintings. But what I wanted to ask you about this time is the Hieronymus Bosch that's just been sold at Goode & Floore's. D'you know anything about it?'

'Now, why would you be asking me about that?'

'Because I'm curious. I happened to be at the sale, and I've never watched anything as important as that go under the hammer before. It was listed in the catalogue as though there was absolutely no doubt about its being by Bosch, but there was no provenance given, which made me wonder. And you were so frank at dinner about some of the goings on in the art world that

I thought you might be able to tell me whether you believe in the attribution.'

'There's not a lot of help I can give you on this one. I haven't seen this particular painting, but you should know that there have been a lot of iffy Bosch panels around for several centuries. He was much copied even in his own lifetime, although it was usually the big allegories that were reproduced, not these rather dull churchy subjects.'

'One of the people who appeared to be bidding for it was the director of the Gregory Bequest. Wouldn't he have known if this were a fake?'

'You'd have thought so.'

Trish waited for more. There was silence on the line. Ah, she thought. He is telling me something.

'So why would he have been bidding for something that looks a bit iffy?'

'I'm afraid I have no idea. How is Antony? I haven't seen him for ages.'

'He's fine,' Trish said, accepting the block. Was Radsden a friend of Toby's? Or was this just professional solidarity of art historians? Either way, she'd better not risk asking obvious questions about Toby's Clouets now. 'Thank you very much for your help. There is just one more thing you might tell me.'

'If I can.'

'Do auction houses keep records of who has bought and sold paintings over the years?'

'Of course, but it's always confidential. In the old days they would provide lists of the people to whom lots had been sold, but the names given were often pseudonyms, so they didn't help anyone much. These days, no saleroom will do even that much. They don't give away any names without permission until fifty years after the sale. Even then it's only the vendor's you'll get. It's the last unregulated market of any kind in this country, you know.'

So that's not going to help me find out who bought the Clouet drawings when Peter Chanting sold them on, Trish thought.

'I see,' she said aloud. 'Then the only other thing I need to ask is: how easy would it be for an art faker to get hold of antique paper that would pass any tests designed to prove whether or not it's as old as it's supposed to be?'

'The Bosch sold by Goode & Floore's is on panel,' Radsden said, with just enough uplift on the last syllable to turn the statement into a question.

'I know. This is for something completely different.'

'Ah. I see. Well, I don't think I want to know where you're going with this or why, but I can tell you that the most obvious source is the flyleaves of books of the right date. They rarely have anything printed on them and are generally what is used,' Radsden said, before quickly adding: 'Or so I understand.'

'I see. Thank you,' Trish said. 'You've been very helpful. I hope we meet again soon.'

'Me too,' he said. 'Let me know next time you're thinking of bidding for a Bosch, and I'll give you some advice that's worth having.'

Trish laughed. 'Me? The only sort of Bosch I could afford is a washing machine.'

'Nice one.' The voice on the other end of the phone had relaxed again. 'Goodbye.'

Helen had been counting the days. Once counting the days would have meant waiting in blissful agony for Jean-Pierre to reappear, as mysteriously as he'd gone. Now it meant trying not to believe what she knew was true. She was only three months late. She'd been late before. It could happen for all sorts of reasons. But when your breasts were swollen and tender and you felt sick in the mornings and you'd been making love, there wasn't much doubt about the reason. She didn't know what to do, but she knew she hadn't long to decide. Soon, in two months at the very most, it would be unmistakable and then she'd be shipped home at once, in disgrace.

Her family wouldn't want to know; they hardly wanted to know her any more as it was, so coarsened did they believe her war service had made her. She had no money of her own. She would never be able to keep herself alive, let alone a child.

Panic made her feel as though lice were cavorting all over her back again. She'd caught them more than once in the front-line dressing stations, but she knew she was free of them now and kept herself that way with the harsh carbolic soap they all used. It was just the fear that made her skin crawl. Just. She nearly laughed at her own stupid word.

'Helen! Helen!' She recognized the voice of her best friend and turned to see what she wanted.

Myrtle was running towards her beckoning. Her cap was slipping sideways and her face was red. One of the doctors, or perhaps the sister, must be screaming for Helen, even though she wasn't supposed to be on duty for another twenty minutes.

'What?' She almost hated Myrtle, not for interrupting her but for not being able to help. 'What is it?'

'Jean-Pierre's back,' Myrtle whispered, although there was no one anywhere near enough to hear either of them shout. 'He's helping Major Jamieson at the moment, but he wants to see you. Come on.' She tugged Helen's wrist.

How was she going to tell him? Helen waddled after Myrtle, wondering if, in her mother's terrible phrase, he would 'stand by her' in her disgrace. Perhaps he would know somewhere she could go, some family who might employ her here in France once the baby had been born.

He saw her as soon as she walked through the flaps of the tented hospital ward, and he smiled. His lips didn't move, but his eyes warmed and told her that something was still all right. She gestured to herself, then out of the tent. Behind the doctor's back, he nodded.

As soon as he could extricate himself from Major Jamieson's clutches, he followed her to the bottom of the old orchard, where a straggling hedge gave them a little privacy. Fat white ducks were picking their way through the scrubby grass.

'Hélène, *ma mie*. Thank God you are still here. I was afraid when they told me you would be on escort duty again that you might—'

'Where have you been all these weeks, Jean-Pierre?' she asked, not naggingly but because she had to know.

'I could not get back sooner. I was trapped on the wrong side of the line.' She shivered, then felt his hands on her hair, stroking her. 'But I am here now. What have you been doing to yourself? Are you ill?'

Nerving herself, reminding herself that he loved her and that he had once told her she had more courage than anyone he knew, she stood up straight, looked him in the eye, and said:

'I am going to have a child. Our child, Jean-Pierre.'

Scorching fury blazed out of his eyes. She took a step backwards, and gasped as her foot caught on something in the ground. Her ankle twisted under her and pulled her even further back. Staggering, she fell heavily on the rock-like ground. It didn't matter. Nothing mattered except his fury. She lay where she had fallen, her face turned into the sharp grass, and the gold of his miniature pressing into the flesh of her chest.

'Hélène. Hélène, *ma mie*.' Amazingly his voice sounded kind again. A second later, she felt his hands running over her back, her head, gently pulling her body round. 'Are you hurt?'

'No.' She managed to wipe her eyes on her sleeve before she turned fully. Somehow she got herself on to her knees, then allowed him to pull her up. 'Jean-Pierre, I'm—'

'Don't talk any more,' he said, laying two fingers against her lips. 'All that matters is that you are all right, not hurt, healthy. You must forgive my shock. I was just so frightened for you. It is too soon.'

'I know this is no world into which to bring a child,' she said, tugging at her hair to tidy it. 'But I couldn't help it. I didn't ever think—'

'No.' He smiled again. 'But I do not understand how you have hidden it for so long, from me and also from them.'

Shocked herself, she looked down, but there was no swelling yet in her abdomen. She put both hands over it.

'Can you tell?'

'Not yet, but to have worked so long in these conditions. Have you not felt unwell?'

'Of course. But what is that to do with anything?'

He stood in front of her, shaking his head. 'I have always said you have more courage than any man I ever knew. We must make arrangements now. We must be married at once.'

So he was going to stand by her. Helen felt weaker than ever in her relief and tears leaked out of her eyes.

'I had hoped to wait until the end of the war, until we could have a proper ceremony with your family present. Now we cannot wait. Do not look so sad, *ma mie*. Come here.'

She lay against his chest, feeling the kind of safety that comes only once or twice in a lifetime.

'There is a *curé* near to here. I will take you to him. He will marry us. Then when the time comes and you must resign from the service, you will tell them that you are now Madame Gregoire, with a husband of your own and a home in London, and you will go there to wait in safety, with our child.'

'But how long must I wait? Why can't you come with me?'

He smiled, spreading his hands in a gesture so typically his that she had to smile also. No one else she had ever known had so effectively demonstrated helplessness.

'I have no *laissez-passer*, *ma mie*, even though I own the house in London. You will be safe there. Eventually, when the war is over and travel is possible again, I will come to you and our child and we will all be happy together.'

Chapter 17

'That was amazing, Miss Maguire. You did great. I never expected to win, you know. Mr Wilkins said we didn't have much of a case.'

Trish smiled at her client's exuberance, but she was pleased. His future in the catering business looked much healthier now that he was going to get damages from the firm that had supplied him with faulty equipment.

'But he did tell me to trust you. And he was right, wasn't he? I can't wait to tell my wife.' The client suddenly lost his head and kissed her soundly.

Matthew Wilkins, the solicitor, shot a worried glance at Trish. She smiled again at both of them. 'I'm really glad you're pleased. It did go well.'

'Thanks to you. Will you come and have some bubbly with us now? My wife's waiting at home to hear the result and she insisted on putting a bottle on ice, you see, whatever Mr Wilkins said.'

'That's really kind,' Trish said. She could see that the solicitor thought all these congratulations were rather exaggerated, but she was touched. 'Unfortunately I have to go and see someone in Godalming while I'm in the area. Will you forgive me?'

'If I must.' He grabbed her right hand between both his own and pumped it up and down, hardly able to bear to let it go.

'Mr Jones,' said the solicitor. 'I think Miss Maguire really does have to leave now.'

'Yes. I know. I'm sorry. And you do look tired. You must have been up all night preparing for today.'

It was true that she hadn't slept much, but it had been Toby Fullwell's problems that had kept her awake, not this man's. She couldn't get them out of her head now, wherever she went and whatever she did. She was even beginning to wonder whether Mer's red-headed giant might be real, after all, and his broken arm something to do with whatever had been terrifying his father. In which case, the need to get the whole problem sorted was even more urgent than she'd thought.

She got rid of the client at last and went back to her car, thinking of everything that had poured through her mind last night as she'd tried to decide what to do about Toby.

Only as grey light had drawn lines around the edge of her bedroom curtains had she realized that she would have to talk to Peter Chanting's father, however reluctant he might be to see her. With that thought had come another, trailing a whole new story of what could have been going on in Toby's life.

In this one, Martin Chanting was an avenger, punishing Toby for driving a wedge between him and his son. In a way it felt more convincing, perhaps because it was so much less dramatic, than the version in which Toby had been using the Gregory Bequest as cover for money-laundering or selling forgeries he'd had made to pay off a crippling drug debt. And it would mean that Mer's giant was a fantasy after all. No one in Martin Chanting's position would deliberately break a child's arm, even if he were taking revenge on the child's father.

Now, only four miles away from Godalming and the house where Chanting lived, Trish prepared herself as carefully as she did for the toughest cross-examinations. Even the adrenaline provided by her win in court couldn't stop her yawning, so she went in search of caffeine. A double espresso in the nearest coffee shop should give her brain the necessary kick to send her on her way and the energy to keep going if she faced serious opposition.

Martin Chanting's house proved to be a sizeable red-brick villa, which looked as though it could have been designed by Lutyens. It seemed too big for one elderly inhabitant, but his wife had died only about a year ago, so he might not have had the energy or will to move yet. Or he could have been clinging to the memories the house contained.

Trish heard the bell clanging inside, but there was no other sound for nearly five minutes. At last a light was switched on, providing a red glow through the leaded lights at either side of the front door, and hesitant steps shuffled towards the door. Hearing effort and difficulty in those steps, she felt guilty about her disruption of the old man's afternoon.

He didn't put the door on its chain or seem at all fragile when he flung it open with a simple 'yes?' He was taller than Trish and stood perfectly straight. Not for him the kind of defeated stoop to which Toby had been reduced. She remembered an old joke about the extrovert actuary being the one who looked at your shoes rather than his own. Smiling, she watched his sharp eyes take in her suit and briefcase.

'Mr Chanting?' she said. 'My name's Trish Maguire, and I—'

'The barrister who telephoned the other day,' he said in a dry, light voice that had no quiver in it at all. She wondered whether it had been fear of the phone that had made him sound so trembly when she called, or whether it had been some kind of disguise.

'Yes. I am sorry to disturb you.'

'You said that last time.' He was leaning against the edge of the door, effectively blocking the opening. 'Along with the fact, I believe, that you were once a friend of my son. He never had any lawyers as friends that I can remember. Were you lying?'

Approving of his directness, Trish nodded. He removed himself from the edge of the door, opened it wider and invited her in, presumably as a reward for belated honesty.

'Thank you,' she said, stepping over the threshold.

Inside the house was a high, square hall with an open fireplace. The first thing Trish noticed was an ugly Knole sofa. Upholstered in crimson cut velvet, with shiny gold cords lashing the finials together, it suited neither its surroundings nor the little she knew of the man who owned it. The incongruity interested her and she wondered whether it could be deliberate, a way of unsettling stray visitors. Or perhaps, she told herself caustically, it represented his wife's taste rather than his own and carried no intentional messages whatsoever.

A comfortable-looking Labrador seemed much more appropriate as it heaved itself up from a torn hearthrug and came to sniff Trish's shoes. There were plenty of white hairs around the dog's muzzle and it moved as stiffly as its owner.

'Do you mind dogs?'

'Not when they're as calm as this one.'

'Good. Then come and sit down and tell me what you really want.'

She dropped her briefcase on an uncomfortable-looking settle under one of the windows and joined him on the sofa.

'And don't apologize again. I dislike it. We must accept that you have disturbed me and go on from there. Your only chance of retrieving yourself is to tell a good enough story to excuse it.'

'I don't think it is a very good story,' Trish said, quickly changing her plan. With this invitation, it would be better to launch straight into it, instead of asking her carefully drafted questions. 'But I'll tell it all the same. Nearly twenty years ago, there were two friends at Cambridge. One had money and flair and courage; the other, expertise and knowledge of art history, along with a desire to please anyone who seemed more powerful than himself.'

She paused, waiting for permission to carry on, but the old man merely nodded.

'Between them, either for profit or perhaps for a joke, they decided to try a little scam. One of them – at this stage, I'm still not sure which it was – could draw. Somehow they acquired some sixteenth-century paper, perhaps from the flyleaf of an old book, and presumably did some research into the kind of crayon or chalk an artist of the time would have used. Having acquired something roughly similar, they produced drawings in the style of François Clouet.'

'So?'

'Am I getting warm?'

'To be crude, Miss Maguire, so what if you are?'

'I'm trying to track down those drawings.'

'Then you have had a wasted journey. To my knowledge, no such drawings exist.'

'But they did once, didn't they?'

'What do you think?'

'I think they must have because I cannot believe so many people would remember the story if they hadn't. Besides, three drawings in coloured chalks, catalogued as being "by François Clouet (known as Jannet)", are recorded as having been sold at Goode & Floore's in 1983. I have been in touch with them, you see.'

'And?'

'And, alas, I have not been able to persuade them to tell me who either the vendor or the purchaser was. But 1983 is the right year for the sale of the three Clouet drawings discovered in Cambridge by your son. I think it would be too much of a coincidence to suggest that they are not the same drawings.'

Martin Chanting's face was expressionless. 'I see. And you

have come here in the expectation that I will tell you the name of the purchaser, have you?'

'Expectation would be putting it a little high,' Trish said and watched a faint smile thicken the creases around his mouth. 'Call it hope.'

'All right. It was, I believe, an American philanthropist, who planned to donate them to his *alma mater*.'

'And yet you say that they do not exist. How come?'

'Perhaps someone else bought them from the philanthropist.'

Trish had spent a long time last night thinking about what she might have done if she'd discovered that a rather older David had participated in a fraud like this.

'In order to destroy them?' she suggested and had to wait again. This time there was no nod or smile to encourage her. 'To protect his son, maybe, from any future charge of fraud? Or even to protect his own reputation?'

'Who will ever know?' Martin Chanting smiled as though he was enjoying her frustration. 'Since the drawings do not exist.'

'Mr Chanting, I wish you'd be frank with me.'

He laughed, still as upright as he had been when he opened the door. He stirred up the Labrador with his foot. The old dog barely raised his head.

'If wishes were horses, beggars would ride,' he said. 'I'm like the dog: too old and tired to hunt any longer. All I want is to be left to snooze in peace.'

'I'll do that in a moment, but please let me ask one more thing.'

'You can always ask.'

'Where *is* your son now? I badly want to talk to him.'

Trish had had fantasies of hearing the old man say he wished he knew, that he had been putting pressure on Toby Fullwell as a way of reaching out to his lost child. She'd even had visions of his dying wife, begging him to make peace with their son and bring him home before it was too late.

'Now? I have no idea,' Chanting said, showing no sign of any of the emotions Trish had hoped he might feel. 'He could be anywhere.'

'You sound as though you don't care.'

'Why should I? I told you. I've not seen him for seventeen years.' Some human feeling twisted the muscles of his face under the blotched skin, but it was closer to rage than any kind of affection. 'He was always a wastrel.'

'In what way?'

'The usual way, Miss Maguire.' The sharpness of his contempt stung. She tried to imagine its effect on a child. 'I could perhaps have forgiven his extravagance and fecklessness if there had been nothing else. Young men do occasionally grow out of that kind of stupidity, even if they have been given too much money too young.'

'Is that what happened to your son?'

'I don't think that is any of your business.'

'I'm sorry,' Trish said, forgetting his dislike of apologies until she saw his twisted face. To retrieve her position, she quickly added: 'What did you mean when you said: "if there had been nothing else"?'

'My son succumbed, in spite of his excellent brain and first-class degree, to some ludicrous mish-mash of invented religion,' he said, speaking much faster and more freely, as though he had wanted an opportunity to justify himself for some time. 'I could never have forgiven that. I dislike religion of all kinds, but I could have stomached Christianity, Buddhism or any other properly considered system of belief. But this! It was neither Eastern nor Western, just a sentimental, self-indulgent muddle of incense, temple bells and nonsense dreamed up by a bunch of British and American, drug-mazed dropouts in Kathmandu.'

'Your only son,' Trish said, still trying on the stories until she found one that would fit. 'That must have hurt. Did the other man involved in the Clouet scam also succumb to this strange religion?'

'I may be seventy-four, Miss Maguire, and long retired, but my brain still works.' His voice had returned to its earlier slow harshness. 'You must have read the interview with Toby Fullwell in the *Sunday News*, just as I did. Why are you pretending to know so little about him?'

She hesitated, remembering his approval of her frankness at the door.

'Are you really Trish Maguire, the barrister?' His tone was goading now, which made her want to resist telling him anything. 'There is one, I know, because I looked her up after you telephoned. But you could easily be an impersonator.'

'I am the real thing,' she assured him, thinking: and I clearly suffer from a surfeit of sentimentality. Why did I think I would find some paternal feeling behind what's happening to Toby? Did I want it so much that I didn't care that it might be perverted?

'Given that you were never a friend of my son's, do I take it that you have some connection with Toby Fullwell?'

'I have barely met him.'

'Then just what exactly are you doing here, Miss Maguire?'

'Asking questions for a friend,' she said, happy to join him in providing answers that answered nothing.

'You can't expect me to fall for that absurd fiction. "A friend" indeed! That is what nervous young men claim when they ask for information at a venereal disease clinic. I must ask you once again to leave. This Peter and I need to set off for our afternoon walk.'

At the sound of his name, or perhaps the word 'walk', the Labrador heaved himself up again and stood panting against the old man's legs as he pushed himself up off his sofa.

And that, thought Trish, is the only sign I'm going to get that there is some warmth left in him somewhere for the son who so disappointed him.

'Come on, Peter.'

Somewhere outside a church poured out a cascade of bells, jangling yet satisfying to Trish, who had always loved the rippling, triumphant sound.

'Those wretched bellringers,' Martin Chanting said, covering his ears. 'It's a new craze round here and they make the evenings hell with their clatter. I wouldn't mind if it was part of an unbroken tradition, but it's not. They'd do better to weave baskets. Quieter and much more useful. Goodbye. We won't meet again.'

Trish went obediently back to her car. She had the key already in the ignition when she started to think properly about the name he'd bestowed on his Labrador. Elderly though it was, it couldn't have been as old as seventeen. Which meant that it had been named after Peter Chanting disappeared.

Would any man have called his dog after his estranged son if he cared as little for the son as Martin Chanting had claimed? Sentimental or not, she just couldn't believe it. And if he cared, he must at least have tried to find him.

Running after him and the dog, she tripped and crashed down on the edge of the pavement, ripping her tights and the skin of her left leg. She was amazed at how much it hurt. As a child she'd regularly grazed both knees, tripping while roller-skating or falling out of trees, and she did not remember feeling anything like this.

She thought of poor Mer and his arm. It must have been agony. She hoped, with a passion she hadn't felt for some time, that the giant had been a fantasy. By the time she had caught up with her quarry, she could feel the warm blood running down her leg. Soon it would clot and stick disgustingly to her skin.

'Yes?' he said, turning when she called his name.

'I accept the fact that you have had no contact with your son,' she said, standing as straight as her bleeding knee would allow, 'and that you do not know where he is at this precise moment.'

She saw the start of a smile playing about his thin lips and knew she was on the right track.

'But I believe you must know more than you suggested about his general whereabouts. Is he still based in Kathmandu?'

'You are a sharp little thing, aren't you?'

She couldn't tell from his tone whether he approved or not. 'I hope so. It's an important skill in my job. Does he still live in Nepal?'

'I don't know. But it is true that he does come back to this country at intervals.'

'How do you know?'

'If it's any of your business, he writes to me occasionally.'

'Ah. Good. Where does he stay when he comes back? With you?'

'Certainly not.' His expression suggested that he had just trodden on a slug. 'He has an interest in a small shop in London, selling imported rubbish from the subcontinent. I imagine there is some kind of accommodation over the shop.'

At last, she thought. 'How can I find it?'

'It is in Clerkenwell, I believe, and he has called it The Chantry.' Chanting's face creased into the kind of contempt that made her throat ache. 'That, of course, is typical of his feckless stupidity. Anyone who knows the English language will assume that it is a shop selling Christian paraphernalia and eschew it on those grounds, or go there in search of hymnals and leave in disgust at the glitter and incense sticks.'

That's easily worth a bruised and bloody knee, Trish thought as she thanked him and limped back to the car.

* * *

David was writing up his latest contribution to the school project on war when Trish got back to the flat, while Nicky was in the kitchen, preparing supper. The air of busyness and the scent of frying onions made the flat seem quite different from the echoing, brick-walled, art-filled refuge it had been for so long. Trish looked at the small dark head, bent over the wide spread of papers and photographs, heard him sigh, and didn't regret the old emptiness. Particularly not now that he seemed more serene and she and George were back on track with each other.

Determined not to disturb the peace, Trish crept up the spiral stairs to her room, where she showered and covered the still oozing graze on her knee with extra-wide Elastoplast. Her jeans felt comfortably tight over it, and she pulled on the thick red cashmere tunic George had given her one Christmas, before reaching for the London Business Telephone Directory.

The Chantry was listed, even though there was no entry with its owner's name. Someone must have records of that somewhere, unless Peter Chanting had been operating it under a false name. Trish padded down the spiral staircase to pull boots on over her thick socks and slipped out of the flat to hail the first cab she saw.

The driver took her to a charming little street near Exmouth Market on the edge of Clerkenwell. It was lined on both sides with small Georgian cottages, some of which had been converted into shops. They had none of the fashionable glamour of their Exmouth Market equivalents, and they looked dustier. There was a newsagent and a small, slightly dingy greengrocer's. Both were still open. Trish didn't think she would want to buy any of the limp, grimy vegetables in the greengrocer's. The potatoes were all sprouting and the bananas looked almost as black as those she'd bought as an impoverished law student.

Two doors along from the greengrocer's was The Chantry, with a squared-off bay window. There were no display lights in the shop, but she could see the mirrored plaques on a Rajasthani shawl glinting in the light of the overhead street lamp. Moving closer, she saw a ravishing brown silk box, embroidered in gold and amber colours with pearls set here and there among the stitchery, and a set of beautiful brass temple bells.

There was a 'Closed' sign on the shop door. Trish peered in through the grimy glass of the window, moving her head, first this way then that, to try to penetrate the gloom of the room beyond the gleaming wares in the window. There seemed to be heaps of fabric and paper lying all over the floor.

She rubbed the window with her sleeve, hoping to get a clearer view, but all she could see was the mess. It looked as though someone had emptied a filing drawer over the floor and then pulled down racks of clothes. She rang the bell beside the shop door, leaning on it for a full thirty seconds, but no one came, so she went into both the other shops in search of information.

Neither the greengrocer nor the newsagent could help. They couldn't remember when the shop had last been open or when they'd seen the owner, but they said it was often closed for days at a time and never had many customers.

Back in the street, Trish tried The Chantry's bell again, then took out her mobile to phone the local police.

'I see,' said the man who had taken her call when she had explained herself, 'so you have never been to this shop before and you have no idea of its normal opening hours. You do not know anything about the owner or any staff he may have. There is no sign of a break-in or any kind of trouble, apart from some mess you think you could see at the back of the shop. And yet you are sure that something serious is going down. Have I got that right?'

'Yes,' Trish said, hanging on to her patience like a lifebelt. Could it have been the expectation of a reception like this that had made Henry Buxford wary of going to the police in the first place, rather than a determination to manipulate any evidence there might be that his godson was involved in something criminal? 'But there's—'

'Never you mind. I have taken a note of everything you have told me and I will pass it on to the Home Beat Officer. Goodbye.'

'Shit!' Trish shouted to the surprise of a straggly-looking stray cat, which slid away under a parked car. She scuffled in her bag for her diary and then phoned Martin Chanting, who did not sound any more concerned by her story than the police officer had been.

'There could be any number of explanations for what you have seen,' he said at last. 'I have to go, Miss Maguire. Goodbye. Please do not telephone again.'

Feeling a fool in three different dimensions, Trish plodded back to St John Street, down through Smithfield with its gaudily painted ironwork and huge refrigerated meat lorries ready for the morning's market, and on towards the bridge and home.

Both legs were aching by the time she'd reached the bridge and her neck felt as though it had sunk two inches into her shoulders. She saw that the police had taken away their yellow signs. Had they found out enough about the body in the river now? Or had they just given up expecting any information?

Much later, after David had gone to bed, Trish settled down to draft a letter to Henry. It took her almost an hour to come up with a version that covered everything she wanted to tell him without sounding absurd. With each word she keyed in to her computer, she saw herself in court defending a charge of libel, and knew that she could not send this as an email.

Dear Henry,

You may already have persuaded Toby to tell you what is going on. I very much hope that you have because I am convinced that there is nothing else *I* can do for you. And something must be done.

If you are still not prepared to go to the police, or Customs & Excise, I think you should seriously consider employing a genuine investigator. I have come to the end of my always limited usefulness and I can see nowhere else to go.

All I have managed to discover is that, irrespective of whatever he may be doing now, Toby has definitely been involved in art fraud in the past. This afternoon I met Martin Chanting (the father of Toby's Cambridge friend), who virtually confirmed my suspicions that the Clouet drawings Toby identified at Cambridge were in fact fakes, deliberately produced for the purpose.

As you know, Toby and Peter Chanting sold the drawings through Goode & Floore's and achieved a record price. I have reason to believe that Peter's father bought them from the purchaser so that he could destroy them and therefore the evidence they represented. Which means, obviously, that we will never be able to prove anything. But I don't think Toby knows this.

I can only imagine the rows that must have taken place between Martin Chanting, his son and Toby, but they ended with Peter's exile to Nepal. His father says they have not spoken since, even though Peter now owns a shop in Clerkenwell and must therefore spend at least some of his time in the UK.

Given that, I imagine that he and Toby must have been in touch again and could be up to their old tricks. The Gregory Bequest is relatively close to Clerkenwell. I'd have thought they could easily have met in the street, even if they hadn't actually planned an encounter.

For a while I thought that Martin Chanting could be behind what has been happening to Toby, taking revenge on him for the loss of his son by forcing Toby to create another fake to sell through Goode & Floore's. I imagined that it wouldn't be hard to expose the modern fake and so ruin Toby's reputation or even have him arrested and tried for fraud.

However, I am now almost sure that his son must be involved in Toby's current problems. Peter seems to have disappeared, leaving his shop in a state of chaos. Whether he went back to Nepal of his own volition, having done what he wanted, or whether someone (?Toby) could have got rid of him in some other way, I do not know. And, once again, I do not have the resources to gather the evidence that would prove anything.

But I am concerned because, as I told you, Toby has recently been showing signs of violence. We know he has been hitting his wife. I have also discovered that his son, Mer, has a broken arm. He's been telling his schoolfriends that a giant attacked him. If his father assaulted him, I can understand why he should have made up the story of the giant to make it seem bearable. A lot of children would rather create a mythical bogeyman than blame one of their parents for hurting them. Of course, the so-called giant could be real and working with whoever has been making Toby himself so afraid. Either way, the child's broken arm seems to me a most serious danger signal.

I ought to have been firmer when we last talked, Henry, but I have to say now that I think the policy of terrifying Toby into making a confession is too dangerous to pursue. I cannot take any further part in it.

Please let me know, however, if there is anything I can ever do for you – in my professional capacity.

With best wishes,
Trish Maguire

Almost satisfied and definitely certain that she couldn't do any better, she added 'Strictly Private & Confidential' at the top of the letter, along with Henry's name and the address of his bank. She printed off a single copy for herself and filed the original on her hard disk and on a floppy, which she added to the others in her small fireproof safe.

Chapter 18

'It's Jay here,' said the junior clerk's voice over the phone later that morning. 'Sir Henry Buxford's on the line. Can you speak to him?'

Trish had been rereading her copy of the letter she had dropped in at Grunschwig's offices on her way into chambers and wondering whether she should pre-empt trouble by telling Antony what she had done or leave it to Henry.

'Yes. Put him through.'

'I have your envelope, Trish. And I wanted to assure you that I will tackle the matter now. I should also like to say how grateful I am for everything you've done, and for the discretion with which you have done it. But I do think your suggestion that Toby might have got rid of his old friend is more than a little Jacobean. As is the idea that he could have deliberately broken his son's arm.'

Thank God he's taking it so calmly, she thought. 'I shall be very relieved if I am wrong,' she said. 'But I know there's something serious going on.'

'I think you're right about that. But I'll handle it from here. I was wondering, though, whether I could persuade you to meet me this evening so that I can thank you in person for what you've done. Will you have one more drink with me?'

It would be pretty graceless to refuse to let him thank me

in whatever way he wants, Trish thought, as she agreed to meet him.

'Good. Then what about the Cork & Bottle again at seven o'clock?'

When she put down the phone, Trish saw that another email had come in from Ivan Gregory.

My dear Miss Maguire,
I have remembered the first time my mother told me about the paintings. I said, I think, that I'd grown up hearing about them, but that's not quite true. I had grown up hearing about my amazing father, the love of her life and great connoisseur, but not that we had his collection in our house. That news came one night in the Blitz.

I had come off duty from fire-watching. I was dog-tired. Up half of every night during the bombing and trying to do two or three men's work at the bank all day took it out of me, even when my asthma wasn't bad. Some bombs were still falling when I got back home, so I filled one flask with tea and another with whisky and soda, collected my novel – Dickens, I think – and took them with some blankets to the cellar.

My mother was already there, and in the kind of state I'd never seen. She'd always been so brave, but that night something had happened. I didn't know until later that one of her favourite patients had killed himself. He had long left the nursing home where she worked, but she visited him in his tiny flat whenever she could. It seemed that the sound of the bombing night after night had brought back all his old shell shock and he had hanged himself. She'd found him that day and had had to organize the removal of the body and so on.

The shock had made her very shaky herself and she was talking much more freely than she ever had before about the trenches and the men she had nursed, and her meeting with my father. She talked about her fear and her horror of some of the wounds she had to deal with and the bliss of being clean and warm and loved by a man like him.

Then she began to tell me how he'd first told her about his paintings, about how they had become lovers and she had become pregnant and they had been married by a French priest in a small village behind the front line.

That was the first occasion, incidentally, that I had heard about their marriage postdating her pregnancy. It didn't seem to matter much then. So I asked what happened to the paintings.

'They are here,' she said, pointing upwards. 'In the attic.'

I took my lantern (it all sounds very primitive, doesn't it?) and climbed up into the roof space. There, stacked under the eaves, were these tubes. Piles and piles of them. Some had brown stains on the outside, which made me think someone must have bled all over them. My father, perhaps. Or some of the wounded men in her care. Then I decided I was being fanciful. The marks could equally have been some form of mould.

When I got down to the cellar again, I asked her why she had never unpacked them. She told me she had never felt she had the right to touch them. They were his and it was her duty to keep them for him. But she also admitted that night that she had lost her faith that she would see him again.

In her distress, she poured out her hatred of the paintings, telling me that they were worth nothing to her without him, that she would willingly set fire to them if that could bring him back. She also confessed that she had been praying the house would receive a direct hit that night so that she would not have to go on without him any longer.

Later in the night, when she was calmer, she apologized and asked if she had hurt me by talking of the destruction of my unknown father's life's work. I told her that I was too busy and too tired at that point to care one way or the other about any damned paintings that belonged to a man I had never known.

I wish I hadn't done that. She turned away, very hurt herself. But when the asthma sewed my lungs together again later that night, she tended me as gently as she always had during my childhood. She was truly a great lady, and she did not have the life she deserved.

Yours etc.
Ivan Gregory

There's a whole network of us, Trish thought, who grew up without fathers. Was it that shared experience that made me like Ivan Gregory as soon as I read his first email? Has he had the same kind of thoughts about his father as I've had about Paddy? And how much has he understood about the significance of his mother's fruitless search for his father's family?

Henry had arrived, once again, before her at the wine bar. This time he had a bottle of Alsatian *pinot gris* in a cooler in front of him, with a plate of smoked-salmon wrapped fish and two forks. She approved of his determined provision of food to go with the wine he chose, but she wasn't hungry.

'I've just had another email from Ivan Gregory. Why didn't you tell me his mother was pregnant before she married Jean-Pierre?' she said as she sat down.

'Because there is no way that could possibly be relevant to Toby's problems,' Henry said, looking surprised. 'And because one of my preoccupations in all this has been to guard Ivan's privacy. I didn't want any gossip in the papers. He might not have read it, but his carers could have, and they might have said something to upset him.'

'You care far more about him than your godson, don't you?'

Henry hesitated. 'My affection for each of them is quite different,' he said stiffly. 'But, of course, I care for Toby, as well as for Margaret and the boys. By the way, you can let yourself off all that anxiety about Mer's arm.'

'Really?'

'Yes. I've been in touch with his mother, who tells me that Mer makes up stories like this one about the giant to get himself out of trouble. She says the accident happened while he was playing alone in the garden of the house in Chelsea where they're staying. Apparently there's an old Victorian cast-iron roller behind a tree, which the boys have been forbidden to touch. It seems likely that Mer was messing about on it and the handle sprang back and caught his arm. Apparently the pattern of bruising is consistent with that.'

'Thank God.' Trish brushed her hand across her forehead and was surprised to find it damp. 'I was worried.'

'I know, but I was sure it was unnecessary. I knew Toby couldn't have done anything like that to his own son.'

'No. Good. Tell me, how did you come to be his godfather?'

'His father was one of my oldest friends.' Henry's voice was still stiff, and it carried no warmth at all. That was so unlike him, that Trish was certain he was hiding something.

She knew enough about the containment of unbearable emotion to watch his hands. His right thumb was stuck deep into his left fist, as it might once have been stuck in the mouth of the child who needed comfort.

'Was?' She made her voice gentle.

'Yes.'

'I'm sorry,' she said, watching pain drag down the corners of his eyes and remembering how much she had once liked him. 'What about Toby's mother? Is she still alive?'

'Yes.' This time the single word made a sound like a drop of water hitting red-hot metal. His hands separated. He picked up his wineglass.

'Then why did you ever need me? Couldn't you have gone to her for information about Toby and his past and what he could be doing now?'

'No.'

'Why not?' This was like trying to make a stone talk. 'You know, if you'd told me more about them all in the first place, I might have come up with something more useful, and more quickly, too.'

Henry took a moment to speak, playing with his glass. At last he looked up at Trish. Her eyes widened at the sight of the held-in loathing in his expression. How like him to be able to show hatred so much more easily than distress!

'Toby's father used to talk about his wife's distorted view of their son's capabilities and potential. I'm sure that has something to do with his emotional fragility now. I wouldn't trust a single thing she said about him.'

Trish remembered Martin Chanting's contempt for his son and wondered if that had provided the link that had made the two undergraduates friends at Cambridge. 'Poor Toby.'

'Yes. His father did his best to help, but he told me once that intervening on the boy's behalf only made his wife more aggressive towards the pair of them. It wasn't – it wasn't a tolerable existence. He stuck it for as long as Toby depended on him, then killed himself just after Toby left university. I have felt as though I was *in loco parentis* ever since.'

Trish wondered whether her own anxieties had been affecting her judgement. All her more extravagant ideas about what Toby could be doing or suffering returned to her mind. Margaret had said she had always had to bolster Toby's confidence and make him believe he was worth something in spite of all his hated mother's bitter criticism, which fitted in with Henry's belated honesty.

Perhaps there never had been anything odd about the sale of the Pieter de Hooch. Perhaps all Toby's fear had come from nothing more than his own lifelong sense of inadequacy.

'Why didn't you warn me that there was a history of suicide in Toby's family,' she asked, 'when you set me on to terrify him?'

'Because it's not relevant. Suicide isn't catching,' Buxford said. His face gave her no clues to what he was thinking. 'Or genetic.'

'I hope you're right.' Trish realized that she wanted Toby's fear to be about something real and criminal, not a hangover from old parental cruelties. She didn't want to be told again that adults never got over what happened to them before they were ten. And she definitely didn't want to discover that she was still so tightly imprisoned in her own past that she could not trust her judgement of other people – or evidence.

'What's upsetting you so much?' Buxford asked.

'Nothing,' she said, fighting to get back some sensation of control over her life and mind. 'You know I've become very suspicious of your Jean-Pierre Gregoire.'

Henry put down the glass he had been nursing between his hands and pushed back the silver wings of hair at his temples.

'Don't go there, Trish.' His voice was unusually rough. 'All you need to know is that he was a collector so affected by a truly horrific war that he wanted his most cherished possessions out of the way of the fighting. Any suggestion to the contrary could do irreparable damage.' Buxford hesitated for a second, then added, pushing an envelope towards her across the table: 'Damage to Ivan's last years, I mean. I am really grateful for the effort you've put into this. Now, drink up, and have some of the fish. It goes well with this particular *pinot gris*.'

Trish ate and drank only enough to be polite.

As Henry made friendly conversation about his early years in the law before he went to the city, she battled with ironic curiosity about the investigation she'd been so keen to drop. There was no reason, of course, why she shouldn't continue her email correspondence with Ivan Gregory. And even though David would not tell her anything about Mer, their head teacher would probably pass on any important news of him. Trish might even hear it from Margaret.

'Trish?' Henry's voice broke through her preoccupations. She had no idea what he'd been talking about or what he wanted.

'I'm so sorry. My mind had slid off on a frolic of its own. What did you say?'

'Nothing of any importance. I was obviously talking too much.'

'Not a word too much. I was just thinking how much I'm going to miss them all. You will tell me what happens in the end, won't you?'

He smiled, and looked friendlier than at almost any time since they'd first met here, before she'd heard anything about Jean-Pierre Gregoire, or met Toby.

'Antony's right about you.'

Trish thought of Antony's complete withdrawal of approval, affection and even ordinary courtesy. He had brushed right past her this morning, refusing even to answer a casual question about the progress of his money-laundering case.

'In what way?'

'Along with the fact that you have this rare ability to mix imaginative perception with solid analytical reasoning,' Henry said, 'he believes you can make yourself care about the most hopeless people. As a misanthrope, he admires that.'

What member of Antony's chambers could want more? Trish asked herself. It would have been reassuring, though, if he'd been able to tell her himself.

'And he can't think why he didn't notice you for so long

while you were being wasted in family law.' Henry pushed himself up from his chair with both hands flat on the table. He leaned over the bottle and glasses to kiss her cheek. 'Good luck, Trish. I know we'll meet again. I hope it's soon.'

When he'd gone, she poured a little more wine into her glass and opened the envelope he'd left her. The size of the cheque made her eyes widen all over again. She didn't see how she could take any money, let alone this much, for what she'd helped to do to Toby Fullwell.

But she couldn't leave the cheque here on the wine-bar table, so she folded it and slid it into her wallet. She ought to get home and do something to make up for neglecting her family. She remembered promising David a trip to the Imperial War Museum. If she didn't take him soon, he'd have finished his war project before they ever saw the exhibits.

After the last Garrick dinner, Toby had known better than to accept another invitation to eat there. But that meant he'd had to let Henry into the flat. Now, here they were sipping some thin sour white wine he'd found at the back of the fridge and picking at the mouldy end of the cheddar truckle he'd been hacking at every night, while Henry asked him questions.

Thank God, he wasn't still going on about Peter. This time he wanted to know about Margaret and the state of their marriage, and why she'd moved out. Which was outrageous. It was none of his business.

Still, Toby answered as freely as he could and thought that would be the end of it. But it wasn't. As soon as he'd persuaded Henry that marriage to Margaret was the most important thing in his life, the bloody man started banging on about drugs again.

At least those questions were easy to answer. Drugs had never held out any lure for Toby. At Cambridge, when every room he'd entered had been sweet and foggy with the smoke of a dozen spliffs, the idea of losing himself in dope had seemed horrible. Even now, when he longed for oblivion, he couldn't have risked it. Ben might phone when he was stoned and trick him into saying or doing something fatal.

'Good. Let's have another bottle,' Henry said. 'I saw you had one in the fridge.'

Toby couldn't understand why anyone would want to drink more of the filthy stuff, but he obediently drove in the corkscrew, thinking of Ben's face while he did it. His hands tightened as he imagined the crack of Ben's cheekbones and a moment later, when he heard the slosh of the wine, he thought of blood pouring out from a vast wound. He sneaked a glance at Henry and saw frightening suspicion in his expression.

'I keep hearing about the shadier side of the art world,' Henry said, holding out his glass, which still looked nearly full. 'Is there really as much forgery and price-rigging as people suggest?'

With the sour fluid prickling against his tongue and his skin pouring sweat, Toby thought of all the spy novels he'd ever read. He tried to remember what they'd said about the best way to resist interrogation.

Ten minutes later, he was giggling at his own jokes about the Russian icon scam of the early 1980s, while Henry sat like a judge in front of him, pouring more and more wine into his glass and waiting for him to break.

Chapter 19

Sam Makins was sitting, staring at the floor, in Trish's room when she got into chambers after lunch next day. He didn't move, even when she greeted him, so she laid a hand on his shoulder.

'Hey, what's up?'

'Tamara O'Connor got the maximum sentence,' he said, still staring at the floor. 'I tried to make them believe she was a victim rather than a villain, but I screwed up. It would probably have been better if I had just made the usual contrition speech.'

Trish squeezed his shoulder, then let him go. 'It's not your fault. Come on, Sam, she was found with twenty-two condoms of cocaine in her gut. There's no getting away from the fact that she was guilty.'

'I know. But she was crying when I went down to see her in the cells afterwards.' At last he looked up at Trish. 'Her face was grey. Her eyes were all over the place and she had no nails left.'

'I can imagine.'

'And she gave me a message for you.'

'Oh?' Trish did not want to hear this, but Sam looked anguished enough to make her do whatever she could for him.

'She said: "Tell Trish Maguire that if I don't get my kids back, I'll kill myself. I don't want to live if I can't have them. Tell her that." '

Trish rubbed both hands through her hair. There wasn't anything to say. Even if Tamara had had a hope of getting them back before she became a mule, she'd blown it now.

'How do you bear it?' Sam asked.

'You don't,' she said. 'You shut yourself off. It's the only way. And then, when you stop being able to do that, you switch to commercial law. Once you've done that, you put all your energies into forgetting all the women like Tamara and all the brutalized and miserable children you've ever represented. Instead you involve yourself in dreary little arguments about exactly what a contract did or didn't mean and which company owes which other company damages.'

'That's awful.'

'Better than cracking up.'

Toby had just about got his hangover under control by three o'clock in the afternoon. He'd drunk litres and litres of water and eaten several cheese sandwiches. Even so, the ringing phone spiked into his residual headache and he rushed to silence it. Then he saw the number of Margaret's mobile on the screen.

'Darling! Thank God! How's Mer?'

'Silent. The doctor says his arm is healing as it should, but he still won't tell us how it happened. All we know is that he had a row with Tim over whose turn it was to choose the TV programme, let himself out into the garden, and came back half an hour later with his arm broken in two places, a lot of bruises and a silly story about a giant grabbing him in the garden. You know what a fantasist he's always been.'

'A giant? Oh, God!' How was he ever going to forgive himself for this? And how was he ever going to forgive himself for hating what he'd once seen as his own father's cowardice? Now that he knew how much courage it took to kill yourself, all his ideas about his father had changed. He sniffed and swallowed.

'Oh, Toby,' said his wife, sounding kinder than usual. 'Don't be silly. You know Mer always makes up stories like that when he's done something he knows is wrong. He'll be fine. It doesn't hurt any more, and the doctor says it'll heal cleanly. You really don't have to worry so much.'

Of course, I do, he thought. Then he coughed and found his voice again: 'Margaret, why haven't you rung before? I've left dozens of messages.'

'I know. It's driving me mad. But it wasn't until today that you sounded like you. I wasn't prepared to talk to you while you were still behaving like a lunatic. I had enough to deal with over Mer and his arm and Tim's nightmares.'

'When am I going to see you?'

'If you can promise me that you really have sorted yourself out,' Margaret said, 'we can talk about a day to come home soon. Will you be at Mer's school play next Thursday? I thought we might discuss it then.'

'Thursday,' he said, feeling shivery with dread and hope, as though someone had run an ice cube across his burning skin. Thursday was D-day.

Ben had promised that if he bought the next fake successfully, whatever it cost, that would be the end of it. Afterwards, so long as Toby kept his mouth shut, Ben had said, the boys would be safe, and no one would come back to him for more favours. By the time the play began on Thursday afternoon, he would know if he had a future.

'Of course, I'm coming to the play,' he said, as his mental picture of Cézanne's hellish landscape melted into his favourite sunny Monet. 'There's nothing in the diary. Nothing else, I mean. I'll be there.'

'OK. How's Jo?'

'What do you mean?'

'Exactly what I asked. When I phoned her the other day to ask her to stop you leaving me all these messages, she started crying and told me you've been bullying her. Is that true?'

'Of course not.' Toby thought of everything Jo had done and felt his blood pressure rising. 'But I can't bear her sloppiness or refusal to take proper messages. An old friend of mine came round twice a few weeks ago and because she wouldn't take his phone number or address I've had no way of finding him. And it's important that I do. I have to know why he wanted to get in touch after so long.'

'That doesn't sound bad enough to justify terrorizing Jo. You need to be careful of her. She's a lot more sensitive than you think and you of all people ought to know what that means. She's also exceptionally efficient under normal conditions, and she does a very good job with the visitors. You'd have difficulty getting anyone else as good for twice the salary the trust pays her. I've told Henry he ought to pay her more. The least you can do is be kind to her.'

'You've seen Henry?' Toby said, wishing he hadn't sounded so sharp. But it was hard not to, now that he knew why his godfather had been asking all those questions yesterday. His face burned as he realized Margaret must have told Henry about their fight and her black eye.

'No,' she said, sounding quite kind. 'But he phones me at intervals to check that we're all right and not needing anything. *He* cares about us.'

'That's not fair.' Toby thought of all the lonely evenings when he'd longed for her. 'You've just told me you hated getting all my messages.'

'True.' That edge was still there in her voice. 'And I suppose the fact that you didn't try to find us physically does at least tell me you're not a wife beater after all. They *always* come after you.'

'What are you talking about? Wife beater? Margaret, you know I'm not.'

'What's that bleeping? It sounds like your other phone. You'd better answer, and I must go anyway. See you at the play. Don't be late.'

She'd gone before he could say anything more. He waited for the answering machine to pick up the call. The sound of Ben's voice made him back against the wall.

'Hi, Toby! I couldn't get through on your mobile, so I thought I'd just remind you that there must be no mistakes at next week's sale. If you're listening to this, pick it up.'

Toby lunged for the receiver: 'Did you break Mer's arm, you bastard?'

'Of course,' Ben said, sounding surprised. 'I told you we'd give you a taster of the kind of punishment you could expect for letting us down. Be thankful you weren't made to watch it. You will be next time. So think about that when you go into the auction next week. And it won't just be an arm, either.'

Toby couldn't speak, and Ben didn't say anything else. When Toby heard the click of Ben's phone, he rewound the answering machine tape and wiped it. He didn't want Jo hearing anything Ben had said.

'What's the matter now?' she asked from behind him. His hands slipped off the controls of the machine as dizziness made him reel.

'Toby, what's going on? Who were you talking to about me hearing something?' She sounded frightened.

He turned to see her staring at him. One of her hands was almost touching his elbow, as though she thought he might fall over.

'You need help,' she said, peering even closer into his face. For once she sounded almost gentle. 'Let me get you a doctor.'

'Don't be stupid.'

'I'm not. You look awful. And I know you're cracking up. You hear voices from people who aren't here. You talk to yourself all the time. You're obviously not sleeping. You're scaring me, Toby. Please let me call your doctor. *Please.*'

'Don't be ridiculous. I'm fine, except for having to deal with the mess you're making of your job. Haven't you finished typing today's letters yet?'

'Of course.' The sympathy in her expression closed in until it was as mean and spiteful as usual. He felt his hands curling into fists.

'They're on your desk, waiting for your signature,' Jo went on as though she was rubbing salt into a deep cut in his flesh. 'But you'll have to post them yourself. I'm going home. I've got a migraine.'

Once she had gone, Toby sat beside the phone. He couldn't think what to do. His skin itched, as though microscopic creatures were crawling all over it, and his eyes kept watering. He wondered if he was suffering from lack of fresh air. Or perhaps it was just the constipation that had made his insides set like concrete.

Sunlight, broken by the bare branches of the garden's trees, was dappling the mossy paving of the garden. It seemed months, years even, since he'd walked anywhere for pleasure. Maybe that was partly why everything seemed so awful. A bit of ordinary exercise in the fresh air might put things in perspective. And it might help his digestion, too. Yes, in a while he'd lock up the gallery and walk across the river.

He was just beginning to feel a faint memory of enjoyment from stretching his legs as he strode across the Millennium Bridge's so-called streak of light when he saw ahead of him Ben's thin, dark woman, walking beside a small boy. At first the child distracted him; then he realized the woman must have brought him with her for cover. They were leaning against the parapet, and she was peering back at the Gregory Bequest Gallery, pointing to it and saying something Toby couldn't hear.

Hanging back, glad of the concealing crowd, Toby waited to

see what she would do next. Had she been there when Ben had broken Mer's arm? Toby began to comfort himself with ideas of what he would like to do to her.

Trish pushed open the corrugated-iron door at the front of the trench exhibit and looked back.

'Are you sure you want to do this?'

'Yes.' David's black eyes were showing a lot more energy than usual. 'Jamie says it's great. Really lifelike. And Mr Thompson thinks we should all see it. For the project, you know.'

'Good. On we go, then.'

The museum was still full, even though it was only about half an hour until closing time. Trish had been amused as they wove their way through the crowds upstairs, between the tanks and the submersibles, to see that there were very few girls in the various family parties and those there were had all been dressed in combat clothes.

The trench door clattered behind them. The darkness seemed almost complete, although there was a small flickering red lamp high up on the trench wall to their right. Guns crashed and voices shouted. Bodies seemed to be all round them. Trish couldn't distinguish which belonged to the crowd and which to the exhibit's figures until she brushed against them.

'Of course, the real thing would have been wet, David,' she said. 'Our feet would be squelching through the mud, and there would be rats running around.' She suppressed all the descriptions she had read of body parts and excrement.

They passed a lens-like glass square in the wall. Trish peered into it and found that it was a periscope, giving her a view of the bleak emptiness of no man's land. David couldn't reach up to it, but they found a child's-eye version a little further on.

Trish's eyes were beginning to adjust to the darkness and she could see a large group ahead of them. Maybe a school party; maybe just a big family. She didn't want to push her way through, so she slowed down as she rounded the next dogleg.

Toby grabbed the boy by the arm and hissed: 'Don't say a word.'

Rather to his surprise, the boy kept his mouth tightly closed. He did pull against Toby's grip, but he made no sound. Toby held on and dragged his captive with him, against the flow of people, till they got to the corrugated-iron entry door.

'We must get to the toilets,' Toby murmured whenever someone protested. Toilet wasn't one of his words, but he assumed it would sound normal to these sightseers, and probably to the dark-haired woman's child as well. 'Can't risk an accident.'

The boy glared up at him with so much hatred that Toby nearly hit him there and then. But he managed not to. Instead, he dragged him down the corridor towards the gents and pushed open the door with his shoulder. He wasn't going to risk letting go. Luckily there was no one at any of the urinals and the doors to all the loos were open. Thank God for that. He dragged the boy into one cubicle and locked the door.

'Don't look so scared,' he said, contemptuous of his quarry's white face and shaking body. What a loathsome little wimp! 'I'm not going to touch you. Not this time anyway. But I want you to give your mother a message.'

'My mother's dead,' the boy said viciously. His black eyes looked enormous, but there were no tears in them. That surprised Toby more than the lie or the spite.

'Rubbish. She brought you here.'

'No, she didn't. I'm on my own.'

'Don't be ridiculous. I'm talking about the woman who came in with you: tall, thin and dark. She called you David. I heard you both talking, so there's no point lying.'

'Only because we met in the queue for the security check.' The piping voice was breathless. And no wonder, producing such a load of rubbish. 'She asked me what my name was and what I'd come to look at. I don't know her. I've never seen her before in my life.'

'You can't be stupid enough to think I'll believe that, but it doesn't matter either way. You can take a message to her whoever she is.'

'She'll probably have gone and I won't find her again. She was on her own, too. No. No, she wasn't.' The boy shoved both hands into his pockets. His voice trembled, but he still wasn't crying: 'I mean she said her boyfriend would be waiting for her. He's big and quite old. He's a policeman called Inspector Lyalt, she said. He's a policeman. She won't be on her own.'

'Never mind her bloody boyfriend. Concentrate. This is the message: tell her to stay out of my life. I know what she's up to. And I know she works with Ben Smithlock. But I won't have it. Make her understand that. OK?'

'No,' the boy said, looking stupid. 'I don't understand and I can't give her any message because I don't know who she is. And I won't ever see her again.'

And then, before Toby realized what he was doing, the child flung himself on the floor, flattening his body like an animal, and crammed himself through the gap under the door. Toby could hear him panting and slipping as he ran across the travertine.

Toby unlocked the door, planning to follow, when he heard footsteps outside. He bent over one of the basins to wash his hands. The newcomer unzipped his trousers and relieved himself into the nearest urinal. He was a total stranger, who didn't even look at Toby and obviously suspected nothing. Toby breathed more easily, dried his hands and left.

Trish almost walked into the tall figure on her left and put out a hand to regain her balance. The hardness against her palm told her she was touching one of the exhibits. She squinted in the darkness to see more.

'Look, he's standing on what they called the firing step. It gave them a chance to shoot over the edge of the sandbags, but it meant they were at risk of getting a bullet in the brain,' she whispered over her shoulder, not wanting to disturb anyone else as she shared her few facts with David. 'They called wounds like that Blighties, or Blighty ones, because they were so serious you got sent home for treatment.'

'Are you a guide then, miss?' said a shrill voice from the level of her waist. 'Where's your badge? The others have all got badges on a chain round their necks.'

Trish peered at the child she'd thought was her brother and saw a quite different, brown-haired boy. She smiled at him, before squinting through the darkness beyond.

'Sorry,' she whispered. 'I thought you were someone else. D'you want to get past me?'

She pushed past him, and the three people behind him, but she still couldn't see the black-eyed pointy face she wanted.

'You'd do better going out the far end and coming back in again,' said an irritable male voice. 'There isn't room for two-way traffic on these duckboards.'

That seemed so sensible that Trish nodded and fought her way out of the trench, checking every child she passed. None of them was the right one.

Outside, the light seemed very bright, and the foyer almost empty. She ran through it, calling his name.

No one answered. Trish told herself not to panic. He was nine, quite capable of surviving a few minutes without her and finding his way back. Even so, she went back through the trench four times, checking all the nooks and twists in case he was there. On one pass, she was momentarily distracted by a glass case to her left, which contained a life-sized model of a VAD in uniform beside all sorts of smaller exhibits.

Peering into the case, she saw a photograph of a train filled with wounded soldiers. Some men were climbing the high steps up into it, helped by nurses in uniform. Beside the train were rows of stretchers, each one containing a bandaged, semiconscious soldier.

'And that,' Trish said aloud, 'is why the paintings had to be stuffed into narrow tubes. Of course!'

'Trish! Trish!' She heard David's voice, whispering and urgent. She looked round and saw him at last, white faced and running towards her from the lavatories.

'Can we go, Trish? I don't like it.'

'Of course. Are you feeling ill?'

'No. But can we go *now*? Please.' He was tugging at her hand. She could feel his palm slippery with sweat and castigated herself for being so insensitive. He'd been so excited by the idea of the exhibit that she hadn't thought carefully enough how male voices shouting and guns and the aura of death might affect him.

'Come on,' she said, tugging in her turn. 'Let's not wait for the lifts. Race you up the stairs?'

He ran and she followed, hating herself. He seemed no less jittery once they'd got outside, so she hailed a taxi and hustled him in. Only then did he begin to calm down.

'What happened in there?'

'Nothing happened. I just didn't like it. And I had to have a pee.' He was silent, until they reached the end of their street, when he added: 'I'm sorry, Trish. It was really kind of you to take me.'

'That's fine. It doesn't matter. Maybe it was all too much after a heavy day at school. Don't give it another thought.'

'No. OK.' He twisted round so that he could peer out of the window, but there was nothing to see except the dark street and the miserable one-legged pigeons who eked out their depressing existence round the parked cars.

'Look, there are lights on in the flat,' he said a moment later. 'Nicky must be in.'

'Yes,' Trish said, hearing the pleasure in his voice and fighting an emotion that wasn't exactly jealousy, but seemed disturbingly like it.

Helen was leaning against the edge of the carriage as the train rattled and swayed. Poor Lieutenant Walters was groaning again. He had two of Jean-Pierre's tubes in his stretcher, on either side of his legs. She'd been afraid they were hurting her patient, but the last time she'd wiped his forehead and given him a sip of water, he'd told her it was his chest and his head that hurt. The last doctor to see him had assured her that nothing they were doing to his legs could trouble him now because of the damage to his spine. He had no feeling below the waist.

'Nurse! Nurse!' It was Captain Coot's rasping voice. She turned, trying to wear the comfortable, confident smile that was the only thing she had to offer most of them.

'We'll soon be there,' she said, looking down at him. She could see from the saliva on his moustache that he'd been biting his lips, trying not to groan. There was sweat all over his greyish skin. Both his arms were broken and had had to be splinted across his chest. 'I'm sorry about the rattling. I've tried to wedge you in tight, but I know it must hurt.'

'Not too bad,' he said. 'There was a letter in my pocket. Could you see if it's still there?'

It didn't seem very likely. His breeches had had to be ripped up the seams so that the wounds in his legs could be dressed. As carefully as possible, she moved Jean-Pierre's tube and felt her way down the side of his body, feeling the stiffening edges of his bloody, ripped breeches. There was the pocket. He flinched and she knew she'd hurt him. But there was a piece of paper in there. She slid her fingers deeper into the torn pocket and pulled it out, carefully replacing the tube.

'Would you like me to read it for you?'

'Yes, please.'

She unfolded it, hoping it wasn't going to be one of the brutal announcements of infidelity or impending marriage to someone else. She couldn't believe how some women were behaving to these men, and tried to hope it was ignorance of what they suffered at the front rather than the conscienceless cruelty it seemed.

'My dear Jim,' she read, tilting the thin sheet to catch the little light there was. 'I wish you were here. I married—'

Helen broke off to check that he wanted her to go on reading. To her amazement he was smiling and nodding slightly.

'I married Rupert yesterday. It was a beautiful day, but I missed you. We both did. And mother wept.'

'I think she'd have wept even if I'd been there,' the captain said, still smiling even though he winced each time the train clacked over a gap in the rails. 'She's an emotional woman, my mother.'

'So this is your sister, is it?'

'Yes. My little sister. Just imagine her getting married. And to such a good chap. He was out with us until he got a Blighty one. But he's well enough to take care of her now. Does she say when they're due back from their honeymoon?'

Helen looked back at the letter. 'Yes. They will have been back four days by now. She should be able to come and see you as soon as the doctors have decided where to send you.' She saw the wound stripes on his hanging sleeve. 'This must be your third time on one of these convoys.'

'Yes.'

She smoothed the thin khaki sheet over him. 'I should think they'll give you an instructor's job now. You won't have to go back again. Not for a fourth time, Captain.'

His eyes filled with tears and he took another big chunk of

his moustache between his teeth. 'Do you think so, Nurse?' he said when he'd got back enough control to let his jaw unclench.

'Yes. You've done your share already, Captain Coot. More than your share. They won't ask you to go out again now.'

'No one can say that until it's over. It could go on for ever so that we all have to go on going back.'

'It will end,' she said, remembering all Jean-Pierre's reassurance.

The tempo of the rattle changed.

'We're slowing down.'

Helen braced herself. This was the moment she most dreaded for herself rather than for any of her patients. What if Jean-Pierre's friend were not at the station to collect the tubes of paintings? What if one of the orderlies asked too many questions? Or one of the doctors insisted on having a tube opened? What if she were arrested?

She thought of Edith Cavell. At least she had been working for her country. Helen felt her child kick in her womb and put her hand over the bump. Someone would notice soon. This had to be the last time, even if she disappointed Jean-Pierre. She couldn't take any more of it.

Captain Coot groaned, cutting off the sound almost as soon as it escaped his lips. This was the important thing. Even more important than Jean-Pierre and his paintings.

'I'm just going to take these bracing tubes away now,' she said carefully, pulling them away. 'I don't want them getting in the way when they move you on to the ambulance.'

As soon as she had a free moment that evening, Trish phoned Buxford. A woman answered and said that her husband was out and could she take a message?

'That's very kind. My name is Trish Maguire.'

'Ah. Yes, Henry has told me all about you. Is this about Toby? Henry said you'd very sensibly backed out of all that.'

'It's only peripherally to do with Toby. Could you say to Henry that I've just realized Helen was a mule.'

'That sounds like code,' Lady Buxford said with a light laugh. 'I'd better write it down. Hold on a moment. Yes, here's a pencil. Did you say: "Helen was a mule"?'

'I did. Thank you.'

Trish put down the phone and went to turn off David's light.

'Will you hear my lines again?' he asked. 'I kept getting them wrong when Nicky tested me this evening.'

He was lying in bed, looking very tired, his white face marked with deep bruises under his black eyes. Even though this anxiety over his part in the play could only be a displacement for whatever had upset him at the museum, Trish thought she knew exactly how he felt.

'Wouldn't you rather have your light out and get some rest so that you're fresh enough to run through the lines tomorrow? We could easily rehearse over breakfast.'

'No. I must try again now.' There was a new shrillness in his voice, and his bottom lip was swollen, as though he'd been chewing it. 'I tell you I kept getting them wrong with Nicky. And in the last rehearsal. It's only days till the play. If I don't get them right before you put out my light, I won't get to sleep. *Please*.'

'Of course, I'll hear your lines,' she said, smiling down at him. 'But you mustn't worry too much if you don't get them right tonight. You were word-perfect last week. I think you've been doing too much worrying and rehearsing. That can make even the best speakers forget what they know perfectly well. You need to be relaxed to do yourself justice. Now, where's your copy of the play?'

He fished it out from under his pillow. Trish, who knew it backwards now, rather approved of the way the English master had updated the familiar story of the homeless stranger calling for help on Christmas Eve. In this version, the first house he tried was a rich banker's and he was turned away with contempt because he was ragged and dirty. David was to be the spokesman for the second house, which in this production was to be a council flat inhabited by the family of a police officer.

'It's cold outside,' Trish said, prompting his first line. 'Have you got a blanket to spare?'

'Come on inside, my friend. There's food here. Hot food. And we've plenty to share.'

David was staring forwards, and his hands were clenched on the edge of his duvet. He gave no expression to the words. Trish remembered Mrs More's saying to her once that he had turned out to be a surprisingly good actor. He didn't look like any kind of actor now. She tried to help him by thinking herself into the part of the tramp:

'I'm too dirty to come into your house.' She thought of poor Mer, whose part she was reading, who ate rust, was terrified of his father and – or – the giant who had broken his arm, and was loathed by everyone in his class. It didn't seem the most suitable part for him. Or had Hester More pinned her hopes on the fact that the despised tramp turned out to be a messianic figure in disguise? Probably. Trish hoped it would work for Mer.

'Dirt is only— No. Sorry, Trish. Only dirt is— No. You see, I can't do it. I can't. I always get the dirt bit wrong. I don't know what to say.'

'You mustn't worry about it. The real line is: "Dirt is only on the outside. What matters is what's inside. I'll take you to the bathroom before we eat, so that you can wash."'

She saw him close his eyes and fight whatever block his mind had put up against these particular words. There were deep lines between his eyebrows and on either side of his mouth. He looked like an old, old man.

A waft of aromatic steam reached her, making her turn away. George was cooking again. She couldn't leave him alone much longer. It was his turn now. She got up off the edge of the bed. David's hand moved, suddenly gripping hers. She covered his with her other one and waited. Neither of them spoke. After a while, his breathing eased and he let her go. She watched him for a moment longer, bent to kiss his forehead, then turned off his light and went to join George.

'That took a long time,' he said. 'Is he all right?'

'Panicking about forgetting his lines. At least that's the presenting anxiety. But there's still a hell of a lot left below the surface he can't bear to let out. And I don't know how to help him do it.' She shook her head. George was probably bored rigid by her anxieties. 'That smells wonderful.'

He put a warm plate in front of her, then laid two covered dishes on the mats between their places. 'Help yourself. It's an experiment. It may be disgusting.'

'If so that'll be a first. It's amazing that you can cook at all after ten hours in the office, let alone this sort of elaborate stuff. How was it today?'

'Hellish. Staff, partners, professional-indemnity insurers and, of course, clients. I had the most appalling row with Jeremy Carfield. He wants something that is simply not possible within the law and he thinks he can get it by yelling at me. He can't, but we can't afford to lose his business either, so I've been walking a tightrope all day.' He patted his generous gut and laughed. 'As you know, I'm not built for tightropes. Honestly, Trish, I sometimes think it's only cooking that keeps me sane. D'you mind?'

'I love it.'

'Liar,' he said, ladling some more sauce over the chicken he'd put on his plate. 'Eat whatever you can or it'll spoil. And tell me how you're getting on with persuading your father to come to the Christmas play.'

'Not well,' Trish said, hating herself for having forgotten to leave another message on Paddy's answering machine.

'Don't beat yourself up, Trish. He'll come round in the end. And you can't force the pace.'

She looked down at her plate. The food wasn't in fact up to George's usual perfectionist standard, and the sauce was far too sweet. She felt her stomach jump and tighten at the thought of eating any more.

'Go on,' he said. 'There's no need to finish it. Go and phone.'

As she went, she thought how easy her life was, with its phones and text messages and emails, compared with Helen Gregory's. She had waited fifty years for a man who never contacted her, and still believed she would see him again.

Trish couldn't imagine such endurance – or self-deception – but then she hadn't been trained through the war to end all wars, when news was as rare as survival on the front line.

Chapter 20

'The great man wants to see you, Trish,' Robert said, breaking into her close study of the disputed clauses of an architect's contract for four multi-storey blocks of flats. 'But he's in a mega strop this morning, so be careful.'

'Thanks for the warning.'

'Pleasure, Trish, but before you go, tell me something.'

'What?'

'Did Peter Chanting jump or was he pushed?'

'What *are* you talking about?'

'Haven't you read the paper this morning? How extraordinary! Presumably childcare at breakfast means you just don't have the chance to keep up. It's no wonder you're losing your touch if you have no idea what's going on in the world outside the nursery.'

The last things she wanted to discuss were blunted edges and maternity-fuddled brains. 'What has Peter Chanting done?'

'Such innocence! You are good at it.' The synthetic admiration in Robert's voice would have sounded excessive in a daytime TV game-show host. 'But will you be able to keep it up when the police come to feel your collar? I hope you've got a really good criminal silk up your sleeve.'

'Stop messing about, Robert, and tell me what you're talking about.'

He laughed. 'You remember that body in the river with a bullet in its head?'

'Yes. Why? Are they saying Chanting killed him?'

'Even more lovely innocence, Trish. I do admire your thespian abilities, you know. But you're wasting time and the great man's not going to be very pleased with you. He was expecting you to whiz off to his room straightaway.'

The sound of Robert's laughter echoed down the dusty corridor behind her and continued to ring in her ears as she opened Antony's door. He looked at her over the top of his half-moon glasses.

'Henry seems to have forgiven you for backing out, but I'm not sure I have. Come in and sit down.'

'There was nothing more I could do,' she said, refusing to give in. But she did take the offered chair.

'Only you could be the judge of that. What concerns me now is what you're going to do with the information you did collect. I find that Robert already knows you've been working for Henry, and I wonder who else does.'

Trish smiled. She wasn't going to bring George into this, or any other inhabitant of her private life. They were none of Antony's business.

'I hope you're not planning to turn the Gregory Bequest's problems into a good story for an entertaining evening in El Vino, Trish.'

She stood up. 'I don't know how much Henry may have shared with you of the little I was able to find out for him, but it is far too serious – and dangerous – to pass on to anyone else. Was there anything else you wanted to discuss this morning?'

'I don't think so.' He sounded blander than the bland now, as he watched her over the top of his half-moon glasses. She wished she knew what was going on in his mind.

She felt like an angry muttering fool as she left his room, but at least she hadn't demeaned herself by begging for reassurance that he wasn't planning to find ways to punish her for her failure to help Henry Buxford.

'Steve?' she said as she looked round the door of the clerks' room, 'have you got a paper this morning?'

Without a word, he leaned towards his wastepaper basket and removed a neatly folded newspaper. Having shaken a cascade of pencil shavings from it, he handed it over. Trish soon found the story Robert had used to tease her under a photograph of a good-looking man with eyes narrowed against the sun and mountains in the background.

> The body found in the Thames by Blackfriars Bridge three weeks ago has been identified as that of Peter Chanting. He lived an exotic life, dividing his time between Nepal and London. He is thought to have been involved in smuggling Shatoosh shawls (see fashion editor's comment on page 23), and been afraid of discovery. The police are not looking for anyone in connection with his death.

'So they think it was suicide, do they?' she muttered, making Steve peer at her as though checking for symptoms of serious illness. 'But how can they? No one could walk naked through London without being spotted.'

As she walked back down the corridor to her cell-like room, wondering what Toby had been doing on the night Chanting's body went into the river, she was mentally drafting a letter to his father. When she reached her desk, she remembered the coldness with which Martin Chanting had talked about his son. She picked up her pen and after several hopeless attempts, produced two simple lines.

Dear Mr Chanting,

The news in today's papers has shocked and saddened me. I am so sorry about your son's death. I wish I could have met him.

Yours sincerely,
Trish Maguire

Toby felt weightless, as though he was floating a few inches from the floor. There seemed to be no brains or blood or anything else in his head. That must be why he felt so light, but nothing except shock explained why the laws of gravity had been suspended.

He read the paragraph in the paper again and again, trying to feel, trying to understand the extraordinary last line. But he couldn't. All he knew was that Peter had been found dead in the Thames on the day after he had come to the house and Jo had turned him away.

Had he killed himself out of guilt for blabbing the Clouet secrets? Or had he tried his blackmail trick on other people, too, and been killed by one of them?

Toby felt something disgusting and looked down. He had forgotten the banana he'd been about to eat for breakfast. He'd squeezed it so hard that the skin had burst and the pulpy flesh was oozing across the backs of his hands.

He heard someone unlocking the front door from outside, and he dropped the mangled mess. He reached mechanically for a cloth and was still holding it, wiping his hands over and over again, as he opened the door to see Jo climbing up the stairs in tears, with a newspaper clutched between her hands.

It was hard to believe he'd ever thought her pretty, with her blotched face and chapped lips.

'And what are *you* crying about?' he said, shocking himself with the cruelty of his voice.

'The man who came to see you that night.' She pointed to the folded newspaper. 'It's him, isn't it? He came here, wanting you, and then when he didn't get to talk to you he killed himself.'

'That's what it looks like, yes. And if you hadn't screwed up, I'd have been able to find out what he wanted, and I might have saved him.'

'Toby, I'm sorry,' she whispered. 'I'm really sorry. I just didn't know it was that important, and I was so angry with you for making all those unfair accusations about lost messages and things that I didn't write down the phone number he gave me. I'm really, really sorry.'

Toby turned on the stairs and went back into the private flat, shutting the door on her. It was the only way he knew to stop himself smashing her face against the wall.

Trish barely noticed the time as she ploughed on through her case notes that afternoon. Her room hardly ever had any daylight in it and so the gathering dark didn't impinge on her consciousness until she looked up and caught sight of her own reflection in the window.

The circle of light thrown by her Anglepoise reading lamp just fitted her neat dark head, white bony face, thin shoulders and long arms, balanced now either side of the neatly piled papers. Stretching her left arm only a fraction meant that the hand was in almost complete darkness.

It didn't matter that she'd spent longer in chambers than she'd meant because Nicky was in charge at home this evening. Trish stretched her aching neck and at last looked at her watch. It was after seven. No wonder her muscles were tight. She rubbed her hands through her hair, forgetting that she'd lost her spikes, and wiped her gritty eyes.

For some reason that reminded her of Paddy. Yet again he hadn't returned her call. She reached for the phone and automatically dialled his number without even thinking about it. This time he answered it himself.

'Paddy?' she said, fighting against the shock of his voice. 'It's me, Trish.'

'And how are you now?' he asked, his voice sounding scarily Irish. He only ever reverted to the lilting accent and intonations of his childhood when he had something to protect.

'I'm fine. Busy.'

'So what's new?'

'Nothing except work. Lots of it.' She smiled. There were some things the two of them didn't even have to explain. He would be quite as busy. They both used work as a life raft. 'I wondered if you'd come to any decision about David's play. It would be great to have you there, and you might enjoy it.'

'D'ye really think it's after being my kind of thing, Trish? I never went to your school to see you act, now did I?'

Don't I know it? she thought. But at least he was putting her and the boy in the same category, in however sidelong a way. 'No reason not to start now. It's a ticketed event. So you'll need to decide in advance.'

'Bella can't come. She has an important meeting. But I suppose I could, Trish.' Now his voice was as English as could be. 'Will that fat solicitor of yours be there?'

Did Paddy always have to bait her? He knew George's name perfectly well, and Trish had protested about the rude description of him often enough. In any case, he wasn't fat; just big. Or well padded. Still, tonight she wasn't going to rise.

'Unless some awful crisis comes up he will. OK, I'll get tickets for the three of us and I'll post you yours so that you can still get in, even if George and I are both held up.'

'What's the boy's part? If you might not be there, there's no point my going if I'm not to know which he is.'

'You'll know him,' Trish said, hearing herself sound as dry as the Sahara. 'But he's the policeman.'

'How suitable.'

Was there a desert even drier than the Sahara? Trish wondered. She wasn't sure that Paddy would honour this commitment, any more than he'd honoured the rest, but she hoped he would.

''Bye now, Trish. Take care of yourself.'

So, she thought: none of the old friendly suggestions of meeting for drinks or a meal. Still, we've made some progress.

She tidied up her desk and slung on her thick dark-grey overcoat. On her way out, she saw that Steve had left his cherished brass reading light on and went in to switch it off. On his blotter was an envelope marked with her name in Antony's writing. She reached over to take it and felt the strap of her shoulder bag slip.

The bag hit Steve's pen pot, scattering his innumerable pens and pencils all over his desk and the floor. Cursing, she put down the envelope and bag and grovelled under the desk to pick them up.

'I know you have to spend a lot of time sucking up to the clerks to get any decent work at all,' said Robert's voice from behind her. The shock made Trish's head jerk painfully against the bottom of the desk. 'But you don't have to go quite that far, do you?'

Trish snaked her way out from under the desk and stood up with as much dignity as a dusty front, messy hair and a handful of leaking pens allowed. There was an ominous cracking sound under one of her shoes, but she wasn't going to give ground by looking down.

'Hello, Robert,' she said, making herself sound casually surprised. 'You still here? It's not like you to work so hard. I thought a proper chap had to look as if his achievements were effortless.'

'Oh, bugger off,' he said, sounding more human than usual.

'Have a good evening.'

For a moment she thought he was going to offer to stay and help, but her partial victory over her father must have turned her brain. Robert smirked and left her to her tidying.

She was afraid she'd trodden on one of Steve's fountain pens in her rush to get upright, but the ugly sound had come only from the transparent plastic casing of a ballpoint, which was easily replaceable. She restored his desk to its usual order, gave his Churchillian brass reading lamp a propitiative stroke, then opened the envelope.

> Dear Trish,
> Henry and his wife are coming to the opera with us on 14 December. We have two spare tickets. Would you and George like to come, too? It's Covent Garden, Richard Strauss's *Daphne*. Very well reviewed.
>
> Antony

Outside she turned up her face to the drizzling rain and wondered just exactly what the invitation meant. Had Henry managed to persuade Antony that her refusal to go on working for him was reasonable? Or was this invitation another bribe to stop her asking any awkward questions about Toby Fullwell's sudden need to shift millions around, or Jean-Pierre Gregoire's for a mule?

The drizzle turned to a deluge. Hunching her chin down into the thick collar of her coat, she hurried home, wondering how much to tell George. He would probably want to accept the invitation if he knew about it. Unlike Trish, he genuinely liked opera, and he might also need a new big client if Jeremy Carfield did withdraw his business as he'd threatened. An opportunity for George to cosy up to Henry Buxford would be helpful. But could she bear to watch him doing it?

She shivered as rain slid down the back of her neck, finding its way between her shirt collar and her skin. It felt like icy little worms, insinuating themselves down her spine. This was definitely not a night for mooning over the view of St Paul's or congratulating herself for living in the centre of one of the most beautiful cities in the world.

Once, when she'd said as much to George, he told her not

to be so smug and to think instead of Venice, or even Oxford, and admit that London was a mishmash of ugliness punctuated by some quite nice parks and a few admirable buildings. She'd thrown a pillow at him.

Toby felt lonelier than ever. He couldn't stop thinking about Peter. The treacherous enemy who had caused all his torments and deserved his death had metamorphosed back into the matchless friend and fellow victim. Toby knew now that he could have saved Peter's life, as Peter had once saved his, if only Jo hadn't let them both down.

In fact, Peter had saved his life more than once. If it hadn't been for him, Toby would never have survived Cambridge long enough to go to Nepal.

He wished he could bring back a mental picture of Peter in those days. But he couldn't really remember anything properly now. His mind kept throwing up images of things that hadn't happened and people who had never existed. Sometimes he had only to shut his eyes now to see Peter on the bridge and himself with a gun in his hand, pointing it at Peter's head.

How could he have seen that if he hadn't been there?

And yet he knew he hadn't been. He hadn't even known that Peter was in England until Jo had described the man who'd rung the bell that appalling afternoon. And he'd never had a gun.

Or had he?

Toby hit his forehead hard with a closed fist, trying to make his mind work. Logic, reason and sequential thought shattered whenever he tried to take a grip of any of them. And every idea split into a million dangerous glittering shards before he could look at it properly.

There seemed to be lots of versions of himself, too, and he didn't know which was real and which was just a distorted reflection in one of the glass splinters. Was he the victim or the villain? Had he been the loathsome, lying, pathetic child of all those old accusations, ruining his mother's life and causing his father's death? Or he had tried as hard as he could to do what she wanted, be what she wanted, and put up with her rages as well as he could without crying too much?

Was he Ben Smithlock's dupe now, or had he somehow called up Ben, like a devil from the hell that was undoubtedly waiting for him when going on living became more frightening than killing himself.

'"To die",' he said aloud, remembering the endless performances of *Hamlet* he'd sat through for one radio arts programme or another. '"To die, perchance to dream." Oh, God forbid!'

He thought that if he could just get the Clouet story straight, and then sleep a night through, he might manage the rest. All he'd retrieved so far was a memory of one winter's afternoon in Cambridge, when he and Peter had been eating toasted Mother's Pride and Golden Syrup, of all peculiar things.

Peter had asked him why François Clouet seemed such a good artist to fake. And Toby had started sketching the kind of elegant but empty coloured chalk portrait Clouet had produced, explaining that people had been commenting on the lack of psychological insight in his work since it had first been produced. One papal nuncio had written in the 1570s about his reluctance to send the Pope any portrait with so little individuality.

Clouet had had a huge studio of craftsmen working for him. Anyone with any real talent for drawing could produce a convincing version, Toby had explained, if only he could acquire the right sort of paper and black and red chalk. The black wasn't charcoal, but a real chalk called carbonaceous shale and it had been found in France.

It was weird how even with his mind splintering on every idea it found, he could remember that: carbonaceous shale found in France. He said it again, like a mantra. Maybe it would straighten the splinters and bring them back together into a whole. Wasn't that what a mantra was supposed to do? Peter would know. He'd have learned that much in the ashram.

Peter had watched him draw that afternoon and admired him and told him there was no one like Toby Fullwell in the whole world, and that together they could beat the whole world, let alone Goode & Floore's.

So why had Peter given all that disastrous information to Ben?

That despairing question suddenly brought all the splinters together, and Toby's mind began to work again, digging an even bigger, more appalling pit. Had Ben been blackmailing Peter, too, and then had him killed because he'd decided to come clean? Or because he'd come to the end of his usefulness? Did they eventually kill everyone they'd forced into working for them?

Toby could see his own naked corpse toppling over the bridge into the Thames. The new fear made him feel as dirty and despicable as when he'd been shitting and sicking up his life at Peter's feet in Nepal.

The phone rang, releasing him for a moment. He looked at the mobile and saw Margaret's number on the small green screen.

Thank God! If he got her back, he might be able to fight the terror and Ben and his memories. Clicking the phone on, he told her he loved her before she could say anything. He heard her gasp, then sniffle a bit. They started to talk properly then, as they had in the old days before Ben had come crashing into their lives. Much later Margaret told him she'd called to remind him about Mer's school play.

'I hadn't forgotten,' he said. It was a lie, but how could anyone remember something like that in all this?

Chapter 21

Two days later, Toby stood once more in the doorway of Goode & Floore's great saleroom, looking round at the people who were already there and pitying them for their ignorance. Some of his panic was under control now. He had come to understand that if Peter had tried to talk to him about what was happening, then he had probably been talking to other people as well, and that must be why Ben had had him killed. It didn't necessarily mean he'd kill Toby, too.

Silence might not save him, but telling anyone what was going on would definitely be fatal. If he did exactly what Ben had demanded and then kept his mouth shut, he might have a chance.

He couldn't see either Henry Buxford or Ben's dark woman this time, and he couldn't feel any malign presence whatsoever. Glad of that much, he checked out his usual seat. It was still empty. That had to be a good omen, too.

Today there were fewer people in the room altogether, and a less dramatic atmosphere. It was even more of a help to see that the auctioneer wasn't Marcus Orgrave. There was a woman on the rostrum, whom Toby had never seen before. He settled back in his chair and waited for lot 65.

Ben appeared just as lot 62 was being knocked down for a respectable enough three hundred thousand pounds. Toby tried to ignore him, but it was all he could do to control his urge to vomit. Ben positioned himself on the other side of the aisle, three rows ahead. Toby jammed the nails of one hand into the palm of the other and fought to swallow the acrid saliva that kept pumping into his mouth.

'Here we have a particularly fine portrait by Gerrit van Honthorst. Unrestored and yet in surprisingly good condition, it would represent a major acquisition for any institution or private collector. Who will start the bidding at five hundred thousand pounds?'

Terrified he was going to throw up, Toby made his bids. When the painting was knocked down at last, he got up, not surprised to hear his knees crack. It always happened when he'd been tense.

It was so long since he'd bid successfully for anything that he'd almost forgotten the drill. But he'd have to go down to the office now to settle up and arrange for one of the specialist art moving firms to bring the painting to the gallery. Then he would have to put it in the darkest corner of the storeroom and pray that no one, particularly Henry Buxford, would ever ask why he hadn't exhibited it.

'Well done.' Ben was right behind him, so close that Toby could feel Ben's breath on his neck. 'You're nearly there now.'

He didn't turn or acknowledge the remark in any way. As soon as he felt Ben leave him, he signed the cheque for the cashier and smiled at her as he handed it over. Turning at last, he saw no sign of Ben and headed in relief for the open air.

He thought he might walk back to Southwark this time. He could do with the exercise, and it might help remind him he was a free man.

There ought to be plenty of time to get home, grab a cheese sandwich and perhaps even a glass of wine, before changing to go to the boys' school. That would make a fitting celebration. And after the play, he'd bring his family home. Maybe, after all, life could begin again.

* * *

Trish realized she would be in danger of being late for the play if she didn't get a move on soon and exhorted herself to hurry up in a loud voice. Naturally Robert happened to be passing at exactly that moment.

'I know, Robert,' she said. 'I know. It's the first sign of madness. Still, at least I'm not looking for hairy palms.'

He was so surprised that she thought of explaining the very mild joke, then decided against it. There wasn't time. She nipped into the loo before she left chambers and took a few extra minutes to ensure that the edges of her dark hair were sharp and there were no smudges on her face. She'd once been in court with a large dark-grey stripe down one cheek, where she'd rested her face on a hand that was grimed with newsprint. No one had bothered to tell her, but she'd noticed amusement on the faces of everyone around her, including the judge, and wondered why. Today all seemed fine. She added some mascara and a slick of lipgloss and left it at that.

Some of the Blackfriars Prep mothers would be wearing the latest Prada creations, with one or two shining in Escada glamour, but most would have rushed from work and be dressed in dark-grey, black or navy suits like hers.

All the effort on her hair was wasted because it started raining two minutes after she left the building, and she had no umbrella. Halfway to the school already, she thought there was no point going back to beg a brolly off one of the clerks, and so she ran, splashing the puddles up her legs, and arrived with dripping hair and face.

The first person she saw was Paddy, looking uncharacteristically nervous as he hovered outside the school hall, pretending to examine the notice board.

'Hi,' Trish said, casually laying a hand on his back. He flinched. Turning to see who had touched him, he glared at her.

'And I thought you were concerned about my heart, Trish. What are you doing, giving me a shock like that? And why are you looking like something the cat brought in?'

'Sorry, Paddy. It's only the rain. How are you?'

'I don't know.'

'Don't worry about it.' She understood exactly what he meant and was encouraged by the lack of the jokes and Irish accent. 'He's a nice child.'

'So you said. Shall we go in or are we waiting for your fat solicitor?' Trish didn't think she had registered her instinctive protest, but her expression must have changed because Paddy went on: 'Ah, come on now, Trish. 'Tis only like calling him the Fat Controller. Do you not remember how we used to read those train books together when you were little?'

'I remember,' she said, tucking her hand into his arm. She wanted to tell him he'd been a good father to her then, but the words wouldn't come. All she could manage was: 'It was fun.'

'Wasn't it?'

'I haven't thought of *Thomas the Tank Engine* for years. It's a pity David's too old for stories like that.'

'D'you mean you still have the books, Trish?' It was so unlike Paddy to ask directly for reassurance that she gave it to him at once.

'Of course. I couldn't have got rid of them. Or *Sam Trolley*. Do you remember that one? It was about a fireman with his horse-drawn fire engine?'

'I do. Look, there's your George.'

Trish squeezed Paddy's arm before letting go to wave.

'Jess is here,' George said. 'I met her outside, parking the car. She said Caro is tied up but still hoping she might make it before the end of the play. Even if she doesn't, David should have a pretty good showing. I know Nicky's planning to come. How are you, Paddy?'

'Fine. Why don't you and I go in and see if Nicky's inside while Trish waits for Jess?'

Toby couldn't believe it. The dark woman was here, still dogging him, and now actually in his sons' school. Ben had promised he would be free after he'd bought the Honthorst this morning. Like every sucker in the world, Toby had believed what he wanted to believe. Now he knew better. His hands curled into claws as he thought about what he'd like to do to the woman. And her brat.

She was thin and quite fragile looking. It would be easy to lure her on to one of the bridges after dark and just tip her over. But then she'd probably be undrownable, like any medieval witch. She'd need concrete boots or a bullet in the brain like Peter's to keep her underwater long enough to kill her. And he wasn't equipped to give her either. Still, he could probably break her neck. Fantasizing about it, seeing her white face bloated and discoloured with the gasses that would distend her drowned body and eventually force it up to the surface, helped to contain his loathing. For now, anyway.

Trish could feel Paddy's nervousness as she sat down next to him. He was almost quivering with it. Maybe that wasn't so surprising. After all, this would be his first sight of his son.

'He's not in the first scene,' she whispered as the curtain went up, hoping to help Paddy relax. He didn't answer.

She waited for the appearance of Mer Fullwell as the tramp and was surprised by his confident acting. He still had one arm in a sling, and he looked very pale, in spite of the greasy stage make-up someone had applied to his thin face.

Nothing she had heard about him had made her think he'd be capable of doing his stuff in front of a hundred-strong audience like this. But he could have been alone in the big room for all the embarrassment he showed. He knocked at the door of the banker's mansion, which was economically suggested by a porticoed doorway painted on wavering canvas.

The boy who answered it and sent him on his way spoke his lines fluently enough, but like the child he was. Mer, on the other hand, had got fully into the skin of his part. Trish wondered whether that came only from skill or whether he had experienced the aching need he was portraying. As the curtain came down, and the audience clapped with encouraging vigour, Trish looked round for Margaret.

There was no sign of her, but Toby was there, only three rows behind Trish's party. He caught her eye and sent her a look of such hatred that she jerked round in her seat.

'What's the matter, Trish?' Paddy asked, sounding worried.

'Nothing,' she muttered. 'Here we go.'

Mer was back, looking even more abject than before, knocking at a plain blue door. It opened inwards. A light came on and David appeared, with a real dog at his side. He'd told Trish that Mr Mills, the art teacher, was going to bring in his golden retriever and they'd try to use it, but that if it barked too much or widdled on the stage it would have to be taken out.

The dog seemed happy. David kept one hand gripped round the lead, waving the other in the familiar over-stiff gesture. But once he started to speak his lines, he settled into the part. Trish relaxed as the well-known words rang out.

'You don't have to mouth them, do you?' Paddy muttered, making her realize what she was doing. 'The boy can't see you from here. And it makes you look ridiculous.'

Trish grinned at him, understanding the anxieties behind his irritated embarrassment. After a moment he nodded and smiled back. At the end of the scene, he said:

'You're right. I would have known him anywhere. He looks like the both of us.'

'Isn't he brilliant?' said Nicky, leaning forwards at the far end of the row.

'Thanks to you and all those rehearsals at home,' Trish answered, still not sure how to deal with her father's unusual vulnerability. 'Paddy, did I tell you there's to be tea and buns backstage for the cast and parents?'

'You know you didn't.'

'I meant to. Will you stay for it?'

'So long as you don't introduce me in any embarrassing way.'

'Just Paddy Maguire?'

'Just that.'

Later she was concentrating so hard on the best way of effecting the meeting between David and his father that she didn't focus on any of the other parents jostling their way towards the queue for the tea table.

'Ben promised today would be the end of it, so what the fuck are you doing here, you bitch?' Toby whispered from behind her, spitting out the words so viciously that she could feel flecks of his saliva on the back of her neck.

She looked round and saw that he was standing less than a foot away. His face was contorted and he was shaking. Everyone else shuffled backwards, giving them room.

'I beg your pardon?' Trish said in tones that meant what the hell do you think you're doing?

His eyes were bulging and his face grew even more red. 'I've seen you following me, day after day, but I never dreamed you'd have the cheek to force your way in here, too.'

'Don't be ridiculous,' Trish said, facing forwards again and moving nearer the tea table.

He grabbed her wrist and forced her arm up behind her back in a half-nelson. Trying to look back again, she found the constraint meant she couldn't turn her head far enough to see his face. Was this how he'd broken Mer's arm?

'Let me go!' she said, horrified to realize what she'd risked by getting involved with Buxford and his sodding godson.

Somehow she had to get Toby off her before David saw what was happening and panicked.

'Only when you promise to keep out of my way,' Toby hissed. She could feel more of his spittle. He pushed her arm higher up her back and made her gasp. 'Promise.'

'Don't be ridiculous!' An agonizing pain shot from her upper arm, right across her back and through her neck, as he wrenched it higher still.

'Promise, bitch!'

'Stop it!' shrieked a child.

Trish had a confused view of David rushing past her. She forced her head as far as she could and caught sight of him dragging at Toby's arm. His head was pressed against Toby's hand for a second before Trish felt his grip on her wrist let go.

'The little shit's bitten me,' Toby yelled and slapped the boy so hard across the face that he sprawled on the floor. Trish grabbed David, hauled him up and put him behind her, wincing as her wrenched arm jagged again. Standing face to face with Toby, she said very clearly:

'Keep back. If you don't back off now, I'll—'

'What's going on?' George said, shouldering his way through the crowd. 'Are you all right, Trish?'

'No,' she said loudly, before explaining what had happened. 'Will you sort this man out while I see to David?'

'Of course. Paddy's here, too. We'll deal with this.'

Toby took two steps back as the two tall men closed in on him. Trish could hear David whimpering behind her and turned to take him in her arms. As she hugged him with her good arm, she felt his heart battering and his hands clutching at her back.

'You can take him into my study,' said a cool voice behind Trish. A second later, Hester More stood in front of her. 'He'll be happier out of this crowd.'

More shaken than she'd ever felt in her life, hating the avid and embarrassed faces all round, Trish urged her brother out of the room, keeping her arm round his shoulders. His face was still jammed into her side and she could feel his lips moving, even through her jacket. Hester unlocked the door of a small room, which was furnished simply with a desk and chair and a soft-looking sofa. Trish gently pushed the child down on it.

'Don't make me go,' he was saying with his eyes tightly closed. 'Don't make me go. Don't make me go. Don't make me go.'

Her heart breaking, Trish put her hands on his head, lifting it so that he could see her face. But he kept his eyes tightly shut. Fat, glistening tears were forced out between his sticky lashes. Making her voice as firm and sure as it had ever been, she said very clearly: 'I'll never make you go. You're safe.'

His eyes flew open. 'But *you're* not. He hurt you. And he said he'd do it again, and I can't stop it, Trish.' His eyes screwed up and he started sobbing as he panted out his worst fear. 'I can't stop him hurting you if you make me go.'

At last she knew exactly where he was now and had been all along. She thought of the old adage that you should beware of what you ask for because you never know in what form it will come. She'd wanted David to shed his shell so that she could get at the hurts and fears she knew he must be hiding. But she'd never wanted it to happen like this, pushing him even further back into a hell in which he felt responsible for his mother's death.

Kneeling in front of him, she wondered whether any words would reach him, and chose the simplest she could find.

'David,' she said very gently at last, 'I will never send you away. But you don't have to protect me. There are grown-ups who will do that.'

He was still crying, and Trish could see that all his energies were needed for the fight to control himself. She hoped the gentleness of her voice would have got through to him, even if he hadn't understood a single word she'd said.

He hiccuped every so often as he battled down the tears. Her attempts to comfort him seemed to be making the process harder, so she kept quiet, waiting for him to open his eyes again.

There was a knock at the door. Trish took her hands from his knees and pushed herself up off the floor. Opening the door, she saw Hester More, holding a tray of tea, milk and miniature doughnuts.

'There's no need for either of you to come out until you want to,' she said in a deliberately ordinary voice. 'Everyone's fine out there, and Mr Fullwell has asked me to say that he made a dreadful mistake. He seems to have thought you were someone else, someone who's been stalking him. He hadn't realized you are David's sister and were here only to watch the play. He asked me to pass on his deepest apologies.'

'Thank you,' Trish said, opening the door more widely. 'Did you hear that? Mrs More says it was a case of mistaken identity. Just as I thought. There's nothing to worry about now.'

David looked up from under his sodden lashes. The tears had glued them into clumps as spiky as her hair had once been. 'I'm sorry, Mrs More. I didn't mean to make a scene.' He sobbed once more, and fought for control as his hands twisted round and round each other. 'I'm really sorry.'

'That's fine,' the Head said casually, as though the episode had been no more important than a lost textbook. 'Here's your milk. Have some of that and a doughnut. They're very good.'

When she had gone, he put down the doughnut he had taken.

'I can't eat anything,' he said as his eyes filled up with tears again. 'My throat's shut itself up again at the top.'

'That's fine,' Trish said, finding the description all too recognizable. 'Don't worry about it. Would you like to go home now? George has the car outside, so we can nip out as soon as you want.'

'Can I wash my face first?'

'Of course. Where's the nearest loo?'

'Mrs More has one through there,' he said, pointing to a door on the other side of the room. 'She lets us use it if we need to when we're talking to her.'

'Fine. I'll go and find George, and we'll come back to pick you up.'

He nodded. She went back into the hall, a little self-conscious and very aware of what he would feel when he had to face people again. George was easy to spot, standing with Paddy, apparently chatting happily to a group of parents who were completely unknown to Trish. She was about to join them, when she felt a hand on her arm.

Turning sharply, she saw Margaret Fullwell, who was breathing as though she'd been running. Her eyes had a bruised look about them, and the skin of her lower lip was broken where she'd bitten through it. A crust of dried blood circled the gash.

'I saw you,' she said, 'when I was taking the boys to the car, so I sent them on. I had to come back and make sure you're all right. You and your brother. I'm sorry about what Toby did. So, so sorry.'

'Please, Margaret; it's not your fault.'

'I thought it was only me Toby was capable of hurting. I never dreamed he'd do it to anyone else. I'm so sorry. I think he really has gone mad, just as his secretary keeps telling me,' Margaret said, her left hand covering her mouth. Above it, her eyes pleaded with Trish for a moment before she turned away.

David must be ready by now, Trish thought, wishing she'd been able to say something that might have comforted Margaret. She caught George's eye and beckoned. He said something to the group around him and came over to her.

'How is he?'

'Dealing with it. I left in him in the Head's bathroom, washing his face. I think we ought to take him home now. Could you collect Nicky and explain to the others? I don't think this is the moment to introduce Paddy into his life, do you?'

'No. And Paddy will understand, but I know he wants to say something to you. Why don't I drive David and Nicky home, and give you a chance to talk?'

Trish nodded and left him, while she went to thank her father for his instinctive help. He kissed her, which was a surprise, and his voice was completely English as he said:

'I was glad to be here. It was little enough to do for you or the boy. Trish, now's not the time, but later, when he's over this, will you let me see him?'

Let you? she thought. When I've been trying to persuade you to do just that for nearly a year?

'You know I will.'

'OK. On your way now,' Paddy said. 'David will need you.'

So something good's come out of this, she thought, rubbing her sore arm as she went in search of her coat. And maybe now that he's been forced to let go, he'll learn to be less frightened by everything he's been keeping so tightly controlled.

Chapter 22

Toby had apologized so much that his throat felt raw. Margaret had told him he'd gone mad. Was she right? Had it happened now, as he'd been afraid it might for so long? It must have. How else could he have mistaken Mer's friend's sister for the satanic woman who'd been dogging him wherever he went? Could it be that the relief of being free of his blackmailers had sent him crashing through the last safeguards of sanity?

Trying to believe in the freedom, trying to breathe carefully and remember that he was once more an ordinary, law-abiding member of the civilized classes, Toby made his way through the diminishing crowd of parents. They were probably all sniggering at him. He was tempted to go without waiting to collect his coat, but he couldn't bear the thought of his own cowardice.

From now on, he would be a different man. He would not give in to pressure from outsiders or his own nightmares. He would remember who he was and behave accordingly. And one day Margaret would come home. He'd show her that he was the same man she had loved when they married and not some mad molester of strange women. He would get her back.

Mrs More came into sight again. Toby tried to smile. She nodded briefly enough to show him that he was of no more importance than a stray woodlouse. He identified his overcoat among all the other good navy wool versions by the scarlet scarf hanging out of the pocket and put on both. It was a struggle to persuade the young games teacher who was running the cloakroom that he'd also left an umbrella, which must be somewhere behind the counter.

'It's an old-fashioned City umbrella,' he said as patiently as he could. 'Tightly rolled, black, with a malacca handle and a gold band round it with my initials: TTF.'

'Oh, that one,' said the young man, apparently holding down laughter with difficulty. Toby had no idea what was so funny about his umbrella. 'Why didn't you say so before? I put it up on this shelf to make sure no one nicked it. Here.'

'Thank you,' Toby said, wondering whether he was supposed to tip the teacher as he would a proper cloakroom attendant. Oh, what did it matter? He couldn't be bothered with anything so trivial.

Outside he was met with a wall of thick, acrid fog, which made him cough. He hadn't seen anything like it since childhood. A boat hooted on the river, sounding like a wounded animal pleading with its mate to bring it some sustenance. Car engines throbbed much closer, and a man swore viciously as he tripped. All the sounds were exaggerated and distorted, and the street lights turned the filthy fog pale green.

'Sorry,' someone muttered ahead of him, then: 'Sod it.'

Toby almost fell, too, as his foot caught on something. Then he found he couldn't move forwards. Someone was pulling at his coat. All the rage that had made him hit that boy flooded up again and he flung himself round to confront his attacker. There was no one there. Ghosts of madness danced round him again, until he realized he still couldn't move forwards. At last he saw that his coat had caught in the wheel of a bicycle chained to one of the lampposts.

'Irresponsible fool!' he muttered to the bike's absent owner, as he bent to free the cloth. It ripped against a broken spoke. Toby nearly cried as he thought of the price of the coat and his pathetic salary, and how unfair it was that he had to pig away on starvation wages when everyone else around him – even that scrawny woman he'd mistaken for one of Ben's watchers – looked so sodding rich. He kicked the bicycle and heard it clang down on to the pavement. Serve its irresponsible owner right.

He was alone in the fog, just as he was alone in his misery. Margaret had abandoned him again. Another boat hooted, and a lorry crashed by, two inches from his nose. He might have been killed.

Here was the pedestrian crossing. He pressed the button for the lights to change, hoping that any more lorries would at least be able to see the red globes against the fog, even if they hadn't seen his red scarf. At last the green man lit up on the far side of the road. If he could see that, the cars must be able to see their traffic lights. He crossed over as fast as he could, huddling his cold chin into the scarf. Margaret had given it to him last Christmas, when she still cared whether he was warm enough or not.

Turning into Baynard Street, which would lead him down to Upper Thames Street and the quickest way home, he thought he heard footsteps behind him. If that bloody woman was after him again, he thought, even if she had nothing to do with Ben, he wouldn't be able to control himself. He stopped to listen more carefully. Yes, there were steps, but they weren't a woman's and they weren't coming from behind him. That was all right. Only in *Alice Through the Looking Glass* could someone follow you from a place you hadn't yet reached.

Light-headed in relief, he breathed carefully and thought he might, after all, be able to deal with all this. It occurred to him at last that Trish Maguire and his dark-haired Nemesis could be the same woman. If Trish Maguire had been taking her brother to school, there was no reason why she might not have been talking to Margaret, or walking about the streets round here. The stalking might have been no more than a product of his own fears, nothing whatever to do with Ben. What a fool he'd been!

The footsteps were coming closer. They were definitely heavier than any tall thin woman's would be. Suddenly a new fear rose out of the swirling fog as a purring, powerful car swished past him. This was just the kind of weather for muggers. He touched the breast of his overcoat, feeling through the soft material to the solidity of his wallet in the inside pocket of his suit.

He could always hand over his mobile if he had to. That was in his right outer pocket. It would be a pain to lose it, but not a disaster. It rang suddenly, betraying its presence and his. He moved back against the high concrete wall, just before the turning into Upper Thames Street.

The fog seemed protective now. No one would be able to see him, pressed against the wall like this. He put the phone to his ear and gave his name as quietly as he could.

The footsteps ahead had stopped, as though their owner was listening. There was a high pile of something covered in thick blue plastic sheeting beside Toby. It looked like a tumulus. He wondered whether anyone had ever dumped a body in a builder's storage heap.

'Toby?' said Ben's voice over the phone. 'That is you against the wall, isn't it? I can't see properly in all this damn fog.'

'Who is this?'

'It's Ben, as you very well know.'

Toby peered through the fog and saw a tall shadow materializing as it grew closer, beckoning. This was definitely Mer's giant and his own nightmare. He didn't need the phone now and stuffed it back in his pocket as he walked down towards the concrete-lined underpass.

Ben put away his own phone. 'What are you playing at?' He sounded colder and more cruel than ever. 'Did you think you could hide in the school? Or were you trying in your usual pathetic way to protect your sons? You won't be able to, you know. We can get to them whenever we want.'

'But you said they'd be safe and I'd be free after I'd bought the painting today. I did it. I did everything you wanted, and I haven't told anyone. Not even about Mer's arm.'

'That's good. But it's not enough. You haven't quite earned your freedom yet.'

'I am not going to buy any more of your fakes. You can do whatever you want to me, but I'm not going to. And if you hurt one of my boys again, I will kill you myself.'

'Don't make me laugh. You couldn't kill a bluebottle. But don't worry, I'm not going to ask you to buy any more pictures. No one in his right mind would let you do that again after the spectacle you made of yourself today. But there is one more thing you have to do for us.'

'I can't do any more for you.'

'I think you'll find you can, when you consider the alternative. Mer screaming on the floor as we take a hammer to his knees.'

'You bastard! I've done everything you asked to establish your boss as a serious collector and your fucking fakes as the real thing,' Toby said, understanding at last that he would never be free. He could see this scene endlessly repeating itself down the years, with Ben promising him freedom after one more small, illegal job.

'God, you are naïve! And stupid. You haven't been buying and selling fakes. At least you may have, but that wasn't the point. You've been helping us move our money around so that it's untraceable. But never mind that now. Your next exercise is to think of someone else like you, with a dirty little secret to protect. That's how we got on to you, you know. Your mate Peter didn't want to tell us anything, but in the end even he cracked.'

'Peter?'

'Peter Chanting. Your partner in the Clouet scam.' Ben peered into Toby's face, as though the fog had thickened so much he couldn't see what was only centimetres from his eyes. 'You didn't know he'd shopped you? How did you think we got on to you?'

'I—' Toby began to cry.

'There's no need for that. He won't be troubling you again, after all.'

'Did you kill him?'

'Of course.' Ben moved further away from the road, into a doorway plastered with notices. Only as they got close to it, did Toby manage to read the warning not to obstruct it. He hadn't realized fog could fill up a tunnel like this. He couldn't see the wall on the far side of the road, and the cars that passed were just vague roaring lumps in the murk. Even their headlights couldn't penetrate the grey-green blur all round.

'Why?'

'He'd started to talk. So take it as a warning of what will happen to you if you ever tell anyone what you've done for us.'

'You bastard!' The thought of all the weeks he'd spent hating Peter made Toby feel as guilty as if he'd fired the gun himself.

'There's no need to be so emotional,' said Ben. 'The sooner you give me the information I need, the sooner you'll be left alone. In your line of work, you must know someone with secrets to hide.'

'Of course I don't.'

'It's surprising how many influential people have them: it could be a fraud like yours, or some tasty little sexual oddity, or even an unexplained death. An amazing number of people seem to have helped friends or family to die. And euthanasia is still illegal, so that would do as well as anything else. All you've got to do is give me the story and the name and address. Once we've checked it out and found it works, you'll be on your own again, free to do whatever you want. Except talk about this, of course. And you know now what'll happen if you do that.'

Toby felt his mouth opening and closing, but he couldn't squeeze any sound out of his larynx, until Ben's laughter freed the blockage.

'I wouldn't put my worst enemy through what I've had to bear,' Toby said very clearly.

'I think you'll find you can. Your Peter said much the same at the start after we'd leaned on him with his false names and his Shatoosh smuggling and his tax avoidance. But in the end he was happy enough to hand you over so that he could protect his old father. Think of your sons, Toby. Mer fainted when his arm was broken, you know, so he didn't feel as much as we'd meant. Next time we'll bring smelling salts to make sure he's conscious throughout.'

Toby's stomach lurched, as though he'd dropped fifty floors in an express lift. The rush-hour cars throbbed on through the fog, their peering drivers unaware that Toby's whole life was up for grabs.

Ben was laughing again. He came closer and patted Toby's shoulder.

'Don't touch me.'

'Have it your own way.' Ben let his hand drop to his side again. 'But let's get out of this tunnel. Fog like this could kill us both.'

And the sooner the better, Toby thought as memories of the last few weeks burst into his brain. All that suffering for this shit of a man? All that unjust hatred of his dearest friend?

'Are you telling me that you've done this to lots of people? More than Peter and me? Just so that you can clean up some dirty money? It's drug money, I suppose. You really are the lowest kind of filth.'

'Come on, Toby, it's only business.'

Almost before he'd thought, Toby had reversed the umbrella he'd been holding. He could remember every detail of his father's stories of the ex-Shanghai policeman who'd once told him how to deal with an attack in the street. His father could have been reciting the instructions into his ear.

'You just push the ferrule up through the chin. It punctures the soft palate without any great force and destroys the brain. Quickest, easiest way to kill anyone in secret, my boy.'

'Toby?' There was surprise in Ben's confident voice, but no fear. Not yet.

Cars were moving four or five feet behind him, but only their lights were visible, like huge boiled sweets melting into the fog.

Toby knew the two of them must be invisible to everyone in the cars. Ben leaned forwards as though to see Toby more clearly. The position was perfect. His chin was stretched forwards, quite unprotected.

This is for Mer, and Margaret, Toby thought as he shoved the umbrella upwards with all his strength. And for Peter. And this one is for me. He twisted the umbrella.

Ben coughed. Toby twisted the umbrella once more, feeling the power of it under his hands, and then pulled it clear, stepping smartly sideways as blood spurted out from Ben's punctured chin.

He must be dead by now, Toby thought, watching the body crumple downwards on to its knees, then face forwards into the blood and dirt. Still the cars growled by. No one stopped. There were no cries, no shrieking brakes, no sirens. He waited a little longer, then wiped the ferrule on Ben's coat so that nothing would drip from it and walked away, looking at his feet in case of any CCTV camera that might just happen to be loaded with film. He didn't think there were any in this part of the tunnel, although there was one at the Puddle Dock end, but he wasn't going to look up to check.

There might be one at the Southwark end, too, he thought and wheeled left to walk back up Baynard Street. There definitely wasn't one there. It meant a slightly longer walk home, but a safer one in the circumstances. And if there were a camera or two in Queen Victoria Street it would be no bad thing to be seen, looking ordinary on his way back home from his sons' school play.

He was surprised to realize that he felt no disgust, no terror and no distress. There was just a vast freedom, as though he'd launched off some rocks to swim in a gloriously empty warm sea.

How could I ever have been so frightened of him? Toby wondered, remembering the days when the sound of Ben's voice had sent him scurrying to the basement to hide.

There'll be time for that later, he told himself.

He knew he must be practical now. There would probably be some of Ben's blood on him, even if he couldn't see it, and he'd have to make sure it didn't betray him. Forensic scientists could find the tiniest traces these days.

He thought of the soles of his shoes, too, as he walked with confident steps towards Mansion House. But he was sure he hadn't trodden in any of the blood, so he couldn't be leaving a trail that way. And he was carrying the umbrella straight out in front of him, holding it by the middle of the shaft so that the ferrule couldn't trail any of Ben's blood or brains on to the pavement if there were any traces he hadn't managed to wipe off. No splatters on his coat would be visible in this weather, so long as he kept away from the street lights and away from the cars.

For the first time in weeks, Toby was glad to know there'd be no one at home. He'd be able to burn everything that might be contaminated with Ben's bodily fluids. He wouldn't be caught out by forensic scientists finding blood splatters on any of his clothes. Of course, the clothes would have to wait until he'd dealt with the umbrella. Obviously that had to go first.

He thought of Peter's voice in the old days telling him that whatever anyone suspected, they couldn't touch him without proof or a confession. Good memories of Peter would see him through this, just as the man himself had seen him through the original fear of discovery, and through the amoebic dysentery. Peter was, and always would be now, his friend.

Toby lifted the umbrella a little further up, to look affectionately at the ferrule. Who would have thought something so ordinary could have been such a life saver? He thought even more affectionately of his father who had given him this most priceless piece of information. It made up for a lot that he hadn't been able to give.

Now, at last, Toby had crossed the line from victimhood

to power. The world would be a better place without Ben. Cleaner, too.

Toby had reached the steps up to Southwark Bridge. He paused again, waiting to make sure no one was following him. For the first time he realized that Ben might have brought someone else to watch his back at the rendezvous he must have planned in the tunnel this evening.

There were no sounds of pursuit and when Toby turned casually, looking first at the pavement as though he'd dropped something, he checked the street and saw no sign of anyone either. Perhaps Ben's contempt had been such that he'd never realized he'd need a bodyguard for a meeting with the despised Toby Fullwell. Even if he had, there wasn't much any of them could do now. Ben was dead and, criminals themselves, his friends could hardly demand help from the police.

Reaching home at last, Toby almost skipped up the first few steps. He could have been alone in the fog, he thought as he took his time finding his front-door keys, and he liked it now.

There were no more ships to be heard on the river. Even the cars seemed to be avoiding the bridge tonight. His keys clattered against the phone in his pocket as he pulled them out. Opening the door and punching in the alarm code was automatic; he didn't even have to turn on the hall light to do it. He walked up the dark staircase to his office on the first floor at the back.

There was an open fireplace there with a working chimney, the only one that was ever used. Smoke in any of the other parts of the gallery might have damaged the paintings, and open fires would have been much too boring for Margaret to have to clean in the flat.

The insurance company hadn't liked the idea of even this hearth being used in such a building and quoted a vast extra premium because of it. Toby had managed to persuade the trustees that it was necessary to have actual flames, as a way of welcoming important visitors and showing them what the house would have been like in its heyday. He'd negotiated a small discount with the insurers to save his face and then had the most beautiful chain-mail curtains made to draw across the whole fireplace whenever the room was to be left unattended while the fire was burning.

Up in the office, he turned on the overhead light and took off all his clothes, leaving them in a heap on the tiled hearth. The shutters were already properly secured so he didn't have to worry about any of the neighbours looking in. He was surprised to find himself so calm. He hadn't felt as well as this for months. His mind was clear, and he knew exactly what he had to do.

There was a small radio on the desk. He turned it on to Radio 4 and was gratified to hear *The Archers*. He hadn't realized how late it was. Nigel and Elizabeth were having another tense marital spat, which made him feel better, too. Nothing in the world had changed outside the circle of his relationship to Ben, and no one would have any idea what had happened. Life – for everyone except Ben, of course – would go on just as it always had.

Toby built his fire in the grate as meticulously as he knew how, until real flames were flickering up around the nasty smokeless briquettes. That made him think of the neighbours and wonder whether they would notice illicit smoke billowing out of his chimneys. Not in the fog, surely. But just in case someone did see and wondered, it might be a good idea to burn some wood.

Even under the clean air act, you were allowed to burn household waste, he thought. And there was an old tea chest downstairs. Tinder dry, it would make the fire burn even more effectively and if anyone ever came asking questions about the smoke, he could show them the metal sides and screws of the tea chest.

Cracking up the tea chest was good fun. First the paper lining went on the fire, scattering the last few tea leaves it had once protected. They'd be useful evidence, too, if anyone ever came looking for clues here. He dismantled the metal sides and then broke up the thin, inflammable wood panels. Once they were properly alight they generated plenty of heat, so he hardly noticed that he was naked.

'Hardly,' he said aloud, chortling, 'or barely.'

Now that the fire was burning merrily, he began to dismantle the umbrella. This would be a long job, he knew, but it was important to do it properly. He fetched a small pair of very sharp scissors from the pencil pot on the desk and snipped the stitching that held the black nylon material round each spoke. Underneath the material, he found the join between the dull black spokes themselves and their shiny caps. They weren't at all difficult to pull apart. He put the rounded gleaming ends in a new envelope with no betraying address written on it. The sharp spokes themselves would go into a John Lewis plastic bag, which also bore no personal identification.

Opening the umbrella to dismantle the mechanism that lifted the spokes gave him a pang of old-style angst. It was supposed to be unlucky to have an open umbrella indoors. Then he chuckled again, amazed at the toughness of his new self.

Toby tried to remember that he had just killed Ben, that a once-breathing, talking, living man was dead in a pool of blood because of him, but it didn't mean anything more than confirmation of his own strength.

Maybe Margaret *was* right and he had gone mad. If so, he couldn't think why he'd fought so hard against the idea for so long. This was great. If this were madness, then give him madness every time. Ben Smithlock had not deserved to live. That was all there was to it. Who was it who'd said that 'moral is what you feel good after'? Hemingway, could it have been? Toby couldn't remember, but it didn't matter.

The Archers had moaned and comforted each other into silence, to be replaced by Mark Lawson and *Front Row*. It was ages since the producers had asked Toby on to *Front Row*.

Somehow, subtly, he'd have to remind them of his existence without looking as though he was begging for work. It would never do for the powerful player he'd discovered beneath his anxieties to beg.

Now the umbrella was almost dismantled. The spokes lay neatly in their bag. He'd have to think of the best place to 'lose' them. He was left with the brass ferrule and the cup-like piece that had held the nylon in place, along with the gold band with his betraying initials. That had probably better go straight into the river. Even if the river police ever dragged the bottom for evidence, they weren't likely to come up with something as small as that, or know what it was if they did. After all, they sometimes turned up whole bodies they could never identify.

The fire was still burning nicely. He put the wooden shaft of the umbrella across his knees to break it. It wouldn't move. All he got from his efforts was a bruise. Still, he thought he looked rather wonderful in the flickering firelight, half kneeling like someone's statue of Vulcan. He'd never noticed how dark and thickly curling his pubic hair looked. Somewhere in the house, there must be a hacksaw. Even a pair of heavy pruning shears might do it. In the meantime, he'd better start burning the clothes so as not to waste the fire's heat.

Margaret's dressmaking shears were sharp and heavy enough to deal easily with the overcoat, but he was surprised at how many layers of different sorts of linings and waddings there were. Fine in a handmade coat, he thought, but not in something off the peg like this. No wonder it had cost such a fortune.

It took a long time to get the whole lot burned and he didn't like to leave the fire to search for a hacksaw. While the coat was burning, he slit up the two pieces of his suit, his shirt, socks and underpants, adding small heaps of the resulting scraps whenever flames managed to get through the mass of overcoat pieces. He should have fed them in more slowly, he realized. But at last the flames began to take control back from the fabric pieces.

No wonder they'd always talked of fire as purifying. It was doing a grand job tonight. He'd have to think what to do with the ash, of course, but getting rid of that somewhere no one would ever link with him shouldn't be beyond his new capabilities.

At last the scraps were all on the fire. The final few were still smouldering, so he drew the iron mesh curtains in front of the grate and went to find his hacksaw. Someone rang the front-door bell as he was halfway down the stairs. He hoped it would be one of the innumerable charity collectors, or perhaps a canvasser rather than someone like Henry. The bell rang again, followed by the sharp, imperious crack of the knocker.

Oh, shit, he thought as he hovered naked, covered in smuts, and indecisive on the stairs. What if they lifted the letter-box flap to peer inside the house? Could they see him from here? For a second he felt some of the old panic returning, then remembered the rules of vision and perspective. No one was going to be able to look up the stairs through a flap as low in the front door as his. One more ring sounded, then silence, then at last the flap of the letter box. He watched a small piece of white paper fluttering down and heard retreating footsteps.

'The smoke,' he muttered. 'Could he have seen the smoke?'

Even if he had, whoever 'he' was, he might think it came from the boiler. As soon as Toby was sure there was no one ready to whip up the flap just as he was bending down to collect the note, he went to see what it was.

There was no envelope. He didn't pick it up because he wasn't sure when he planned to be known to be back in the house. But it was easy to see it was from Henry. Toby would have known those emphatic, confident black letters anywhere. On the side that lay uppermost, he could read:

'. . . and she's worried, Toby. She asked me to come and talk to you. She said you assaulted Trish Maguire at the school play. I know Trish well, Toby, so you have embarrassed me as well as Margaret. What has been going on to make you behave like this? Please phone as soon as you get in. We *need* to talk.'

Well fuck you, Henry, he thought. You can't expect me to come running just because you're embarrassed.

This was going to need some careful working out, he realized. Someone might easily have seen him come in this evening, so he'd better leave via the garage and quickly so that he could claim to have gone out before Henry arrived. On the other hand, it would be awful to run into Henry in one of the surrounding streets now. And he wasn't ready to go out yet in any case. He still had the inflammable parts of the umbrella to burn, then he had to collect the ash in an airtight bag, then he had to clean the fireplace and then he had to clean himself. No, he couldn't go out yet.

If there were ever any questions, he'd have to say he'd taken some strong painkillers to deal with a stress-induced headache after the scene at the school and fallen too deeply asleep to hear the front-door bell. They might well believe that, especially if he did take some pills to show up in any blood test.

Up in the bathroom, he found the Co-dydramol Margaret had been prescribed after her fibroids operation and took two, before speeding up his search for the hacksaw. If the pills were likely to make him sleepy, he wanted to have all the tricky parts of the job done before they acted. There was no sign of the hacksaw, but he did find a Stanley knife. That made reasonably quick work of the wooden shaft of the umbrella, and the two pieces he ended up with fitted neatly on top of his small fire. They burned well, too. Now it was just the nylon.

That was so thin he didn't think it would need cutting up like the heavy overcoat so he dumped the whole lot on top of the fire, only to see the sodding stuff melt.

His courage deserted him. For a hideous second he thought he could hear laughter, but it was only the wind in the chimney. Wind! If there were wind strong enough to make that kind of noise, it would probably blow away the fog. He had to get this done before the fog went and the next driver passing by found Ben's body.

Burning nylon smelled disgusting, Toby discovered, as well as leaving sticky evidence all over your fireplace. He didn't know what to do. There was another tea chest in the cellar. The pills were beginning to work, too, and he felt his mind blurring. Not yet, he screamed in silence. Hang on a bit longer.

He scraped his thighs as he clambered upstairs with the second tea chest. It hurt, and he knew he was oozing blood. But he got the box in pieces without too much more damage, except to the same torn hangnail he'd ripped when he'd rushed over to the garage in case Ben had locked Mer in it. Still, the wood did help the fire flare up and start to deal with the nylon, even though the smell of that was still horrible. He'd have to clean the fireplace, too. But it would have to be cold for that. His eyes kept closing. Damn! Why had he had to be so clever with the pills?

The wind laughed in the chimney again. He couldn't sit on the clients' sofa to wait for the fire to finish its work and then cool down or he'd have to start cutting up the sofa cover to burn it and the evidence it held, and the whole cycle would go on for ever. The only place he could rest was the bath, where water would wash away any clues he might have had left on his skin.

Staggering a little, he let himself into the bathroom, remembering to pull down the blind before he switched on the light. He flung a whole handful of Margaret's latest scented granules into the hot water and got in after them. They crunched under his bum and he realized he should have given them time to dissolve. Too bad. He'd needed to lie down.

At last, he thought as he slid down the bath until even his chin was submerged in hot water. With the sweet-smelling steam washing the burning-nylon smell from his nostrils and his back and legs stretched out, he leaned his head back against the tiled shelf behind the bath and let his eyes close. It would only be for a minute or two.

Chapter 23

1920

Helen could count the pieces of coal she had left now, and the sight of the eighteen lumps terrified her. She'd had to light the fire again tonight because Ivan had felt like a marble statue in a winter garden when she'd touched him. But the eighteen lumps wouldn't last for many more days, even if she had a fire only when he absolutely had to get warm.

She'd heard nothing from Jean-Pierre since he'd said goodbye outside the station in France, laid his hand against her belly and said:

'Call him Ivan. It sounds good in both the languages, and he will belong to both our countries.'

'And if the baby's a girl?' she'd said, coquettish as any adoring new wife, who could be confident of having her husband around to look after her and their child. Now she hated the silly innocent credulous fool she'd been.

'Then call her Caroline. That works well, too. And whatever happens, you must take care of yourself, Hélène. I will come as soon as I can, but it may take some time. I have asked Thomas to bring you money to the house and I will send more whenever you need it. Wait for me, Hélène.'

He'd kissed her and she'd waited as she'd promised him. It was true Thomas had come with money, twice. There had been great wedges of notes, pounds and francs, as though Jean-Pierre had just sent over everything he could lay his hands on. When she'd counted the first batch, she'd had the first intimation that he might not be expecting to join her for years. There had been nearly four hundred pounds. The second delivery had been less, not much more than one hundred. But it was long gone now.

She had never had any way of getting in touch with Thomas, or known what his other name might be, and she had no address for Jean-Pierre, except the house of the *curé*, who had married them. She had tried writing to Jean-Pierre there, but had no reply, except a note from the *curé* in spiky French handwriting.

He had answered her covering letter with the news that he had not seen her husband since she had left France and had only his old address, from which letters were now being returned. The *curé* promised to keep her letter behind the clock in the salon until Jean-Pierre should reappear. For all she knew it was there still.

Ivan coughed. It was just a small cough, but it was enough to distract her. Not tonight, she begged in silence. No choking fit tonight. Please. I'm too tired to cope with that, too.

If Jean-Pierre didn't come soon, she would have to find work and she didn't know how. Nursing was the only thing she knew and she had already had to leave the service because of her marriage. She had broken her contract and had been left in no doubt by the sister who'd received her confession that she had transgressed in every possible way. Not only had she married without leave, but she was much too far gone in her pregnancy to have waited until her wedding night, which put her beyond the pale. And to cap it all, she had married a Frenchman.

But someone in London must need a nurse, experienced, willing to do anything for only enough pay to feed herself and her child. That was the next difficulty. She had a child and no one to care for him while she worked.

There was her family, of course, living only three or four miles to the west in Kensington. But she wasn't going to them unless she had no alternative whatsoever. Ivan coughed again. This time the cough was followed by the terrifying whooping gasp that told her no one had listened to her silent prayers.

This punishment was far worse than anything she deserved: having to watch her son battle for breath in pain and terror. It didn't matter that she was so hungry she sometimes felt that her insides must be eating themselves or that she was always cold except when she held Ivan in her arms. The only thing that mattered now was to calm herself enough to give him the confidence he needed to breathe. She fought herself until she knew she could help him, then bent to pick him up out of his small bed.

He tensed in her arms, hardly breathing, as her whole mind was split apart by the thought she'd been trying to ignore: what if Jean-Pierre were dead?

Toby dreamed of icebergs banging into him as he drifted on a collapsing raft in an icy sea. His foot hit the taps and his head sank into the water as he woke. Spluttering, he fought his way to the surface of the bath again. His finger ends were a pale-yellowish mass of wrinkles, and his member was shrivelled almost to nothing against the coarse dark hair between his thighs.

Horrified to see that there was pale-grey light bulging round the edges of the blind, he pushed himself up against the sides of the bath, feeling even colder as the frigid water cascaded off his body, and grabbed a towel. Even that was cold. The heating wouldn't come on again until seven-thirty. He rubbed his body hard, wincing in spite of the friction-induced warmth, and stepped out on the bath mat, carefully shaking each foot over the sinking bathwater before he risked wetting the mat.

Margaret's dark-green towelling dressing gown hung on the back of the door. He pulled it round himself, glad for once that she was so much broader than he, and pattered down to the office and the fire. It was safely out, although the vile, throat-rasping smell of burning nylon still hung all over the room. He put one clean hand against the sticky black side of the grate. Good, that was cold, too. Now all he had to do was clean up. He looked at the clock. Six-forty. He had nearly two hours before Mrs Pegg, the daily, was likely to appear. That should be enough to get the place clean enough to show no signs of what he'd been doing.

But it wasn't quite. He was still on his knees, still wearing Margaret's dressing gown, and scrubbing at the hearth when he heard the sound of a key in the lock. He mustn't be found here. The place now smelled of bleach rather than burned nylon. He'd just have to hope that Mrs Pegg would have breathed in so many of her own cleaning fluids on the way up to the first floor that she wouldn't notice. He scrabbled together all the cloths he'd been using and piled them into the black bag he'd brought up with him. Holding the skirts of the dressing gown together in one hand and grasping the neck of the black bag in the other, he crept out of the room and upstairs to dress.

There was a cheval mirror on the top landing. In its reflection he saw a figure so exotically bizarre that he stopped in fascination. The dark-green towelling, which looked so good on Margaret with her dark-red hair and white skin, turned him sallow. There were black smuts all over his face and his hair stood up on end, as though an electric current had been run through him. His eyes were red-rimmed and there were strange new lines in his skin, as though someone had taken a metal grid and pressed it deep into his flesh.

He'd have to have another bath and quickly. Keeping well away from the banisters, he called down:

'Mrs Pegg?'

'No. It's Jo.'

He peered through the open door of the boys' bedroom and saw sleety rain spattering the window. The fog had gone, though.

'I slept late,' he shouted down the stairs. 'I'm just going to have a bath. Do you need anything from me just yet?'

'I can cope. I'll deal with the post first. Would you like me to make you some coffee?'

'No. Don't worry about that,' he said, surprised by the ordinariness of her voice. 'I'll have some later. Mrs Pegg should be here by now. She's very late. See to her when she comes, will you?'

'OK.'

The water was hot again as it gushed out of the tap, and so was the towel rail. He'd been cleaning for nearly three hours. No wonder he looked extraordinary. His back was aching and his fingers felt as though someone had rubbed them all over with wire wool. He didn't know how a woman like Mrs Pegg bore it. She must be well over sixty, and this was what she did all day. She must be strong as a horse.

He got into the bath and started washing, sinking down under the surface to get all the smuts out of his hair, and scouring every millimetre of his skin with the obsessive care of a surgeon in a hospital ridden with flesh-eating bacteria. Halfway through, he heard the front-door bell ring, but Jo could deal with that. He had to get clean.

Dried and dressed, he bundled the black bag full of rags into a second bag and thrust it under the bed, along with the two plastic carriers of umbrella spokes and spoke-ends. As soon as Jo and Mrs Pegg had gone, he'd disguise those in some way, maybe inside a briefcase, and get them safely out of the house. And then, no one, even if they'd found a way to suspect him of having something to do with Ben's death, would be able to prove it.

That reminded him that someone must have found the body by now, so he switched on the radio. Too late. He was listening to *Woman's Hour*. He'd have to wait until the eleven o'clock news.

Now, he thought, I'm not the madman in the dressing gown, or the killer of Ben Smithlock. I am Toby Fullwell, connoisseur, director and employer. Time to do my stuff.

As he went downstairs, he thought of Noël Coward at the end of *The Italian Job*, processing down the gaol stairs to the cheers of all the cons lining the landings, and took on some of his regality.

'Morning, Jo. I'm sorry I wasn't ready when you came. Anything interesting in the post?'

'Not really. A few bills. Oh, and an MP wants to bring a party of constituents round the gallery next month. What do you feel about that?'

'Depends on the MP.' Toby laughed. He was going to be OK. Life would continue, and get better every day. 'Is it one of the civilized ones?'

Jo handed him the letter and he was pleased to see that it was indeed from one of the most civilized of them all, John Flanagan. They'd met at one of Henry Buxford's dinners. What could be a more perfect beginning to his new life? Toby reached for the phone to ring the number of the House of Commons. He was a player at last.

'Are you sure you're up to school today, David?'

'Yes.' He sounded irritable. Trish didn't know what to do. His shell was firmly back in place, but now that she had seen the screaming, weeping vulnerability it hid, she feared it even more.

He obviously hadn't slept well, and his eyes were still swollen, but he sounded cheerfully teasing when he said: 'And *you* should be in chambers by now.'

'You're right about that.' She knew she was frowning from the sensation of tightness above her nose and made herself smile instead. The last thing she wanted was for him to think she was angry with him. 'You've got the number there and my mobile, so if you need anything, just—'

'I won't.' He bit back something else, coughed and looked at the floor. 'I just want to be ordinary, Trish.'

'Good for you,' she said, feeling inadequate in the extreme.

George had gone home to his own house in Fulham last night, under protest, which was probably just as well. If he'd been there, Trish would have tried to involve him, and this had to be the boy's decision.

He looked at her from under his lashes and produced a valiant approximation of a smile. 'It's the last day of term, Trish. I can't miss it. And we've got rowing practice in the gym, too. You know I like that.'

Trish nodded, also knowing how hard he was working to reassure her. 'All right. But promise that if you don't feel well, or anything—'

'I promise. And you must, too.'

'Yes.' She knew that Nicky would take him all the way to school and that Hester More would ensure that he was safe all day. He'd shown no signs of drowsiness or dizziness, or even headache, and he hadn't been sick, so it didn't seem likely that Toby's tremendous slap across his face had done him any physical harm. 'I'll pick you up this afternoon. Have a good day.'

'And you, Trish,' he said. 'Nicky said she'd be here in a few minutes, and I'll be fine till then.'

Trish was going to be late as it was, so she made him promise not to open the front door to anyone until Nicky had arrived and then ran.

Once on Blackfriars Bridge, she felt the full force of the wind. It blew the ends of her hair sharply into her eyes and picked up puddles of dirty rainwater to fling against her tights, as well as pushing her briefcase hard against her calves. Head down, she kept up a good pace until she was back between the buildings of New Bridge Street. The blast weakened at once.

Steve caught her on her way into chambers with the news

that Antony wanted her and that there had been a delivery of flowers, which he'd put in her room.

'Could you tell Antony I'm just dropping off my things and I'll be with him in a sec?' she called, needing to wipe herself down and comb her hair before she saw anyone else.

The first thing she saw as she opened the door to her little room was an artfully simple dark-wicker handleless basket, planted with white orchids and silky olive-green moss. In the shabbiness of her room the arrangement looked as glamorous as a Fabergé jewel, and nearly as artificial. Stroking one petal and finding it was real, she ripped open the thick envelope to read:

'Trish, I am so sorry about what happened yesterday. Will you telephone me when you've got time? With my best wishes, Henry.'

She appreciated the gesture and longed to know what he'd heard and how much he knew, but that would have to wait until Antony was finished with her.

'I'm sorry I'm late,' she said as she walked into his room.

'After what Henry told me this morning, I'm impressed you're here at all. Is your brother all right?'

'I hope so.'

'Both Henry and I feel seriously responsible for what happened yesterday. I wish I'd never passed on his original request, and he, of course, is wishing that he'd hauled his godson straight off to a psychiatrist as soon as he knew something was wrong. He's clearly suffering from some form of neurotic paranoia.'

Trish felt as though he'd dug his pen into her stomach. 'I must say I hate the fact that he lives so close to my flat. I'll always dread running into him now, whenever I leave here or the flat. You know, I used to think London was vast and impersonal. Now it feels like a goldfish bowl.'

'More like a pond full of piranhas, I'd say.' Sympathy had softened Antony's voice. Trish felt the muscles over her nose contracting again and tried to stop the frown before it tied up her face completely. 'Considering the latest news.'

'Oh, God! What's happened now?'

'Haven't you read the papers yet?'

Trish shook her head.

'A man was killed yesterday, in the tunnel by Blackfriars. It sounds like another murder.'

'Oh, shit! It used to feel so safe here. Now it's like a war zone. Was this one shot, too?'

'They haven't said, but—' The phone on Antony's desk rang. He picked it up, listened, then waved Trish out of the room. As she left, she heard him say:

'Terrific work, Robert. I think we'll be able to swing it now. Well done.'

Back at her own desk, Trish phoned Nicky's mobile to ask how David had seemed when she dropped him at school, and whether either of them had heard anything about the murdered man found at Blackfriars.

'I'm still at the Paddington left-luggage office,' Nicky said, her voice high with strain. 'I was going to phone you anyway because they can't find your package. I keep making them go back to look again, but they say without the ticket there's nothing they can do.'

'Nicky, what's going on? What are you talking about?'

'Your package at Paddington.' She could have been talking to an idiot.

'I haven't got a package at Paddington. Is David all right? He must be very worried about being so late for school.'

'Didn't you take him?'

'No.' Trish was holding the edge of her desk and forcing herself to speak calmly. 'Nicky, you know you were supposed to take him this morning.'

'Yes. But he phoned me while you were in the shower this morning and said you'd asked him to call me because you hadn't got time to do it yourself. You were taking him to school early and you wanted me to go to Paddington to collect this package that's been left for you there with your name on it.'

Trish's heart was beating at twice the normal speed, and her mouth was completely dry, but her mind was absolutely clear. She let go of the edge of the desk and felt the blood rushing painfully back into her whitened knuckles.

'He made up the whole thing. He's up to something. We have to find him. Now. Nicky, get straight home in case he goes back there. I'll get on to Caro Lyalt.'

'Let me come with you. Please.'

'No. Someone's got to be at home in case he goes there. I'll let you know the minute something happens, but go straight on home now. As fast as you can, Nicky.'

Trish's fingers hit the buttons on her phone like hailstones on a metal roof. In a few seconds she was talking to Hester More.

'Well, I was surprised that you hadn't phoned,' the Head said with lunatic calmness, 'but I assumed you'd decided you couldn't leave David for a moment. I was waiting to hear from you.'

'You mean you haven't seen him at all today?' Trish had to be certain of his disappearance before she set the police on to David, even in the person of his beloved godmother.

'He has not been in any part of the school's property at all today,' she said with her usual pedantic clarity.

'I'm about to call in the police, so if he does show up, call me at once.' Trish cut the connection, then pressed in the code for Caro's direct line.

The first good thing of the day was that she answered it herself after the second ring and listened to the whole of Trish's explanation without asking any questions.

'In normal circumstances, I'd have said it was too early to do anything,' Caro told her. 'But given the child's history and this definite campaign to deceive you and Nicky, it's clear he has a plan. Could he have been so scared by what happened at the school yesterday that he's run away?'

'It's possible.' Trish was glad Jess had told Caro everything that had happened after the Christmas play. It saved a lot of explanations. 'Although he kept assuring me he was all right, but then he would, wouldn't he, if he was working out how to get away?'

'Have you any idea where he could have gone?'

'He has got some friends at school, but that's where they'll be, so he can't be with them.'

'What about old friends, from his past life?'

'There's Joe, who was at the junior school with him. We used to get him to tea quite often, then it sort of fizzled out. I suppose David could have gone back there, trying to get away from all this to the only other place he knows. I'd better drive up there right away.'

'Trish, slow down a minute. There's no need to go rushing anywhere yet. Do you know Joe's mother's phone number? And the school's?'

'Yes, of course.' Trish grabbed her diary, silently blessing Caro's common sense. 'I'm going mad. I'll ring them now and let you know.'

'Good. But we should also have a fall-back. Where else might he have gone?'

'I've no idea. Unless— Oh, God! You don't think he could have gone after Toby, do you?'

'Toby? Trish, you're going to have to give me more.' Caro's voice was very calm, and very sure. 'Who is Toby?'

'The man from yesterday,' Trish said, adding everything else she knew, including David's pathetic pleas last night, and her belated understanding of quite how responsible he felt for his mother's death.

'Don't worry too much,' Caro said, still sounding calm. 'I'll deal with Toby, while you look into Joe and his mother.'

'No, let me go to the gallery. I've been before, and—'

'If everything you've said is true, the further you stay away from him, the better. I have the resources to deal with this. You don't, so get phoning.' Caro cut the connection before Trish could say anything else.

She had to hang on for ages before anyone answered the phone at the North London junior school, and then for several minutes while the secretary checked and found that David's old friend Joe was in school that day, and just now in the middle of a class. His mother had her answering machine on at home, but it gave a mobile number. Trish phoned that, but reached only the voice mail. She left a message, then sat, staring at the phone, willing it to ring.

'What's up, Trish?' The sound of Robert's voice made her look away from the door. She didn't want to deal with him now. 'You seem a bit distracted.'

'Problems at home.'

'Oh, right. I assumed you'd been listening to stories of this body they found in Upper Thames Street. It would spook me if I walked home through the dark the way you do.'

Trish still didn't look round. He was right, though. Even a confrontation with Toby might be less dangerous for David than walking alone through these streets after dark, if a murderer were on the loose. She thought of his old fears of a serial killer.

Her fingers were aching as they wound in and out of each other, and her jaw was tight. She had to believe that Caro would find him soon.

'Have they identified the corpse yet?' Robert's voice buzzed in her ear, like a mosquito in the night. 'The bulletin I heard just said a man with no ID. Sounds amazingly like Peter Chanting's. Did you have a hand in this death, too?'

Trish looked up at the window and saw Robert's face reflected there. Even the rippled shadows showed her his gloating grin.

'Don't,' she burst out before she could stop herself. 'I know you're not serious, but I can't take it this morning. I'm too raw. Just leave me alone.'

'Trish?' His voice was quite different from usual. With the tears of temper in her eyes, she knew she couldn't turn round. She felt his arm on her shoulder. 'Trish, it was only meant to be a joke.'

She stared out at the gloomy light well and swallowed. But she had to sniff, too.

'Oh, God, Trish, don't go and cry on me.'

'Just leave me alone for a bit, will you?'

'All right,' Robert said. She could hear him backing away from her. 'But you must tell me if I can help.'

That made it harder to hold on, so she nodded.

'OK. Right. Fine. Well, 'bye,' he said, shutting the door behind him with the tiniest clicking sound.

Trish leaned forwards against the cold glass. All she could do now was wait for news.

Chapter 24

1925

On her way out of the bedroom, Helen paused by the cheval mirror, which was a mistake. She had lost so much weight that her clothes hung off her. Her face was gaunt and there were already thick grey streaks at her temples. She was only thirty-three.

'Don't start moping,' she said aloud. 'You've got to look confident today.'

She straightened her aching shoulders, ignored the fraying cuffs of her coat and the cracks in the leather of her shoes, and went downstairs to collect the tube with one of Jean-Pierre's paintings in it. Every night for the past week she had woken in a sweat of anxiety, with the question eating at her heart: was it fair to sell one, just one, of the paintings, in order to get proper care for Ivan?

Her part-time job paid for no more than necessities. In six years more he could leave school and find employment in the City, but until then she had to have money for his food and clothes, and for doctors. His choking fits became more terrifying every year and he was dangerously thin.

There was a long queue for the bus, and so she could not get on the first two that drew up at the stop. At last she was on her way, holding the tube far more carefully than she had been able to do when she had brought them all over from France with the convoys of wounded. As the bus lumbered westwards, she gazed out at the once-familiar landmarks. It was hard to remember she had ever been a young lady trained to behave as though she were incapable, delicate and needing shelter from anything dangerous or distasteful.

Here was Piccadilly. The bus went on to Knightsbridge and Kensington rather than going up Bond Street, so she would have to get off at the next stop and walk. When she had first hatched this plan, she had been afraid she might run into her mother or sister, but the reflection she had seen in the cheval glass had told her she need not worry. She looked nothing like the girl they had known, or even the angry exhausted nurse who had given them so much of a shock on her leave in 1915.

'Oh, Jean-Pierre,' she whispered and saw her breath misting the glass. Someone else rang the bell and the bus squealed to a halt. She had forgotten everything, even that this was a request stop.

She scrambled out of the double seat, apologizing as she stepped on the well-polished shoe of the man who had shared it. He looked curiously at her and she realized she must have been talking aloud to herself. That kept happening now. Sometimes with Ivan asleep, she would walk around the huge, dusty, horrible house talking to the walls and the lamps, begging them to help with her son or to tell her how to find Jean-Pierre.

There was a puddle just beside the bus's platform, but she managed to avoid it, which was strange. There weren't many kinds of clumsiness she had avoided recently. The picture was still securely in its tube and wrapped in brown paper, neatly tied with clean string. She had nothing to be ashamed of there, even though her clothes marked her out as little better than a beggar.

The gallery looked exactly as she remembered it from her girlhood, the big gleaming window revealing a small oil landscape in an ornate frame balanced on a miniature easel. The rest of the window was empty, the floor and walls lined with pale-gold velvet. She could see a wide plane of pale-gold carpet beyond and a beautifully dressed young man sitting at a desk halfway down the long room. Coughing, remembering everything she had seen and done in the war to give her courage, she pushed open the gallery door.

She caught the end of the tube in the door and had to tug it free, which did nothing for her poise.

'May I be of service, madam?' said the young man in a voice that told her what a fool she had already made of herself.

'I have a painting here,' she said, dredging up the old confident Kensington voice, 'which I am considering selling. I should like to know whether you would be interested in buying it.'

'We buy very little from members of the public,' he said languidly. But he did come closer to her. 'Would you like to unwrap it?'

'If you could show me somewhere I could lay it. It is rather large.'

'And clearly not framed.'

'No. My . . . my late husband had it sent to London for me in this tube. I have never had it framed.' She couldn't tell this horrible young floorwalker the story of Jean-Pierre and his paintings.

'I see.' He was looking over her shabby hat, as though he couldn't bear to lower himself even to meet her eyes. He led her to a backroom, that was far more brightly lit than the gallery. A long plan chest filled the further wall. 'Please unwrap your picture there.'

She struggled so hard with the knots she had tied in the string, that the young man lost patience and leaned forwards and cut it for her. Angry now, she tore the brown paper away, borrowed his knife to cut the tapes that closed the tube at top and bottom and fairly shook out the canvas. As she unrolled it on the flat top of the plan chest a few flakes of paint fell out.

The canvas showed a dark-browed madonna in an orange

frock, seated against an arched stone window. The child on her lap looked as unlikely as most old master babies.

'Ah yes, I see,' said the young man. 'Yes, I do see. I suggest that you parcel it straight up again and take it home. Your local pawn-broker might give you a fiver for it, if you're lucky. It is not the kind of work we handle.'

Helen had never been spoken to with such contempt in her life.

'But it is exactly the kind of work you sell,' she said. 'You specialize in old masters.'

'My dear lady, what makes you think that this is an old master? A Derby winner does not come out of a . . . a hill farm in Wales.'

She turned her back on the curling, flaking canvas and faced him, glad to see a spark of surprise in his eyes. He could have been no more than twenty-two or -three, she thought. He had not fought in the war. He had not learned what he was capable of, or how even the bravest of men could be reduced to weeping, shaking invalids by daily fear.

'Just because I am poor, there is no need to assume that I am a fool. This is an old master painting, the property of my late husband, who was a French collector before the war. If he had not been killed, I would not have been reduced to these shifts, and it would never have crossed my mind to sell any of his collection.'

Something, perhaps a scruple of the shame he should have felt, moved him to say that he would consult one of his senior partners.

Helen waited, hoping the anger would see her through. But the man who came to talk to her was so much less contemptuous, so polite and so kind that she lost it and was once more on fire with humiliation. This man took much greater care as he looked at the painting, but his verdict was little different from the first.

He told her gently that it was the work of a gifted amateur, painting in the style of the Italian Renaissance, perhaps in the last century or perhaps at the beginning of this one.

'Perhaps it was even your husband himself, who painted it. Many French gentlemen, connoisseurs of course, took pleasure in reproducing the work of great artists. See here, and here.' He pointed to the painting of the madonna's face with a well-manicured finger. 'And again the sky. These are the giveaway points, madam. I am very sorry to have to tell you, that this is not an original work.' He smiled at her most kindly and asked if she had come far.

'Thank you, no. Not far. But I had best be going now.' She started to gather together the torn wrappings.

'Please do not trouble yourself. One of the porters will repack it for you.'

'Thank you.'

'I am sorry I could not give you more encouraging news. Thank you for letting us see the painting. Good day.'

He left her with his disdainful assistant and a porter dressed in a brown linen coat, who proceeded to reroll and wrap the painting for her. All she wanted to do was grab it and get herself home to cry in peace. She did not know what to do. The disdainful young man, perhaps rebuked for his rudeness, made polite conversation throughout the elaborate wrapping process. But all Helen could think about was Jean-Pierre and his motives for making her take all those dozens of tubes of worthless paintings in the trains full of wounded and dying men.

Had there been something else in the tubes, something Thomas had removed before he took the tubes to the house by Southwark Bridge? If so, what could it have been? What had she brought in to England from France? And how had she been mad enough to believe Jean-Pierre's protestations of love? No wonder he had never come to see her and Ivan. No wonder she had had no answers to the letters she had sent to the *curé* who had married them and the mayor of the town where Jean-Pierre claimed to have lived.

Had she ever actually been married?

And what *had* she brought into England in Jean-Pierre's tubes along with the worthless paintings?

The only saving grace to all of this, was the knowledge that Jean-Pierre's country had been an ally of her own in the war. Whatever she had brought in for him, it could not have made her a traitor to her country.

'Would you like me to call you a cab?' The disdainful young man was almost shouting. Helen realized he must have asked the question several times. She shook her head, not bothering to speak again. The porter held out the tube. She pulled on her worn and mended gloves and took it from him, only just remembering to thank him. No one escorted her through the gallery or opened the door for her. Alone, she walked past the paintings that were doubtless on sale for thousands of pounds, and alone she went back to the house that Jean-Pierre had bought.

On that thought, she stopped, causing an angry fat man behind her to mutter about inconsiderate women causing trouble to decent men. Why would Jean-Pierre have bought a house for her and Ivan if he had wanted her only as a courier for whatever he had secreted in the tubes of rubbishy pictures?

But if anything he had told her was real, why had he never written? And why had Thomas disappeared after the second delivery of money? *Was* Jean-Pierre dead?

'But what were you thinking of, Toby?' Henry Buxford looked and sounded as though he'd forgotten how to speak English.

Toby couldn't understand why Henry was making such a big deal of his little spat with Trish Maguire at the school. If he only knew what had happened later! It was hard to keep the laughter inside his head.

'It was the most trivial event,' he said eventually. 'Slightly embarrassing, I'll admit, but I've apologized to all and sundry. I suppose I could send her a note as well if that would make you feel better.'

The front-door bell rang and Toby moved as though to answer it.

'Your secretary can deal with that,' Henry said, snapping the office door shut so that Toby couldn't get out. 'You and I have to get this sorted fast. I hope Trish Maguire isn't planning to sue you for assault. Just in case she is tempted, tell me precisely what was going on in your mind when you grabbed her.'

'Virtually nothing. I've told you: it was trivial. She wasn't hurt.'

'But it was a very public incident, and you followed it by picking on a 9-year-old child and hitting him in front of about a hundred witnesses. That is not trivial, Toby. And if it does come to court your recent record isn't going to help, is it?'

Toby flinched. There was no way Henry could know about Ben Smithlock, so what was he talking about now?

'Don't play the innocent. You've been hitting Margaret, haven't you? Too many people saw her black eye for you to try to pretend. Toby, I've never thought of you as a violent man. What on earth has been going on? You have got to tell me now.'

'Nothing's been going on. I keep telling you. Margaret's black eye was an accident. And I mistook your friend Trish Maguire for the tall, thin, dark-haired woman who's been stalking me for the last few weeks. Asking questions about the origins of the collection, and generally loitering in a suspicious manner wherever I go.' He couldn't understand why Henry looked so ill. 'I must find out who it is who rang the bell. I can see you're worried about this lawyer friend of yours, but work must go on.'

'That's true,' Henry said. 'But there is a great deal we need to discuss yet, about your recent activities. Go on downstairs and find out what's happening, then come back up here. All right?'

'Well, yes, if you've really got the time to wait.'

'I haven't, but I'm going to.' Henry was feeling in his pocket for his mobile. 'Get on with it. I'm just going to call my secretary.'

Toby ran downstairs to find Jo working at the computer. She seemed to have reformed, too.

'Who was that?'

'Only Mer's friend, come to collect his football boots.'

'What?' Toby heard the snap in his voice and smiled to mitigate its effect on the open-mouthed Jo. He didn't need her to tell him he'd gone mad again. He made his voice quieter: 'What friend?'

'I don't know. But it was a young boy in school uniform, who said that Mer is his friend and needs his boots. Oh and that he'd left them in the basement.'

Toby saw his hand snaking out to grip her shoulder and made it freeze before it could do any damage.

'Is he still in the basement?'

'No, of course not. The phone was ringing, so I just unlocked the door for him, came back to answer it. When I'd dealt with the caller, I went down to see if the boy needed any help, but he'd already gone. So I locked up again. Here are the keys.'

Toby couldn't understand what she was talking about, but he knew he had to check the basement at once.

'Go and take Sir Henry a pot of coffee and tell him I'll be up in a moment,' he said.

The basement door was properly latched and locked, but that didn't mean anything. Toby opened it quietly and listened. He could hear scuffling. There were no mice or rats in the cellar after all the poison he'd put down, so the boy had to be still there, whatever Jo thought. He must have hidden when he heard her coming down to check on him. Closing the door quietly behind him, Toby crept down the stairs, bending to get the first possible sight of what was going on.

'You loathsome little shit,' he said between his teeth as he saw the boy surrounded by curling canvas and torn paper. 'What the hell do you think you're doing?'

He didn't see the scalpel in the boy's hand until he reached out to grab him and the blade sank itself into his hand. Hot blood poured out, bringing pain screaming through his brain.

Chapter 25

When the phone rang at last, Trish just stared at it. She'd been waiting for so long that she didn't believe in the sound. Then her hand moved.

'I've got him,' Caro's voice said into her aching ear a second later. 'He's safe. There are things to sort out, but he is safe.'

Trish's spine sagged, and the determination that had kept her going seeped away.

'Where are you?' she said, pushing Henry's orchids out of the way. There were yet more tears in her eyes and she felt very shaky.

'At your flat,' Caro said. 'With David. He wants to talk to you very much. Shall I put him on?'

'Yes, please.' Trish sniffed while she had the chance. Then Caro came back on the line, saying:

'OK. Here he is.'

Then came her brother's voice, pleading and afraid: 'Trish? Trish, I'm really sorry.'

'It's all right. Whatever it is, it's all right, so long as you're not hurt. I'm coming straight home now. I'll be with you in about ten minutes. Will you tell Caro?'

She left her briefcase where it was, but grabbed her handbag automatically and was out of the building before anyone could stop her. There was a stitch in her side before she'd even reached the bridge and lack of oxygen was making her so dizzy that she had to stop to catch her breath.

At last she was home and at the top of the iron staircase. The door opened before she could get her key in the lock. Caro stood beside it, looking much more serious than Trish had expected. But all her attention was on the child, whose small white face showed absolute fear. Forgetting everything George had said about what young boys could take, she grabbed him and held him safe against her.

Amazingly his arms went round her back again.

'I'll make some tea,' Caro said.

Questions were spurting into Trish's mind, but they would have to wait. David let her go much sooner than she wanted, but she obediently pulled away and smiled at him.

'Let's sit down.' She led the way to one of the squashy black sofas. After a moment he joined her, but he chose a spot a careful two feet away from her. 'Can you tell me what happened?'

He bit his lip and looked at his shoes. 'I didn't mean it.'

'What? What didn't you mean?'

'I didn't mean to hurt him.'

Trish felt her mouth opening, but she held back the protest. Caro walked round the open fireplace, carrying a tray.

'He was in the basement storeroom of the gallery when the director startled him. David happened to have a scalpel in his hand and the director suffered cuts in his hand and arm. No serious damage was done, although there was quite a lot of blood, which frightened everybody.'

Caro's voice was careful and stern enough to tell Trish there was more to this than she had been able to say in the boy's presence.

'But why were you in the gallery at all?'

He kicked the sofa with his heels. 'Mer said his Dad had treasure in the basement.'

'Yes, I know. You told me. But it was only pictures.'

'I thought there was something more inside the tubes. I wanted to know so we could tell the police and make them stop him hurting you again. So I was cutting them open. That's why I had the knife.'

Trish had to work hard to keep her face from showing shock. The thought of a frightened 9-year-old boy with a scalpel in a room full of Rembrandts was far worse than any cuts in Toby Fullwell's arm.

'The paintings are all fine,' Caro said, interpreting some of Trish's thoughts. 'Tea?'

'I'm not sure I could swallow it. David —'

'I think perhaps not now, Trish. And you *should* have tea.' Caro brought her a mugful and handed David a glass of apple juice.

Later, when Nicky was giving him his supper, Caro took Trish outside. The wind was still rushing between the buildings, but it was dry and there was no one to overhear them there.

'What's going to happen now?' Trish asked, dizzy with relief that her brother had not quite reached the age of criminal responsibility. 'Did he really not damage the paintings?'

'Not more than anyone would in opening them up like that. He didn't slash them or anything. He simply unrolled them, and he only cut Toby out of terror. But that's not the most important thing at the moment. I had got an emergency search warrant, just in case Toby resisted our attempts to look for David.'

'Did he?'

'He wasn't in a position to resist with his hand dripping blood like that, but he behaved so oddly that, once he was on his way to casualty, I asked my officers to make a search of the building. What they found means that some of our colleagues are now interviewing him. I can't say any more.'

'This is mad, Caro. You have to tell me what you're talking about. You can't leave me hanging like this.'

'Trish, this is a police matter. You know I can't tell you any more.'

'And what do you expect me to do? Leave it there? Did you find something in amongst the paintings?'

'No.'

'But there was evidence of a crime?'

'We found evidence that might be connected with an ongoing investigation, yes.'

'Is David implicated?'

'No, of course he isn't. He was just behaving like James James Morrison Morrison in that A. A. Milne poem.'

Trish had far too much banging around in her brain to identify that, so Caro obliged.

'You know, the child who didn't want his mother going out without him to protect – or monitor – her.'

'Oh, shit.'

'As far as I understand the little David was prepared to tell me, he was trying to get evidence that could be used to put Toby away for a while and so keep him off you. That's why I've been so careful to stress the nature of the wound to Toby's arm. I'm sure it was accidental. The secretary said she heard Toby yelling something about "I'll get you, you loathsome little shit" before she heard Toby scream. I don't want David persuading himself or you or anyone else that he deliberately stuck the scalpel into Toby. That would be the worst possible outcome of this. He's scared enough already.'

'Caro, I don't understand any of this.'

'I know you don't. As soon as I can tell you any more, I will. But I don't think you're going to have to worry about Toby any longer. Oh, by the way, there was a man at the gallery, who might be able to tell you more. Bloke called Buxford.'

'Ah. Thanks, Caro. For everything. You know how grateful I am that you stepped in, don't you?'

'Of course.' Caro put her strong arm around Trish's shoulders and kissed her. 'I'm glad you came to me. I have to go now. But if you're worried about anything, phone me. I don't think there will be any repercussions, but if there are, I'll do whatever I can to sort them out. OK?'

'He's under the age of criminal responsibility,' Trish said. 'Thank God. Love to Jess.'

'I doubt if I'll be seeing Jess for some time. I've got to get back to work.'

More mystified than ever, Trish went back to the flat. George had arrived while she was talking to Caro and was being given a brief account of the day's dramas by Nicky as she chopped onions in the kitchen.

'David wants to tell you something, Trish,' Nicky said, turning a tearful face at the sound of her voice. Trish blew George a kiss, longing to fling herself into his arms and let him sort everything out, and went back to her brother's bedroom.

He was lying propped up against his white pillows, looking fragile and wounded. His black eyes were enormous, and the long lashes looked very dark against his pallid skin.

'Hi,' Trish said, striving for a cheery tone. 'How're you feeling?'

'Not too bad.' He was whispering. 'There *was* something in two of those tubes apart from paintings.'

'What?'

'Yes. Envelopes. One in each of the two tubes. I kept them for you. No one else knows about them. I put them up my jersey as soon as I found them, and Mer's Dad didn't know. Nor Caro. Nor anyone.'

'Right,' Trish said, smiling to hide all her anxieties. This was beginning to sound more like revenge than an attempt to prove Toby guilty of serious crime, as Caro believed. 'Where are they now?'

'I put them under my Scrabble board before Nicky could see them. Over there.'

Trish kneeled on the floor to reach under the bottom shelf of the bookcase for the pile of board games. The Scrabble was the second from top. David had obviously taken care that no one should find it too easy to grab his loot. Lifting off the lid of the box, as though it might contain explosives, she saw only the board and the dark-green bag of spelling tiles.

'They're under the board.' His voice promised such treats that she had to turn to smile at him. She wasn't sure she'd be able to bear it if his activities today brought social workers back into their lives. Caro's Delphic utterances suggested Toby was suspected of a crime so much more serious that anything David had done to him would be well outweighed, but Trish of all people knew that police suspicion was proof of nothing whatsoever.

'Go on,' he said, with excitement bubbling in his voice. 'Open them, Trish. See what they are.'

The two envelopes were foxed and flat enough to reassure her that there could be nothing in them except paper. They were also sealed. One was addressed 'To Whom It May Concern'; the other, to 'Madame Hélène Gregoire'.

'I don't think I can. They're not ours to open.' This might not have been the ideal moment for a lesson in right and wrong, but she couldn't shirk it. 'If you found them in the rolls of paintings, then they belong to the owners of the gallery. I'm going to phone one of them now to tell him that we've got the letters.'

He shuddered.

'Not Mer's Dad, but the chairman, who is in charge of them all.'

As she watched, his face returned to the frozen politeness she had come to fear. Then he slid down the bed under his duvet and literally turned his face to the wall. Trish felt her tendons cracking and the Procrustes icon enlarged itself in her mind until she could see almost nothing else.

'He has the right to open them. We haven't.'

David didn't answer. Trish put away the Scrabble, then paused for a moment by his bed to brush her hand across his hair.

'I'm really grateful that you wanted to bring me something,' she said, trying to reassure him yet still not give him the wrong message. 'And I know how frightened you must have been in that basement. But we have to do the right thing now.'

He still did not move.

Outside his room, she poured out some of her feelings in a sigh that would have moved all the fog in London last night. Then she phoned Henry.

'And I have the two envelopes here,' she said after she had described what her brother had done. 'They're addressed in writing that looks French to me and they look old enough to have been written by Jean-Pierre. I can't leave the child tonight. Shall I call a bike to bring them to you?'

'No.'

Oh, help, she thought. Now I have really screwed things up.

'No, Trish, I wanted to come and see you anyway because I have things I have to tell you. Will you be in your flat if I come straight round?'

'Yes, but—'

'Good. I'll be as quick as I can. I've got the chauffeur waiting downstairs for when you called.'

George, she thought as the phone went dead. George and Nicky next. She went back to the kitchen, where about a kilo of onions had been reduced to tiny particles under Nicky's knife.

'You need to know what's going on,' Trish said. 'And there isn't much time before the next instalment.'

'We're itching to know,' George said. 'But you look like death. Go and have a shower while we open a restorative bottle.'

'There isn't time. Henry Buxford's coming.'

'You can shower in two seconds flat. I've seen you do it. Get on upstairs. I'll come with you and you can talk while you're drying. You don't mind, do you, Nicky?'

''Course not. I'll finish making the tart.'

'She's a saint, that woman,' Trish said as she fumbled her way up the spiral stairs, giving George the merest outline of what had been going on.

She'd told him quite a lot of the rest between emerging like an otter from the shower and dressing in plain black trousers and the scarlet cashmere tunic. She left her feet bare.

'Like a penitent?' George suggested.

'Maybe,' she said. 'I'm beyond decoding what my psyche's doing to us all these days. Oh, help, there's the bell. We must go down.'

Nicky had let Henry Buxford in and was standing beside him with his bulky coat in her arms, offering him white wine or whisky. He chose whisky, breaking off his thanks to greet Trish.

She took both his outstretched hands and peered uncomprehendingly at his anxious face.

'There are no words – and certainly no orchids – to tell you how sorry I am that I involved you in all this, that I didn't listen to what you said, and then put you and the boy at such risk. I can only throw myself on your mercy.'

'It's fine,' she said, looking over her shoulder at George.

'I think it's possible that Trish is more in the dark than you think,' he said. 'I certainly am. Can you tell us what's going on?'

'Didn't you know? Toby's been arrested for this murder in the Blackfriars tunnel.'

'Good God!'

'Yes. The police found parts of a deliberately destroyed umbrella in his study. The whole room was stinking of bleach and there were peculiar traces of carbonized nylon in the grate. He had obviously been trying to burn the fabric of the umbrella.

That, combined with various other pieces of evidence, has led them to believe that the wound they found under the corpse's chin might have been made with an umbrella.' Henry looked sick. 'An umbrella which penetrated and destroyed the brain.'

'Henry, you don't have to tell us all this,' Trish said, remembering all her efforts to warn him of what scaring Toby might do. Even she hadn't imagined anything like this.

'I owe you a great deal more than that, Trish. I have asked Antony to recommend suitable counsel for Toby and obviously his case will be fought with the utmost rigour, but I—' He broke off, covering his eyes with his hand.

She wasn't aware that she was moving until she found herself standing beside him, patting his shoulder.

'Look,' she said, 'I'm not blameless in all this. If I'd—'

'Don't try to make me feel better. You couldn't. No one could. Anyway, that's the root of my confession, and the branches are that it looks as though you were right about everything.'

She was beyond speech now and merely gaped at him.

'The murdered man is known to the authorities,' he told her. 'He's suspected of being the money-laundering manager for a growing drugs-importing operation. He has been under intermittent surveillance by Customs & Excise, as well as the National Crime Squad. Unfortunately no one was following him in the fog yesterday, and no one had picked up the fact that he was in touch with Toby. Obviously I haven't said anything, but you and I know that he must have been, and why, Trish.'

'I think we should all have a drink,' George said, getting up off the sofa, 'and try to look at this less excitably.'

'Yes. And maybe open the letters David found.' Trish collected the two crackling envelopes from her desk and offered them to Henry. 'If you are going to do that, I'd like to get him out of bed so that he can witness it.'

He took them and nodded. Trish fetched David. By the time they'd got his dressing gown on and tied around his minimal waist, Henry had opened the first envelope and was skimming through it. Trish saw that he was blushing until his whole face was claret coloured. After a moment, he recovered and handed her the sheet.

> To Whom It May Concern
> I write this in case I cannot be present to show you that my wife knows nothing of the origin of these paintings. She has no idea that she has been transporting stolen property to England. She is wholly innocent of everything I have ever done.
>
> This is my statement, with my signature witnessed by a notary. I do not know whether it can be a valid document in an English court, but I trust that you will accept it and not punish my wife for crimes she has not committed.
>
> Jean-Pierre Gregoire

Trish couldn't read the name of his witness, but that didn't seem to matter. She couldn't look at Henry's humiliation either.

'I don't know what to say. You were right about that, too. Helen was indeed a mule.'

'Please, Henry, it doesn't matter.' She had her arm around her brother's shoulders now and felt him lean against her. With that sensation, nothing else mattered.

'Yes, it does. Not just because of what you and your boy have suffered, but because if I had listened properly to you, and not tried to frighten Toby into talking, I might have got to him before he—' Henry glanced at the boy, then back at Trish and said quietly: 'before he crossed the line.'

Remembering his stories of Toby's father, his best friend, Trish had to distract him.

'What's in the other letter?'

He shivered and handed it to her. She held it so that David could read it, too.

Hélène, ma mie,

If you are reading this, then one or both of the two worst things has happened. Either the authorities have intercepted you on your way back from France or I am dead. Either way, you must know that even though I came looking only for a courier, I found a woman I loved.

The love was real, Hélène, even though my name and our marriage were not. Do not forget, ever, that I have loved you more than I believed possible.

Take care of our child. Love him as I would have loved you both.

'Jean-Pierre'

'Ivan will be glad to know his father had some feeling for his mother,' Trish said, hardly able to bear the thought of Helen Gregory's wasted life as the lonely victim of a thieving, art-smuggling conman. 'Henry, don't tear yourself up. You couldn't have known any of this.'

'Perhaps not. But Toby will go to prison for life because of my arrogance. If I'd done what you advised and had him followed by a professional investigator, this could never have happened.'

Trish suppressed the comment that if Toby's barristers were any good, they would almost certainly get him off on provocation, or at the very least go for a psychiatric defence.

She passed the letters on to George, who was practically throbbing with impatience.

Much later, when the three of them had explained the significance of the letters to David and answered all his questions, Henry took the two documents away. George poured himself another drink, while Nicky went back to the onion tart she had been making and Trish escorted David back to his room. Sitting on the edge of his bed, she helped him to tell her everything he had seen and felt and done in Toby's basement.

'And I was pleased when the knife went into his hand,' he said at last, shuddering again. 'Because of what he did to you yesterday.'

Trish put her own hands around both of his so that he would know she would always hold on to him, however scared he made her, and whatever he did. 'I can understand that because you must have been frightened as well as very angry, but it mustn't happen again. No more knives. Ever. Whatever happens.'

He looked up at her, the black eyes that were so like her own unblinking. She couldn't read anything in them.

At last he said: 'He took me away from the trench, you know, that day we went to the museum.'

'*What?*'

'You know, when I said I didn't like it and we had to leave? He'd pulled me into the loo and tried to make me give you a message.'

'But why didn't you tell me then?'

His head dropped and his eyes slid sideways so that he couldn't look directly at her. After a while, he said: 'I thought I could make it not be real if I didn't tell you. And I didn't want you to be scared, too.'

Trish remembered Margaret Fullwell's telling her about the anti-sneaking culture at the school.

'That was kind of you,' she said simply. 'But I do wish you'd said something. Nothing like this will ever happen again, but if there's ever anything that worries or frightens you, please tell me. There will nearly always be things I can do to help. And even if there aren't, I will know who can help us. All right?'

He nodded, but she couldn't be sure he meant it.

Later still, when he was asleep and Nicky had gone to her flat across the road, George said: 'I don't want to sound too much like Pollyanna, Trish, but you do see what those letters mean, don't you?'

'That I'm a prophetic genius?' she said, trying to make a joke and failing. 'No, it's all right. I am taking this seriously. In fact what it means is that one crime always attracts a whole lot more, just as I've always believed. If Jean-Pierre hadn't made Helen smuggle his stolen paintings into England, Toby would never have been in a position to use them for money-laundering, and he would never have been driven to commit murder.'

'True, but that wasn't what I meant either.'

'No? Then what? That it's dangerous to push vulnerable people? That's definitely true. I can see why Henry was distraught at what he and I have done to Toby.'

George kissed her. Still holding the back of her head in one big capable, comforting hand, he said:

'I think Toby would probably have done something similar even if neither of you had put him under pressure. I don't share your view that any one of us could turn violent under the right stress. I think the capacity for violence is either inborn or inculcated very early in life. But that's not what I meant either. Trish, don't those letters from Jean-Pierre show you that not everyone lies about love?'

She felt the familiar tugging between her eyebrows, then his finger, trying to smooth away the frown.

'Don't you think they show that it's time to get over your terror of believing people care about you? People like David and Paddy?' he asked. 'And me?'

This was much too important to take seriously. Trish let her frown relax and kissed him.

'The evidence is purely circumstantial, m'lord,' she murmured when she could speak again.

A mobile rang. They both looked round and traced the sound to George's little Nokia.

'Leave it,' Trish said, 'and come to bed. It's been another long day.'

'I can't. It could be a client.' He put the phone to his ear. The voice that came through was so loud that Trish could hear it, too.

'George? Jeremy Carfield here. Some idiot police officers have arrested me. I'm at Southwark Police Station and this is my one phone call.'

'What's the charge?'

'Selling coke. They were tracking a street dealer, thought they saw something pass from me to him, and hauled us both off in one of their sodding white vans. And now they're treating me as if *I* was some sad loony off the street. Come and get me out of here.'

'I'll get one of our crime specialists, Jeremy. He'll do you far better than—'

'I want you, George. Now.'

He looked at Trish, who nodded. 'I know. He's a client.'

'And if that's Trish Maguire with you, tell her to drop round to see how Angelique's doing. She'll be in a panic by now, wondering where I am, and these baboons won't let me make two phone calls.'

'I'll see that your wife is informed,' George said, 'and I'll be with you as soon as the traffic allows.' He clicked off the phone to see Trish already on her landline to Nicky, asking whether she would come back to babysit. 'You don't have to do it, Trish. He's not your client.'

Trish looked at him. After everything they'd said to each other – and not quite said – she wasn't going to make him do this alone. 'What's yours is mine, George.'

While they waited for Nicky, she told him about the Procrustes icon, which was flickering madly away on the edge of her mind, like the jagged arcs of light that signalled a migraine.

'God, how I hate drugs!' she burst out.

'I know.'

Nicky unlocked the door before he could say any more. They saw she was wearing her rose-splattered pyjamas under her coat.

'I thought I'd make up a bed on the sofa, if that's OK, Trish,' she said, yawning. 'It makes more sense than sitting up till you get back.'

'Very sensible. I must look around for a bigger house, so that we can all have bedrooms under the same roof,' Trish said lightly. 'Come on, George. You could drop me off at the Carfields' flat on your way to the nick. We'll be as quiet as we can when we come back, Nicky. Sleep well.'

As they walked down the iron staircase, with their footsteps setting up a resonating clang, George said:

'I hope you're proud of the way you beat the pair of them.'

'Toby and his victim?'

George laughed, the sound fat with satisfaction. 'No. Henry and Antony. They tried to use you, then they tried to threaten you – in their customary ultra-civilized way – and in the end they tried to bribe you. But you just went on regardless till you got to the end. You showed them. Well done.'

'I wouldn't have got to the solution without David's intervention.'

He slung a friendly arm around her shoulder. 'I don't think either of us could get anywhere very far without him now.'